NEAL SHUSTERMAN
UNWHOLLY

BOOK 2 IN THE UNWIND DYSTOLOGY

SIMON & SCHUSTER BFYR

New York   London   Toronto   Sydney   New Delhi

SIMON & SCHUSTER BFYR

An imprint of Simon & Schuster Children's Publishing Division
1230 Avenue of the Americas, New York, New York 10020

Black market organ statistics courtesy of www.havocscope.com
"Belgian Surgeons Harvest Organs After Euthanasia" by Michael Cook, © BioEdge Web
Journal, May 14, 2010
"Hoodies, Louts, Scum: How Media Demonises Teenagers" by Richard Garner, © The
Independent, March 13, 2009
"34 Children Abandoned Under Nebraska's Safe-Haven Law" by Nate Jenkins, © The
Associated Press, November 14, 2008
SIMON & SCHUSTER BOOKS FOR YOUNG READERS
and related marks are trademarks of Simon & Schuster, Inc.
For information about special discounts for bulk purchases, please contact
Simon & Schuster Special Sales at 1-866-506-1949 or business@simonandschuster.com.
The Simon & Schuster Speakers Bureau can bring authors to your live event.
For more information or to book an event, contact the Simon & Schuster Speakers Bureau
at 1-866-248-3049 or visit our website at www.simonspeakers.com.
Also available in a SIMON & SCHUSTER BFYR hardcover
Interior design by Hilary Zarycky based on a design by Al Cetta
The text for this book was set in Fairfield.
Manufactured in the United States of America
This SIMON & SCHUSTER BFYR paperback edition October 2013
16 18 20 19 17
The Library of Congress has cataloged the hardcover edition as follows:
Shusterman, Neal.
UnWholly / Neal Shusterman.
p. cm. Sequel to: Unwind.
Summary: Thanks to Connor, Lev, and Risa, and their high-profile revolt at Happy Jack
Harvest Camp, people can no longer turn a blind eye to unwinding. Ridding society of
troublesome teens and, in the same stroke, providing much-needed tissues for transplant
might be convenient, but its morality has finally been brought into question. However,
unwinding has become big business, and there are powerful political and corporate interests
that want to see it not only continue, but expand, allowing the unwinding of prisoners and
the impoverished. Cam is a teen who does not exist. He is made entirely out of the parts of
other unwinds. Cam, a 21st century Frankenstein, struggles with a search for identity and
meaning, as well as the concept of his own soul, if indeed a rewound being can have one.
When a sadistic bounty hunter who takes "trophies" from the unwinds he captures starts to
pursue Connor, Risa and Lev, Cam finds his fate inextricably bound with theirs.
ISBN 978-1-4424-2366-4 (hc) ISBN 978-1-4424-2368-8 (eBook)
[1. Fugitives from justice—Fiction. 2. Survival—Fiction. 3. Revolutionaries—Fiction.
4. Identity—Fiction. 5. Science fiction.] I. Title.
PZ7.S55987Uv 2012] [Fic]—dc23] 2012002729
ISBN 978-1-4424-2367-1 (pbk)

For Charlotte Ruth Shusterman
Love you, Mom

ACKNOWLEDGMENTS

I never dreamed that *Unwind* would turn into additional books, but I just couldn't escape the strange world it encompasses. I owe a continuing debt of gratitude to David Gale, Navah Wolfe, Justin Chanda, Anne Zafian, and everyone in Simon & Schuster's editorial department. Also Paul Crichton and Lydia Finn for organizing publicity and book tours, Michelle Fadlalla and Venessa Williams for their work on school and library conferences, Katrina Groover in managing editorial, Chava Wolin in production, and Chloë Foglia in design.

I thank my children for their endless patience while Dad disappears deep into his head, and Marcia Blanco, my extraordinary assistant, who keeps me sane and somehow keeps me organized! Many thanks to Wendy Doyle and Heidi Stoll for their tireless work on the Shustermania newsletter. Another nod to Wendy, and to my son Jarrod, for transcribing my story ramblings whenever I find myself in a digital dictatorial phase. Thanks to my critique group, the Fictionaires, for helping to guide my words—particularly Michelle Knowlden, for our wonderful collaboration on the "UnStrung" short story, and my "Big Sis" Patricia, for catching me when I McFall.

I am indebted to the countless educators out there who are finding ways of using my books in the classroom, and the many fans who tell me how my books affect their lives—fans like Veronica Knysh, whose e-mail brought me to tears and made me remember the reason why I write.

Thanks to Andrea Brown, Trevor Engelson, Shep Rosenman, Lee Rosenbaum, Steve Fisher, and Debbie Deuble-Hill: my proverbial "people," who run my career with a collectively enlightened hand (and keep me from running it into the ground!). My gratitude also goes out to Marc Benardout, Catherine Kimmel, Julian Stone, and Charlotte Stout, whose unflinching belief in *Unwind* and *UnWholly* will most certainly result in an incredible film!

And finally I thank my parents, Milton and Charlotte Shusterman, for always being there, even when they can't be.

And the answer is . . .

As Unwind *and* UnWholly *represent a world turned upside down, what better way to keep you up to speed than giving the answer before the question, like on a certain quiz show? Read the answers, and see how many questions you can get right! Get enough right and you may get to tear up your own unwind order! (Warning: Skipping the game may leave you feeling a bit unwound while reading. . . .)*

This is the process by which an individual is dismantled. By law, 99.44 percent of a person must be used and kept alive in transplant.

What is unwinding?

America's second civil war—also known as the Heartland War—ended when the pro-life and pro-choice armies came to this agreement, which made life inviolable from conception to the age of thirteen but allowed for the "retroactive abortion" of troubled teenagers.

What is the Unwind Accord?

When a mother does not wish to keep a newborn baby, she has the legal option to leave the baby on someone else's doorstep. The baby then becomes the legal responsibility of the people in that home. This is the common term for the leaving of the baby.

What is storking?

When a person is unwound, since virtually all of them is still alive, they are not considered to be dead, but to be living in this state.

What is the divided state?

These are licensed facilities in which Unwinds are prepared for a divided state. While each facility has its own particular personality, they are all designed to provide a positive experience for youth designated for unwinding.

What are harvest camps?

This northern Arizona harvest camp, in a town named after the joyful lumberjacks who founded it, has recently been closed due to terrorist activity.

What is Happy Jack Harvest Camp?

This is a slang term for the clinic within a harvest camp where unwinding is performed.

What is a Chop Shop?

These young terrorists have introduced an undetectable chemical into their circulatory system that makes their blood explosive. They get their name because they detonate by bringing their hands together in powerful applause.

What are clappers?

This is the common term for the law enforcement officers who work for the National Juvenile Authority and are responsible for the policing of Unwinds.

What are Juvey-cops, or Juvies?

The act of chemically rendering someone unconscious by use of tranquilizer bullets or darts. It is the preferred method utilized by juvenile enforcement officers, because using bullets on Unwinds is both illegal and damages their vital organs, thereby reducing their value.

What is tranq'ing?

From the French word for "beef"—and probably the origin of the slang expression "buff"—this is the common term for a soldier, or a muscular teen on track for a military career.

What is a boeuf?

Originally a military term, it means "away without leave" but has more recently been used as a term for runaway Unwinds.

What is AWOL?

This organization fights unwinding by rescuing AWOL Unwinds. However, it's not as well organized as people think.

What is the ADR or Anti-Divisional Resistance?

This secret (not so secret) sanctuary for AWOL Unwinds is at a massive airplane salvage yard in the Arizona desert.

What is the Graveyard?

Also known as Connor Lassiter, this runaway Unwind from Ohio is believed to be responsible for the revolt at Happy Jack Harvest Camp, and is presumed dead.

Who is the Akron AWOL?

Derived from the term meaning "ten percent," this is a child designated from birth for unwinding, usually for religious reasons.

What is a tithe?

This tithe became a clapper who didn't clap, and by doing so, put a face on the resistance movement.

Who is Lev Calder?

This is the last name given to parentless children raised in state homes.

What is Ward?

A survivor of Happy Jack Harvest Camp, this former state ward became a paraplegic, because she refused to have her damaged spine replaced by the spine of an Unwind.

Who is Risa Ward?

Wishing you a nail-biting, sleep-depriving, thought-provoking read!

Neal Shusterman

Part One

Violations

The only way to deal with an unfree world

is to become so absolutely free that your very

existence is an act of rebellion.

—*Albert Camus*

1 · Starkey

He's fighting a nightmare when they come for him.

A great flood is swallowing the world, and in the middle of it all, he's being mauled by a bear. He's more annoyed than terrified. As if the flood isn't enough, his deep, dark mind has to send an angry grizzly to tear into him.

Then he's dragged feetfirst out of the jaws of death and drowning Armageddon.

"Up! Now! Let's go!"

He opens his eyes to a brightly lit bedroom that ought to be dark. Two Juvey-cops manhandle him, grabbing his arms, preventing him from fighting back long before he's awake enough to try.

"No! Stop! What is this?"

Handcuffs. First his right wrist, then his left.

"On your feet!"

They yank him to his feet as if he's resisting—which he would, if he were more awake.

"Leave me alone! What's going on?"

But in an instant he's awake enough to know exactly what's going on. It's a kidnapping. But you can't call it kidnapping when transfer papers have been signed in triplicate.

"Verbally confirm that you are Mason Michael Starkey."

There are two officers. One is short and muscular, the other tall and muscular. Probably military boeufs before they took jobs as Juvey-rounders. It takes a special heartless breed to be a Juvey-cop, but to specialize as a rounder you probably need to be soulless as well. The fact that he's being rounded for

3

unwinding shocks and terrifies Starkey, but he refuses to show it, because he knows Juvey-rounders get off on other people's fear.

The short one, who is clearly the mouthpiece of this duo, gets in his face and repeats, "Verbally confirm that you are Mason Michael Starkey!"

"And why should I do that?"

"Kid," says the other rounder, "this can go down easy or hard, but either way it's going down." The second cop is more soft spoken with a pair of lips that clearly aren't his. In fact, they look like they came from a girl. "The drill's not so hard, so just get with the program."

He talks as if Starkey should have known they were coming, but what Unwind ever really knows? Every Unwind believes in their heart of hearts that it won't happen to them— that their parents, no matter how strained things get, will be smart enough not to fall for the net ads, TV commercials, and billboards that say things like "Unwinding: the sensible solution." But who is he kidding? Even without the constant media blitz, Starkey's been a potential candidate for unwinding since the moment he arrived on the doorstep. Perhaps he should be surprised that his parents waited so long.

Now the mouthpiece gets deep in his personal space. "For the last time, verbally confirm that you are—"

"Yeah, yeah, Mason Michael Starkey. Now get out of my face, your breath stinks."

With his identity verbally confirmed, Lady-Lips pulls out a form in triplicate: white, yellow, and pink.

"So is this how you do it?" Starkey asks, his voice beginning to quaver. "You arrest me? What's my crime? Being sixteen? Or maybe it's just being here at all."

"Quiet-or-we-tranq-you," says Mouthpiece, like it's all one word.

A part of Starkey wants to be tranq'd—just go to sleep and if he's lucky, never wake up. That way he won't have to face the utter humiliation of being torn from his life in the middle of the night. But no, he wants to see his parents' faces. Or, more to the point, he wants *them* to see *his* face, and if he's tranq'd, they get off easy. They won't have to look him in the eye.

Lady-Lips holds the unwind order in front of him and begins to read the infamous Paragraph Nine, the "Negation Clause."

"Mason Michael Starkey, by the signing of this order, your parents and/or legal guardians have retroactively terminated your tenure, backdated to six days postconception, leaving you in violation of Existential Code 390. In light of this, you are hereby remanded to the California Juvenile Authority for summary division, also known as unwinding."

"Blah, blah, blah."

"Any rights previously granted to you by the county, state, or federal government as a citizen thereof are now officially and permanently revoked." He folds the unwind order and shoves it into his pocket.

"Congratulations, Mr. Starkey," says Mouthpiece. "You no longer exist."

"Then why are you talking to me?"

"We won't be for much longer." They tug him toward the door.

"Can I at least put on shoes?"

They let him go but stay on their guard.

Starkey takes his sweet time tying his shoes. Then they pull him out of his room and down the stairs. The Juvey-cops have heavy boots that intimidate the wood of the steps. The three of them sound like a herd of cattle as they go down.

His parents wait in the foyer. It's three in the morning, but

they're still fully dressed. They've been awake all night antici-
pating this. Starkey sees anguish on their faces, or maybe it's
relief, it's hard to tell. He hardens his own emotions, hiding
them behind a mock smile.

"Hi, Mom! Hi, Dad!" he says brightly. "Guess what just
happened to me? I'll give you twenty guesses to figure it out!"

His father takes a deep breath, preparing to launch into the
Great Unwinding Speech that every parent prepares for a wayward child. Even if they never use it, they still prepare it, running the words through their minds while on lunch break, or
while sitting in traffic, or while listening to some moronic boss
blather on about price points and distribution, and whatever
other crap that people in office buildings have meetings about.

What were the statistics? Starkey saw it on the news once.
Every year the thought of unwinding passes through the mind
of one in ten parents. Of those, one in ten seriously considers it, and of those, one in twenty actually goes through with
it—and the statistic doubles with every additional kid a family
has. Crunch those juicy numbers, and one out of every two
thousand kids between the ages of thirteen and seventeen will
be unwound each year. Better odds than the lottery—and that
doesn't even include the kids in state homes.

His father, keeping his distance, begins the speech. "Mason,
can't you see that you left us no choice?"

The Juvey-cops hold him firm at the bottom of the stairs,
but they make no move to get him outside. They know they must
allow the parental rite of passage; the verbal boot out the door.

"The fights, the drugs, the stolen car—and now being
expelled from yet another school. What's next, Mason?"

"Gee, I don't know, Dad. There are so many bad choices I
can make."

"Not anymore. We care enough about you to end your bad
choices before they end you."

That just makes him laugh out loud.

And then there's a voice from the top of the stairs.

"No! You can't do this!"

His sister, Jenna—his parents' biological daughter—stands at the top of the stairs in teddy bear pajamas that seem too old for her thirteen years.

"Go back to bed, Jenna," their mother says.

"You're unwinding him just because he was storked, and that's unfair! And right before Christmas, too! What if I had come storked? Would you unwind me also?"

"We are not having this discussion!" yells their father, as their mother begins to cry. "Go back to bed!"

But she doesn't. She folds her arms and sits at the top of the stairs in defiance, witnessing the whole thing. Good for her.

His mother's tears are genuine, but he's unsure whether she's crying for him or for the rest of the family. "All these things you do, everyone told us they were a cry for help," she says. "So why didn't you let us help you?"

He wants to scream. How could he possibly explain it to them if they can't see? They don't know what it's like to go through sixteen years of life knowing you weren't wanted; a mystery baby of uncertain race storked on the doorstep of a couple so sienna-pale, they could have been vampires. Or to still remember that day when you were three years old and your mom, all doped up on pain medication from your sister's cesarean delivery, took you to a fire station and begged them to take you away and make you a ward of the state. Or how about knowing every Christmas morning that your gift is not a joy, but an obligation? And that your birthday isn't even real because they can't pinpoint when you were born, just the day you were left on a welcome mat that some new mother took too literally?

And what about the taunts from the other kids at school?

In fourth grade Mason's parents were called into the principal's office. He had flipped a boy off the top platform of the jungle gym. The kid had suffered a concussion and a broken arm.

"Why, Mason?" his parents had asked, right there in front of the principal. "Why did you do it?"

He told them that the other kids were calling him "Storky" instead of Starkey, and that this was the boy who had started it. He naively thought they'd rise to his defense, but they just dismissed it as if it didn't matter.

"You could have killed that boy," his father had reprimanded. "And why? Because of words? Words don't hurt you." Which is one of the hugest criminal lies perpetrated by adults against children in this world. Because words hurt more than any physical pain. He would have gladly taken a concussion and a broken arm if he never had to be singled out as a storked child ever again.

In the end, he got sent to a different school and was ordered to have mandatory counseling.

"You think about what you did," his old principal had told him.

And he did what he was told, like a good little boy. He gave it plenty of thought and decided he should have found a higher platform.

So how do you even begin to explain that? How do you explain a lifetime of injustice in the time it takes the Juvey-cops to herd you out the door? The answer is easy: You don't even try.

"I'm sorry, Mason," his father says, tears in his eyes as well. "But it's better for everyone this way. Including you."

Starkey knows he'll never make his parents understand, but if nothing else, he'll have the last word.

"Hey, Mom, by the way . . . Dad's late nights at the office

aren't really at the office. They're with your friend Nancy."

But before he can begin to relish his parents' shocked expressions, it occurs to him that this secret knowledge could have been a bargaining chip. If he had told his father he knew, it could have been ironclad protection from unwinding! How could he be so stupid not to have thought of that when it mattered?

So in the end he can't even enjoy his bitter little victory as the Juvey-cops push him out into a cool December night.

The Juvey squad car leaves the driveway with Starkey locked in the backseat behind a bulletproof barrier. Mouthpiece drives while Lady-Lips flips through a fat file folder. Starkey can't imagine his life could have that much data.

"It says here you scored in the top ten percentile in your early childhood exams."

The mouthpiece shakes his head in disgust. "What a waste."

"Not really," says Lady-Lips. "Plenty of folks will get the benefit of your smarts, Mr. Starkey."

The suggestion gives him an unpleasant chill, but he tries not to show it. "Love the lip graft, dude," Starkey says. "What's the deal? Did your wife tell you she'd rather be kissed by a woman?"

Mouthpiece smirks, and Lady-Lips says nothing.

"But enough lip service," says Starkey. "You boys hungry? Because I could go for a midnight snack right about now. Some In-N-Out? Whaddaya say?"

No answer from the front seat. Not that he expects one, but it's always fun to mess with law enforcement and see how much it takes to irritate them. Because if they get ticked off, he wins. What's that story about the Akron AWOL? What did he always say? Oh yeah. "Nice socks." Simple, elegant, but it always undermined the confidence of any figure of false authority.

The Akron AWOL—now *there* was an Unwind! Sure, he died in the attack on Happy Jack Harvest Camp almost a year ago, but his legend lives on. Starkey longs for the kind of notoriety that Connor Lassiter has. In fact, Starkey imagines Connor Lassiter's ghost sitting by his side, appreciating his thoughts and his every action—not just approving, but guiding Starkey's hands as he wriggles his handcuffs down to his left shoe—just low enough to fish out the knife from the lining. The knife he's saved for special occasions like this.

"Come to think about it, In-N-Out Burger does sound good right about now," says Lady-Lips.

"Excellent," says Starkey. "There's one up ahead on the left. Order me a Double-Double, Animal Style, and Animal fries, too, because, hey—I'm an animal."

He is amazed that they actually pull into the all-night drive-through. Starkey feels like the master of subliminal suggestion, even though his suggestion was not all that subliminal. Still, he is in control of the Juvey-cops . . . or at least he thinks he is until they order meals for themselves and nothing for him.

"Hey! What's the deal?" He pounds his shoulder against the glass that separates their world from his.

"They'll feed you at harvest camp," says Lady-Lips.

Only now does it hit home that the bulletproof glass doesn't just separate him from the cops—it's a barrier between him and any part of the outside world. He will never taste his favorite foods again. Never visit his favorite places. At least not as Mason Starkey. Suddenly he feels like hurling up everything he's eaten, backdated to six days postconception.

The night shift cashier at the drive-through window is a girl Starkey knows from his last school. As he sees her, a whole mess of emotions toy with his brain. He could just lurk in the shadows of the backseat, hoping not to be seen, but that would make him feel pathetic. No, he will not be pathetic. If he's going down, then it will be in flames that everyone must see.

"Hey, Amanda, will you go to the prom with me?" He shouts loud enough to be heard through the thick glass barrier.

Amanda squints in his direction, and when she realizes who it is, she turns up her nose as if she's smelled something rancid on the grill.

"Not in this life, Starkey."

"Why not?"

"A, you're a sophomore, and B, you're a loser in the back of a police car. And anyway, don't they have their own prom at the alternative school?"

Could she possibly be any denser? "Uh, as you can see, I've graduated."

"Pipe down," says Mouthpiece, "or I'll unwind you right into the burgers."

Finally Amanda gets it, and suddenly she becomes a little sheepish. "Oh! Oh, I'm sorry, Starkey. I'm really sorry. . . ."

Pity is something Mason Starkey can't stand. "Sorry for what? You and your friends wouldn't give me the time of day before, but now you're sorry for me? Save it."

"I'm sorry. I mean—I'm sorry that I'm sorry—I mean . . ." She sighs in exasperation and gives up, handing Lady-Lips a bag of food. "Do you need ketchup?"

"No, we're good."

"Hey, Amanda!" Starkey shouts as they drive away. "If you really want to do something for me, tell everyone I went down fighting, will you? Tell them I'm just like the Akron AWOL."

"I will, Starkey," she says. "I promise."

But he knows she'll forget by morning.

Twenty minutes later they're turning into the back alley of county lockup. No one goes in the front way, least of all the Unwinds. The county jail has a juvenile wing, and in the back of the juvey wing is a special box within a box where they hold Unwinds awaiting transport. Starkey's been in regular juvey enough to know that once you're in the Unwind holding cell, that's it. End of story. Even death row inmates don't have such tight security.

But he's not there yet. He's still here, in the car, waiting to be transferred inside. Right here is where the hull of this little ship of fools is thinnest, and if he's going to sink their plans, it has to happen between the car and the back door of the county jail. As they prepare for his "perp walk," he thinks about his chances of breaking free—because as much as his parents may have imagined this night, so has he, and he's made up a dozen valiant escape plans. The thing is, even his day-dreams are fatalistic; in every anxiety-filled fantasy, he always loses, gets tranq'd, and wakes up on an operating table. Sure, they say they don't unwind you right away, but Starkey doesn't believe it. No one really knows what goes on in the harvest camps, and those who find out aren't exactly around to share the experience.

They pull him out of the car and flank him on either side, grasping his upper arms tightly. They are practiced in this walk. Lady-Lips grips Starkey's fat file in his other hand.

"So," says Starkey, "does that file show my hobbies?"

"Probably," says Lady-Lips, not really caring either way.

"Maybe you should have read it a little more closely, because then we'd have something to talk about." He grins. "You know, I'm pretty good with magic."

"That so?" says Mouthpiece, with a twisted sneer. "Too bad you can't make yourself disappear."

"Who says I can't?"

Then, in his finest Houdini fashion, he raises his right hand, revealing the cuff no longer on it. Instead, it dangles free from his left hand. Before they can even react, Starkey slides the penknife he used to pick the lock out of his sleeve, grips it in his hand, and slashes it across Lady-Lips's face.

The man screams, and blood flows from a four-inch wound. Mouthpiece, for once in his miserable life of public disservice, is speechless. He reaches for his weapon, but Starkey is already on the run, zigzagging in the shadowy alley.

"Hey!" yells Mouthpiece. "You're only making it worse for yourself."

But what are they going to do? Reprimand him before they unwind him? The Mouthpiece can talk all he wants, but he's got no bargaining position.

The alley turns to the left and then to the right like a maze, and all the while beside him is the tall, imposing brick wall of the county jail.

Finally he turns another corner and sees a street up ahead. He charges forward, but just as he emerges into that street, he's grabbed by Mouthpiece. Somehow he made it there before Starkey. He's surprised, but he shouldn't be, because doesn't every Unwind try to run? And couldn't they build a twisting alley specifically designed to waste your time and give the Juvey-cops an advantage that they never really lost?

"You're through, Starkey!" He crushes Starkey's wrist enough to dislodge the knife and brandishes a tranq gun with trigger-happy fury. "Down on the ground, or this goes in your eye!"

But Starkey does not go down. He will not humble himself before this legalized thug.

"Do it!" says Starkey. "Tranq me in the eye and explain to the harvest camp why the goods are damaged."

Mouthpiece turns him around and pushes him against the brick wall, hard enough to scrape and bruise his face.

"I've had enough of you, Starkey. Or maybe I should call you *Storky*." Then Mouthpiece laughs, like he's a genius. Like every moron in the world hasn't already called him that. "Storky!" he snorts. "That's a better name for you, isn't it? How do you like that, Storky?"

Blood boils hotter than water. Starkey can vouch for that, because with adrenaline-pumped fury, he elbows Mouthpiece in the gut and spins around, grabbing the gun.

"Oh no, you don't."

Mouthpiece is stronger—but maybe animal-style beats strength.

The gun is between them. It points at Starkey's cheek, then his chest, then to Mouthpiece's ear, then under his chin. They both grapple for the trigger and—*Blam!*

The concussive shock of the blast knocks Starkey back against the wall. Blood! Blood everywhere! The ferrous taste of it in his mouth, and the acrid smell of gun smoke and—

That was no tranq bullet! That was the real thing!

And he thinks he's microseconds away from death, but he suddenly realizes that the blood isn't his. In front of him, Mouthpiece's face is a red, pulpy mess. The man goes down, dead before he hits the pavement and—

My God, that was a real bullet. Why does a Juvey-cop have real bullets? That's illegal!

He can hear footsteps around the bend, and the dead cop is still dead, and he knows the whole world heard the gunshot, and everything hinges on his next action.

He is partners with the Akron AWOL now. The patron saint of runaway Unwinds is watching over his shoulder, waiting for Starkey to make a move, and he thinks, *What would Connor do?*

Just then another Juvey-cop comes around the bend—a cop he has never seen and is determined to never see again. Starkey raises Mouthpiece's gun and shoots, turning what was just an accident into murder.

As he escapes—truly escapes—all he can think about is the bloody taste of victory, and how pleased the ghost of Connor Lassiter would be.

Affordable financing is available, so don't wait for that next bad report card. Take action now! Call The NeuroWeave Institute today for your free quote. Our results are 100 percent guaranteed or your money back.

The NeuroWeave Institute: When education fails, we'll give you straight As!

To be an AWOL Unwind is one thing, but to be a cop killer is another. The manhunt for Starkey becomes more than just your typical Unwind chase. It seems the whole world is put on alert. First Starkey changes his look, dying his straggly brown hair red, cutting it bookworm-short, and shaving off the little victory garden goatee that he's been cultivating since middle school. Now when people see him, they might get a feeling they've seen him before, but not know from where, because now he looks less like a face from a wanted poster and more like someone you'd see on a Wheaties box. The red hair is a bit of a disconnect with his olive complexion, but then, being a genetic hodgepodge has served him well all his life. He's always been a chameleon who could pass for any ethnicity. The red hair just adds one more level of misdirection.

He skips town and never stays anywhere for more than a day or two. Word is that the Pacific Northwest is more sympathetic to AWOL Unwinds than Southern California, so that's where he's headed.

Starkey is prepared for life as a fugitive, because he has always lived in a kind of protective paranoia. Don't trust anyone, not even your own shadow, and look out for your own best interests. His friends appreciated his clear-cut approach to life, because they always knew where they stood. He would fight to the end for his friends . . . as long as it was in his own interest to do so.

"You have the soul of a corporation," a teacher once told

him. It was meant as an insult, but he took it as a compliment. Corporations have great power and do fine things in this world when they choose to. She was a glacier-hugging math teacher who got laid off the following year, because who needs math teachers when you can just get a NeuroWeave? Just goes to show you, hugging a chunk of ice gets you nothing but cold.

Now, however, Starkey's one with the huggers, because they're the kind of people who run the Anti-Divisional Resistance, harboring runaway Unwinds. Once he's in the hands of the ADR, he knows he'll be safe, but finding them is the hard part.

"I've been AWOL for almost four months now and haven't seen no sign of the resistance," says an ugly kid with a bulldog face. Starkey met him while hanging out behind a KFC on Christmas Eve, waiting for them to throw out the leftover chicken. He's not the kind of kid Starkey would hang with in real life, but now that real life has flipped into borrowed time, his priorities have changed.

"I've survived because I don't fall for no traps," Dogface tells him.

Starkey knows all about the traps. If a hiding place seems too good to be true, it probably is. An abandoned house with a comfortable mattress; an unlocked truck that happens to be full of canned food. They're traps set by Juvey-cops for AWOL Unwinds. There are even Juvies pretending to be part of the Anti-Divisional Resistance.

"The Juvies are offering rewards now for people who turn in AWOLs," Dogface says, as they stuff themselves sick with chicken. "And there are bounty hunters, too. *Parts pirates*, they call 'em. They don't bother with collecting rewards—they sell the AWOLs they catch on the black market—and if you think regular harvest camps are bad, you don't wanna know about the illegal ones." The kid swallows a mouthful so big, Starkey can see it going down his

17

gullet like a mouse being swallowed by a snake. "There never used to be parts pirates," he says, "but since seventeen-year-olds can't be unwound no more, there's a shortage of parts, and AWOLs fetch a huge price on the black market."

Starkey shakes his head. Making it illegal to unwind seventeen-year-olds was supposed to save a fifth of the kids marked for unwinding, but instead it forced a lot of parents to make their decision earlier. Starkey wonders if his parents would have changed their mind if they had another year to decide.

"Parts pirates are the worst," Dogface tells him. "Their traps aren't so nice as the ones the Juvies set. I heard this story about a trapper who got put out of business when fur was made illegal. So he took his heaviest animal traps and retooled them for Unwinds. Man, one of those traps snaps around your leg, and you can kiss that leg good-bye." He snaps a chicken bone in half for emphasis, and Starkey shivers in spite of himself. "There are other stories," Dogface says, licking chicken grease from his dirty fingers, "like this kid in my old neighborhood. His parents were total losers. Strung-out druggies who prolly shoulda been unwound themselves, if they had unwinding back in the day. Anyway, on his thirteenth birthday, they sign the unwind order and tell him about it."

"Why would they tell him?"

"So he'd run away," Dogface explains, "but see, they knew all his secret hiding places, and they told a parts pirate where to find him. He caught the kid, sold him, and split the fee with the kid's parents."

"Son of a bitch!"

Dogface shrugs, and flicks away a chicken bone. "The kid was a stork-job anyways, so it was no great loss, right?"

Starkey stops chewing, but just for a moment. Then he grins, keeping his thoughts to himself. "Right. No great loss."

That night the dogfaced kid takes Starkey to a drainage tunnel where he's been hiding out, and once the kid falls asleep, Starkey gets to work. He goes out into a nearby neighborhood and leaves a bucket of chicken at some strangers' front door, rings the bell, and runs.

There's no chicken in the bucket, though. Instead there's a hand-drawn map, along with the following note:

Need money? Then send the Juvey-cops here, and you'll collect a fat reward. Happy holidays!

Right around dawn, Starkey watches from a nearby rooftop as Juvies storm the drainage tunnel and pull out the dogfaced kid like so much earwax.

"Congratulations, asshole," he says to himself. "You've been storked."

ADVERTISEMENT

"When my parents signed the unwind order, I was scared. I didn't know what would happen to me. I thought, 'Why me? Why am I being punished?' But once I got to BigSky Harvest Camp, all that changed. I found other kids like me and was finally accepted for who I was. I found out that every single part of me was precious and valuable. Thanks to the people at BigSky Harvest Camp, I'm not afraid of my unwinding anymore.

"The divided state? Wow. What an adventure!"

Every AWOL Unwind will steal. It's an argument that the authorities like to use to convince the public that Unwinds are rotten apples from skin to core—that criminality is part of their very nature, and the only way to separate them from it is to separate them from themselves.

Theft, however, is not about predisposition when it comes to Unwinds. It's simply a matter of necessity. Kids who would never steal a penny find their fingers stickier than molasses and full of all sorts of pilfered goods, from food to clothes to medicine—the various things they need to survive—and those who were already prone to crime simply become even more so.

Starkey is no stranger to criminal activity—although until recently most of his crimes were misdemeanors of the rebellious sort. He shoplifted if a shopkeeper looked at him suspiciously. He tagged bits of his own personal philosophy, which usually involved some choice four-letter words, on buildings that stood for the very things that ticked him off. He even stole a car from a neighbor who always made his young children go inside whenever Starkey came out. He took that guy's car on a joyride with a couple of friends. Fun was had by all. Along the way he sideswiped a row of parked cars, losing two hubcaps and a bumper. Their ride ended when the car jumped a curb and mounted a very unresponsive mailbox. The damage was just enough to have the car labeled a total loss, which was exactly what Starkey wanted.

They never could prove it was him, but everybody knew. He had to admit, it wasn't one of his shining moments, but he knew he had had to do something to a man who didn't think Starkey was good enough to breathe the same air as his own children. The guy simply had to be punished for that kind of behavior.

All of it seemed to pale now that he was a murderer. But no—It would do him no good to think of himself that way. Better to think of himself as a warrior: a foot soldier in the war against unwinding. Soldiers were given medals for taking out the enemy, weren't they? So even though that night in the alley still plagues him in moments of insecurity, most of the time his conscience is clear. His conscience is also clear when he begins parting people from their wallets.

Starkey, imagining himself as a big-time Las Vegas magician someday, used to amaze friends and terrify adults by making their watches disappear off their wrists and turn up in other people's pockets. It was a simple parlor trick, but one that had taken lots of time to perfect. Making wallets and purses disappear followed the same principle. A combination of distraction, skilled fingers, and the confidence to get it done.

On this night, Starkey's mark is a man who comes stumbling drunk out of a bar and slips an overstuffed wallet into the wide pocket of his overcoat. The drunk fumbles with his keys on the way to his car. Starkey strolls past, bumping him just hard enough to dislodge the keys, and they fall to the ground.

"Hey, man, I'm sorry," Starkey says, picking up the keys and handing them to him. The man never feels the fingers of Starkey's other hand in his pocket, lifting the wallet at the same moment Starkey's handing him the keys. Starkey strolls off whistling to himself, knowing the man will be halfway home before he realizes that his wallet is gone, and even then, he'll think he just left it at the bar.

Starkey turns a corner, making sure he's out of sight before he opens the wallet, and the second he does, a jolt of electricity courses through him with such power his feet fall out from under him and he's left semiconscious on the ground, twitching.

A stun-wallet. He's heard of such things but never saw one in action until now.

Within seconds, the drunk is there, not so drunk after all, with three others whose faces he can't make out. They lift him up and shove him into the back of a waiting van.

As the door is pulled closed and the van accelerates, Starkey, only barely conscious, sees the face of the drunk/not-drunk man looking down at him through an electrically charged haze.

"Are you an Unwind, a runaway, or just a lowlife?" he asks.

Starkey's lips feel like rubber. "Lowlife."

"Great," says the un-drunk. "That narrows it down. Unwind or runaway?"

"Runaway," mumbles Starkey.

"Perfect," the man says. "Now that we've established you're an Unwind, we know what to do with you."

Starkey groans, and some woman beyond his limited peripheral vision laughs. "Don't be so surprised. Unwinds all got this look in their eye that lowlifes and runaways don't. We knew the truth without you saying a thing."

Starkey tries to move, but he can barely lift his limbs.

"Don't," says a girl he can't see from somewhere behind him. "Don't move or I'll zap you even worse than the wallet did."

Starkey knows he's fallen for a parts pirate's trap. He thought he was smarter, and he silently curses his luck . . . until the man who pretended to be drunk says, "You'll like this safe house. Good food, even if it does smell a little."

"Wh-what?"

Laughs from everyone around him. There may be four or five people in the van. But his vision still isn't clear enough to get an accurate count.

"I love that look on their faces," the woman says. Now she comes into his field of vision and grins at him. "You know how they tranq escaped lions so they can bring them back to safety before they get themselves in a heap of trouble?" she says. "Well, today you're the lion."

PUBLIC SERVICE ANNOUNCEMENT

"Hi, kids! Watchdog Walter here, eyes open and nose to the ground! Not everyone can be a bloodhound like me, but now you can join my Junior Watchdog Club! You'll receive your own Junior Watchdog kit, and a monthly newsletter with games and tips on spotting crime in your own neighborhood, from suspicious strangers to Unwind 'danger-houses!'

With you on the job, bad guys and AWOLs don't stand a
chance! So join today! And remember, Junior Watchdogs—
eyes open and nose to the ground!"

Sponsored by Neighborhood Watch Inc.

The safe house is a sewer pump station. Automated. No city
workers ever show up unless something breaks.

"You get used to the smell," Starkey is told as they bring
him in, which he finds hard to believe—but it turns out to be
true. Apparently one's sense of smell realizes it's going to lose
the battle and just goes with it—and, as they told him in the
van, the food makes up for it.

The whole place is a petri dish of angst, generated by kids
whose parents gave up on them, which is the worst kind of
angst there is. There are fights and ridiculous posturing on a
daily basis.

Starkey's always been a natural leader among sketchy outcasts and borderline personalities, and the safe house is no
exception. He quickly rises in the social ranks. Word of his
escape act is already churning out smoke in the rumor mill,
helping his status from the very beginning.

"Is it true you shot two Juvey-cops?"

"Yep."

"Is it true you shot your way out of lockup with a machine
gun?"

"Sure, why not?"

And the best part is that the storked kids—who, even
among Unwinds, are treated like second-class citizens—are
now the elite, thanks to him!

Starkey says the storks get served first? They get served
first. Starkey says they get the best beds, farthest from the
stinking vents? They get the best beds. His word is law. Even
those running the place know that Starkey is their greatest

asset, and they know to keep him happy, because if he becomes an enemy, then every Unwind there is an enemy too.

He starts to settle in, figuring he'll be there until he's seventeen—but then in the middle of the night they're rounded up and taken away by the ADR—shuffled like a deck of cards to different safe houses.

"This is the way it works," they're all told. The reason, Starkey comes to understand, is twofold. One, it keep the kids moving closer to their destination, wherever that might be. Two, it splits them apart to keep any alliances from becoming permanent. Kind of like unwinding the mob rather than the individuals to keep them in line.

Their plan, however, backfires with Starkey, because in each safe house he manages to earn respect, building his credibility among more and more kids. In each new location he comes across Unwinds who fancy themselves alpha males, trying to take charge, but in truth they're just betas waiting for an alpha to humble them into submission.

In every instance, Starkey finds his opportunity to challenge, defeat, and rise above. Then there's another midnight ride, another shake-up, and a new safe house. Each time Starkey learns a new social skill, something to serve him, something to make him even more effective at gathering and galvanizing these scared, angry kids. There could be no better leadership program than the safe houses of the Anti-Divisional Resistance.

And then come the coffins.

They show up at the final safe house: a shipment of lacquered wood caskets with rich satin linings. Most kids are terrified; Starkey is just amused.

"Get in!" they're told by armed resistance fighters who look more like special ops. "No questions, just get in. Two to a box! Move it!"

Some kids hesitate, but the smarter ones quickly find a partner like it's a sudden square dance, and nobody wants to be stuck with someone too tall, too fat, too unwashed, or too randy—because none of those things would fare well in the confines of a coffin—but no one actually gets in until Starkey gives the nod.

"If they meant to bury us," he tells them, "they would have done it already." As it turns out, he's more persuasive than the guys with the guns.

He chooses to share his little box with a wisp of a girl who is giddy at having been chosen by him. Not that he particularly likes her, but she is so slight that she'll barely take up any room. Once they're wedged in together in a tight spoon position, they're handed an oxygen tank and then closed into the darkness of the coffin together.

"I've always liked you, Mason," says the girl, whose name he can't recall. He's surprised that she knows his first name, since he never uses it anymore. "Of all the boys in the safe houses, you're the only one who makes me feel safe."

He doesn't respond; he just kisses her on the back of her head, to maintain his image as the safest port in her storm. It's a powerful feeling to know you make others feel safe.

"We . . . *could*, you know . . . ," she says coyly.

He reminds her that the ADR workers were very clear. "No extracurricular activities," they had said, "or you'll use up your oxygen and die." Starkey doesn't know if it's true, but it certainly is a good argument for restraint. Besides, even if someone were stupid enough to tempt fate, there's not enough space to move, much less generate any sort of friction, so the point is moot. He wonders if it's some sort of twisted joke the adults are having, shoving hormonal teens into tight quarters but making it impossible to do anything but breathe.

"I wouldn't mind suffocating if it was with you," the girl says, which is flattering, but makes him even less interested in her.

"There'll be a better time," he tells her, knowing that such a time will never come—at least not for her—but hope is a powerful motivator.

Eventually they settle into a sort of symbiotic breathing rhythm. He breathes in when she breathes out, so their chests don't fight for space.

After a while, there's a jarring motion. With his arm now around the girl, he holds her a little more tightly, knowing that easing her fear somehow eases his own. Soon there's a strange kind of acceleration, like they're in a speeding car, but the angle changes, tilting them.

"A plane?" asks the girl.

"I think so."

"What now?"

He doesn't answer because he doesn't know. Starkey begins to feel light-headed and, remembering the oxygen tank, turns the valve so that it slowly hisses. The coffin isn't quite air tight, but closed tightly enough that they would suffocate without that oxygen, even in the pressurized hull of a plane. In a few minutes the stress-induced exhaustion puts the girl to sleep, but not Starkey. Finally, an hour later, the sudden jar of landing jolts the girl awake.

"Where do you think we are?" the girl asks.

Starkey is feeling irritable from the tight quarters but tries not to show it. "We'll find out soon enough."

Twenty minutes of anticipation, and finally the lid is unlatched and opened, resurrecting the two of them from the dead.

There's a smiling kid with braces above them.

"Hello, I'm Hayden, and I'll be your personal savior today," he says brightly. "Oh look! No vomit or other unpleasant bodily fluids. Lucky you!"

With barely any blood circulating in his feet, Starkey joins a limping procession out of the jet's cargo hold and into the blinding day. What he sees before him as his eyes adjust seems more like a mirage than anything real.

It's a desert filled with thousands of airplanes.

Starkey's heard of places like this, airplane boneyards where decommissioned aircraft go to die. Around them are teens in military camouflage, carrying weapons. They're not unlike the adults back at the last safe house, just younger. They herd the kids into a loose formation at the bottom of the ramp.

A Jeep drives up. Clearly this is the approach of someone important, someone who will tell them why they're here.

The Jeep comes to a halt, and out steps an unremarkable-looking teenager in blue camouflage. He's Starkey's age or maybe a little bit older, and he has scars on the right half of his face.

As the crowd gets a good look at him, people begin to murmur with excitement. The kid raises his hand to quiet them down, and Starkey spots a shark tattoo on his arm.

"No way!" a fat kid next to Starkey says. "You know who that is? That's the Akron AWOL! That's Connor Lassiter."

Starkey scoffs, "Don't be ridiculous, the Akron AWOL is dead."

"No, he ain't! He's right there!"

The very idea sends a surge of adrenaline through Starkey's body, finally bringing circulation back to his limbs. But no—as he looks at this teen trying to rein in the chaos, he realizes this couldn't be Connor Lassiter. This kid does not look the part at all. His hair is tousled, not coolly slicked back, the way Starkey always imagined it would be. This kid looks too open and honest—not quite innocent, but he has nowhere near the level of jaded anger that the Akron AWOL would have. The only thing about him that could even slightly resemble Starkey's image of

27

Connor Lassiter would be the slight smirk that always seems to be on his face. No, this kid before them, trying to command their respect, is nobody special. Nobody at all.

"Let me be the first to welcome you to the Graveyard," he says, delivering what must be the same speech he delivers to every batch of new arrivals. "Officially my name is Elvis Robert Mullard . . . but my friends call me Connor."

Cheers from the Unwinds.

"Told you so!" says the fat kid.

"Doesn't prove anything," says Starkey, his jaw set and teeth clenched as the speech continues.

"You're all here because you were marked for unwinding but escaped, and thanks to the efforts of a whole lot of people with the Anti-Divisional Resistance, you've made it here. This will be your home until you turn seventeen and can't be unwound. That's the good news. . . ."

The more he speaks, the more Starkey's heart sinks, and he comes to realize the truth of it. This *is* the Akron AWOL—and he's not larger than life at all. In fact, he barely lives up to reality.

"The bad news is that the Juvenile Authority knows about us. They know where we are and what we're doing—but so far they've left us alone."

Starkey marvels at the unfairness of it all. How could this be? How is it possible that the great champion of runaway Unwinds is just some ordinary kid?

"Some of you just want to survive to seventeen, and I don't blame you," Connor says. "But I know that many of you would risk everything to end unwinding forever."

"Yeah!" Starkey shouts out, making sure it's loud enough to draw everyone's attention away from Connor, and he starts pumping his fist in the air. "Happy Jack! Happy Jack! Happy Jack!" He gets a whole chant going in the crowd. "We'll blow up every last harvest camp!" Starkey shouts. Yet even though he's riled them up, one look from Connor throws a wet blanket over the whole crowd, silencing them.

"There's one in every crowd," says Hayden, shaking his head.

"I'm sorry to disappoint you, but we will *not* be blowing up Chop Shops," Connor says, looking right at Starkey. "They already see us as violent, and the Juvies use public fear to justify unwinding. We can't feed into that. We're not clappers. We will not commit random acts of violence. We will *think* before we act. . . ."

Starkey does not take the reprimand well. Who is this guy to shut him down? He keeps talking, but Starkey's not listening anymore, because Connor has nothing to say to him. But the others listen, and that makes Starkey burn.

Now, as he stands there, waiting for the so-called Akron AWOL to shut up, a seed starts to take root in Starkey's mind. He has killed two Juvey-cops. His legend is already set, and unlike Connor, he didn't have to pretend to die to become legendary. Starkey has to smile. This airplane salvage yard is filled with hundreds of Unwinds, but in the end, it's no different from the safe houses—and like those safe houses, here is just one more beta male waiting for an alpha like Starkey to put him in his place.

2 · Miracolina

The girl has known since before she can remember that her body has been sanctified to God.

She has always been aware that on her thirteenth birthday she would be tithed and would experience the glorious mystery of having a divided body and a networked soul. Not networked in the computer sense—for the pouring of one's soul into hardware happens only in the movies, and never to good results. No, this would be a *true* networking within living flesh. A stretching of her spirit among the dozens of people touched by her divided body. There are people who say it's death, but she believes it to be something else—something mystical, and she believes it with every ounce of her soul.

"I suppose one cannot know what such division is like until one experiences it," her priest once told her. It struck her as odd that the priest, who was always so confident in church dogma, spoke of uncertainty whenever he talked about tithing.

"The Vatican has yet to take a position on unwinding," he pointed out, "and so until it is either condoned or condemned, I can be as uncertain about it as I please."

It always made her bristle when he called tithing unwinding, as if they were the same thing. They're not. The way she sees it, the cursed and unwanted are unwound—but the blessed and the loved are tithed. The process might be the same, but the intent is different, and in this world, intent is everything.

Her name is Miracolina—from the Italian word for "miracle." She was named this because she was conceived to save her brother's life. Her brother, Matteo, was diagnosed with leukemia when he was ten. The family had moved from Rome to Chicago for his treatment, but even with harvest banks all over the nation, a marrow match could not be found for his rare blood type. The only way to save him was to create a match—and so that's exactly what his parents did. Nine months later Miracolina was born, doctors took marrow from her hip and gave it to Matteo, and her brother was saved. Easy as that. Now he's twenty-four and in graduate school, all thanks to Miracolina.

Even before she understood what it meant to be a tithe, she knew she was 10 percent of a larger whole. "We had ten embryos in vitro," her mother once told her. "Only one was a match for Matteo, and that was you. You were no accident, *mi carina*. We chose you."

The law was very specific when it came to the other nine embryos. Her family had to pay nine women to carry them to term. After that, the surrogates could do as they pleased—either raise the babies or stork them to a good home. "But whatever it cost, it was worth it," her parents had told her, "to have both Matteo and you."

Now, as her tithing approaches, it comforts Miracolina to know that she has nine fraternal twins out there—and who knows? Maybe a part of her divided self will go to help one of these unknown twins.

As to why she is being tithed, it has nothing to do with percentages.

"We made a pact with God," her parents told her when she was young, "that if you were born, and Matteo was saved, we would show our gratitude by gifting you back to God through tithing." Miracolina understood, even at an early age, that such a powerful pact was not easily broken.

Lately, however, her parents have become more and more emotional at the thought of it. "Forgive us," they begged her over and over again—quite often in tears. "Please forgive us for this thing we've done." And she would always forgive them, even though the request baffled her. Miracolina always felt blessed to be a tithe—to know, without question, her destiny and her purpose. Why should her parents feel sorry for giving her a purpose?

Perhaps the guilt they feel is for not throwing her a big party—but then, that had been her own choice. "First of all," she told her parents, "a tithing should be solemn, not loud. Secondly, who's going to come?"

They couldn't dispute her logic. While most tithes come from rich communities, and belong to the kinds of churches that expect tithing, theirs is a working-class neighborhood that's not exactly tithe-friendly. When you're like those rich families, surrounding yourself with like-minded people, there are plenty of friends to support you at a tithing party—enough to offset the guests who find it uncomfortable. But if Miracolina had a party, everyone there would feel awkward. That's not how she wanted to spend her last night with her family.

So there's no party. Instead she spends the evening in front of the fireplace, sitting between her parents and clicking through favorite scenes from favorite movies. Her mom even prepares her favorite meal, rigatoni Amatriciana. "Bold and spicy," her mom says, "just like you."

She sleeps that night, having no unpleasant dreams, or at least none she can remember, and in the morning she rises early, dresses in her simple daily whites, and tells her parents that she's going to school. "The van doesn't come for me until four this afternoon, so why waste the day?"

Although her parents would prefer she stay home with them, her wishes come first on this day.

At school, she sits through classes, already feeling a dreamy distance from it all. At the end of each class, the teacher awkwardly hands her all her collected classwork and grades, calculated early.

"Well then, I guess that's that," each teacher says in one way or another. Most of them can't wait for her to get out of their room. Her science teacher is the kindest, though, taking some extra time with her.

"My nephew was tithed a few years ago," he tells her. "A wonderful boy. I miss him terribly." He pauses, seeming to go far away in his thoughts. "I was told his heart went to a firefighter who saved a dozen people from a burning building. I don't know if it's true, but I'd like to believe it is."

Miracolina would like to believe it too.

Throughout the day, her classmates are just as awkward as her teachers. Some kids make a point to say good-bye. Some even give her uncomfortable hugs, but the rest say their farewells from a safe distance, as if tithing is somehow contagious.

And then there are the other ones. The cruel ones.

"See you *here and there*," a boy says behind her back during lunch, and the kids around him snicker. Miracolina turns, and the boy tries to hide behind his gaggle of friends, thinking he's safe within that cloud of rank middle-school perspiration—but she recognized his voice and knows exactly who it is. She pushes through his friends to coldly face him.

"Oh, you won't see me, Zach Rasmussen . . . but if any part of me sees you, I will definitely let you know."

Zach's face goes a little green. "Get lost," he says. "Go get tithed." But still there's that look of uneasy fear beneath his idiotic bravado.

Good, thinks Miracolina, *I hope I've given him a few nightmares.*

Her school is a huge one, so even though tithes aren't common in her neighborhood, there are four others, all dressed in white like her. There used to be six, but the oldest two are already gone. These remaining tithes are her true friends. These are the ones to whom she feels a need to say one last good-bye. Oddly, they're all from different backgrounds and faiths. Each is a member of a splinter sect of their particular religion—a sect that takes its commitment to self-sacrifice very seriously. Funny, Miracolina thinks, how these same religions fought over their differences for thousands of years, and yet in tithing, they all come together as one.

"We are all asked to give of ourselves—to be charitable and selfless," says Nestor, her tithe friend closest to her in age, only a month short of his own tithing. He clasps her hands, giving

33

Miracolina a warm good-bye. "If technology allows us a new way to give, how could it be wrong?"

Except there are people who *do* say that it's wrong. More and more people these days. There's even that ex-tithe out there—the one who became a clapper, who people hold up as an example. Well, how stable can *he* be? After all, he became a clapper, for goodness' sake. The way Miracolina sees it, if someone would rather blow themselves up than be tithed, well, that's like stealing from the collection plate, isn't it? It's just plain wrong.

When the school day ends, she walks home just like on any other day. As she comes onto her street, she sees her brother's car in the driveway. She's surprised at first—he goes to school five hours away—but she's happy Matteo's come to see her off.

It's three o'clock, an hour until the van comes, and her parents are already crying. She wishes they weren't, that they could take this as stoically as she, or even Matteo, who spends his time chatting about only the good memories.

"Remember that time we went to Rome, and you wanted to play hide-and-seek in the Vatican Museum?"

Miracolina smiles at the memory. She had tried to hide in Nero's bathtub—this huge maroon stone bowl that could practically fit an elephant. "The security guards had a fit! I thought they'd take me to the pope, and he'd spank me—so I ran."

Matteo laughs. "You went missing for, like, an hour—Mom and Dad were pulling their hair out."

Missing isn't the word for it, though. You don't go missing in a museum—you just get temporarily absorbed by the walls. She remembers moving through the crowds of the Vatican, until she found herself standing in the middle of the Sistine Chapel, gazing up toward Michelangelo's masterpiece, which covered the walls and ceiling. And there in the center was the divine link between heaven and earth. So close was Adam's hand to the hand of God, both straining to touch each other, but the impossible weight of gravity kept Adam from truly touching the heavens.

She stood there, looking up, forgetting that she was supposed to be hiding, for who could hide in a place that was all about revealed mystery? And that's exactly where her family found her; amid hundreds of tourists, staring up at the greatest work of art ever created by the hand of man—humanity's grandest attempt to touch perfection.

She was only six, but even then, the images of the chapel spoke to her, although she had no idea what they said. All she knew was that she herself was just like this beautiful place, and if someone could go inside her, they would see glorious frescoes painted on the walls of her soul.

The van arrives ten minutes early and waits out front. There's a brightly painted logo on the van's side that reads WOOD HOLLOW HARVEST CAMP! A PLACE FOR TEENS!

Miracolina goes to her room to get her suitcase—a small one filled with just a few sets of tithing whites and some basic necessities. Now her parents cry and cry, begging again for her forgiveness. This time, however, it just angers her.

"If tithing makes you feel guilty, that's not my problem," she tells them, "because I'm at peace with it. Please have enough respect for me to be at peace with it too."

It doesn't help matters. It just makes their tears flow in a steadier stream.

"The only reason you're at peace with it," her father tells her, "is because we made you feel that way. It's our fault. It's all our fault."

Miracolina looks at them and shrugs. "So change your mind, then," she suggests. "Break your pact with God and don't tithe me."

They look back at her like she's giving them a glorious

gift, a reprieve from hell. Even Matteo is hopeful.

"Yes, that's what we'll do!" her mother says. "We haven't signed the final papers yet. We can still change our minds!"

"Fine," says Miracolina. "Are you sure that's what you want?"

"Yes," says her father with intense relief. "Yes, we're sure."

"Positive?"

"Yes."

"Good, now you can be guilt free." Miracolina picks up her suitcase. "But regardless of what you choose, I'm going anyway. That's *my* choice."

Then she hugs her mother, father, and brother and leaves without looking back—without even saying good-bye, because good-byes imply an end, and more than anything else in this life, Miracolina Roselli wants to believe that her tithing is a beginning.

It's a three-hour drive to Wood Hollow Harvest Camp. The van is all plush leather seats and pop music pumped through expensive speakers. The driver is a man with a salt-and-pepper beard, a big smile, and just enough of a gut to be jolly. Santa Claus in training.

"Excited for your big day?" Chauffeur-Claus asks as they drive away from Miracolina's home and family. "Did you have a big tithing party?"

"Yes, and no," she says. "I'm excited, but no party."

"Aww . . . that's too bad. Why not?"

"Because tithing shouldn't be about me."

"Oh," is all Chauffeur-Claus can say to that. Miracolina's response is the perfect conversation killer, which is fine. The last thing she wants is to recap her life for this man, no matter how jolly he is.

"There are drinks in the cooler," he tells her. "Help yourself." And then he leaves her alone.

Twenty minutes into the drive, instead of turning onto the interstate, they enter a gated community.

"One more pickup this afternoon," Chauffeur-Claus tells her. "Tuesdays are lean, so it's just this stop. Hope you don't mind."

"Not at all."

They stop at a house that's at least three times larger than her own, where a boy in white waits out front with his family. She does not watch as he says his good-byes. She looks out of the other window, giving them their privacy. Finally Chauffeur-Claus opens the door, and in comes a boy with straight dark hair, perfectly trimmed, bright blue eyes, and skin as pale as bone china—as if he had been kept out of the sun all his life to keep his skin pure as a baby's bottom for his tithing.

"Hi," he says shyly. His tithing whites are shiny satin and trimmed in fine gold brocade. This boy's parents spared no expense. Miracolina's tithing whites, on the other hand, are simple raw silk, unbleached so their whiteness won't be so blinding that it draws attention to itself. Compared to hers, this boy's whites are like a neon advertisement.

The seats in the van aren't in rows—they all face center, to encourage camaraderie. The boy sits across from Miracolina, thinks for a moment, then reaches across the gap, offering his hand for her to shake. "I'm Timothy," he says. She shakes his hand. It's clammy and cold, like the way your hands get before a school play.

"My name's Miracolina."

"Wow, that's a mouthful!" Then he chuckles, probably mad at himself for saying it. "Do people call you Mira, or Lina, or something to shorten it?"

"It's Miracolina," she tells him. "And no one shortens it."

"Okay, well, pleased to meet you, Miracolina."

The van starts up, and Timothy waves good-bye to his large family still outside, and although they wave to him as well, it's clear that they can't even see him through the dark glass. The van pulls out and begins to wind out of the neighborhood. Even before they leave the gate, Timothy begins to look uncomfortable, like he's got a stomachache, but Miracolina knows if his stomach bothers him, it's just a symptom of something else. This boy has not found peace with his tithing yet. Or if he had, he lost it the moment the van door closed, cutting the umbilical to his old life. As insulted as she is by his lavish whites and exclusive neighborhood, Miracolina begins to feel sorry for him. His fear hangs in the air around them like a web full of black widows. No one should journey to their tithing in terror.

"So, the ride is like three hours, or something?" Timothy asks, his voice shaky.

"Yes," says Chauffeur-Claus brightly. "There's an entertainment system with hundreds of preprogrammed movies to pass the time. Help yourselves!"

"Yeah, okay, sure," says Timothy. "Maybe later, though."

For a few minutes, he seems lost in his own thoughts. Then he turns to Miracolina again.

"They say tithes get treated really well at harvest camp. You think it's true? They say it's lots of fun, and we're with tons of other kids just like us." He clears his throat. "They say we even get to choose the day when we . . . when we . . . well, you know . . ."

Miracolina smiles at him warmly. Usually tithes like Timothy go to harvest camp in a limo—but she knows why Timothy didn't, without having to ask. He didn't want to make the journey alone. Well, if fate has brought them together on this momentous day, she will be the friend he needs.

"I'm sure harvest camp will be just the experience you want it to be," she tells him, "and when you choose your date, you'll choose it because you're ready. That's why they let us choose. So it's *our* decision, no one else's."

Timothy looks into her with those piercing perfect eyes. "You're not scared at all, are you?"

She chooses to answer his question with another question. "Have you ever been on an airplane?" she asks him.

"Huh?" Timothy is thrown by the change of subject. "Yeah, a bunch of times."

"Were you scared the first time you flew?"

"Yeah, sure, I guess."

"But you went anyway. Why?"

Timothy shrugs. "I wanted to get where I was going, and my parents were with me and said it would be okay."

"Well," says Miracolina, "there you go."

Timothy looks at her, blinking with a kind of innocence Miracolina doesn't think she ever had. "So then, you're not scared?"

She sighs. "Yes, I'm scared," she admits. "Very scared. But when you trust that it will all be okay, you can enjoy the fear.

You can use it to help you instead of letting it hurt you."

"Oh, I get it," says Timothy. "It's like a scary movie, you know? You can have fun with it because you know it's not real no matter how scared it makes you." Then he thinks about it a bit more. "But getting unwound *is* real. It's not like we're going to walk out of the theater and go home. It's not like I'm going to get off a plane and be in Disneyland."

"Tell you what," Miracolina says, before Timothy can drag himself back into his pit of spider-filled despair. "Let's watch one of those scary movies and get it all out of our systems before we get to harvest camp."

Timothy nods obediently. "Yeah, sure, okay."

But as she scrolls through all the preprogrammed movies, none of them are scary. They're all family films and comedies.

"It's okay," says Timothy. "To tell you the truth, I don't like scary movies anyway."

In a few minutes, they're on the interstate making good time. Timothy contents himself with video games to keep his mind from going to dark places, and Miracolina puts in her earphones, listening to her own eclectic mix of music, rather than the van's vapid pop tunes. There are 2,129 songs in her iChip, and she's determined to listen to as many as she can before the day she enters the divided state.

About two hours and thirty songs later, the van exits the interstate and turns down a scenic road winding through dense woods. "Just half an hour now," Chauffeur-Claus tells them. "We made good time!"

Then, as they come around a bend, he slams on the brakes, and the van screeches to a halt.

Miracolina takes off her earphones. "What's going on? What's wrong?"

"Stay here," orders Chauffeur-Claus, no longer jolly, and he jumps out of the van.

Timothy already has his nose pressed against the window, looking out. "This can't be good."

"No," agrees Miracolina. "It can't."

Just off the road in a ditch is another Wood Hollow Harvest Camp van, but this one is overturned, wheels to the sky. There's no telling how long it has been there.

"He must have blown a tire or something, and skidded off the road," says Timothy. But none of the tires look blown.

"We should call for help," says Miracolina—but no one brings a phone to harvest camp, so neither she nor Timothy has one.

Just then there's a commotion outside. Half a dozen people dressed in black with faces hidden by ski masks come leaping out of the woods from all directions. The chauffeur is hit with a tranq bullet to the neck and goes down like an overstuffed rag doll.

"Lock the door!" shouts Miracolina, and doesn't wait. She pushes Timothy out of the way to get to the driver's unlocked door—but she's not fast enough. Just as she reaches for the lock, the door is pulled open, and the assailant hits the button that pops all the locks. All the van's doors are pulled open at once by the masked attackers. Clearly these attackers have done this before and have gotten good at it. Timothy screams as hands reach in, pulling him out. He tries to wriggle free, but it's useless. If his fear is a web, then the spiders have got him.

Two more figures reach for Miracolina, and she drops to the floor, kicking at them.

"Don't you touch me! Don't you touch me!"

Her fear, which had been so well under control, explodes from her now, because this violation of her journey is a far greater unknown than harvest camp. She kicks, and bites, and claws in terror and outrage, but it's no use—because in the end, she hears the telltale *pffft* of a tranq gun firing. She feels

41

the sharp jab of the tranq bullet as it embeds itself in her arm, and the world goes dark as she spirals helplessly into that timeless place where all sedated souls go.

Waking up after being tranq'd is not a pleasant experience. With consciousness comes a splitting headache, a terrible taste in one's mouth, and the disturbing feeling that something has been stolen from you.

Miracolina awakes to the sound of someone crying beside her, begging for mercy. She recognizes the voice as Timothy's. He's definitely not the kind of boy built to handle something like this. She can't see him, though, because her eyes are covered by a thick blindfold.

"It's all right, Timothy," she calls to him. "Whatever's going on, it's going to be okay." Hearing her voice makes his pleas and sobs settle into whimpers.

Miracolina shifts to feel the position of her body. She's sitting upright, and her neck aches from the position in which it had hung while she slept. Her hands are behind her back, tied together. Her legs are tied to the chair she sits in. Not painfully, but tight enough to ensure she won't break free.

"Okay," says the voice of a boy in front of them. "You can take off their blindfolds."

Her blindfold is pulled off, and although the light around her is not bright, it's still painful to keep her eyes open. She squints, slowly letting her eyes adjust and focus.

They're in some sort of grand, high-ceilinged ballroom. Crystal chandeliers, artwork on the walls—it looks like the kind of place where French royalty would have entertained high society before getting themselves beheaded. Except that this place is falling apart. There are holes in the ceiling through which pigeons freely fly in and out of the daylight. The paintings are peeling with weather damage, and the rank smell of mildew fills the air. There's no telling how far they've been taken from their destination.

"I'm really sorry we had to do it this way," the boy sitting in front of them says. He's not dressed like any sort of royalty. Even moldy royalty. He wears simple jeans and a light blue T-shirt. His hair is pale brown, almost blond, and too long—like he hasn't had a haircut in recent memory. He seems to be her age, but the tired look around his eyes makes him appear older, like he's seen many more things than anyone ought to see at their age. He also seems a little bit frail in some indefinable way.

"We couldn't risk you getting hurt, or figuring out where we were taking you. It was the only way to safely rescue you."

"Rescue us?" says Miracolina, speaking up for the first time. "Is that what you call this?"

"Well, it might not feel that way at the moment, but yes, that's exactly what we've done."

And all at once, Miracolina knows who this is. A wave of rage and nausea courses through her. Of all the unfair things to happen to her, why did she have to face *this*? Why did she have to be captured by *him*? She feels the kind of anger, the kind of hatred she knows is not good for her soul, especially this close to her tithing—but try as she might, she can't purge herself of the bitterness.

Then Timothy gasps, and his watery eyes go wide.

"You're him!" he says with the kind of enthusiasm boys like Timothy usually save for encounters with sports stars. "You're that tithe who became a clapper! You're Levi Calder!"

The boy across from them nods and smiles. "Yes, but my friends call me Lev."

3 · Cam

Wrists. Ankles. Neck. Strapped down. Itching. Itching all over. Can't move.

He flexes his hands and feet in the bonds. Side to side, up and down. It scratches the itch, but makes it burn.

"You're awake," says a voice that's familiar, and yet not. "Good. Very good."

He turns his neck. No one. Just white walls around him.

The scrape of a chair. Closer. Closer. The person who spoke comes into blurry view, moving her chair into his line of sight. Sitting. Legs crossed. Smiling, but not smiling. Not really.

"I was wondering when you'd wake up."

She wears dark pants and a blouse. Pattern of the blouse too blurry to make out. And the color. The color. He can't put a finger on the color.

"ROY-G-BIV," he says, searching. "Yellow. Blue. No." He

grunts. His throat hurts when he speaks, and the words come out raspy. "Grass. Trees. Devil puke."

"Green," the woman says. "That's the word you're looking for, isn't it? My blouse is green."

Can the woman read minds? Maybe not. Maybe she's just clever. Her voice is gentle and refined. There's an accent to it. Slightly British, perhaps. It automatically makes him want to trust her.

"Do you recognize me?" she asks.

"No. Yes," he says, feeling his thoughts cinched in bonds tighter than the ones that secure him to the bed.

"Fair enough," says the woman. "This is all very new to you—you must be frightened."

Until that moment, it hasn't occurred to him that he should be frightened at all. But now that the crossed-legged, green-shirted woman says he must be, then he must be. He tugs against his bonds in fear. The burning itch begins to hurt even more, and it brings forth a jagged shattering of memories that he must speak aloud.

"Hand on stove. Belt buckle—no, Mom, no! Falling from bike. Broken arm. Knife. He stabbed me with a knife!"

"Pain," says the cross-legged woman calmly. "'Pain' is the word you're looking for."

It is a magic word, for it calms him down. "Pain," he repeats, hearing the word as it spills from strange vocal cords, and over unfamiliar lips. He stops struggling. The pain fades to burning, and the burning fades to an itch once more. But the thoughts that came along with the pain are still there. The burned hand; the angry mother; the broken arm; and a knife fight that he never fought, and yet somehow did. Somehow, all these things happened to him.

He looks again to the woman, who studies him coolly. Now that his focus is better, he can see the pattern of the blouse.

"Paste . . . palsy . . . hailey."

"Keep trying," says the woman. "It's in there somewhere."

His brain twitches. He struggles. Thinking feels like a race. A long, grueling Olympic race. What is that race called? It starts with an *M*.

"Paisley!" he says triumphantly. "Marathon! Paisley!"

"Yes, I imagine this is as exhausting as a marathon for you," says the woman, "but it was worth the effort." She touches the collar of her blouse. "You're right, it *does* have a paisley pattern!" She smiles, this time for real, and touches his forehead with her fingertip. He can feel the tip of her nail. "I told you it was in there."

Now that his thoughts are beginning to settle, he realizes that he does recognize the woman, but has no idea from where.

"Who?" he asks. "Who? Where? When?"

"How, what, and why," she adds with a smirk. "Your question words have all returned."

"Who?" he demands again, not appreciating the joke at his expense.

She sighs. "Who am I? You can say I'm your touchstone, your connection to the world—and in a sense your translator, because I can understand you, where few others can. I'm an expert in metalinguistics."

"Meta . . . meta."

"It's the nature of the language you speak. Metaphoric associations. But I can see I'm confusing you. It's not for you to worry about. My name is Roberta. But you wouldn't know that, because I never told you my name in all the times you've seen me."

"All the times?"

Roberta nods. "You can say you've only seen me once, yet you've also seen me many, many times. What do you think of that?"

It's a marathon again as he searches through his mind for the word he wants to say. "Gollum in the caves. Answer, or you can't cross the bridge. What's black and white and red all over?"

"Work for it," says Roberta. "I know you can do it."

"Riddle!" he says. "Yes, marathon but worth it! The word—riddle!"

"Very good." Roberta gently touches his hand. He takes a long look at her. She is older than him. He knows this, even though he has no idea how old he actually is. She's pretty, in a motherly sort of way. Blond hair with a hint of brown roots, and just a little makeup. Her eyes seem younger than the rest of her face. But that blouse . . .

"Medusa," he says. "Crone. Witch. Crooked, rotten teeth."

She stiffens a bit. "You think I'm ugly?"

"Uuuugly!" he says, savoring the word. "No, not you! Ugly green paisley ugly."

Roberta laughs, relieved, and glances down at her blouse. "Well, I guess there's no accounting for taste, is there?"

Accounting! Accountant! My father was an accountant! No—a policeman. No—a factory worker. No—lawyer, construction worker, pharmacist, dentist, unemployed, dead. His thoughts are all true, and all false. His own mind is a riddle that he can't hope to solve. He feels the fear that Roberta told him he must feel. It wells up again, and he begins to struggle once more against his bonds. They're not just bonds, though; some of them are bandages.

"Who?" he asks again.

"I already told you," Roberta says. "Don't you remember?"

"No! *Who?*" he asks. "*Who?*"

Roberta raises her eyebrows in understanding. "Oh. Who are *you?*"

He waits anxiously for an answer.

"Well, that's the million-dollar question, isn't it? Who *are* you?" She taps her fingertips on her chin, considering it. "The committee could not agree on a name. Of course, everyone has an opinion, the pompous buffoons. So, while they're dickering about it, perhaps you can choose one for yourself."

"Choose?" But why must he choose a name? Shouldn't he already have one? He runs a series of names through his mind: Matthew, Johnny, Eric, José, Chris, Alex, Spencer—and although some of them seem more likely than others, none of them hold the sense of identity that a true name should have. He shakes his head, trying to push something—*anything*—about himself into its proper place, but shaking his head only makes it hurt.

"Aspirin," he says. "Tylenol-aspirin, then count the sheep."

"Yes, I imagine you must still be tired. We'll up your pain medication, and I'll leave you to get some rest. We'll talk more tomorrow."

She pats his hand, then strides out of the room, turning off the light and leaving him alone with thought fragments that won't as much as shake hands with one another in the dark.

The next day—or at least he thinks it's the next day—he's not quite so tired, and his head doesn't hurt as much, but he's still just as confused. He now suspects that the white room that he took for a hospital room is not. There were enough hints in the architecture to suggest he was in some private residence that had been retrofitted for the convalescence of a single patient. There is a sound beyond the window that he can hear even when the window is closed. A constant rhythmic roar and hiss. Only after a day of hearing it does he realize what it is. Crashing waves. Wherever he is, it's on a seashore, and he longs to see the view. He asks and Roberta obliges. Today is the day he gets out of bed.

Two strong uniformed guards come in with Roberta. They

undo his bonds and help him to his feet, holding him beneath his armpits.

"Don't be afraid," Roberta says. "I know you can do this."

The first moment of standing gives him vertigo. He looks to his bare feet, seeing only toes sticking out from beneath the pale blue hospital gown he wears. Those toes seem miles beneath him. He begins to walk, one labored step at a time.

"Good," says Roberta, walking along with him. "How does it feel?"

"Skydiving," he says.

"Hmm," says Roberta, considering this. "Do you mean dangerous or exhilarating?"

"Yes," he answers. In his mind he repeats both words, remembering them, pulling them from a massive box of unsorted adjectives and filing them in their proper place. There are so many unsorted words in the box, but bit by bit, it's all beginning to slide into coherent formation.

"It's all in there," Roberta has told him more than once. "It's just a matter of finding it."

The two guards continue to hold him beneath his armpits as he shuffles along. A knee buckles, and their grip grows tighter.

"Careful, sir."

The guards always call him "sir." It must mean that he commands respect, although he can't imagine why. He envies their ability to simply "be" without having to work at it.

Roberta leads them down a hallway that, like the distance to his feet, seems like miles, but is only a dozen yards or so. Up above, in the corner of the ceiling, there's a machine with a lens that zeroes in on him. There's a machine like that in his room, too, constantly watching him in silence. *Electric eye. Cyclops lens.* He knows the name for the device. It's on the tip of his tongue. "Say cheese!" he says. "It puts on ten pounds. Rolling . . . and . . . action! A Kodak moment."

"The word you're looking for starts with a *c*, and that's all the help I'll give you," Roberta says.

"Cuh—cuh—Cadaver. Cabana. Cavalry. Canada."

Roberta purses her lips. "You can do better."

He sighs and gives up before frustration can overwhelm him. Right now, it's hard to master walking, much less walking and thinking at the same time.

Now they come through a door to a place that is both inside and out.

"Balcony!" he says.

"Yes," Roberta tells him. "That one came easy."

Beyond the balcony is an endless sea, shimmering in the warm sun, and before him are two chairs and a small table. On the table are cookies and a white beverage in a crystal pitcher. He should know the name of that beverage.

"Comfort food," Roberta tells him. "Your reward for making the journey."

They sit facing each other with the food between them and the guards at the ready, should he need their help, or should he try to hurl himself off the balcony to the jagged rocks below. There are soldiers with dark, heavy weapons positioned strategically on those rocks—there for his protection, Roberta tells him. He imagines that should he hurl himself down to them, the guards on the rocks would also call him "sir."

Roberta pours the white liquid from its crystalline pitcher into crystalline glasses that catch the light, refracting it and splintering it in random projections on the stonework of the balcony.

He takes a bite of cookie. Chocolate chip. Suddenly the intensity of the flavor drags more memories out of hibernation. He thinks of his mother. Then another mother. School lunch. Burning his lip on a freshly baked Toll House. *I like them best chewy and hot. I like them best hard and almost burnt. I'm allergic to chocolate. Chocolate is my favorite.*

He knows all these things are true. How could they all be true? If he's allergic, how could he have so many wonderful chocolate memories?

"The marathon riddle continuing," he says.

Roberta smiles. "That was almost a complete sentence. Here, have something to drink."

She holds the glass of cold white liquid to him, and he takes it.

"Have you given any thought to your name?" Roberta asks, just as he takes a sip—and all at once, as the flavorful fluid dislodges a piece of soft cookie from the roof of his mouth, more thoughts fly in. The combination of tastes forces a hundred thoughts through a sieve, leaving behind diamonds.

The electric eye machine. He knows what it's called! And the white stuff, it's from a cow, isn't it? Cow juice. Starts with an *M*. Electric eye. "Cam!" Cow juice. "Moo!"

Roberta looks at him strangely.

"Cam . . . Moo . . . ," he says again.

Her eyes sparkle, and she says, *"Camus?"*

"Cam. Moo."

"Camus! What a splendid name. You've outdone yourself."

"Camera!" he finally says. "Milk!" But Roberta isn't listening anymore. He has sent her to a more exotic place.

"Camus, the existential philosopher! 'Live to the point of tears.' Kudos to you, my friend! Kudos!"

He has no idea what she's talking about, but if it makes her happy, then it makes him happy. It feels good to know that he's impressed her.

"Your name shall be Camus Composite-Prime," she says with a grin on her face as wide as the shimmering sea. "Won't the committee just die!"

From then on, each of his days begins and ends with therapy. Painful stretching followed by guided exercises and weight lifting that seem specifically designed to cause him the greatest amount of pain.

"The healing agents can only do so much," says his physical therapist—a deep-voiced bodybuilder with the unlikely name of Kenny. "The rest has to come from you."

He is convinced this therapist enjoys watching him suffer.

Thanks to Roberta, those who don't just call him "sir" now call him Camus, but when he thinks of the name, all that comes to mind is a big black-and-white whale.

"That's *Shamu*," Roberta tells him over lunch. "You're *Camus*; it rhymes, but has a silent S."

"Cam," he tells her, not wanting to sound like a sea mammal. "Make it Cam."

Roberta raises an eyebrow, considering it. "We can do that. We can most certainly do that. I'll let everyone know. So how are your thoughts today, Cam? Feeling a bit more cohesive?"

Cam shrugs. "I have clouds in my head."

Roberta sighs. "Maybe so, but I can see your progress, even if you can't. Your thoughts are becoming a little clearer each day. You can string together longer strands of meaning, and you understand almost everything I say to you, don't you?"

Cam nods.

"Comprehension is the first step toward clear communication, Cam." Roberta hesitates for a second, then says, "*Comprends-tu maintenant?*"

"*Oui, parfaitement*," says Cam, not knowing that something was different about it until the words came out of his mouth. He realizes that yet another door of mystery has opened inside his head.

"Well," says Roberta, a mischievous smirk on her face, "for the time being, let's go one language at a time, shall we?"

New activities are added into his day. His afternoon naps are pushed back to make room for hour-long sessions sitting at a table-size computer desktop filled with digital images: a red vehicle, a building, a black-and-white portrait—dozens of pictures.

"Drag to you the images you recognize," says Roberta on the first day of this ritual, "and say the first word that each image brings to mind."

Cam feels overwhelmed. "Scantron?"

"No," Roberta tells him, "it's not a test, it's just a mental exercise to find out what you remember and what you still need to learn."

"Right," says Cam. "Scantron." Because her answer is the very definition of a test, isn't it?

He looks at the images and does as he's told, pulling the objects he recognizes closer. The portrait: "Lincoln." The building: "Eiffel." The red vehicle: "Truck fire. No. Fire truck." And on and on. As he pulls an image away, another sprouts to replace it. Some he has no problem identifying, others have no memories associated with them at all, and still others tug at the edge of his mind, but he can't find a word to attach to them.

Finally, when he's done, he feels even more exhausted than he does after physical therapy.

"Basket," he says. "Crumpled paper basket."

Roberta smiles. "Wasted. You feel wasted."

"Wasted," Cam repeats, locking the word in his mind.

"I'm not surprised—none of this is easy, but you've done well, haven't you? And you are to be commended!"

Cam nods, more than ready for a nap. "Gold star for me."

Each day more and more is asked of him, both physically and mentally, but no explanation is given for any of it. "Your success is its own reward," Roberta tells him, but how can he relish any success if he has no context with which to measure it?

"The kitchen sink!" he tells Roberta at dinner one day. It's just the two of them. It's always just the two of them. "The kitchen sink! Now!"

She doesn't even have to probe to figure out what he means. "In time you'll know everything there is to know about yourself. Now is not that time."

"Yes, it is!"

"Cam, this conversation is over."

Cam feels the anger well in him and doesn't know what to do with it, and he can't put enough words together to take it away.

Instead it goes to his hands, and before he knows what he's doing, he's hurling a plate across the room, then another, then another. Roberta has to duck, and now the whole world is flying dishes and silverware and glass. In an instant the guards are on him, pulling him back to his room, strapping him to the bed—something they haven't done for over a week.

He rages for what feels like forever, but then, exhausted, he calms down. Roberta comes in. She's bleeding. It's just a small cut above her left eye, but it doesn't matter how small it is. He did it. It was his fault.

Suddenly all his other emotions are overwhelmed by remorse, which he finds is even more powerful than anger.

"Broke my sister's piggy bank," he says in tears. "Crashed my father's car. Badness. Badness."

"I know you're sorry," Roberta says, sounding as tired as him. "I'm sorry too." She gently takes his hand.

"You'll be restrained until morning for your outburst," she tells him. "Your actions have consequences."

He nods, understanding. He wants to wipe away his tears, but he can't, for his hands are secured to the bed. Roberta does it for him. "Well, at least we know you're every bit as strong as we thought you'd be. They weren't kidding when they said you were a baseball pitcher."

Immediately Cam's mind scans his memory for the sport. Had he played it? His mind might be disjointed and fragmented, so finding what it contains is always difficult, but it's easy to know what memories don't exist at all.

"Never a pitcher," he says. "Never."

"Of course not," she says calmly. "I don't know what I was thinking."

Bit by bit and day by day, as more things fall into place in Cam's mind, he begins to realize his terrifying uniqueness. It is night now. His physical therapy has left him, for once, feeling more exhilarated than exhausted—but there was something Kenny the therapist had said. . . .

"You're strong, but your muscle groups don't work and play well with others."

Cam knew it was just an offhand joke, but there was a truth to it that stuck in Cam's craw, the way food often did. The way his throat didn't always agree to swallow what his tongue was pushing its way.

"Eventually your body will learn the alliances it has to

make with itself," Kenny had said—as if Cam was a factory full of strike-prone workers, or worse, a clutch of slaves forced into unwanted labor.

That night Cam looks at the scars along his wrists, like hairline bracelets, visible now that the bandages have been removed. He looks down to the thick, ropy line stretching down the center of his chest, then forking left and right above his perfectly sculpted abs. Sculpted. Like a piece of marble hewn into human form—an artist's vision of perfection. This cliffside mansion, Cam now realizes, is nothing more than a gallery, and he is the work on display. Perhaps he should feel special, but all he feels is alone.

He reaches toward his face, which he has been told not to touch. That's when Roberta comes in. She knows he's been taking stock of his body, having spied on him through the camera lurking in the corner of the room. She is accompanied by two guards, for they can already tell Cam's emotions are starting to surge and threaten a tempest.

"What's wrong, Cam?" asks Roberta. "Tell me. Find the words."

His fingertips graze his face, which is filled with strange textures, but he's afraid to truly *feel* his face, for fear that in his anger he might tear it apart.

Find the words. . . .

"Alice!" he says. "Carol! Alice!" The words are wrong, he knows they're wrong, but they are the closest he can get to what he wants to say. All he can do is circle, circle, circle the point, lost in orbit around his own mind.

"Alice!" He points to the bathroom. "Carol!"

A guard grins knowingly, but knowing nothing. "Maybe he's remembering old girlfriends."

"Quiet!" snaps Roberta. "Go on, Cam."

He closes his eyes, forcing the thought to take shape, but

the only form that comes is the ridiculous shape of—

"*Walrus!*" His thoughts are useless. Pointless. He despises himself.

But then Roberta says, ". . . and the Carpenter?"

He snaps his eyes to her. "Yes! Yes!" Somehow, as random as those two things are, they make perfect sense.

"'The Walrus and the Carpenter,'" says Roberta, "an absurd poem that makes even less sense than you!"

He waits for her to connect at least some of the dots for him.

"It was written by Lewis Carroll. Who also wrote—"

"Alice!"

"Yes, he wrote *Alice in Wonderland*, and *Through the*—"

"*Looking Glass!*" Cam points to the bathroom. "*Through the Looking Glass!*" But he knows that's not the word people use for it anymore. The modern word is—

"Mirror!" he shouts. "My face! In the mirror! My face!"

There is not a single mirror anywhere in the mansion, or at least in the rooms he's allowed in. Not a single reflective surface anywhere. It could not be an accident. "Mirror!" he shouts triumphantly. "I want to look in a mirror. I want to look now! Show me!" It is the clearest statement and the highest level of communication he has yet to achieve. Surely Roberta will reward that!

"Show me now! *Ahora! Maintenant! Ima!*"

"Enough!" says Roberta, with calculated force in her voice. "Not today. You're not ready!"

"No!" He touches his face with his fingers, this time hard enough that it begins to hurt. "It's Dauger in the iron mask, not Narcissus at the pool! Seeing will lighten the load, not break the camel's back!"

The guards look to Roberta, ready to leap in, to restrain him, to tie him once more to his bed, where he can't hurt himself. But Roberta does not give the order. She hesitates. Considers. Then she finally says, "Come with me." She turns and strides out of the room, leaving Cam and his guards to follow.

They leave the wing of the mansion that has been carefully designed for his protection, journeying to places that seem far less clinical. Rooms with warm wooden floors instead of cold linoleum. Framed artwork instead of bare white walls.

Roberta tells the guards to wait at the door, and she leads Cam into a living room. There are people present: Kenny, and some members of his therapy staff, as well as others whom Cam doesn't know; professionals of some sort who work behind the scenes of his life. When they see him, they rise from their leather chairs and sofas, alarmed by his presence.

"It's all right," Roberta tells them. "Give us a few minutes alone." They drop whatever they're doing and scurry out. Cam would ask Roberta who they are, but he already knows. They're like the guards at his door, and the guards on the rocks, and the man who cleans his messes, and the woman who rubs lotion on his scars. All these people are there to serve him.

Roberta leads him to a full-length mirror against a wall. He can see himself now head to toe. He sheds the hospital gown and stands there in his shorts, looking at himself. The shape of his body is beautiful; he is perfectly proportioned, muscular and trim. For a moment he thinks maybe he is Narcissus after all, absorbed in vanity—but as he steps closer and more into the light, he can see the scars. He knew they were there, but to see them all at once is overwhelming. They are ugly, and they're everywhere—but nowhere are they more pronounced than on his face.

That face is a nightmare.

Strips of flesh, all different shades, like a living quilt stretched across the bone, muscle and cartilage beneath. Even his head—clean-shaven when he awoke, but now filling in with peach-fuzz hair—has different colors and textures sprouting like uneven fields of clashing crops. His eyes ache from the sight of himself, and tears cloud them.

"Why?" is all he can think to say. He turns from his reflection, trying to disappear into his own shoulder, but Roberta gently touches that shoulder.

"Don't look away," she says. "Have the strength to see what I see."

He forces himself to look again, but all he can see are the scars.

"Monster!" he says. That word comes from so many different bits of memory, he needs no help finding it. "Frankenstein!"

"No," Roberta says sharply. "Never think that! That monster was made from dead flesh, but you are made of the living! That creature was a violation of all things natural, but you, Cam, you are a new world wonder!"

Now she looks into the mirror with him, pointing out his many miraculous parts. "Your legs belonged to a varsity runner," she tells him, "and your heart to a boy who could have been an Olympic swimmer, had he not been unwound. Your arms and shoulders once belonged to the best baseball player any harvest camp had ever seen, and your hands? They played guitar with rare and glorious talent!" Then she smiles and catches his gaze in the mirror. "As for your eyes, they came from a boy who could melt a girl's heart with a single glance."

There is a certain pride in the way she speaks of him. It's a pride he cannot yet feel himself.

Roberta puts a finger to his temple. "But the best of it all is right in here!" She moves her finger around the multitextured fuzz of his hair, pointing out different spots on his cranium, like travel destinations on a globe.

"Your left frontal lobe holds the analytical and computational skills of seven kids who tested at the genius level in math and science. Your right frontal lobe combines the creative cores

59

of almost a dozen poets, artists, and musicians. Your occipital lobe holds neuron bundles from countless Unwinds with photographic memories, and your language center is an international hub of nine languages, all waiting to be reawakened."

She touches his chin, turning him to face her. Her eyes, which seemed so far away in the mirror, are now only inches from his. They are hypnotic and overpowering.

"*Anata wa randamu de wa nai*, Cam," she says. "*Anata wa interijento ni sekkei sa rete imasu.*"

And Cam knows what she's saying. *You are not random, Cam. You are intelligently designed.* He has no idea what language it is, but he knows what it means, all the same.

"Every part of you was handpicked from the best and the brightest," Roberta tells him, "and I was there at each unwinding, so you would see me, hear me, and know me once all the parts were united." She takes a moment to think about it, and sadly shakes her head. "Those poor kids were too dysfunctional to know how to use the gifts they were given—but now, even divided, they can finally be complete through you!"

Now that she speaks of unwinding, fragments of memories flood him.

Yes, he had seen her!

Standing beside the operating table without as much as a surgical mask to cover her face, because the point, he now realizes, was for her to be seen and remembered. But it wasn't just one operating room, was it?

An identical memory
from dozens of different places in his mind.
But it's not his mind, is it?
It's their minds.
All of them.
Crying out.
Please, please make this stop,

until there is no voice to beg,
no mind to scream.
At that singular moment
When "I am" becomes "I'm not . . ."

He takes a deep, shuddering breath. Those final memories are a part of him now, spliced together, like the skin of his face. The memories are impossible to bear, and yet he bears them. Only now does he realize how strong he truly must be to hold the memory of a hundred unwindings without crumbling to nothing.

Roberta bids him to look around at the wealthy spoils of the cliffside mansion. "As you can see by your surroundings, we have very powerful backing to support you, so that you may continue to grow and prosper."

"Backing? From who?"

"It doesn't matter who. They're friends. Not just your friends, but friends of a world we all want to live in."

And though it is all beginning to come together, his whole life beginning to slide into place, one thing still plagues him.

"My face . . . it's horrible . . ."

"Not to worry," Roberta says. "The scars will heal—in fact, the healing agents are already taking effect. Soon those scars will vanish completely, leaving the faintest of lines where the grafts meet. Trust me on this; I've seen the projection of what you will look like, Cam, and it is spectacular!"

He traces his fingers along the scars on his face. They are not as random as he had thought. They are symmetrical, the different skin tones forming a pattern. A design.

"It was a choice we made to give you a piece of every ethnicity. From the palest sienna-Caucasian, to the darkest umber tones of unspoiled Africa, and everything in between. Hispanic, Asian, Islander, Native, Australoid, Indian, Semitic—a glorious mosaic of humanity! You are everyman, Cam, and the truth of it is evident in your face. I promise you, when those scars heal, you will be the new definition of handsome! You will be a shining beacon, the greatest hope for the human race. You will show them that, Cam! By the mere virtue of your existence, you will show them!"

As he thinks of this, his heart accelerates, pounding powerfully in his chest. He imagines all the races this heart of his has won—and although he has no memory of being a star swimmer, his heart knows what his mind does not. It longs to be in the pool once more, just as his legs long for the track.

Right now, however, those legs buckle beneath him, and he finds himself on the ground, wondering how he got there.

"Too much stimulation for one day," Roberta says.

The guards, who have been watching from the door, race in and help him up.

"Are you all right, sir? Should we call for help, ma'am?"

"That won't be necessary. I'll tend to him."

They bring him to a plush sofa. He's shivering now, not just from the chill in the air, but from the revelation of knowing his own personal truth. Roberta grabs a throw blanket and covers him. She orders the room be made warmer, and she sits beside him like a mother comforting a feverish child.

"There are big plans for you, Cam. But you don't have to worry about that now. Right now, all you have to do is build that amazing potential; rope in all those parts of your mind that are still stray; teach every part of your body to work in concert. You are the conductor of a living orchestra, and the music you're going to make will be beyond spectacular!"

"What if it's not?" he asks.

Roberta leans over, kissing him gently on the forehead. "Simply not an option."

Cam's dreams are always lucid. He always knows that he's dreaming, and until now his dreams have been a source of intense frustration. They don't follow dream logic—they don't follow any logic—they are disjointed, disconnected, and confused. Snippets of randomness strung together by the cobweb of his unconscious mind. His dreams feel like channel surfing through mental stations so quickly, it's impossible to grasp the concept of any one thought-byte. Maddening! However, now that he knows the nature of his being, Cam finds that he's able to ride the wave.

Tonight he dreams he's in a mansion. Not the one overlooking the ocean, but one in the clouds. As he moves from room to room, it's not just the decor that changes, but the world as well—or rather, the life he's living within that world. In a kitchen, there are siblings he recognizes sitting at a table waiting for dinner. In a living room, a father asks him a question in a language that didn't make it into his brain, so he can't answer.

And then there are the hallways—long hallways with rooms on either side, containing people he knows but only slightly. These are rooms he will never enter, and those people will never be more than images, trapped in those rooms. No further memory of them exists, or at least not within the cortical tissue he received.

In each room and hallway he moves through, Cam feels an intense surge of loss, but it's balanced by the anticipation of the many rooms ahead.

At the end of the dream, he finds a final door opening on a balcony with no railing. He stands at the edge, looking down into billowing clouds below, shredded and reformed by the forces of some sentient wind. Within him a hundred voices— the voices of those who are a part of him—all speak to him, but their many voices have blurred into an unintelligible rumble. Still, he knows what they're trying to tell him. *Jump, Cam, jump!* they're saying. *Jump, because we know you can fly!*

In the morning, still high from the dream, Cam pushes himself harder than he ever had before in physical therapy. He feels the burn in his muscles now rather than the strain on his healing wounds.

"You're at the top of your game today," Kenny tells him as he treats Cam's joints with a repeating cycle of ice and heat to speed the healing. Kenny, Cam has learned, was a top trainer for the NFL, but the powerful friends of whom Roberta spoke hired him to train a single client, offering him top dollar.

"Money talks," Kenny had to admit. "Besides, it's not every day you get to be part of history in the making."

Is that what I am? Cam thinks. *Future history?* He tries to imagine the name Camus Composite-Prime taught in future classrooms, but it doesn't stick. It's the name. It sounds too clinical, like the subject of an experiment rather than the result. He ought to shorten it. Camus ComPri. The images of race cars speeding around a bend soars through his mind. The Grand Prix. That's it! *Camus Comprix.* Silent *S*, silent *X*—a name that holds as many secrets as he!

He grimaces as Kenny ices his shoulder, but today, even that pain feels good.

"Pie-marathon, no more basket!" he says, then clears his throat and allows the thought to congeal, gathering the proper words. "This marathon I'm on . . . now it's as easy as pie. Not feeling wasted at all."

Kenny laughs. "Didn't I tell you it'd get easier?"

This afternoon Cam sits on the balcony with Roberta, and they're served lunch on silver trays. Each day the foods have greater variety, but they're always in small portions. Shrimp cocktail. Beet salad. Chicken curry with couscous. All delicious challenges to his taste buds, sparking micro-memories and forcing neural connections to accompany his acute senses of taste and smell.

"All a part of your healing," Roberta tells him as they eat. "All a part of your growth."

After lunch, they sit for their daily ritual before the digital tabletop, taking in images to stimulate his visual memory. The images are more complicated now. Nothing so easy as the Eiffel Tower or a fire truck. There are obscure works of art that Cam must identify—if not the actual work, then at least the artist. Scenes from plays.

"Who is the character?"

"Lady Macbeth."

"What is she doing?"

"I don't know."

"Then make something up. Use your imagination."

There are images of people in various walks of life, and Roberta asks Cam to imagine who they might be. What they might be thinking. Roberta doesn't allow him to speak until he has taken a moment to find the proper words.

"Man on a train. Wondering what's waiting at home for dinner. Probably chicken again. He's sick of chicken."

Then, amid the pictures strewn across the computer table-top, Cam sees an image of a girl that catches his attention. Roberta follows his eyes to the image, and she immediately tries to wipe the image away, but Cam grabs her hand and stops her.

"No. Let me see."

Reluctantly Roberta takes her hand from the image. Cam drags it toward him, rotates it, and enlarges it. He can tell the picture was not taken with the girl's permission. It's framed at an odd angle. Perhaps taken secretly. A memory flashes. This same girl. On a bus.

"That picture is not supposed to be here," Roberta says. "Can we move on now?"

"Not yet."

Cam can't quite tell where the picture was taken. It's outdoors. Dusty. The girl plays a piano under something dark and metallic that shades her. The girl is beautiful.

"Clipped wings. Broken heaven." Cam closes his eyes, remembering Roberta's order that he find the proper words before he speaks. "She's like . . . an angel damaged when she fell to earth. She plays music to heal herself, but nothing can heal her brokenness."

"Very nice," says Roberta unconvincingly. "On to the next one."

Roberta reaches over and tries to drag the picture away again, but Cam slides it to his corner of the table, out of her reach. "No. Stays here."

The fact that Roberta is bothered by this just makes Cam more curious. "Who is she?"

"Nobody important." But clearly from Roberta's reaction she is.

"I will meet her."

Roberta chuckles bitterly. "Very unlikely."

"We'll see."

They get on with their mental exercises, but Cam's mind stays on the girl. Someday he will find out who she is and meet her. He will learn everything he needs to know, or more accurately, unify and organize all the things that are already there in his fragmented brain. Once he does, he'll be able to speak to this girl with confidence—and then, in his own words, and in whatever language he needs to, he'll be able to ask her why she looks so sad, and what unfortunate twist of fate has left her in a wheelchair.

Part Two

Whollies

34 CHILDREN ABANDONED UNDER NEBRASKA'S
SAFE-HAVEN LAW

by Nate Jenkins, The Associated Press
Friday, November 14, 2008

LINCOLN, Neb. (AP) Nebraska officials geared up Friday for a special legislative session designed to deal with a unique "safe haven" law whose unintended consequences have allowed parents to abandon nearly three dozen children as old as 17.

As the session to correct the law approached, a 5-year-old boy was dropped off at an Omaha hospital on Thursday night. Earlier in the day, a woman dropped off two teenagers at another Omaha hospital, but one of them, a 17-year-old girl, fled. Authorities have not found her yet.

As of Friday afternoon, 34 children had been abandoned under the Nebraska law, five of them from other states.

Nebraska was the last state to enact a safe-haven law, intended to take in unwanted newborns. But unlike laws in other states, Nebraska's doesn't include an age limit.

Some observers have interpreted the current law as applying to children as old as 18.

The full article can be found at: http://articles.nydailynews.com/2008-11-14/news/17910664_1_safe-haven-law-omaha-hospital-unique-safe-haven-law

4 · Parents

They're together as they open the door. A father and mother, dressed for bed. Worry lines fill their foreheads as they see the nature of their visitors. This is an anticipated yet unexpected moment.

A Juvey-cop stands at the door with three plainclothes officers to back him up. The lead Juvey-cop is young. They all seem young. They recruit them earlier and earlier these days.

"We're here to process Unwind subject 53-990-24. Noah Falkowski." The parents glance at each other in alarm.

"You're a day early," the mother says.

"The schedule has been pushed up," the lead cop tells her. "We have the contractual right to change the pickup date. Can we please have access to the subject?"

The father takes a step forward to look at the name on the officer's uniform.

"Look here, Officer Mullard," he says in a loud whisper, "we're not prepared to surrender our son just yet. As my wife has told you, we were expecting you tomorrow. You'll have to come back then."

But E. Robert Mullard waits for no one. He barges into the house, with his team following behind him.

"Good God!" the father says. "Have some decency."

Mullard lets out a guffaw. "Decency? What do you know about decency?" Then he looks down the bedroom hallway. "Noah Falkowski!" he calls loudly. "If you're back there, come out now."

A fifteen-year-old boy peeks out of a bedroom doorway,

takes one look at the guests, and slams his door. Mullard signals to the brawniest of his cohorts. "He's all yours."

"I'm on it."

"Stop him, Walter!" the woman begs her husband. Walter, put on the spot, turns to Mullard with a vengeance. "I want to talk to your superior."

And then Mullard pulls out a gun. "You're in no position to make demands."

It's clearly just a tranq pistol, but considering that nasty business about the Juvey-cop killed with his own gun, Walter and his wife aren't about to take any chances.

"Sit down," Mullard says, nodding toward the dining room. The couple hesitates. "I said sit down!" And then two of Mullard's team force them to sit in two dining room chairs. The father, a reasonable man, assumes he's dealing with another reasonable young professional like himself.

"Is this all really necessary, Officer Mullard?" he asks, in a calmer, more accommodating tone.

"My name isn't Mullard, and I'm not a Juvey-cop."

Suddenly it hits the man how obvious this is. He knew this kid was too young to have that kind of authority. The scars on his face made him seem a little . . . well . . . *seasoned*, but still he was too young. How could Walter have been so easily fooled? And isn't there something familiar about this young man's face? Has he seen him before, possibly in the news? The man is rendered speechless by this unexpected turn of nonprofessional events.

5 · Connor

The best part of these missions is the look on the parents' faces when they realize that the tables have been turned. How their eyes dart down toward the tranq gun aimed at them, suddenly realizing that their unwind order is now nothing but a piece of paper.

"Who are you?" asks the father. "What is it you want?"

"We want what you no longer want," Connor tells him. "We want your son." Then Trace, the muscular team member he sent after Noah, comes out of the bedroom holding the struggling kid.

"They don't make bedroom locks like they used to," Trace says.

"Lemme go," shouts the kid. "Lemme go!" Connor goes to him while Hayden, also on the rescue team, pulls a tranq gun to make sure the couple doesn't get any ideas.

"Noah, your parents were about to unwind you," Connor tells him. "In fact, the Juvies are coming tomorrow—but luckily for you, we came first."

There's a horrified look on the kid's face. He shakes his head, denying the possibility. "You're lying!" Then he looks to his parents, not so sure anymore. "He's lying, right?"

Connor doesn't let the parents answer. "The truth—you owe him that much."

"You have no right to do this!" the mother yells.

"The truth!" demands Connor.

Then the father sighs, and says, "Yes, what he says is true. I'm sorry, Noah."

Now Noah casts a furious gaze at his parents, and then turns to Connor. Connor can see tears building behind his fury.

"Are you going to hurt them?" Noah asks.

"Do you want me to?"

"Yes. Yes, I do."

Connor shakes his head. "Sorry, that's not what we do. Someday you'll be grateful we didn't."

Noah looks down. "No, I won't."

Trace, no longer having to hold Noah quite so tightly, escorts him back to his bedroom so Noah can shove a few things into his backpack; what little he can salvage from fifteen years of life.

While the rest of Connor's team checks out the home, making sure there is no one else present to call the police or otherwise foul up the mission, Connor hands a pad and pen to the father.

"What's this for?"

"You're going to write down the reasons you decided to have your son unwound."

"What's the point?"

"We know you have reasons for doing it," Connor says. "I'm sure they're stupid; I'm sure they're selfish and seriously screwed up, but they're still reasons. If nothing else, it'll help us to know what kind of pain in the ass Noah is, so maybe we can deal with him better than you did."

"You keep saying we," the mother asks. "Who's we?"

"We're the ones saving your son's freaking life. That's all you need to know."

The father looks down pitifully at the little notepad.

"Write," Connor says. Neither he nor the mother look up as Trace escorts Noah out of the house into the waiting car.

"I hate you!" he yells back at them. "I never meant it when I said it before, but now I do."

Connor can tell it cuts deeply into these parents, but not as deeply as the scalpels of a Chop Shop.

"Someday, if he makes it to seventeen, he may give you a shot at forgiveness. If he does, don't throw that chance away."

They say nothing to that. The father just looks down at the pad, scribbling and scribbling. When he's done, he hands it back to Connor. Rather than a manifesto, the man has written down his excuses in efficient bullet points. Connor reads them out loud, as if each one was an accusation against them.

"'Disrespect and disobedience.'"

Those are always the first reasons. If every parent unwound a kid due to disrespect, the human race would go extinct in a single generation.

"'Destructive behavior to self and property.'"

Connor knows a bit about self-destructive behavior and did his share of vandalizing in times of frustration. But most kids get over that, don't they? It never ceases to amaze him how everything—even unwinding—is geared toward the quick fix. Connor looks at the third bullet point and has to laugh.

"'Lack of personal hygiene'?"

The woman throws her husband an angry gaze for writing that.

"Ooh, I like this one!" Connor says. "'Diminished prospects for future.' Sounds like a stock report!"

At every rescue mission, Connor reads aloud the reasons, and each time he wonders if it's the same list his parents would have written. This time, the last reason chokes Connor up a bit.

"'Our own failure as parents.'"

And then he gets mad at himself. These parents haven't earned his sympathy. If it's *their* failure, then why should their son have to pay for it?

"Tomorrow, when the Juvey-rounders come for him, you'll tell them that he ran away, and you don't know where he went. You won't talk about us, or what happened here today, because if you do, we'll know. We monitor all the police frequencies."

"And if we don't comply?" the father asks, showing the same kind of disobedience he condemned his son for.

"In case you have any thought of reporting this, we've uploaded a nice identity cocktail for the two of you onto the net."

That makes them both look even more ill than they already do.

75

"What kind of cocktail?"

Hayden's the one who answers, proud because it was his idea.

"We send out a single code over the net, and bingo, your names become linked to a dozen known clapper cells. Your digital footprint will be so tangled in terrorism, you'll spend years trying to get Homeland Security off your collective asses."

The couple nod a solemn acceptance.

"Fine," the man says. "You have our word."

The threat of identity cocktails is always very effective— and besides, whether these kids go with Connor or they're unwound, the parents get what they want. Their unmanageable kid becomes somebody else's problem. Reporting Connor and his team would just make Noah their problem again.

"You have to understand, we were desperate," says the mother with a high quotient of self-righteousness. "Everyone told us that unwinding was the best thing to do. Everyone."

Connor tears up the list of excuses and drops it on the floor, locking eyes with her.

"So, in other words you decided to unwind your son because of peer pressure?"

Finally the two of them crumble, feeling the appropriate weight of shame. The father, who had started out so defiant, suddenly bursts into tears. It's the mother who holds it together enough to offer Connor one last excuse.

"We tried to be good parents . . . but there's a point at which you give up trying."

"No, there's not," Connor tells her. Then he turns to go, leaving them with the worst punishment of all: having to live with themselves.

Connor and his team drive off in an intentionally nondescript minivan with a false license plate. Noah Falkowski is understandably grim as he looks out the window, watching his neighborhood go by for the last time. He doesn't seem to know who they are. He doesn't seem to care. Connor's glad Noah doesn't recognize him. While the Akron AWOL has a legendary reputation in some circles, his face was in the news much less than Lev's. Plus, with everyone thinking he's dead, it's easier to go incognito.

"Relax," Connor tells him, "you're among friends."

"I got no friends," says Noah. And for now, Connor lets him feel sorry for himself.

The Graveyard is true to its name this late at night. Airplane tail fins stand as monumental and as quiet as tombstones. Kids are on watch patrol with tranq-loaded rifles, but other than that, there's no sign that the place is home to more than seven hundred AWOL Unwinds.

"So why are we here?" Noah asks as the rescue party pulls down the main aisle—the busiest "street" of the Graveyard, flanked by a series of large aircraft that make up the core of their living space, each one named by Unwinds who have long since left. Names like Crash Mamma, for one of the main girls' dorms; the ComBom, a veteran World War II bomber that's become their computer and communications center; and of course IHOP, the International House of Purgatory, where new arrivals like Noah stay until they're given a job and integrated into the Graveyard.

"The Graveyard's where you'll live until you turn seventeen," Connor tells Noah.

"Like hell I will," the kid says. Typical. Connor just ignores him.

"Hayden, get him a bedroll and escort him to *IHOP*. We'll see what kind of work he's suited for in the morning."

"So what am I, a stinking AWOL now?" asks Noah.

"AWOLs is what *they* call us," says Hayden. "We call

ourselves Whollies. As to whether or not you stink, I think we all can agree that you need to visit our bathing facilities at your earliest possible convenience."

The kid grunts like a mildly irritated bull, and Connor grins. It was Hayden who actually came up with the term "Whollies," because "Unwind" and "AWOL" were negative labels put on them by the world. "You should be a spin doctor," Connor told Hayden, to which he facetiously replied, "Spinning makes me nauseous; I'd puke on my patients."

Hayden, Connor, and Risa were the only three Whollies remaining who had been harbored in Sonia's safe house way back when. That experience bonded them as if they were life-long friends.

Noah toddles off with Hayden to the International House of Purgatory, and Connor takes a few moments to enjoy some rare peace and quiet. He looks to AcMac, the jet where Risa sleeps. The lights are out, just like the others, but he suspects she has already peered out at the sound of their approach, to make sure that Connor has arrived home safe and sound.

"I'm not sure if these missions of yours are noble or stupid," Risa once told him.

"Why can't they be both?" he responded. The fact is, saving individual kids is somehow far more satisfying for him than the daily ins and outs of running the Graveyard. These side trips keep him sane.

When he was left in charge, it was only supposed to be temporary. The Anti-Divisional Resistance was supposed to find a suitable replacement for the Admiral—someone who could present an image that the public could believe would be running an airplane salvage operation. But then they realized that they didn't need that. They had people in the Graveyard's front office—a trailer near the entrance—and those employees ran the business end of things. As long as Connor kept the kids working, fed, and quiet, the ADR found no reason to hire someone else.

"Surveying your domain?"

Connor turns to see Trace coming up to him.

"It's not mine, I only work here," Connor tells him. "The new kid settled in?"

"Yeah—a real complainer. He says the blanket's too rough."

"He'll get over it. We all do."

Trace Neuhauser is an air force boeuf who gave it up to join the resistance when his sister was unwound. He's AWOL from his unit for six months now, but still a boeuf in every sense of the word. He's all steroid bulk, with a tunnel-vision education in the martial sciences.

Connor never liked boeufs. Maybe because they know their purpose in the world, and generally serve it well. Seeing them always made Connor feel useless. That a boeuf has become such a close friend proves that people change. Trace is twenty-three but seems to have no problem taking orders from a seventeen-year-old.

"Chain of command knows no age restrictions," he once told Connor. "You could be six, but if you were my superior, I'd still do as I was told."

Maybe that's why Connor likes him; because if a guy like that can respect Connor's lead, maybe he's not such a lousy leader after all.

The next day begins as every day begins in the Graveyard. With things to be done. "The Firefighters' Treadmill," the Admiral called it: an endless trot to stomp out nuisances. "Leadership is about keeping toilets flushing," the Admiral once said. "Unless you're on the battlefront. Then it's about staying alive. Neither are pleasant."

On the main aisle, kids are already lounging beneath the recreation jet, watching TV, or playing video games. Still more have begun their shifts, dismantling or rebuilding aircraft parts, as per the orders coming in from the front office. Sometimes it's easier for Connor to think that it's all going on in spite of him, rather than because of him.

As soon as Connor is spotted on the main aisle, the barrage begins.

"Hey, Connor," says a kid running up to him, "not to complain, but, like, can we get some better food here? I mean, I know beggars can't be choosers and all, but if I gotta eat beef-flavored stew with no actual beef in it one more time, I think I'm gonna hurl."

"Yeah, you and everyone else," Connor tells him.

"Mr. Akron," says a girl, fourteen or so—he can't get over the fact that so many of the kids, particularly the younger ones, are not only ridiculously respectful, but think that Akron is somehow part of his name—"I don't know if you know this, but the fans in Crash Mama ain't working no more, and it's way too hot at night."

"I'll send someone to fix them," Connor tells her. Then a third kid comes up complaining that there's too much trash, and can't he do something about it.

"I swear, half the time I feel like a janitor," he tells Trace. "I need a dozen more hands just to keep this place afloat."

"You do have a dozen hands," Trace reminds him. "But you've got to be willing to use them."

"Yeah, yeah," says Connor, having heard it before. He shouldn't be mad at Trace for pointing these things out—after all, that's why he keeps Trace so close: to advise him on how to be in charge. Connor has already accepted the odd reality that he's some sort of leader, but, as the Admiral pointed out, it's a pretty thankless job.

After the Admiral left him in charge, Connor had set up a power structure: an inner circle, an outer circle, and everyone else. Those in his inner circle are supposed to make sure things like food supplies and sanitation are being taken care of, because Connor has much more pressing things to deal with. Things like keeping them all in one piece.

"I'll call a meeting after I meet with the rep from the resistance," Connor tells Trace. "And I'll make sure tasks are being delegated."

"Maybe," says Trace, "you need to take a look at who you're delegating to."

Connor never knew he could handle this kind of responsibility, but now that he knows, he wishes he could go back to just being responsible for himself. There are so many things he feels he still needs to do. Thanks to Lev, and his misguided clapper cell, Connor avoided being unwound, but he still doesn't feel entirely whole.

6 · Risa

There is only one permanently disabled resident of the Graveyard. Since the disabled are a protected class, they're never at risk for being unwound, so they never turn up at the Graveyard with all the other kids who ran from their unwind order. It's a testimony to the swiss-cheese nature of public compassion. Lucky for those to whom grace is extended, but unlucky for those who wind up in the holes.

Risa is disabled by choice. That is to say, she refused surgery that would repair her severed spine, because it involved giving her the spine of an unwound kid. It used to be that spinal damage was irreversible, and if that was the card you were dealt, you spent the rest of your days with it. She wonders if it's harder to live like that, or to live knowing you can be fixed but choose not to.

Now she lives in an old McDonnel Douglas MD-11, for which they built a wooden switchback ramp to the main hatch. The plane has been aptly named Accessible Mac, or AcMac for short. There are about ten kids with sprained ankles or other temporary conditions who currently share AcMac with Risa, each in sections divided by curtains, providing the illusion of personal space. Risa has the old first-class cabin of the jet, which is forward of the hatch. It gives her a larger living area, but she can't stand the fact that it singles her out. The whole lousy jet singles her out—and although her shattered spine is a well-earned war wound, it doesn't change the fact that she is constantly condemned to receive special treatment.

The only other plane with a ramp is the infirmary jet, where she works. It leaves Risa with a very limited choice of interior spaces, so she spends her free time outside when she can stand the heat.

Every day at five o'clock, Risa waits for Connor beneath a stealth bomber they've nicknamed Hush Puppy. Every day, Connor is late.

The bomber's expansive black wings create a huge wedge of shade, and its radar-resistant skin wicks heat right out of the air. It's one of the coolest spots in the Graveyard, in more ways than one.

She finally sees him approaching: a figure in blue camo that sets him apart from anyone else in the Graveyard. "I thought you weren't coming," Risa says as he reaches the shade of Hush Puppy.

"I was supervising an engine dismantling."

"Yeah," says Risa with a grin. "That's what they all say."

Connor brings his tension with him to these daily encounters with her. He says being with her is the only time he gets to

82

feel normal, but he never truly relaxes. In fact, since she first met him, she's never known him to relax. It doesn't help to know that their legends are out there, living lives of their own. Stories of Connor and Risa have already grown deep roots in modern folklore, for few things are more compelling than an outlaw romance. They are Bonnie and Clyde for a new era; the subjects of bumper stickers and T-shirts.

Hard to imagine that so much notoriety came from merely surviving the blast at Happy Jack Harvest Camp. Merely because Connor was lucky enough to be the first Unwind ever to walk out of a Chop Shop in one piece. Of course, as far as the rest of the world knows, Connor died there and Risa is missing—either dead herself, or in hiding deep within some AWOL-friendly nation, if there even is such a thing anymore. She wonders how her legend would hold up if people knew she was right here in the Arizona desert, sunburned and dirty.

A breeze blows beneath Hush Puppy's belly, getting even more dirt in Risa's eyes. She blinks it away.

"Are you ready?" Connor asks her.

"Always."

Then Connor kneels before Risa's wheelchair and begins to massage her legs, trying to coax circulation to those parts of her that can no longer feel. It's part of their daily ritual together, this physical contact between them. It's coolly clinical, yet strangely intimate at the same time. Today, however, Connor is detached. Distant.

"Something's bothering you even more than usual," Risa says. A statement of fact, not a question. "Go on, spill it."

Connor sighs, looks up at her, and asks the big question.

"Why are we here, Risa?"

She considers the question. "Do you mean why are we here philosophically, as a species, or why are we here, doing this in full view of anyone who cares to watch?"

"Let them watch," he says. "I don't care." And clearly he doesn't, because privacy is the first casualty when you live in the Graveyard. Even the small private jet Connor claimed as his quarters has no curtains on its windows. No, Risa knows that this has nothing do with their daily ritual, or the grand question of humanity. It has to do with survival.

"What I mean is, why are we still here in the Graveyard? Why haven't the Juvies tranq'd and yanked us all?"

"You've said it yourself—they don't see us as a threat."

"But they should," Connor points out. "They're not stupid . . . which means that there's some other reason why they haven't taken this place down."

Risa reaches over, rubbing Connor's tense shoulder. "You think too much."

Connor smiles at that. "When you met me, you accused me of not thinking enough."

"Well, your brain is making up for lost time."

"After what we've been through—after what we've seen—can you blame me?"

"I like you better as a man of action."

"Action has to be well thought out. You taught me that."

Risa sighs. "Yes, I suppose I did. And I created a monster."

She realizes that both of them have been profoundly changed in the wake of the Happy Jack Harvest Camp revolt. Risa likes to think that their spirits have been galvanized like iron in a furnace, but sometimes it feels like they've only been damaged by those harsh flames. Still, she's glad she had survived to see the far-reaching effects of that day. Like Cap-17.

Even before Happy Jack, there had been a bill in Congress calling for the lowering of the legal limit of unwinding by a whole year, to one's seventeenth birthday instead of eighteenth. The "Cap-17" bill had never been expected to pass—in fact, most people didn't even know about it until Happy Jack

made the news—and until poor Lev Calder's face became plastered on the cover of every major magazine: the innocent boy
clothed all in white. A bright-eyed, clean-cut kid smiling out
from a school picture. How the perfect child became a clapper
was a question that made parents everywhere stop and take
notice . . . because if it could happen to Lev, who's to say that
their own child might not turn their blood explosive someday
and detonate themselves in a burst of rage? And the fact that
Lev chose *not* to detonate himself troubled people even more,
because they couldn't just file him away as a bad seed. They
had to accept that he had a soul—a conscience—which meant
that maybe society had a hand in making him a clapper. And
then suddenly—as if to assuage everyone's feelings of cultural
guilt—the Cap-17 bill became law. No one could be unwound
after their seventeenth birthday.

"You're thinking about Lev again, aren't you?" Connor asks.

"How do you know?"

"Because whenever you do, time stops, and your eyes go to
the dark side of the moon."

She reaches down to touch his hands, which have stopped
massaging, and he gets back to coaxing her troubled circulation.

"It's because of him that the Cap-17 law passed, you know,"
Risa says. "I wonder how he feels about that."

"I'll bet it gives him nightmares."

"Or," suggests Risa, "maybe he sees the bright side of it."

"Do you?" Connor asks.

Risa sighs. "Sometimes."

Cap-17 should have been a good thing, but in time, it
became clear that it was not. Sure it was a victorious morning
that next day, when the news showed thousands of seventeen-
year-olds being released from harvest camps. It was a triumph
of human compassion, and a great victory for those against
unwinding, but that same feeling of victory allowed people to

turn a blind eye again to the whole problem. Unwinding was still there, but people could now look the other way, believing their consciences were clean.

And then came the media blitz, a flood of advertisements designed to "remind" people how much "better" things were since the Unwind Accord. "Unwinding: the natural solution," the ads said, or "Troubled teen? Love them enough to let them go," and, of course, Risa's favorite, "Experience a world outside of yourself: Embrace the divided state."

The sad truth about humanity, Risa was quick to realize, is that people believe what they're told. Maybe not the first time, but by the hundredth time, the craziest of ideas just becomes a given.

Which brings her back to Connor's question. With a major shortage of Unwinds in the system after Cap-17, and a public accustomed to getting all the parts they want whenever they want them, why hasn't the Graveyard been raided? Why are they still here?

"We're here," Risa tells him, "because we are. And we should just be thankful for that while it lasts." Then she gently touches his shoulder, signaling it's time to end the massage. "I'd better get back to the infirmary jet. I'm sure there are plenty of scrapes, black eyes, and fevers to take care of. Thank you, Connor." As many times as he does this for her, she's always embarrassed that she needs it.

He rolls down the loose-fitting legs of her khaki pants and puts her feet back on the wheelchair's footrests. "Never thank a guy for putting his hands all over you."

"Not all over," Risa says coyly.

Connor throws her a sly little grin, letting it carry the weight of anything he might have said to that.

"I think I'd like our times together even more," she tells him, "if you were actually here."

Connor reaches up to touch her face—but he stops himself, switches hands, and touches her with the left instead of the right. The one he was born with. "I'm sorry, it's just—"

"—your brain making up for lost time. I know. But I do look forward to a day we can be together and not be filled with all these dark thoughts. Then we'll know we've won."

Then she pushes off toward the infirmary jet, maneuvering over the rugged ground on her own, as always, refusing to be pushed by anyone, ever.

7 · Connor

A representative from the Anti-Divisional Resistance shows up the next afternoon—three days late for his scheduled meeting with Connor. He's disheveled, paunchy, and drenched in sweat.

"And it's not even summer," Connor says—hoping to make the point that the sweltering Arizona summer is just a few months away. The ADR had better get their act together, or there are going to be a lot of angry AWOLs. That is, the ones who survive the heat.

They meet in the retired Air Force One, which used to be the Admiral's personal quarters but now serves only as a conference room. The man introduces himself as Joe Rincon, "But call me Joe. No formalities in the ADR." He sits at the conference table and pulls out a pad and pen to take notes. He's already glancing at his watch, as if there's somewhere else he would rather be.

Connor has a whole list of gripes from every corner of the Graveyard. Why are the food shipments so few and far between? Where are the medical supplies they requested? How about air conditioner and generator parts? Why are they not being warned when planes show up with new arrivals—and for that matter, why are the numbers coming in so light? Five or ten at a time, when the planes used to come in with fifty or more. With food supply being a constant issue, Connor doesn't mind the low numbers, but it troubles him. If fewer AWOLs are being found by the resistance, that means the Juvies—or worse, the so-called parts pirates—must be finding them first.

"What's wrong with you people? Why does the ADR keep ignoring all our requests?"

"There's really nothing to worry about," Rincon says, which sends up a red flag for Connor, because he never said anything about being worried. "Things are still being reorganized."

"Still? No one ever told us things were being reorganized at all. And what do you mean by reorganized?"

Rincon blots his sweaty forehead with his shirtsleeve. "Really, there's nothing to worry about."

Over the course of a year, Connor has come to understand the Anti-Divisional Resistance better than he wanted to. When he was just an AWOL, he had no choice but to trust that the ADR was a well-oiled rescue machine—but it was nothing of the sort. The only thing that ran smoothly was the Graveyard— the Admiral had made sure of that, and Connor, following in his footsteps, keeps it that way.

He should have realized things with the ADR were not as they appeared as soon as they accepted the Admiral's suggestion that Connor be the one to run the place, rather than installing a more experienced adult. If they were so willing to let a teenager manage their AWOL sanctuary, something was wrong somewhere.

There was a crazy time when kids were coming in every few days. The Graveyard boasted more than two thousand kids, and the ADR sent shipments of everything they needed on a regular basis. Then, when Cap-17 passed, Connor was ordered to immediately release all the seventeen-year-olds—who were a large percentage of the Graveyard population—but he made a command judgment to do it slowly, releasing them in increments, so they didn't flood the city of Tucson with more than nine hundred homeless teenagers. The fact that they wanted him to just let all those kids go at once should have been another sign that the ADR leadership was faltering.

Connor had released them over a period of two months, but the ADR cut their supplies immediately, as if those kids had suddenly ceased to be their problem. Between the released seventeen-year-olds, kids sent out on work programs that had been set in place by the Admiral, and kids who deserted when there wasn't enough food, the Graveyard population had dropped to about seven hundred.

"I see you've planted yourself quite a garden—and you're raising chickens as well, yes?" Rincon says. "You must be fully sustainable by now."

"Not even close. The Green Aisle produces only about one-third of the food that we need, and with the ADR flaking on our food shipments, we've had to resort to raiding market delivery trucks in Tucson."

"Oh dear," says Rincon. That's all, just "Oh dear," and he starts to gnaw on the end of his pen.

Connor, whose patience has been frayed since day one, is tired of beating around the bush. "Are you going to tell me something useful, or are you just here to waste my time?"

Rincon sighs. "It comes down to this, Connor: We believe the Graveyard has been compromised."

Connor cannot believe what this fool is telling him. "Of course it's been compromised! I'm the one who told you it was compromised! The Juvies know about us, and since the day I took over, I've been saying we need to relocate!"

"Yes, we're working on that, but in the meantime we can't

keep pouring valuable resources into a facility that could be taken out by the Juvies at any moment."

"So you're just going to let us rot here?"

"I didn't say that. You seem to have everything under control. With any luck, the Juvies will never find a need to invade—"

"With any luck?" Connor stands and storms from the table. "The resistance should be about action, not luck. But do you take action? No! I send you my plans to infiltrate harvest camps, and ideas on how to free kids in nonviolent ways that won't piss people off and create a backlash—but all I hear from the ADR is 'we're working on it, Connor,' or 'we'll take it under advisement, Connor.' And now you're telling me to rely on luck for our survival? What the hell is the ADR good for?"

Rincon takes this as his cue to end the meeting—something he's clearly wanted to do since the moment he arrived. "Hey, I'm just the messenger—don't take this out on me!"

But there are some things Connor simply cannot help, and he finds himself swinging Roland's fist at "Call-Me-Joe" Rincon's face. The punch connects with the man's eye, and he stumbles backward into the bulkhead. He looks at Connor not with contempt, but with fear, as if Connor might not stop there. So much for nonviolence. Connor backs off.

"There's my message," he says. "Please take it back to the people who sent you."

There's a wingless Boeing 747 airliner that has been gutted, like just about every other plane in the Graveyard, and retrofitted with gym equipment. It's been named GymBo, although some call it "the fight deck" since so many brawls seem to break out there.

This is where Connor goes to get out his frustrations.

A big punching bag before him, he pounds it like a prizefighter hell-bent on a first-round knockout. He imagines the faces of all the kids who pissed him off that day. All the ones who have excuses for not doing what they're supposed to do. And he spreads his anger further to people like Rincon, and the Juvey-cops that he's had to face, to the smiling counselors at the harvest camp who tried to make unwinding seem like a wholesome family-friendly activity, and finally to the faces of his parents, who set in motion the clockwork that landed him here. For them he can't hit that bag hard enough and yet can't stomach the guilt he feels for feeling that way.

The punches from his left hand are nothing compared to those from his right. He looks at the shark tattoo staring at him from the forearm; that tiger shark even uglier than the real thing. He has to admit to himself that he's gotten used to it, but he'll never like it. The color of the hair that grows on that arm is also thicker and darker than that of his other arm. *He's here,* Connor tells himself. *Roland is here with every punch I throw with his hand.* And the worst part about it is that throwing those punches feels good—as if the arm itself is enjoying it.

He moves toward a bench press, and a couple of kids who had been sharing it make way for him—a perk of being in charge. He looks at the weight, adds another five pounds on either side, then leans back, ready to pump. Every day he does this, and every day this is the part he hates the most . . . because nowhere is the difference between his left arm and his right clearer than on the bench press. The arm he was born with struggles to raise that bar. And suddenly he realizes that even now he's still fighting Roland.

"Need someone to spot you?" says a kid behind him. Connor tilts his neck to see standing above him the kid everyone just calls Starkey.

"Yeah, sure," says Connor. "Thanks." He goes for another set, already feeling his natural arm aching but not wanting to give into it . . . but after seven reps it starts to give out, and

Starkey has to help him get the barbell back onto the cradle.

Starkey points at the shark on his right arm. "You get that after Happy Jack?"

Connor sits up, nursing the burn in his muscles, and looks at the tattoo. "It came with the arm."

"Actually," says Starkey, "I was talking about the arm. The way I figure it, if the guy who's so against unwinding has an Unwind's arm, it probably wasn't by choice. I'd love to hear how it happened."

Connor laughs, because no one's ever asked the question so blatantly. It's actually a relief to talk about it.

"There was this kid—a real tough guy. He tried to kill me once but couldn't go through with it. Anyway, he was the last kid unwound at Happy Jack. I was supposed to be next, but that's when the clappers blew up the Chop Shop. I lost my arm and woke up with this one. Trust me, it wasn't my choice."

Starkey takes in the story and nods, not offering any judgment.

"Badge of honor, man," he says. "Wear it out loud."

Connor tries to get to know every kid who arrives, at least a little bit, so they don't feel like just a number waiting to be caught and unwound. So what does he know about Starkey? He's got personality, and a smile that's a little hard to read. He's got wavy red hair that didn't start that way, as evidenced by dark roots that have grown almost an inch since he arrived a month ago. He's a little short, solid, not scrawny. Stocky, that's the word—like a wrestler—and yet he has a confidence that makes him seem taller. There are also rumors that he killed a Juvey-cop or two while escaping, but they're only rumors.

Connor remembers the day Starkey arrived. Every group of new arrivals has at least one kid who thinks blowing up harvest camps is a good idea. Actually, most of them probably think that, but most kids are too intimidated upon arrival to shout it out. The ones who do turn out to either be problems or over-achievers. Starkey, however has kept a very low profile since his arrival. He's assigned to mess duty as a food server, and in the evenings he goes around performing little magic tricks for anyone who's interested. That makes Connor think back to his own first AWOL night. He was given shelter by a trucker who showed him an arm grafted on at the elbow. It was the arm of an Unwind that came with an ability to do card tricks.

"You'll have to let me see some of your magic tricks, Starkey," Connor says, and Starkey seems a little surprised.

"You know everyone's name here?"

"Only the ones who make an impression. Here, let's switch," says Connor. "I'll spot you." They switch positions, and Starkey tries to lift the weight but can barely do two reps.

"I think I'll pass."

Starkey sits up, taking a long look at him. Most people can't hold eye contact with Connor. It's either the scars or his legend that are too intimidating for them. Starkey, however, doesn't look away. "Is it true that you risked getting caught to save a storked baby?"

"Yeah," Connor says. "Not one of my brightest moments."

"Why'd you do it?"

Connor shrugs. "Seemed like a good idea at the time." He tries to laugh it off, but Starkey's not laughing.

"I was a storked baby," Starkey tells him.

"I'm sorry to hear that."

"No, it's all good. I just want you to know I respect you for what you did."

"Thanks." Outside, someone calls for Connor in that my-problem-is-earth-shattering tone of voice that he hears on a regular basis. "Duty calls. Take it easy, Starkey." And he leaves, feeling a little bit better than when he came in.

But what he doesn't see is what happens after he's gone:

Starkey lying back on the bench press, doing twenty reps of that same weight without even breaking a sweat.

After the sun sets, Connor calls a meeting of his inner circle— a group of seven that Hayden has dubbed the Holy of Whollies, and the name stuck. They meet in Connor's private jet at the north head of the main aisle, rather than the old Air Force One, which still reeks of his meeting with Call-Me-Joe, the resistance rep.

It wasn't Connor's idea to have his own private jet any more than it was his idea to wear blue camo. They were both Trace's suggestions to help solidify Connor's image as the fearless leader.

"What the hell kind of army wears blue camouflage anyway?" he griped when Trace first suggested it.

"It's for air attacks by jetpack," Trace told him. "Never actually attempted, but it works in theory."

The idea was to set Connor apart from everyone else. The Admiral had his uniform, all festooned with war medals; Connor needed something to match his own leadership style, whatever that might be. Although he wasn't too thrilled to be running the place like a boot camp, the Admiral had already set things up as a military dictatorship. It wasn't broke, so Connor didn't try to fix it.

It had been suggested that Connor take over the old Air Force One, but that was the Admiral's style, not Connor's. Instead he settled on a small, sleek corporate jet from the outskirts of the graveyard, and had it towed to the north end of the main aisle.

Connor occasionally hears kids grumbling about it: "Look at him living like a king, while the rest of us get nothing but a bedroll."

"Nature of the beast," Trace is always quick to remind him.

"Respect doesn't come without a little resentment."

Connor knows he's right, but he doesn't have to like it.

The Holy of Whollies arrive mostly on time for the meeting. Once inside, they swivel side to side in the plush leather chairs, for no other reason than that they can. They enjoy the jet far more than Connor does.

Six out of seven are present. Risa, who's the Graveyard's chief medic, refuses to enter Connor's jet until she can roll in on her own—and a wheelchair ramp just to access Connor's jet seems like an extravagance.

Trace, always the first to arrive, is head of security, as well as Connor's strategic adviser.

Hayden is master of the ComBom, running computer and radio communications, monitoring the outside world, police frequencies, and all communication with the resistance. He also has a radio station for the Whollies, with a signal that barely reaches half a mile. He calls it "Radio Free Hayden."

There's a big bruiser of a girl everyone calls Bam, who is in charge of food services. Her real name is Bambi, but anyone who calls her that ends up being treated by Risa in the infirmary.

There's Drake, a rural kid who is the Sustainability Boss, which is just a fancy term for the guy who runs the farm, or the Green Aisle, which was entirely Connor's idea. The food it produces has more than once taken the edge off hunger pangs when ADR food shipments have been too small or nonexistent.

Next is John, a gum-chewing kid with a restless leg who's in charge of maintenance and waste management, and finally Ashley, who claims to be very "person centered" and deals with "issues"—and since just about every kid being tagged for unwinding has issues, she's probably the busiest of the bunch.

"So what's this about?" Bam asks. "Because I got stuff to do."

"First off," Connor tells them, "I met with the ADR dude today. We can expect more of the same."

"More o' nothin' is still nothin'," Drake says.

"You got it. We've pretty much known we've been on our own for a while—now it's official. Deal with it."

"What about supplies and stuff we can't scavenge from other planes?" asks John, his leg bouncing more fiercely than usual.

"If we can't get cash from the front office to buy it, we'll have to creatively find it." Creatively finding is Connor's euphemism for stealing. He's had to send kids as far as Phoenix to creatively find things the ADR won't supply. Things like hard-to-find medications and welding torches.

"I just got word that a new jet is being retired here next Tuesday," Hayden tells them. "I'm sure when we gut it, we'll find a lot of things we need. Coolant compressors, hydraulic thingamajiggies, and all that other hardcore mechanical blue-collar stuff."

"Is the baggage compartment gonna be stuffed full of Whollies?" someone asks.

"No plane arrives without mystery meat," Hayden says. "No telling how many kids there'll be, though."

"I hope there aren't any coffins this time," Ashley says. "Do you have any idea how many kids had nightmares from that?"

"Oh please, coffins are so last month," says Hayden. "This time it's beer kegs!"

"The bigger issue," says Connor, "is having an escape plan. We can't rely on the ADR to save us if the Juvies decide it's time for fresh parts."

"Why don't we just bail now," asks Ashley, "and find a new place to be?"

"It's not that easy to move seven hundred kids—and doing it would be like sending up a flare to every Juvey-cop in Arizona.

Hayden's team has been doing a pretty good job tracking the threat level, so we'll have at least some warning before a raid—but if we don't have an exit strategy, we're screwed no matter what."

Bam throws a glare at Trace, who never says much at these meetings. "What does *he* think?"

"I think you should do whatever Connor tells you to do," Trace says.

Bam snorts. "Spoken like a true army boeuf."

"Air force," says Trace. "You'd be wise to remember that."

"The point is," says Connor, coming between them before Ashley can launch into her anger management speech, "that we all need to be thinking about how to kick out of here on a moment's notice if we have to."

The rest of the meeting deals with the minutiae of management. Connor wonders how the Admiral could stomach conversations about sanitary napkin supply, when the threat of harvest camp was a clear and present danger every minute of every day. "It's all about delegation," Trace has said—which is the real reason why Connor had called this meeting.

"You can all go," Connor finally tells everyone, "except for Bam and John—we still have things to talk about."

Everyone files out, and Connor has John wait outside, while he talks privately to Bam. Connor knows what he must do, he just doesn't want to do it. Some people take joy in dishing out bad news, but Connor was never like that. He knows what it's like to be pulled up short, to be told that you're useless, that you're better off unwound.

Bam stands with arms folded, sweating attitude. "So, what's up?"

"Tell me about the tainted meat loaf."

Bam shrugs like it's nothing. "What's the big deal? The generator to one of the refrigerators blew out. It's fixed now."

"How long was the power out?"

"Don't know."

"So you had no clue how long the thing was without power, and you still served the food inside?"

"How was I supposed to know people would get sick? They ate it, so it's their problem."

Connor imagines the punching bag and makes a fist with his right hand. Then he looks at the shark, and forces his hand to relax. "More than forty kids were down for over two days—and we're lucky it wasn't worse."

"Yeah, right, so I won't let it happen again." Bam says it in such a rude tone of voice, Connor can imagine her saying it that same way to her teachers, her parents, the Juvies, every authority figure in her life. Connor hates the fact that he's one of those authority figures now.

"There won't be a next time, Bam. I'm sorry."

"You're getting rid of me just because of one stupid screwup?"

"No one is getting rid of you," Connor tells her. "But you won't be running food service anymore."

She burns him a long, hateful glare, then says, "Fine. To hell with you. I don't need this crap."

"Thank you, Bam," he says, having no idea what possessed him to thank her. "Send John in on your way out."

Bam kicks the jet hatch open and storms out. She turns to John, who waits nervously outside, twisted in a full body flinch from her angry exit.

"Go on in," Bam growls at him. "He's firing you."

That night Connor finds Starkey doing close-up magic for a bunch of Whollies beneath the recreation jet.

"How does he do that?" kids ask as he makes bracelets disappear from wrists and appear in other people's pockets. When he's done, Connor approaches him.

"You're pretty good. But as the guy in charge, I should ask you to tell me how it's done."

Starkey only smiles. "A magician never reveals his secrets, not even to the guy in charge."

"Listen," says Connor, cutting to the chase, "there's something I want to talk to you about. I've decided to shake things up in the Holy of Whollies."

"A change for the better, I hope," Starkey says, gripping his stomach. Connor chuckles because he already knows Starkey sees where this is going, but that's okay.

"How would you like to be in charge of food?"

"I love food," Starkey says. "And I'm not just saying that."

"Do you think you can handle a team of thirty and get food on the tables three times a day for everyone else?"

Starkey waves his hand and makes an egg appear out of thin air, then hands it to Connor. He saw the egg trick a few minutes earlier, but now its relevance makes it even more entertaining.

"Great," says Connor. "Now conjure up seven hundred more for breakfast." And he walks away, chuckling to himself, knowing that Starkey does have what it takes to make things happen, and make them happen right.

For once Connor's sure he's made the right decision.

8 · Risa

In the early evenings, when the desert begins to cool, Risa plays piano beneath the left wing of Air Force One. She plays pieces that she knows by heart and pieces from sheet music that have found their way into the Graveyard.

As for the piano itself, it's a black baby grand Hyundai—which made her laugh when she first saw it. She didn't think

Hyundai made pianos—but then, why should that surprise her? Multinationals can make anything they want if people will buy it. She once read that Mercedes-Benz had gotten heavy into artificial hearts before the Unwind Accord made such technology pointless. "The Pulsar Omega," the advertisement went. "Take luxury to heart." They invested a fortune in the product, only to lose every penny once unwinding began, and artificial hearts went the way of pagers and CDs.

Tonight she plays a forceful yet subtle Chopin sonata. It pours out like a ground fog, echoing within the hollow fuselages where the Whollies live. She knows it comforts them. Even those kids who claim to despise classical music have come asking her why she isn't playing when she's skipped a night. So she plays for them, but not really, because it's herself that she's playing for. Sometimes she has an audience sitting before her in the dust. Other times, like tonight, it's just her. Sometimes Connor comes. He'll sit beside her, yet somehow be distant, as if afraid to invade her musical space. The times Connor comes are her favorite, but he does not come often enough.

"He's got too much on his mind," Hayden has told her, making the excuses that Connor should make for himself. "He's a man of the people." Then he added with a smirk, "Or at least of two people."

Hayden never passes up a chance to throw a verbal barb about Connor's uninvited appendage. It ticks her off, because some things are no laughing matter. Sometimes she catches Connor looking at the arm with an expression that is so opaque, it frightens her. Like maybe he's going to pull out an ax and chop the thing off right in front of everyone. Even though he also bears a replacement eye, the match is perfect, and the source unknown. It holds no power over him . . . but Roland's arm is different, holding heavy emotional baggage in its powerful grasp.

"Are you wondering if it'll bite you?" she once asked as he gazed at that shark. Startled, Connor went a little bit red, as if he had been caught doing something he shouldn't. Then he just shrugged it off. "Nah, I was just wondering when and why Roland got this stupid tattoo. If I ever come across the person who got that particular brain cell, maybe I'll ask." Then he walked away from her, ending the conversation.

If it weren't for those daily leg massages, Risa would think that Connor has forgotten about her completely. But even those massages aren't the same. They feel perfunctory now. Like the only reason he's there is because he made a promise to himself that he would be—not because he truly wants to be.

Thinking about Connor makes her miss a chord—the same damn chord she missed at her life-or-death recital that left her on a bus, speeding her off to be unwound. She growls, then takes her fingers off the keys and draws a deep breath. Her music carries, which means her frustration is being broadcast just as clearly as Radio Free Hayden.

What bothers her most is that she cares. Risa was always able to take care of herself, both physically and emotionally. At the state home, either you developed several layers of personal armor or you were eaten alive. When had that changed? Was it when she was forced to play music as kids were led into the building beneath her to be unwound? Was it when she made the choice to accept a shattered spine, rather than having it replaced by the healthy spine of an Unwind? Or maybe it was before that, when she realized that, against all sense and reason, she had fallen in love with Connor Lassiter?

Risa finishes the sonata, because no matter how she's feeling, she cannot leave a piece of music uncompleted. Then, when she's done, she fights the dry, craggy terrain beneath her wheels and rolls toward a certain private jet.

9 · Connor

Connor dozes in a chair that's too comfortable to remain fully awake in, but not comfortable enough to be fully asleep. He's jarred alert by a thud against the side of his jet. By the time the second one comes, he realizes it's off to his left. By the time the third one hits, he realizes someone is throwing things at his plane.

He looks out of a window, but in the darkness he sees only his own reflection. Another thud. He cups his hands over his eyes, pressing his face against the glass. The first thing he sees are the curved blue streaks reflecting moonlight. A wheelchair. Then he sees Risa hurling another rock, which hits right above the window.

"What the hell?"

He opens the hatch, hoping she'll stop the barrage. "What's wrong? What's happened?"

"Nothing," she says. "I was just trying to get your attention."

He chuckles, not yet getting her frame of mind. "There are better ways."

"Not lately."

She moves forward and backward a bit in her chair, crushing a dirt clod that had her tilted at a slight angle. "Not going to invite me in?"

"You're invited. You're always invited."

"Well, then maybe you should have put up a ramp."

And although he knows he's going to regret saying it, he says it anyway. "Maybe you should let someone carry you."

She rolls a bit closer but not enough to close the space between them—just enough to make it painfully awkward. "I'm not an idiot. I know what's going on."

Risa might want this talk right now, but Connor is in no mood. After firing Bam and John, he just wants to end this day and find dreamless sleep until whatever fresh hell awaits in the morning.

"What's going on is that I'm trying to keep us all alive," he says with a little too much irritation in his voice, "and I don't see that as a problem."

"Yes, you're so busy keeping us alive. Even when you're not busy, you're busy—and when you do actually talk to me, it's all about the ADR, and how hard it is for you, and the weight of the world on *your* shoulders."

"Oh, for God's sake, Risa, you are not the kind of fragile girl who needs a guy's attention to feel whole."

Then the moon comes out from behind a cloud again, and he can see tears glistening on her face. "There's a difference between needing attention and being intentionally ignored."

He opens his mouth to say something, but his brain fails him. He could talk about their daily circulation massages, but she has already pointed out that even then, he's mentally checked out.

"It's the wheelchair, isn't it?"

"No!" he tells her. "It has nothing to do with that."

"So you admit there's a reason."

"I didn't say that."

"What then?"

He steps down from the jet. Three steps that separate his world from Risa's. He kneels before her, trying to look into her eyes, but now they're hidden in shadow. "Risa, I care about you as much as I ever did. You know that."

"Care about me?"

"Love you, okay? I love you." The words don't come easy for Connor. They wouldn't come at all if they weren't true, so that's how he knows they are. He does love her deeply—that's not the problem. And the wheelchair isn't the problem, and neither is his job of running the Graveyard.

"You don't behave like a boy when he's in love."

"Maybe because I'm not a boy," he tells her. "I haven't been for a good long time now."

She thinks about that, and quietly says, "Then show me how you feel the way a man does. And make me believe it."

The challenge hangs heavy in the air. For a moment he imagines himself lifting her out of the chair and carrying her into his jet, all the way to his room at the back, and gently laying her down on his bed, being for her the man he claims to be.

But Risa will not be carried. Under any circumstances. Ever. And he wonders if maybe this is not entirely his fault. Maybe she's partially to blame for this invisible rift between them.

With no other way to prove his feelings, he reaches forward with his own hand, pushes the hair back from her face, then leans in, giving her a powerful kiss. He puts the whole weight of their relationship and all their built-up frustration into that single superheroic kiss. It should be enough to say everything he can't . . . but when he pulls away, he feels her tears on his cheek, and she says:

"If you wanted me with you, you would have built a ramp."

Back inside, Connor lies on his bed in the dark, the moonlight painting cold bars of light across his bed. He's angry. Not at Risa, because she's right. It would have been nothing to build a ramp to his jet. He could have done it in half a day.

But what if he had?

What if Risa really could be with him in every possible way—and what if the shark on his arm truly did have a mind of its own? Roland attacked her—he tried to force himself on her, and she must have been looking at that damned shark when

---

he did it. She said it didn't bother her, but it bothers Connor enough to keep him awake night after night. Because what if when they were alone together, in the heat of that passionate moment they both wanted—what if he lost control? What if that hand held her too tight, tugged her too hard—what if it hit her, and hit her again, and again, and wouldn't stop? And how could he ever truly be there with her if all he could think about were all the things that arm had done, and all the things it still might do?

Better not to let it happen.

Better to make sure she's never that close.

So you don't build a ramp. You don't visit her in her jet, and when you do have physical contact, it's out in the open where it's safe. And when she rolls away from you in tears, you let her go, thinking whatever she wants to think, because that's better than admitting to her that you're too weak to feel safe with your own arm. Then, alone in the dark of a private jet, you smash your fist furiously against a wall until your knuckles are raw and bloody, but you don't care, because even though you can feel the pain, you know they're not *your* knuckles at all.

10 · Starkey

Starkey spends his days working his particular brand of magic—and he knows that the best magic tricks take practice, patience, and very careful misdirection. Undetectable sleight of hand. For more than a month he has not betrayed his ambitions. To have done so would have made Connor suspicious. Instead he networked among the Whollies, studying the alliances, the friendships, and the power structure—and at last, through careful planning, Starkey has inserted himself in the right place at the right time to gain Connor's favor without him ever knowing that it was all part of Starkey's long-term plan.

Now he's in the highest echelon of the Graveyard, and although it's only food service, it keeps him in direct contact with all seven hundred kids. He has more power, more access, and he begins to do things that previously might be thought of as suspicious, but now come with the territory of being one of the Holy of Whollies.

One afternoon Starkey wanders innocently into the Com-Bom, the Graveyard's computer and communications center, which Hayden runs. Its radio equipment was initially designed to pull in and decode enemy frequencies—which it still does, although now the enemy is the National Juvenile Authority. At any given time it's manned by half a dozen Whollies, who have been handpicked by Hayden for their computer skills.

"I'm not the tech geek everyone makes me out to be," Hayden tells him. "I'm just very good at taking credit for other people's work. I think I get it from my father—he was uniquely skilled at stomping on fingers as he climbed the corporate ladder." Hayden studies Starkey for a moment, and Starkey just smiles back.

"Something wrong?"

"No," Hayden says. "I was just wondering if you're thinking of stealing my position. Not that I care. I wouldn't mind working food service for a while, but it would help me to know what your intentions are."

"I just want to know how stuff works around here, that's all."

"Oh," says Hayden, "you're one of *those*." Starkey doesn't know what kind of "those" he's talking about, but he doesn't care as long as Hayden tells him what he wants to know.

"I have an ethnically diverse team here," Hayden tells him proudly, going around the room. "Tad is Japanese, Hailey is umber, Jeevan is Indian—and Esme is half-Hispanic. I think her other half must be extraterrestrial, because she's too damn smart to be all human." Esme preens proudly for a moment, then gets back to work cracking coded communications. "We have Nasim, who's Muslim, working side by side with Lizbeth, who's Jewish, and guess what? They're in love."

"Bite me," says Nasim, then Lizbeth punches him just hard enough to make it clear that it's true.

Hayden points out the various monitoring consoles. "There's a communications monitoring program running on this one. It can pull keywords out of anything from e-mails to phone conversations. It can warn us if the Juvey-cops are up to something major. Kind of an early warning system originally developed to fight terrorism, but isn't it nice to know we can now use it for civilian purposes?"

"So what do we do if it says things are getting dangerous?"

"Damned if I know," Hayden says. "That's Connor's department."

There's a console from which Hayden creates playlists and runs interviews for his Radio Free Hayden show.

"You realize that it doesn't broadcast any farther than you can shout," Starkey tells him with a smirk.

"Of course not," Hayden says. "If it did, then the Juvies could pick it up."

"If no one is listening, then who's it for?"

"First off," says Hayden, "your assumption that no one is listening is incorrect. I estimate I have at least five or six listeners at any given time."

"Yes," says Tad. "He means us."

"And second," Hayden says, not denying it, "it's preparing me for a career in broadcasting, which I plan to pursue once I turn seventeen and get out of this place."

"Not hanging around to help Connor, huh?"

"My loyalty has the half-life of unpasteurized milk," Hayden tells him. "I'd take a bullet for Connor, and he knows it. But only until I'm seventeen."

It all seems pretty straightforward until Esme says, "I thought you already were seventeen."

Hayden shifts his shoulders uncomfortably. "Last year didn't count."

Next to Jeevan is a printout. A list of names, addresses, and dates. Starkey picks it up. "What's this?"

"Our good man Jeeves here is responsible for getting us a list of all the kids slated for unwinding from here all the way to Phoenix."

"These are the kids for your rescue missions?"

"Not all of them," Hayden says. "We pick and choose. We can't save everyone, but we do what we can." He points out the highlighted names—the ones chosen for rescue—and as Starkey looks over the list, he starts to get angry. There's information about each kid, including birth dates—except for the ones who don't have a birth date. Instead a stork date is listed. None of the storked kids are highlighted.

"So you and Connor don't like saving storked kids?" Starkey asks, not even attempting to hide the chill in his voice.

Hayden looks genuinely perplexed and takes the list to look at it. "Hmm, I hadn't noticed. Anyway, it's not part of our criteria. We look for only-children in dimly lit suburban neighborhoods. It means fewer people to squeal on us, and less of a chance of being seen. See, brothers and sisters can't keep their mouths shut, no matter what we threaten them with. I guess mothers who stork babies mostly give them to people who are parents already. Hard to find a storked only child."

"Well," says Starkey, "maybe we need to change the criteria."

Hayden shrugs like it's nothing, like it doesn't really matter, and it just makes Starkey angrier. "Take it up with Connor," he says, then goes on with his grand tour of the communications center, but Starkey's not listening anymore.

• • •

The revelation in the ComBom gives Starkey a game-changing idea. One by one he singles out all the storked kids in the Grave-yard. It's not an easy task, because most storks want to keep their storking a shameful secret. Starkey, however, makes no secret of his own doorstep arrival, and soon the storked kids begin to seek him out, seeing him as their champion.

As it turns out, a full fourth of the Graveyard population are storks. He keeps that information to himself.

The girl named Bam, who at first hated him because he took her place in the Holy of Whollies, warms to him quickly because she's a stork as well. "If you want your revenge on Connor, be patient," he tells her. "It will come." She reluctantly takes his word for it.

One day Starkey catches Connor when he's busy supervising the dismantling of an engine.

"Is there a buyer for it, or are they gonna put it up for sale?" Starkey asks pleasantly.

"They asked for it in the front office, that's all I know."

"The engine says Rolls-Royce—I thought they only made cars."

"Nope."

Starkey keeps chatting about pointless stuff, until he's sure that Connor is irritated at having to divide his attention between the engine and Starkey. That's when Starkey pulls out what he's been hiding up his sleeve.

"Listen, I've been thinking . . . you know I was storked, right? And well, you know, it's nothing big, but I thought it might be nice to make some special reserved time just for storked kids at the Rec Jet. Just to show them they won't be discriminated against anymore."

"Yeah, yeah, sure," Connor says, as he stares at the engine, happy to be ending the conversation. He never even realizes what he's just given away.

Starkey calls his little group the Stork Club and stakes out the hour between seven and eight every evening. While everyone's looking somewhere else, a new class distinction rises within the Graveyard. The Stork Club is the only minority with special members-only time at the Rec Jet. It's a taste of privilege that these kids have never had before—and Starkey wants them to gobble it up. He wants them to get used to it. He wants them all to expect it—and to know that Starkey can deliver.

Since Starkey runs food services, members of the Stork Club start replacing others in serving positions, and dole out larger servings to other storks with a wink. In the Holy of Whollies, the only ones who seem wise to these little creeping alliances are Ashley, whose job it is to root out social flare points, and that obnoxious Sherman kid who replaced John as head of waste and sanitation. It turns out Ralphy was easily bribed to look the other way, and as for Ashley, Starkey pretty much has it under control.

"What if giving storks special treatment creates resentment in the general population?" Ashley asks him as he supervises dinner one night.

"Well," Starkey tells her with a mildly seductive smile, "the general population can kiss my ass."

It makes Ashley blush just a little bit. "Just try to keep a low profile, okay?"

Still beaming charm, he says, "It's what I do best," and serves her a nice heaping portion, all the while calculating how she might secretly play into his plans.

"You're a hard guy to read," she tells him. "I'd really like to get inside your head."

To which he responds, "The feeling's mutual."

Each night, during "the stork hour" at the Rec Jet, Starkey plants tiny seeds of discontent over games of pool and Ping-Pong. Nothing so blatant as fomenting a revolution, just innocent suggestions to encourage certain directions of thought.

"I think Connor's done a good job for a guy who's not all that smart," he tells them offhandedly. Or, "I really like Connor. He's not much of a leader, but isn't he a great guy?"

Starkey never shows any open defiance; that would be counterproductive. It's not about tearing Connor down, it's about rotting out his roots. He won't even suggest that he should be the one taking Connor's place. That suggestion will eventually come from other storks—and all on their own, without any prompting from him. He knows it will happen, because he knows that every storked kid, deep down, dreams of a world where they're not considered second-class citizens. That makes Starkey more than just the leader of a club. It makes him the hope for storked salvation.

Part Three

Windows of
the Soul

Collected on the Internet, October 2011:

Kidney and other organ prices on the global criminal markets are based upon publicly available reports and are quoted in U.S. dollars. The price represents the amount either paid to the seller of the organ or the price paid by the buyer for the organ.

Average paid by kidney buyer: $150,000
Average paid to seller of kidney: $5,000
Kidney broker in Yemen: $60,000
Kidney broker in the Philippines: $1,000 to $1,500
Kidney buyer in Israel: $125,000 to $135,000
Kidney buyer in Moldova: $100,000 to $250,000
Kidney buyer in Singapore: $300,000
Kidney buyer in United States: $30,000
Kidney buyer in China: $87,000
Kidney buyer in Saudi Arabia: $16,000
Kidney seller in Bangladesh: $2,500
Kidney seller in China: $15,000
Kidney seller in Egypt: $2,000
Kidney seller in Kenya: $650
Kidney seller in Moldova: $2,500 to $3,000
Kidney seller in Peru: $5,000
Kidney seller in Ukraine: $200,000
Kidney seller in Vietnam: $2,410
Kidney seller in Yemen: $5,000
Kidney seller in the Philippines: $2,000 to $10,000
Liver buyer in China: $21,900
Liver seller in China: $3,660

Courtesy of www.havocscope.com

11 · Smoker

The boy is certain he's going to die.

He sprained his ankle falling into the pit, maybe even broke it. Now it's swollen and blue, and has been that way for days. It's bad, but it's not the worst of his problems.

The pit is more than ten feet deep, and even if his ankle were fine, he'd never be able to climb out. For five days he's been screaming for help, and now his voice is nothing but a dry rasp.

And all because of those stupid cigarettes.

It had been weeks since he had a smoke. His supplier had been arrested again, and although there were kids at school who bragged about smoking, no one would offer him a cigarette, or even give him the name of a dealer. That's why he came to this part of town—a warehouse district of unused, rotting buildings, many of which were condemned, but no one wanted to waste the money or energy it would take to tear them down.

He knew if he was ever going to score himself some smokes again, this was the place to do it. Even if it was just one or two from some skank nic addict, it would be worth it. That day was the third time he detoured through the warehouse streets on the way home from school, and nothing. No one. It seemed not even the nic addicts found the warehouse district worthy of their attention.

So imagine his surprise when he saw an open door, and cigarette butts strewn on the ground in front of it, like they had no better place to be.

He stepped into the rotting building. The huge space

smelled of evolving mold, and paint chips littered the ground like a fall of leaves.

Then he saw it—way at the back of the warehouse was a mattress. It was dirty, shredded, probably the digs of some homeless dude. Nothing was remarkable about it. What was remarkable was the unopened carton of cigarettes sitting on the mattress.

He couldn't believe his luck! He looked around to make sure there was no one there, then hurried to the mattress, and, stepping onto it, reached for the cigarette carton.

Even before he touched the carton, the mattress fell out beneath his feet and plunged into the pit. Although the mattress had mostly broken his fall, his right ankle hit the ground unprotected. He almost blacked out from the pain, and when his vision cleared he realized what had happened.

He was furious. His initial thought was that this was some sort of practical joke—as if his buddies from school would be looking down at him at any moment, pointing and laughing, calling him an idiot. But he quickly came to understand that this was not a joke at all. This was a trap.

But if this was a trap, why had no one come for five days?

There had been a jug of water and a box of crackers at the bottom of the pit on the day he fell in, along with a ceramic pot to relieve himself in. Whoever set the trap didn't want him to starve, but he did not do well with the rationing. The food and water was gone in three days, and now there's nothing left but a lousy carton of cigarettes, which he can't smoke because there aren't any matches. At one point he tried to eat the tobacco right out of the wrapper, figuring it might have some nutritional value, but it only made him dry-heave.

Now, with day five coming to an end, he's convinced no one's coming for him. No one's going to find him until it's too late.

Then, just before dark, he hears footsteps crunching the paint chips on the warehouse floor.

"Hey," he tries to yell, "over here!" His voice is barely a hiss, but it's enough. A face appears, looking down at him.

"My God, what are you doing down there? Are you okay?"

"Help . . ."

"Hold tight," says the man. He goes away and comes back a few moments later with an aluminum ladder, which he lowers into the pit. Although the boy has no strength to even stand, some secret reserve of adrenaline fuels his climb and helps him bear the pain of putting weight on his ruined ankle. In half a minute he's out of the pit, throwing his arms around the stranger who saved him.

The man sits him down. "Here, have something to drink," he says and hands the boy a water bottle. The boy guzzles it like it's the only water in the world. "How long have you been down there?"

"Five days." He gags as he tries to swallow the water, almost throwing it up, but he manages to keep it down.

The man kneels to him, shaking his head. "AWOL Unwinds are always getting themselves into trouble. You gotta be more careful."

The boy shakes his head. "I'm not an Unwind."

The man grins and nods knowingly. "Yeah, yeah, that's what they all say. Don't worry. Your secret is safe with me."

Then the boy feels a sudden prick on his arm.

"Ouch!" He sees a drop of blood on his forearm, which the stranger collects with a small electronic device. "What are you doing?"

The man ignores him, looking at the readout of the device. The boy's aunt is a diabetic, and she checks her blood sugar with something like it, but the boy suspects this device has a different purpose, although he's not sure what that purpose is.

"Hmm," says the man, raising an eyebrow, "it looks like you're telling the truth. Your DNA doesn't match any of the kids in the AWOL Unwind database."

"Oh, I get it. You're a Juvey-cop!" He's relieved, because a Juvey-cop is safe. A Juvey-cop will take him home to his parents, who must be worried sick.

"Well . . . I *was* a Juvey-cop," the man says, "but I'm no longer in that line of work." Then he holds out his hand to shake. "The name's Nelson. And you are?"

"Bennett, Bennett Garvin." Only now that he's had some water and some time does he focus enough attention to get a good look at Nelson. He's unshaven, his nails are dirty, and it appears he hasn't been taking good care of himself. But the most startling thing about him are his eyes. There's a strange disconnected intensity about them that doesn't match the rest of him. In fact, the eyes don't even match each other. Two different shades of blue. It's unnerving.

"Could you call my parents?" Bennett asks. "Let them know you've found me?"

The faint smile never leaves Nelson's face. "Oh, I don't think that will be happening today."

Bennett doesn't say anything as he struggles to grasp the situation—but having not eaten, and with the water not yet in his system, everything seems a little fuzzy.

"I can't let you go now that you've seen me." Then Nelson grabs him roughly, squeezing his arm, poking his side, and putting a dirty hand in Bennett's mouth to check his teeth like a horse. "Aside from that nasty ankle, you're a top-notch specimen. A little dehydrated, but nothing a few more water bottles won't take care of. And the black market harvesters don't care whether you're an official Unwind or not—they pay just the same."

"No!" Bennett tries to pull free, but he doesn't have the strength. "Please don't hurt me!"

Nelson laughs. "Hurt you? I wouldn't think of it. The better your condition, the more you'll be worth to me."

"My parents have money. They'll pay you."

"I don't do ransoms," he tells him, "but I'll tell you what—
I like your eyes, they're very expressive. And because I like
your eyes, I'll give you a fighting chance." Nelson points to the
entrance. "If you can get to the front door before I tranq you,
I'll let you go. Hell, I'll even give you a ten-second head start."
He hauls Bennett to his feet. "Ready, set, go!"

Bennett does not need a second invitation. He takes off
across the expanse of the warehouse, feeling dizzy, feeling like
his feet won't move. But somehow, he makes them go.

"One!"

His ankle throbs, but he ignores it. His lungs ache, but he
doesn't care. He knows this is life\and death. The pain is only
temporary.

"Two!"

Paint chips crush beneath his feet like eggshells.

"Three!"

Water sloshes in his belly, making it ache even worse, but
he doesn't let it slow him down.

"Four!"

The door to the warehouse is open wide. The twilight spill-
ing through the door is as glorious as the bright light of a mid-
day sun.

"Five!"

A few yards to go—he's almost there!

"Six-seven-eight-nine-ten!"

Even before he realizes he's been cheated, the tranq dart hits
him right in the back of his neck, delivering a full dose directly
into his brain stem. His legs buckle beneath him, and suddenly
that door that seemed so close might as well be a million miles
away. His eyes cross, his vision blurs, and he smells musty tox-
icity as the side of his head hits the ground. He fights to keep
conscious, while above him looms the shadow of Nelson, a dark

ghost in a fading field of vision. . . . And the moment before he loses consciousness, he hears Nelson say:

"I really do like your eyes. I like them much more than the ones I have now."

12 · Nelson

J. T. Nelson knows he'll never get rich selling careless kids to black market harvesters. Even back when his catches were legitimate, there was no real money in it—but then it didn't matter. When he was a Juvey-cop, he was willing to accept a steady salary, health benefits, and the promise of a pension. He had been more than satisfied with his place in life, maintaining order and bringing AWOLs to justice. But all that changed on the day the Akron AWOL took him out with his own tranq gun. Nearly a year later, he still can't get the image of Connor Lassiter out of his mind: that smug, arrogant look on his face as he shot the tranq bullet into Nelson's leg.

For Nelson, that was a shot heard round the world.

From that moment on, his life was a living hell. He was the butt of jokes—not just in his department, but around the nation. He was held up to ridicule, as the cop responsible for letting the infamous Unwind go. So Connor Lassiter became legend and Nelson lost his job, and his self-respect. Even his wife left him.

But he only wallowed for a little while. He was full of anger but knew how to take anger and mold it into something useful. If the Juvenile Authority no longer wanted him, he might as well be in business for himself. Black marketeers don't laugh at him for having let Connor Lassiter get away, and they ask no questions.

At first it was just AWOLs. They were quick to fall for his

various traps like the stupid kids they are. Then he caught his first runaway, a kid whose DNA didn't show up on the AWOL Unwind database. He thought the black marketeers would turn him away, but they didn't care. As long as the subject was healthy, he got his price. There were even kids like the one he caught today, who were just unlucky. He's happy to take them, too. His conscience doesn't bother him.

What bothers him are their eyes.

That's what he has the most trouble with. The way they look at him. Those fearful, pleading expressions, always hopeful down to the last second, as if he might have a change of heart. Those eyes plague him in his dreams. They're windows of the soul, aren't they? But in those early days as a parts pirate, when he looked at his own eyes in the mirror, he didn't see what he saw in theirs. His "windows" showed no such expression of soulfulness, and the more he looked at his own empty eyes, the more jealous he became. He wanted some of that innocence, that desperate hope for himself. So one day he went to his black market contact and claimed the eyes of his latest catch as part of his payment. He was only able to negotiate himself a single eye, but at least that was better than nothing. After that first operation, when he looked at himself in the mirror, he would see in that eye a shred of humanity, and for a little while, he'd be high on hope. It would remind him of the idealistic young man he had once been many years before. One problem, however: Now he had one blue eye and one brown. That wouldn't do.

So he claimed another, but that eye didn't quite match the first. So he claimed another, and another, and with each operation he felt a sliver of innocence return to him. He knows that someday soon he'll find the eyes that will make him perfect, and then he can finally rest . . . because by seeing the world through other's eyes, Nelson is bit by bit becoming whole.

• • •

The black marketeer wears an expensive European suit and drives a Porsche. He looks more like a legitimate businessman than a shady figure who deals in flesh. He doesn't hide the fact that his business has made him rich. Instead he flaunts his wealth with the entitled disregard of royalty. Nelson envies him his style.

He goes by the name Divan, like some sort of fashion designer, and doesn't refer to himself as a black marketer, but as an "independent supplier." His offshore harvest camp is hidden and mysterious. Not even Nelson knows where it is, and he suspects its operation has none of the strict regulations of American harvest camps.

He meets Nelson in Sarnia, a Canadian town just across the bridge from Port Huron, Michigan. Divan cannot step on American soil. There are numerous warrants out for his arrest. But the Canadians, bless them, have been far more tolerant.

Divan takes possession of the boy with the damaged ankle in the back of a car dealership that he uses as his front. As he looks the boy over, he frowns at the swollen ankle and wags a finger at Nelson—all part of his standard ploy to barter Nelson down. The boy, conscious now but still groggy from a heavy dose of tranqs, mumbles incoherently, and although Nelson ignores him, Divan pats him gently on the cheek.

"Don't you worry about a thing," he tells the boy. "We are not barbarians." It's one of the lines he always uses. It conveys no real information to the boy but somehow comforts him. It's calculated, like everything else about Divan.

The boy is taken away, a price is negotiated, and, as is his custom, Divan pays Nelson in cash from a money clip filled with countless bills. Then he claps Nelson on the back jovially. Nelson gets more respect as a parts pirate than he ever did from his superiors as a juvenile enforcement officer.

"I can always count on you to bring me what I need. Not all

my associates are so consistent. Now that the Juvenile Authority is offering rewards for AWOL Unwinds, I find fewer come my way."

"Goddamn Cap-17 law," Nelson says.

"Yes. Let's hope it's not a sign that society is slipping back to its old, less civilized ways."

"Not a chance," Nelson tells him. "People won't go back there."

He was just a child when the Unwind Accord was passed and the war ended—but it's not the war that sticks in his mind from those days. It's the fear of the ferals. With the failure of the public school system, the nation was overrun by teenagers out of work, out of school, and with nothing to do even before the war. In fact, that fear triggered the war more than anything else. One side claimed the ferals were created by the collapse of family values, while the other side claimed the ferals were a product of rigid beliefs that no longer met the world's needs. Both sides were right. Both sides were wrong—but it didn't matter when people were terrified to go into the streets at night from fear of their own kids.

"Unwinding didn't just end the war," Nelson points out to Divan. "It ripped out the weeds. Kept them from choking the rest of us out. Fear of the AWOLs will keep both of us in business."

"I sincerely hope you're right." Divan opens his mouth as if to say more, but thinks better of it.

"Is there something you're not telling me?"

"Nothing to trouble yourself with. Just rumors. We'll talk more upon your next visit. And if you could, please keep in mind that I'm experiencing a shortage of girls. Ones with red hair in particular. Also umbers—either gender. And, of course, I'll always pay a high price for 'People of Chance.'"

"I'll keep it in mind," says Nelson, already scheming a way of fulfilling Divan's request. He'd yet to capture a Native American kid, but one of these days those so-called "People of

Chance" would bust and leave Nelson with not just a winning hand, but an entire winning body.

As he drives back across the bridge and onto American soil, his spirits are high. If Divan has worries, they're unfounded. Although Nelson has, in recent days, chosen the life of an outsider, he still feels he has a finger on the pulse of the times. With so much of the civilized world employing the practice of unwinding, how could anyone deny that it is a viable alternative for the troubled, the useless, and the unwanted? Like the ads say, "Unwinding isn't just good medicine—it's the right idea."

It was the very rightness of the idea that made Nelson become a Juvey-cop to begin with. The knowledge that he would leave the world a cleaner, brighter place by dredging the dregs from the streets was what propelled him into the police academy. Eventually, though, his ideals were replaced by an abiding hatred for those marked for unwinding. They were all alike, these Unwinds; sucking valuable resources from those more deserving, and clinging to their pathetic individuality, rather than accepting peaceful division. They insisted on living lives no one else felt were worth the effort. As an officer of the law, the rules of conduct held him back—but as a parts pirate, he could take care of business much more effectively. So, as much as he blamed Connor Lassiter for ruining his life, perhaps the boy had done him a favor. Still, it is supremely satisfying to know that the Akron AWOL died an ignoble death at Happy Jack Harvest Camp. It gives Nelson hope that maybe there truly is justice in the universe.

13 · Connor

A retired 787 arrives with only fourteen Whollies packed in empty beer barrels in the hold. Connor wonders if someone in the resistance is just getting bored, or if the barrels were really the most inconspicuous way to ship them. The kids all exit the hold cramped and hunched from the ride, and Connor delivers his usual rallying speech, troubled by the diminishing number of kids in each arriving plane.

Then, after they've been brought to the IHOP jet for assessment, and to get them ready for life in the Graveyard, Connor returns with Trace to the 787. It's the old Boeing Dreamliner, the first one of its kind to arrive at the Graveyard. It was once heralded as the salvation of the aviation industry, and it certainly served its purpose, but there's always something newer, faster, and more fuel-efficient ready to take any jet's place.

"She's still impressive," says Trace, as they walk through the passenger compartment, which is already sweltering in the Arizona sun. "A classical beauty."

"You think you could fly this plane if you had to?" Connor asks him as they size up the Dreamliner.

Trace grins. "I've been flying Cessnas since I was sixteen, and military aircraft for a year before I joined the ADR, so yes, I could fly a commercial airliner. Hell, I could make it do loop-the-loops."

"Good. You may need to do loops if we're being targeted."

Trace puzzles over this for a second, then grins. "Escape jet?"

"If we gut it, we can fit everyone in. Won't be comfortable, but it'll work."

"I'll research the specs and see if it can handle the weight."

"We'll gut the cabin, then have the front-office guys post it all for sale," Connor tells him. "We'll include the engine parts and the cockpit console on the sale list, but we won't really dismantle any of the plane's actual working parts."

Trace gets it without having to be told. "So, to anyone keeping tabs on us, it'll appear that the jet has totally gone to salvage, but we'll know it's still operational."

"Exactly. Then we'll tow it to the main aisle—make it seem like we're using it as a dormitory jet."

"Brilliant."

"No," says Connor, "desperate. Now, let's get out of this thing before we fry."

Trace drives Connor back to the main aisle from the runway. In addition to being head of security in the Graveyard, he's Connor's acting bodyguard and chauffeur. Not Connor's idea, any more than the private jet and the blue camo, but it helped create that illusory leadership pedestal. From the beginning, though, Connor hated the idea of being set apart.

"Get used to it," Risa told him. "You're not just some random Unwind anymore; to these kids, you *are* the resistance. You need to project the image of someone in charge." He wonders if she still feels that way, now that being in charge doesn't leave enough room in his life to truly be there for her. He wonders if he should invent himself some illness just so he can visit her in the infirmary jet. Is that proper behavior for a leader?

"The Dreamliner is a good idea," Trace says, bringing Connor back to the here and now. "But I know there are other things on your mind."

"Always," Connor tells him.

"I know you're worried about the Juvies, and why they're still leaving us alone." Trace waits a moment, then adds, "I think I know why, but you're not going to like it."

"When have I ever liked anything about the Juvies?"

"It's not about them as much as it's about *you*."

"I don't follow."

"You will." They hit a bump, and Connor reflexively grabs onto the door. Trace makes no apologies for his driving. "See, Connor, the kids here, even though they've been legally made nonentities, that doesn't make them worthless. They're as valuable as diamonds. Do you know why diamonds are so expensive?"

"I don't know—because they're rare?"

"No, they're *not* rare. In fact, there are so many of them, they could be as cheap as the fake ones. But there's this thing called the diamond consortium. All the owners of all the world's diamond mines get together, and you know what they do? They hide their diamonds in this huge vault in this huge bank in Sweden or Switzerland or wherever. Thousands upon thousands of them. And hiding them creates the illusion that diamonds are rare, driving the prices through the roof."

The Jeep hits another pothole, and this time Connor absorbs the impact without bracing himself. He follows Trace's line of thought, beginning to worry about where it's leading.

"So," says Trace, "after the Cap-17 law passed, there was a shortage of Unwinds, right? The price for every kind of transplant doubled—tripled even. But people pay the price, because everyone's used to getting the parts they want, when they want them. They'll go without food, but they won't go without their parts."

"So what does that have to do with me?"

"You tell me."

Connor considers what Trace had said, and the truth hits him. "We're the vault! And as long as we pull AWOLs off the street, it keeps the price high. Is that what you're saying?"

"Better that all those AWOLs are here, nice and safe, than caught by parts pirates and sold on the black market. That would just drive the price down."

Connor thinks back to that day he was caught and hauled off to Happy Jack Harvest Camp. It had been a shock when the Juvey-cop interrogating him admitted that they knew all about the Graveyard but turned a blind eye, because going after the kids here wasn't worth the effort.

But this is different.

This makes Connor a willing part of the system. To know that he actually plays into some unwinding consortium's plan makes Connor feel dirty—worse than dirty.

And then, when the deeper revelation hits him, it's like a knockout blow. The final punch that leaves him flat on the canvas.

"How long," he asks Trace, "have you been working for the Juvies?"

Trace just drives the Jeep, keeping his eyes straight ahead, and doesn't answer for at least ten seconds. Finally he says, "Don't ask questions you don't want the answer to."

14 · Dolores

While World War II aircraft enjoy the privilege of permanent museum displays, Korean War fixed-wing aircraft are mostly unloved and forgotten. Since it was the first war to feature extensive use of helicopters, those are the aircraft that get all the attention.

There's a sorry bomber from the Korean War that sits two aisles off the main aisle. The Admiral put it there, and although Connor has moved planes around it, Dolores, as she is called, never moves and is never opened. Her hatch has been retrofitted with a key lock, and Connor has the only key, which he wears around his neck like a latchkey child.

Dolores is the arsenal. She's filled with the kind of weapons that troubled teens should not, under any circumstances, have access to. Unless of course they're in uniform. The idea that the Graveyard would someday have to defend itself like the Warsaw Ghetto hung over the Admiral's head, and now hangs over Connor's. There's not a day he doesn't think about it—not a day he doesn't finger that key around his neck like a cross. Today, however, he visits Dolores for another reason—to defend the Graveyard not from attack, but from infiltration. Today he goes in to find himself a .22 caliber pistol and a cartridge of bullets.

15 · Connor

Trace sleeps in a rusty old DC-3, overseeing the roughest, most troublesome kids. It's an unofficial detention hall, with Trace as the unofficial guard. Since the old propeller plane has a nonfunctioning lavatory, its occupants have to use a portable that sits at the bottom of the gangway stairs. Its lock is broken. Connor broke it a few hours before.

After curfew he and two of the toughest Whollies he could scrounge up wait in the shadows of a neighboring plane, watching.

"Tell us again why we're taking out Trace?"

"Shh!" Connor tells them, then whispers, "Because I say we are."

Connor is the only one with a gun. It's loaded. The goons are just backup, because he knows he can't take Trace alone. The plan is to corner him, cuff him, and keep him as a sort of prisoner of war . . . but Connor has resolved that he'll use the gun if it becomes necessary.

Never wield a weapon unless you're willing to use it, the Admiral once told him. If Connor is going to maintain order in this place, he has to go by the Admiral's playbook.

Every twenty minutes or so, someone comes out to use the restroom. Trace isn't one of them.

"Are we supposed to wait here all night?" complains the tough kid holding the cuffs.

"Yes, if we have to." Connor begins to wonder if Trace's

military training included superhuman bladder control, until Trace comes down a few minutes after midnight.

They wait until the door of the portable closes, and then they quietly approach with Connor in the lead. He puts the pistol in his right hand—Roland's hand—feeling the coldness of its handle and firmness of its trigger. He takes the safety off, takes a deep breath, and then swings the door open.

Trace stands there, staring right at him, not caught off guard in the least. In a single move he kicks Connor's legs out from under him, grabs the gun out of his hand, twists him around, and pushes him cheek-first into the dirt, wrenching Roland's arm painfully behind his back. Connor can feel the seam of the graft threatening to tear loose.

With Connor in too much pain to move, Trace brings down the other two kids before they can run, leaving them unconscious in the dust. Then he returns his attention to Connor.

"First of all," says Trace, "ambushing a man taking a dump is beneath you. Secondly, never take a deep breath before attacking someone, because it gives you away."

Connor, still in pain, spins around to face him, and as he does, he feels the muzzle of the gun pressed to his forehead. Trace holds the gun to Connor's head for a moment more, his face stern, then takes it away. "Don't feel too bad," Trace says. "I'm not just an air force boeuf, I was special ops. I could have killed you nine different ways before you hit the ground." He ejects the clip—but as he does, Connor grabs Trace's wrist, tugs him off balance, wrenches the gun from him, and aims it at Trace again as he gets to his feet.

"There's still a bullet in the chamber," Connor reminds him.

Trace backs away, hands up. "Well played. I guess I'm rusty." They stand there frozen for a moment, and Trace says, "If you're going to kill me, do it now—because I *will* get the advantage again." But Connor's resolve is gone, and they both know it.

"Did you kill the other two?" asks Connor, looking at how the once-tough kids lay twisted and unconscious on the ground.

"Just knocked them out. Not much honor in killing the defenseless."

Connor lowers the gun. Trace doesn't rush him.

"I want you gone," Connor tells him.

"Tossing me out will be a very bad move."

Hearing that just makes Connor angry. "As far as I'm concerned, you're the enemy. You work for *them*."

"I also work for you."

"You can't have it both ways!"

"That's where you're wrong," Trace says. "Playing both sides is a time-honored strategy."

"I'm not your puppet!"

"No," says Trace, "you're my commanding officer. Act like it."

Another kid comes clambering down the stairs to use the portable. He catches sight of Trace and Connor, and the two kids still rag-dolled on the ground. "What's the deal?" the kid says as he takes in the situation.

"When it's your business, I'll tell you," Connor says.

Then he sees the gun in Connor's hand. "Yeah, sure, no problem," he says, and goes back up the stairs.

Connor realizes the distraction would have given Trace plenty of time to turn the tables again, but he didn't. It moves them one step closer to trust. Connor gestures to Trace with a wave of the gun. "Walk." But at this point the gun is just a prop, and they both know it. They move farther from the main aisle and down an aisle of mothballed fighter jets. No Whollies here to eavesdrop on their conversation.

"If you work for them," Connor asks, "then why did you tell me all the things you told me?"

"Because I'm their eyes and ears, but my brain is my own— and whether you believe it or not, I like what you're doing here."

"What have you told them about this place?"

Trace shrugs. "Mostly what they already know. That things are under control here. That a new shipment of AWOLs arrives every few weeks. I assure them that the place is not a threat, and no one's planning to blow up any more harvest camps." Then Trace stops walking and turns to Connor. "What's more important are the things I *don't* tell them."

"Which are?"

"I don't tell them about your rescue missions, I don't tell them about your escape plan . . . and I don't tell them that you're still alive."

"What?"

"As far as they know, this place is being run by Elvis Robert Mullard, a former security guard from Happy Jack—because if anyone knew that *you* were the one in charge, the Juvey-cops would raid this place in an instant. The Akron AWOL is too much of a threat for them to ignore. So I make this place sound like a nursery, and I make you sound like a nanny. It keeps them happy, and it keeps all these kids alive."

Connor looks around them. They're far from the main aisle now. If Trace wanted to, he could probably break Connor's neck and bury him, and no one would ever know. Does that mean that Connor actually trusts Trace in spite of his obvious betrayal? He isn't sure of anything anymore, not even his own motivations.

"None of this changes the fact that you're working for the Juvey-cops."

"Wrong again. I don't work for the Juvies, I work for the people who own them."

"No one owns the Juvenile Authority."

"All right, then, maybe not own, but control. You want to talk about puppets? Every single Juvey-cop is on a string they don't even know about. Of course I don't know who's pulling

132

the strings. All I know is that I got taken away from a promising future in the air force and got sent here."

Connor grins in spite of himself. "Sorry to mess with your career track."

"The point is, I don't report to anyone in the air force; I report to civilians in suits, and that ticks me off. So I did a little research and found out that I work for a company called Proactive Citizenry."

"Never heard of it."

Then Trace drops his voice to a whisper. "I'm not surprised— they keep a low profile, and that provides a cover that gives the military plausible deniability. Think about it; if the brass don't know who they're actually working for, then if something goes wrong, the military can always claim ignorance, court-martial me, and come away clean."

Now things are becoming a little clearer to Connor, or at least clearer as to why Trace decided to play both sides. They turn and begin walking back toward the main aisle.

"I'm disillusioned, Connor. The way I see it, you've been more fair and more trustworthy than whoever it is I work for. Character counts for a lot in this world, and when it comes to Proactive Citizenry, shady doesn't even begin to describe them. So I'll do my job for them, but I put my trust in you."

"How do I know you're not lying to me now?"

"You don't. But so far you've survived because of your instincts. What do your instincts tell you right now?"

Connor thinks about it and realizes the answer is easy. "My instincts tell me that I'm screwed no matter what I do. But that's normal for me."

Trace accepts his answer. "We have more to talk about, but I think that's enough for one day. You should probably put some ice on that shoulder. I wrenched it pretty hard."

"I hadn't noticed," Connor lies.

Trace reaches out his hand to shake, and Connor considers what shaking that hand means. It could be the creation of their own secret society to battle Proactive Citizenry, whatever that is . . . or it could mean Connor has been entirely duped. In the end, he shakes Trace's hand, wishing that just once, there could be a clear course of action.

"Before today you were just a pawn doing what *they* wanted you to do," Trace tells him. "Deep down you knew it—you sensed it. I hope the truth has set you free."

16 · Risa

Before her shift begins each morning, Risa spends time beneath the wing of the Rec Jet, chatting with other kids who've become her friends. She has more friends here than she did back at the state home, but at the same time she feels more like an older sister than a friend. They revere her like some angel of mercy—not just because she's the medical authority, but because she's the legendary Risa Ward, the Akron AWOL's partner in crime. She suspects they think, deep down, she can heal things that are broken inside.

She used to spend time at the Rec Jet in the evening, after her shift, but the Stork Club put an end to that. She has half a mind to demand equal time for the state wards, but knows that fueling a division of the Graveyard into factions won't do anything but cause trouble. Thanks to Starkey, there's enough of that going on without her help.

Farther away, she can see Connor step down from his jet. He walks along the main aisle, head down, hands in his pockets, deep in whatever dark cloud is troubling him today. Immediately he's set upon by kids who need his attention for one reason or another. She wonders if he ever manages to find a spare second for himself anymore. He certainly doesn't have it for her.

He looks up and catches Risa's gaze. She turns away, feeling guilty, as if she's been spying on him, and chides herself for feeling that way. When she looks up again, he's heading toward her. Behind her kids have begun to gather in front of the TV. Something on the news has caught their attention. She wonders whether Connor is coming to see what the commotion is about or coming to see her. She's pleased when it turns out to be the latter, although she tries not to show it.

"Busy day ahead?" she asks him, offering him a slight smile, which he returns.

"Nah, just lying around watching TV and eating chips. I gotta get a life."

He stands there with his hands in his pockets, looking around, although she knows his attention is on her. Finally he says, "The ADR says they'll send those medical supplies you asked for in the next few days."

"Should I believe it?"

"Probably not."

She knows this is not the reason why he came over to her, but she doesn't know how to coax things out of him anymore. She knows she has to do something before this distance between them gets ingrown.

"So what's the problem of the week?" she asks.

He scratches his neck and looks off, so he doesn't have to look her in the eye. "Sort of the same, and sort of you-don't-want-to-know."

"But," says Risa, "it's big enough for you to tell me that you can't tell me."

"Exactly."

Risa sighs. It's already getting hot, and she's not looking forward to pushing her way to the infirmary jet in the heat. She has no patience for Connor being enigmatic. She's about to tell him to come back when he actually has something to say, but her attention is snagged by the grumble coming from the crowd around the TV, which has grown since she last looked. Both she and Connor are pulled closer by the gravity of the crowd.

The news report is an interview with a woman, rather severe-looking, and even more severe-talking. Coming in the middle, Risa can't make heads or tails of what she's talking about.

"Can you believe it?" someone says. "They're calling this thing a new life form."

"Calling what a new life form?" Connor asks.

Hayden is there and turns to both of them. He looks almost queasy. "They've finally built the perfect beast. The first composite human being."

There are no pictures, but the woman is describing the process—how bits and pieces of almost a hundred different Unwinds were used to create it. Risa feels a shiver go as far down her spine as she can feel. Connor must have the same reaction, because he grasps her shoulder, and she reaches up to grasp his hand, not caring which hand it is.

"Why would they do such a thing?" she asks.

"Because they can," Connor says bitterly.

Risa can feel the heaviness of the vibe around her, as if they're all watching some awful global event unfolding before their eyes.

"We need to get the escape plan ready," Connor says. Risa knows he's talking more to himself than to her. "We can't do a dry run, because the spy sats will pick it up, but everyone needs to know what to do."

Risa feels the same blast of communal intuition. Suddenly getting the hell out of the Graveyard sounds like a very good idea. Even without a safe destination.

"Composite human . . . ," someone grumbles. "I wonder what it looks like."

"C'mon, haven't you ever seen Mr. Potato Head?"

There's a smattering of nervous laughter, but it doesn't lighten the mood.

"Whatever it looks like," Risa says, "I hope we never see it."

17 · Cam

With a finger he traces the lines of his face, down the side of his nose to his cheek. Left, then right. Out from the symmetrical starburst of flesh tones on his forehead, then beyond to the lines that spread beneath his hairline. He dips his finger into the graft-grade healing cream again and spreads it across the lines running down the nape of his neck, his shoulders, his chest, and every other place he can reach. He can feel the tingling as the engineered microorganisms in the cream do their job.

"Believe it or not, the stuff is actually related to yogurt," the dermatologist told him. "Except, of course, that it eats scar tissue." It also costs five thousand dollars a jar, but, as Roberta has told him, money is no object when it comes to Cam.

He's been assured that when treatment is done, he'll have no scars at all, just hairline seams where every little bit of himself meets.

His cream-spreading ritual takes half an hour, twice a day, and he's come to enjoy the Zen-like nature of it. He only wishes there were something that would heal the scars in his mind, which he can still feel. He sees his mind now as an archipelago of islands that he labors to build bridges between—and while he's had great success engineering the most spectacular of bridges, he suspects there are some islands he'll never reach.

There's a knock at his door. "Are you ready?" It's Roberta.

"Reins in your fist," he tells her.

A pause, and then, "Very funny. 'Hold your horses.'"

Cam laughs. He no longer needs to speak in metaphors—he's created enough bridges in his mind to bring some normality to his speech—but he enjoys teasing Roberta and trying to stump her.

He dresses in a tailored shirt and tie. The tie's muted colors, yet bold, fractal pattern, were specifically chosen to project a sense of aesthetic composition; a subliminal suggestion that an artistic whole is always greater than the sum of its parts. He fumbles with the tie. While his brain knows how to tie it, his virtuoso fingers obviously had never learned to do a Windsor knot. He must focus and overcome the frustrating lack of muscle memory.

Roberta knocks again, a little more insistently now. "It's time."

He takes a moment to admire himself in the mirror. His hair is just about an inch long now. A virtual coat of many colors; streaks extending out from the focal point of multiple skin tones on his forehead. Blond runs down the middle, blending to amber on both the left and right. Shades of red and brown arc back from his temples, then give way to jet black above his ears, and tight, dark curls at his sideburns. "All the famous hairstylists will be trampling one another to get to you," Roberta said.

Finally he opens the door before Roberta's knocking becomes frantic. Her dress is a little more elegant than the slacks and blouse she usually wears, but still very understated. It's all calculated to keep the focus on him. For a moment she seems annoyed at him, but now that she gets a good look at him, her irritation melts away.

"You look spectacular, Cam." She smoothes out his shirt and straightens his tie. "You look like the shining star you are!"

"Let's hope I don't give birth to complex elements."

She looks at him quizzically.

"Supernova," he says. "If I'm a shining star, let's hope I don't blow up." He wasn't even trying to stump her. "Sorry—it's just the way I think."

She gently takes him by the arm. "Come, they're waiting for you."

"How many?"

"We didn't want you to be overwhelmed by your first press conference, so we limited it to thirty."

His heart beats heavily, and he must take a few deep breaths to slow it down. He doesn't know why he should be so nervous. They have prepared him with three mock press conferences already, where questions were hurled at him in multiple languages. In each one of those he did just fine—and this time it will be only in English, so he has one less variable to worry about.

This one, however, is real. This time he's about to be officially introduced to a world that is unprepared for him. The faces he saw at those fake press conferences were friendly ones pretending not to be, but today he will be facing actual strangers. Some will just be curious, others amazed, and some might be flat-out horrified. Roberta told him to expect this. What he's worried about are the things that not even she can predict.

They walk down the hall to a spiral staircase that leads to the main living room—a staircase he had not been allowed to use for his first weeks, until his coordination improved. Now, however, he could dance his way down those stairs if he chose to. Roberta tells him to wait until she announces him. She goes down first, and Cam can hear the rumble of chattering reporters die down. The lights dim, and she begins her presentation.

"Since time immemorial, mankind has dreamed of creating life," Roberta begins, her voice amplified and larger than

139

life. Flashes of light reach the top of the stairs. Cam can't see the images from her presentation, but he knows them. He's seen it all before.

"But the great mystery of life itself has been elusive," Roberta continues, "and every dream of creation has ended in humbling failure. There's a good reason for that. We can't create what we don't understand, so until we understand what life is, how can we ever create it? No—instead it is the task of science to take what we already have and build on it. Not create life, but perfect it. So we put forth the question, how can we recombine both our intellectual and physical evolution into the finest version of ourselves, the best of all of us combined? As it turns out, the answer was simple once we knew the right question." She pauses to build the suspense. "Ladies and gentlemen, I present to you Camus Comprix, the world's first fully composite human being!"

At the sound of applause, Cam begins his descent down the spiral staircase, posture proud but gait casual. The audience is still in shadows as he descends, and all the lights are focused on him. He can feel the heat of the spotlights, and although he's in a familiar place, it's as if they've transformed the living room into a theater. He hesitates halfway down, takes a deep breath, and continues, making it seem that his pause was intentional—a photo-op tease, perhaps, because this is one press conference where no cameras are allowed. His presentation to the public is being carefully orchestrated.

The applause gives way to astonishment as the crowd gets a good look at him. There are gasps and whispered chatter as he descends to the microphone. Roberta steps aside, giving him the floor, and by the time she does, there is absolute silence in the room as they all stare at him, trying to process what they're seeing: a young man who is, as Roberta put it, "the best of all of us." Or at least the best of various unwound teens.

In the charged silence, he leans toward the microphone and says, "Well, I have to say, you're a very well put-together group."

Chuckles all around. He's surprised by the amplified timbre of his own voice, a resonant baritone that sounds more confident than he actually is. The lights come up over the group of reporters, and with the ice broken, the first hands rise with questions.

"Pleased to meet you, Camus," says a man in a suit that's seen better days. "I understand you're made up of almost a hundred different people—is that true?"

"Ninety-nine to be exact," Cam says with a grin. "But there's room for one more."

The group of reporters laughs again, less nervously than the first time. He calls on a woman with big hair.

"You're clearly . . . um . . . a *unique* creation." Cam can feel her disapproval like a wave of heat. "How does it feel to know you were invented rather than born?"

"I was born, just not all at the same time," he tells her. "And I wasn't invented, I was reinvented. There's a difference."

"Yes," says someone else. "It must be quite a weight to know that you're the first of your kind. . . ."

This line of questioning was addressed in the mock conferences, and Cam knows his answers by heart. "Everyone feels like they're one of a kind, don't they? That makes me no different from anyone else."

"Mr. Comprix—I'm an expert in dialects, but I can't place yours. You keep shifting in and out of vocal styles."

Cam hasn't considered this before. It's hard enough to put thoughts into words, without thinking about how those words are coming out. "Well, I suppose that all depends on which brain cells I'm wrangling."

"So then your verbal eloquence came hardwired?"

Again, the kind of question he's expecting. "If I were a

computer, it would be hardwired, but I'm not. I'm a hundred percent organic. Human. But to answer your question, some of my skills came from before, others have come since, and I'm sure I'll continue to grow as a human being."

"But you're not a human being," someone shouts from the back. "You might be made from them, but you're no more human that a football is a pig."

Something about this statement—this accusation—cuts him in an unguarded place. He's not prepared for the emotion it brings forth.

"Bull seeing red!" Cam says. It comes out before he can funnel it through his language center. He clears his throat and finds the words. "You're trying to provoke me. Perhaps there's a blade you're hiding behind your cape, but it won't keep you from getting gored."

"Is that a threat?"

"I don't know—was that an insult?"

Murmurs from the crowd. He's made it interesting for them. Roberta throws him a warning glance, but Cam suddenly feels the rage of dozens of unwound kids swelling in him. He must give it voice.

"Is there anyone else out there who thinks that I'm somehow subhuman?"

And as he looks out to the thirty reporters, hands go up. Not just the big-haired woman and the heckler from the back, but others as well. As many as a dozen. Do they really mean it, or are they all just matadors flapping the cape?

"Monet!" he shouts. "Seurat! Close to the canvas, their work looks like splotches of paint. But at a distance you see a masterpiece." Someone controlling the media screens pulls up a spontaneous Monet, but rather than punctuating his point, it makes his comments seem contrived. "You people are all small-minded and have no distance!"

"Sounds like you're very full of yourself," someone says.

"Who said that?" He looks around the crowd. No one will take credit. "I'm full of everyone else—and that's spectacular."

Roberta approaches and tries to take over the microphone, but he pushes her away. "No!" he says. "They want to know the truth? I'm telling them the truth!"

And suddenly the questions come like bullets.

"Did they tell you to say all this?"

"Is there a reason why you were made?"

"Do you know all their names?"

"Do you dream their dreams?"

"Do you feel their unwindings?"

"If you're made of the unwanted, what makes you think you're any better?"

The questions come so fast and with such intensity, Cam can feel his mind begin to rattle itself into fragments. He doesn't know which one to answer—if he can even answer any of them.

"What legal rights should a rewound being have?"

"Can you reproduce?"

"*Should* he reproduce?"

"Is he even alive?"

He can't slow his breathing. He can't capture his own thoughts. He can't see clearly. Voices make no sense, and he can see only parts, but not the larger picture. Faces. A microphone. Roberta is grabbing him, trying to focus him, trying to get him to look at her, but his head can't stop shaking.

"Red light! Brake pedal! Brick wall! Pencils down!" He takes a deep, shuddering breath. "Stop?" It's a plea to Roberta. She can make this go away. She can do anything.

"Looks like he's not wound too tight," someone says, and everyone laughs.

He grabs the microphone one more time, his lips pressed against it. Screeching. Distorted.

"I am more than the parts I'm made of!"

"I am more!"

"I am . . ."

"I . . ."

"I . . ."

And a single voice says calmly, simply, "What if you're not?"

" . . ."

"That's all for now," Roberta tells the jabbering crowd. "Thank you for coming."

He cries, unable to stop. He doesn't know where he is, where Roberta has brought him to. He is nowhere. There is no one in the world but the two of them.

"Shhh," she tells him, gently rocking him back and forth. "It's all right. Everything will be all right."

But it does nothing to calm him. He wants to make the memory of those judgmental faces go away. Can she cut it out of his mind? Replace the memory with some random thoughts of another random Unwind? Can they do that for him? Can they please?

"This was just a first salvo from a world that still needs to process you," Roberta says. "The next one will go better."

Next one? How could he even survive a next one?

"Caboose!" he says. "Closed cover. Credits roll."

"No," Roberta tells him, holding him even more tightly. "It's not the end, this is just the beginning, and I know you'll rise to meet the challenge. You just need a thicker skin."

"Then graft me one!"

She chuckles like it's a joke, and her laughing makes him laugh too, which makes her laugh only louder, and suddenly in the midst of his tears he finds himself in a fit of laughter, yet angry at himself for it. He doesn't even know why he's laughing, but he can't stop, any more than he could stop crying.

Finally he gets himself under control. He's exhausted. All he wants to do is sleep. It will be that way for him for a long time.

PUBLIC SERVICE ANNOUNCEMENT

"Have you ever stopped to think about all the people helped by Unwinding? Not just the recipients of much-needed tissues, but the thousands employed in the medical profession and supporting industries. The children, the husbands and wives of people whose lives are saved by grafts and transplants. How about soldiers wounded in the field of duty, healed and restored by the precious parts they receive? Think about it. We all know someone who has been positively touched by unwinding. But now the so-called Anti-Divisional Resistance threatens our health, our safety, our jobs, and our economy by disregarding a federal law that took a long and painful war to achieve.

"Write to your congressperson today. Tell your legislators what you think. Demand that they stand up against the ADR. Let's keep our nation and our world on the right path.

"Unwinding. It's not just good medicine, it's the right idea."

—Paid for by the Consortium of Concerned Taxpayers

Cam is in full mental and emotional regression. All kinds of theories for his backward slide are postulated and debated. Perhaps his rewound parts are rejecting one another. Perhaps his new neural connections are overloaded with conflicting information and have begun to collapse. The fact of it is that he has simply stopped talking, stopped performing for them—he's even stopped eating and is now on an IV.

All nature of tests have been done on him, but Cam knows the tests will show nothing, because they can't probe his mind. They can't quantify his will to live—or lack of will.

Roberta paces in his bedroom. At first she showed great concern, but over the past few weeks, her concern has mildewed into frustration and anger.

"Do you think I don't know what you're doing?"

He responds by tugging his IV out of his arm.

Roberta comes to him quickly and reconnects it. "You're being a stubborn, obstinate child!"

"Socrates," he tells her. "Hemlock! Bottoms up."

"No!" she shouts at him. "I will not allow you to take your own life! It's not yours to take!"

She sits in a chair beside him, calming herself down. "If you won't live for yourself," she begs him, "then do it for me. *Thrive* for me. You've become my life, you know that, don't you? If you die, you'll be taking me with you."

He won't look her in the eye. "Unfair."

Roberta sighs as Cam watches the relentless drip, drip, drip of the feeding tube that's keeping him alive. He's hungry. He's been hungry for a long time, but it's not enough to motivate him to eat. What's the point in maintaining your life when it's in question whether you're even alive at all?

"I know the press conference was a mistake," Roberta admits. "It was too soon—you weren't ready—but I've been out there doing some pretty effective damage control. The next time you face the public, it will be different."

Only now does he meet her eyes. "There won't be a next time."

Roberta smiles slightly. "Ah! So you *can* put together a coherent thought."

Cam squirms and looks away again. "Of course I can. I just choose not to."

She pats his hand, her eyes moist. "You're a good boy, Cam. A sensitive boy. I will make sure we don't forget that. I'll also make sure you get whatever you want—whatever you need. No one will force you to do anything you don't want to do."

"I don't want the public."

"You will when it's yours," Roberta tells him. "When they're trampling one another just to get a look at you. Not as some oddity, but as a star. A celebrated star. You need to show the world what I know you're capable of." She hesitates for a moment, preparing to tell him something. Perhaps something she's afraid he's not ready for. "I've been giving this a great deal of thought, and I believe what you need is someone to go out there with you. Someone who has completely accepted you and can draw the public's curiosity in a more positive way. Dampen their judgment."

He looks up at her, but she dismisses the idea before he can even propose it. "No, it can't be me. I'm seen as your handler. That won't do. What you need is a pretty little planet revolving around your star. . . ."

The idea intrigues him. It makes him realize that he hungers for more than mere sustenance. He hungers for connection. He's seen no one his age since his creation. His age, he's decided, is sixteen. No one can tell him any different. To have a companion—one who was born, not made—would bring him one step closer to being truly human. Roberta has calculated right this time. This gives him a fair measure of motivation. Once more he reaches for his IV line.

"Cam, don't," pleads Roberta. "Please, don't."

"Don't worry." He disconnects the IV and gets out of bed for the first time in weeks. His joints ache almost as badly as his seams. He walks to the window and peers out. He wasn't even aware of the time of day until now. Dusk. The setting sun hides behind a cloud just above the horizon. The sea shimmers, and the sky is a brilliant canvas of color. Could Roberta be right? Could he have as much of a claim on this world as anyone else? Could he have more?

"Self-determination," he decrees. "I will make decisions for myself now."

"Of course, of course," Roberta says. "And I'll be here to advise you."

"Advise, not order. Not control. I will choose what I do, and when I do it. And I will choose my own companion."

Roberta nods. "Agreed."

"Good. I'm hungry," he tells her. "Have them bring me a steak." Then he reconsiders. "No . . . have them bring me lobster."

"Whatever makes you happy, Cam." And Roberta hurries off to do his bidding.

18· Risa

Risa is woken up in the middle of the night by the sound of feet pounding up AcMac's ramp. She's hoping this late-night visitor isn't for her, but it always is. No one comes here in the middle of the night unless there's some kind of medical emergency requiring her attention.

Kiana pulls back the curtain and barges in. "Risa, a couple of kids just got brought in. It's bad, real bad."

Kiana's a sixteen-year-old who works the infirmary's night shift, lives for drama, and always blows everything out of proportion. Having been purged from a family of doctors, she has a chip on her shoulder when it comes to proving what a good junior medic she is, so her exaggerations are usually just to make herself look better when she solves the emergency. The fact that Kiana has come to get Risa and isn't trying to take all the glory herself means the situation must truly be serious.

"A couple of kids were messing with an engine turbine," Kiana tells her, "and the whole engine came down. . . ."

Risa pulls herself out of bed and into her chair. "What were they doing messing with an engine turbine in the middle of the night?"

"I think it was some sort of dare."

"Incredible." Half the injuries Risa sees are either self-destructive or just plain stupid. She often wonders whether it's just the nature of Whollies, or if it's the same in the outside world.

When she arrives at the infirmary jet, every medic, both on and off duty, is already there. While a couple are older teens who stayed behind when they reached seventeen, the rest are just kids who have been trained to treat minor injuries, nothing more. The sight of blood doesn't scare Risa anymore. What scares her are her own limitations—and from the moment she rolls in, she knows she's way out of her depth.

In the corner one kid grimaces and groans with an obviously dislocated shoulder—but he's getting only minimal attention, because the kid on the table is much worse off. His side has a huge, jagged wound through which Risa can see at least one protruding rib. He quivers and moans. Several kids frantically try to stem the bleeding, applying pressure to key arteries, and one kid with shaking hands tries to fill a syringe.

"Lidocaine or epinephrine?" Risa asks.

"Lidocaine?" he says, like it's a question.

"I'll administer. There are epinephrine injectors already prepared."

He looks at her like he got caught in the school hallway without a pass.

"Adrenaline!" she says. "It's the same as adrenaline."

"Right! I know where those are!"

Risa tries to focus in, not allowing herself to be overwhelmed by the larger picture, and gives the injured boy the first shot, which will ease the pain.

"Did anyone call the doctor?" Risa asks.

"Like three times," says Kiana.

There's a doctor who comes out to the Graveyard when they have something on their hands they can't handle. He does it free of charge, no questions asked, since he's sympathetic to the resistance; however, he takes their calls only when he wants to. Even if they're able to reach him, however, Risa knows what he'll say.

"We have to get him to a hospital."

Once she says it, all the kids there are visibly relieved, because now this boy's life will not be in their hands. With all the injuries at the Graveyard, only twice before have they had to send a kid to a hospital. Both times the injured kid died. Risa is determined that it will not happen again.

"Hurts bad," the kid says, between gasps and grimaces.

"Shh," says Risa, and she sees his eyeballs begin to roll. "Stay focused on me." She gives him the epinephrine shot, which should slow his bleeding and hopefully keep him from going into shock. "Tell me your name."

"Dylan," he says. "Dylan Ward."

"Really? I was a ward too. Ohio State Home Twenty-Three."

"Florida Magnolia. Florida state homes don't got numbers. They're named after flowers."

"Figures."

Dylan Ward is thirteen, maybe fourteen. He has a bad cleft lip, and looking at it makes her angry, because like her, he was a ward of the state—and while parents won't unwind a kid on his looks alone, the state homes have no problem unwinding kids they don't want to look at. For Risa, saving him now is a matter of honor. She tells Kiana to get the ambulance.

"It has a flat," Kiana tells her.

Risa growls in frustration. "Fix it!"

"Don't leave," Dylan says, putting all his trust in her.

"I won't," she reassures him.

The ADR keeps promising to permanently station a doctor at the Graveyard, but that has yet to happen. She knows the resistance has other priorities, but when a kid is bleeding out, it's a pretty lame excuse.

"Am I gonna die?" Dylan asks.

"Of course not," she tells him. In truth, Risa has no idea whether he'll live or die, but that's not very comforting to hear, and no one wants the truth when they ask that question.

Risa rolls her way over whatever debris is on the floor and down the plane's rear ramp, where a bunch of kids have gathered to fret.

One kid comes forward. It's Starkey. Ever since Connor put him in charge of food service, he thinks his nose belongs in everything. "Is there anything I can do?"

"Not unless you have powers of teleportation and can get us to a hospital."

"Sorry," he says, "my tricks are just tricks."

That's when Connor runs up.

"I heard about the accident. Is everyone okay?"

Risa shakes her head. "One kid we can take care of, but the other"—again a shiver of memory—"has to go to a hospital."

Connor's lips go thin, and his legs start to shake like they did back when he was in the safe houses. He stops his fear response by pounding his fist into his hand, and he nods. "Okay," he says, "okay, we'll do what has to be done." Only then does he seem to notice that Starkey's there. "Is Starkey helping you?"

"Not really," says Risa. Then, just to get rid of him, she says, "He can help fix the flat on the ambulance."

Starkey looks insulted for a moment, then smiles. "Right, no problem." And he trots off.

The ambulance is a seatless minivan, jury-rigged with medical equipment. Dylan is rushed down the stairs and loaded inside. One of the other medics will drive, and Kiana will tend to Dylan in the back. The boy calls for Risa, but she can't get in with him. Once more she silently curses her wheels.

Starkey still lingers. He turns to Connor. "You mean you're not going?" Starkey asks.

"The Admiral never left the Graveyard until he was carried out," Connor tells him. "I lead by his example."

Starkey shrugs. "It makes you look like a coward."

Connor throws a quick glare at him.

"Hey, I'm just saying."

"I don't care what it looks like," Connor says forcefully. "I do what I have to keep this place alive."

"Sorry, I mean no disrespect, I guess I just have a lot to learn about being in charge."

Starkey nods respectfully to Risa and leaves, but what he said sticks in her mind like gum on her shoe—or at least how it used to get on her shoe when her feet actually touched the ground. Connor is right, of course. If he went to the hospital, it would be a foolhardy show of bravado—the sign of an arrogant leader, not a responsible one. But Risa, on the other hand, has nothing holding her back but her wheelchair. And when has she ever let that stop her?

"I'm going this time," she tells Connor.

Connor throws up his hands. "Risa, no one expects you to go. No one is going to think you're a coward if you don't." He looks over at the minivan. "And getting you there, it's too much—"

"Too much of a burden?" Risa finishes.

"I was going to say too much effort when every second counts for this kid."

But her mind is set. "After what happened the other times," she tells him, "I have to go."

"It won't change the outcome either way," Connor points out.

"I know," she tells him, even though she's not entirely sure he's right. He backs away as two of the medics lift her chair into the van.

"Even if they catch me, they can't unwind me," she reminds him. "I'm seventeen. And besides, the disabled can't be unwound."

"What if they recognize you?"

"Oh, please," Risa says. "It's our names that people know, much more than our faces. I'll be fine." Then she offers him a slim but sincere smile, and he reluctantly returns it. It doesn't bridge the gap between them, but at least it marks the spot where the bridge might be built. She closes the van's back door without saying good-bye, because they share a secret superstition, never saying good-bye to each other. Risa will soon regret that she didn't.

It's a bumpy ride out of the Graveyard with no paved roads, just the hardpan desert flattened by the wheels of jets. There's more than a mile to the gate. In the back, Dylan moans with every bump. As they approach, the guards on duty, notified of the emergency, quickly open the gate.

Once they're on paved roads, the ride is easier, and Dylan quiets down. Risa comforts him and monitors his vital signs.

The first time they had to bring a kid to the hospital, Kiana went with one of the other medics—a kid who panicked whenever Band-Aids didn't stick—but he was the only other medically-experienced kid willing to venture out of the Graveyard on what was potentially a suicide mission. That first time, a new arrival had climbed to the tail of a cargo jet on a dare. He fell and cracked his skull. Risa would have gone, but everyone convinced her there was no point and it was too impractical. Kiana and the nervous medic had taken the boy to the hospital with a whole fake story of what happened and documents to back up a fake identity. The boy died in the hospital. The second time it was a girl with a burst appendix. Again the girl was rushed to the hospital, again Risa stayed behind, and again the girl died.

Risa doesn't know what her presence at the hospital can do. All she knows is that she can't sit back and wait to hear about another kid's death.

Kiana helps Risa out of the back, then single-handedly carries Dylan into the ER waiting room, with Risa rolling in behind her. Now Risa must display her acting skills. She thinks about her friends in the band who had been playing in the Chop Shop when it blew—the ones who died—and the memory brings necessary tears to her eyes. Then she dredges up a character that saved her once before: the ditzy girl who talks in questions.

"Hello, can somebody help us? My brother was on the roof fixing tiles? And he fell from the roof and got hurt real bad? And we didn't know what to do? So we brought him here, but there's a lot of blood and we're really scared? Can you help us?"

She hopes the tears plus the ditz can scramble anyone's BS detectors as effectively as Hush Puppy once scrambled radar. There are rumors that the Juvies have started using DNA decoders in the field. She can only hope that they haven't trickled down to hospitals yet.

Emergency room staff drop whatever they're doing and rush to their aid. In a second Dylan's on a gurney, being wheeled through the AUTHORIZED PERSONNEL ONLY doors.

"Is he going to be okay?" asks Risa, in panic that's only partially feigned. "Because our parents are out of town? And we didn't know what to do?"

"We'll take care of him, honey," says a nurse in a comforting tone. "Don't you worry." The nurse glances at Kiana, who has Dylan's blood on her clothes, then heads off into the emergency room.

The doors swing closed, and Risa rolls over to the admissions desk, with a carefully planned wallet of false information, organized to appear disorganized, and intentionally designed to make Risa appear helpless and flustered.

"We'll sort this all out later," the admissions clerk says, giving up and getting on to the next person in line.

An hour of waiting with no word. Kiana's been pacing, no matter how much Risa tells her to calm down, but perhaps being nervous just plays into their cover story. Finally the same nurse comes out into the waiting room. The woman is slightly teary-eyed, and Risa feels a pit in her stomach, as if Dylan, who she didn't know before today, really is her brother.

"Honey, I'm afraid the news isn't good. You're going to have to prepare yourself."

Risa grips the wheels of her chair, feeling a well of emotion beginning to bubble from deep inside her. Kiana puts her head in her hands.

"I'm sorry," the nurse says, "but your brother was just too badly injured. We did everything we could. . . ."

Risa just looks at her in disbelief and shock. The nurse puts her hand on Risa's, patting it gently. "I can't imagine what you must be feeling right now, but we're going to have to notify your parents. We've been trying, but no one picks up at the numbers you gave us. Do you have any other way of contacting them?"

Risa, her hair dangling in front of her face, shakes her head.

"Well then," says the nurse, "we'll have to keep trying. In the meantime, if there's anyone else you can call . . ."

"Can you give us a few moments?" Risa asks quietly.

"Of course, dear." The nurse squeezes her hand reassuringly and goes back through the emergency room doors, where Dylan's body waits to be claimed by parents that don't exist.

Risa wipes her tears away, trying to find comfort in the fact that she did the best that she could.

And then Kiana says, "It's just like the other times."

That makes Risa look up, and something occurs to her. She wonders *how* similar it is.

"Kiana . . . you *do* know we're supposed to go to a different hospital each time, right?"

By the look on Kiana's face, Risa can tell she never learned that particular protocol. "Shouldn't it be the closest hospital in an emergency?" Kiana asks.

The sudden dread that Risa feels is balanced with an equal amount of hope. "The other times you were here, did you see that same nurse?"

"I think so. At least once. That's bad, isn't it?"

"Yes and no. I'll be back."

Risa rolls herself toward the AUTHORIZED PERSONNEL doors and pushes her way through. She finds herself in a hallway that's more starkly lit and even less inviting than the waiting room.

While hundreds of people flow through an emergency room, there aren't many teenage kids with parents who mysteriously can't be reached, and whose "siblings" vanish upon pronouncement of death. This nurse must have recognized Kiana—there is no question in Risa's mind. Which means there's more than one level of deception here.

"Excuse me," someone says from farther down the hall, "you're not supposed to be in here."

But Risa doesn't care. She rolls into a large room marked RECOVERY. It's subdivided by curtains into cubicles with hospital beds, and she begins to pull back each curtain one by one. An empty bed. An old woman. Another empty bed, and finally, Dylan Ward. His wound has been dressed; an IV leads into his arm. He's unconscious, but a monitor shows a steady heartbeat. He's anything but dead.

Just then the nurse comes up behind Risa and turns her chair around. The woman is nowhere near as teary-eyed as before.

"You need to leave right now, or I'll call security."

Risa locks the brake, so the chair can't be wheeled away. "You told me he was dead!"

"And you told me he was your brother."

"We're taking him and leaving," Risa says, with authority enough in her voice to make it stick if she had any leverage whatsoever. Unfortunately, she doesn't.

"He's in no condition to travel—and even if he was, I would never turn an AWOL Unwind over to anyone but the Juvenile Authority."

"Is that what you did with the others? Gave them to the Juvey-cops?"

"That's my business," the nurse tells her, as cold as can be.

"At least give me the courtesy of knowing if the other two are still alive."

The nurse looks at her hatefully, then says, "They're alive. But probably in a divided state by now."

Risa wishes she could get out of her wheelchair and slam this woman into the wall. Burning gazes fry the air between them like microwaves.

"You think I don't know what goes on down there at the Graveyard? I know; my brother's a Juvey-cop. It's a wonder they don't round you all up and send you off where you belong!" And she points off, as if knowing the exact direction of the nearest harvest camp. "People out there are dying for lack of parts, but you and your selfish friends in the resistance would rather let good people die."

So here it is, thinks Risa. The rift between two completely different versions of right and wrong. This woman sees Risa as a filthy outlaw, and nothing will ever change that.

"Are you really doing this to help society," Risa snaps, "or is it for the reward money?"

The woman breaks her gaze, and Risa knows the truth. The woman's moral high ground has split beneath her, and she's fallen into the chasm.

"You go back and tend to your dirty horde," the nurse says. "Do that and I'll pretend you were never here."

But Risa can't go. She can't leave Dylan to be unwound.

Just then a Juvey-cop comes into the emergency room.

"Over here," calls the nurse, and looks back to Risa. "Leave now, and I'll let you and your friend in the waiting room go. Maybe you can't be unwound, but you most certainly can be locked up."

But Risa is not going anywhere.

The nurse greets the cop, who by his looks is very obviously her older brother. He spares a long, curious glance at Risa before looking at the boy in the bed.

"This him?" he asks.

"We've stabilized him, but he's lost a lot of blood. He won't be ready for transport for a while."

"Keep him sedated," says the cop. "Best that he doesn't wake up until he's at the harvest camp."

Risa grips her chair, knowing what she's going to do at least ten seconds before she does it. Ten seconds of silent personal terror, but no indecision whatsoever.

"Take me," she says. "Take me instead."

She knows Connor won't approve. She knows he'll be furious, but she can't muddy her resolve with thoughts of him now. This is about saving Dylan Ward.

The cop studies her—clearly he knows exactly who she is and exactly what her offer means.

"From my understanding, you're seventeen, Miss Ward, and seeing that you're in a wheelchair, we couldn't unwind you anyway. So what possible value do you have?"

She smiles, finally having the upper hand. "Are you kidding me? A notorious member of the Anti-Divisional Resistance who knows exactly what happened at Happy Jack that day?"

He takes a moment to consider her point. "I'm not an idiot," he says. "You'll never cooperate. You'd rather die than cooperate."

"Perhaps," admits Risa, "but why should that matter to you? No matter how uncooperative I am, you'll still get credit for bringing me in, won't you?"

She can practically hear his mind clicking and whirring. "What's going to stop me from capturing both you and the kid in the bed?"

"If you try," Risa says calmly, "then you lose the prize. I have a subcutaneous cyanide pill in my palm." She holds out her hand for him to see. "It's right under the skin. All I have to do is bring my hands together to crack it open." Then she mimes a wide clap, stopping just short of her palms touching. "You see," she says with a grin, "there's more than one type of clapper."

There is, of course, no such pill under her skin, but he doesn't have to know that. Even if he suspects she's bluffing, he's not sure enough to risk it.

"If I die right here, right now," Risa says, "you won't be known as the cop who brought me in, but the cop who let me die while in your custody." Then she smiles again. "That's almost as bad as getting shot in the leg with one's own tranq pistol, isn't it?"

The man frowns at the thought of being associated in any way with that other unfortunate Juvey-cop.

The nurse is not happy with any of this. She crosses her arms. "What about my reward money?" she asks.

Then her brother turns to her like an older brother should and says, "Shut it, Eva, all right? Just shut it."

And with that, the deal is done.

Dylan's chart will remain marked with his bogus records, and when he's fit to travel, he'll be released to Kiana, no questions asked.

But as for Risa, her life now lies on a different path.

19 · Cam

A suitable partner for Camus Comprix—one with all the right qualities—is not easy to find. More than two hundred girls go through the interview process. All of them have strong credentials. There are actresses and models, scholars, and high-society debutantes. Roberta has left no stone unturned in drumming up the perfect planet for her star.

The final twenty are brought to Cam for his assessment in a cushy fireside interview in the grand living room. They are all well-dressed, pretty, and smart. Most of them talk about their résumés as if applying for an office job. Some look at him with no qualms, while others can't look him in the eye at all. There's one girl who fawns all over him, putting off more heat than the fireplace.

"I would love to be your first," she says. "You can *do* that, can't you? I mean you're . . . *complete*, right?"

"More than complete," he tells her. "In fact, I have three."

She just stares at him dumbfounded, and he decides not to tell her he's joking.

He finds himself attracted to some, left cold by others—but in none of them does he find the spark of connection he has hoped for. By the time he gets to the last girl, a Boston scholar with New York fashion sense, he just wants to get this day over with. The girl is one of those who is intrigued by his face. She doesn't just look at him, though, she studies him like a specimen under a microscope.

"So what do you see when you look at me?" he asks.

"It's not what's on the outside—it's the inside that matters," she responds.

"And what do you think is inside?"

She hesitates, then asks, "Is this a trick question?"

Roberta is exasperated when he refuses to accept a single one of them. Dinner between the two of them that night is all clattering silverware and intense cutting of meat. They barely look at each other across the table. Finally Roberta says, "We're not looking for your soul mate, Cam, just someone to fill a role. A consort to help ease you into public life."

"Maybe I'm not willing to settle for that."

"Being practical is not the same as settling."

Cam slams his fist down. "My decision! You will not force me."

"Of course I won't—but—"

"Conversation over." Then the meal goes back to severe silverware. Deep down he knows she's right, which just makes him furious. All they need to make Roberta's scheme work is an attractive, personable girl holding his hand, convincing the public that there's so much about Cam to love. But he finds no bit of actor in him. Perhaps he can feign it, but he dreads the moments alone when he has to face the emptiness of a false relationship.

Emptiness.

That's what people believe is inside him. A great void. And if he can't find a soul mate among the girls paraded before him, does that mean they're right, and he has no soul?

"Incomplete," he says. "If I'm whole, why do I feel like I'm not?" And as usual, Roberta has a calming platitude intended to ease his mind, but as time goes on her rote wisdom leaves him flat and disappointed.

"Wholeness comes from creating experiences that are

solely yours, Cam," she tells him. "Live your life and soon you'll find the lives of those who came before won't matter. Those who gave rise to you mean nothing compared to what you are."

But how can he live his life when he's not convinced he has one? The attacks in the press conference still plague him. If a human being has a soul, then where is his? And if the human soul is indivisible, then how can his be the sum of the parts of all the kids who gave rise to him? He's not one of them, he's not all of them, so who is he?

His questions make Roberta impatient. "I'm sorry," she tells him, "but I don't deal in the unanswerable."

"So you don't believe in souls?" Cam asks her.

"I didn't say that, but I don't try to answer things that don't have tangible data. If people have souls, then you must have one, proved by the mere fact that you're alive."

"But what if there is no 'I' inside me? What if I'm just flesh going through the motions, with nothing inside?"

Roberta considers this, or at least pretends to. "Well, if that were the case, I doubt you'd be asking these questions." She thinks for a moment. "If you must have a construct, then think of it this way: Whether consciousness is implanted in us by something divine, or whether it is created by the efforts of our brains, the end result is the same. We *are*."

"Until we are not," Cam adds.

Roberta nods. "Yes, until we are not." And she leaves him with none of his questions answered.

Physical therapy has evolved into full-on training sessions with machines, free weights, and cardio. Kenny is the closest thing Cam has to a friend, unless you count Roberta and the guards who call him "sir." They talk openly about things that Roberta would probably want to monitor.

"So the great girlfriend search was a bust, huh?" Kenny

asks while Cam pushes himself on the treadmill.

"We have not yet found a consort for the creature," Cam says, mimicking Roberta's accent.

Kenny chuckles. "You got a right to be choosy," he tells Cam. "You shouldn't accept anything less than what you want."

Cam reaches the end of his workout, and the machine begins its slowdown. "Even if I can't have what I want?"

"All the more reason to demand it," Kenny advises. "Because then maybe they'll get closer to the mark."

Sound logic, perhaps, although Cam suspects it will do nothing but set him up for disappointment.

That night he goes alone to the tabletop computer screen in the living room and starts digging through photo files. Most of it is random stuff—the images Roberta still tests him on, although not as frequently as before. None of it is what he's looking for. He finds a file that features the head shots of all the girls who interviewed. Two hundred smiling, pretty faces, with attached résumés. After a while, they all begin to look alike.

"You won't find her in there."

He turns to see Roberta standing on the spiral staircase, watching him. She descends the rest of the way.

"Deleted?" he asks.

"Should be," Roberta says, "but no."

She touches the screen, logs in, and opens up files that had been locked to Cam. In just a few seconds she drags out not just one, but three photos and sighs. "Is this who you were looking for?"

Cam looks at the pictures. "Yes." The other two photos, like the one he had already seen, seem to have been taken without her knowledge. He wonders why Roberta is now willing to show him these pictures of the girl in the wheelchair, when she was so much against it before.

"Bus," says Cam. "She was on a bus."

"Her bus never made it to its destination. It was run off the road and hit a tree."

Cam shakes his head. "I didn't get that memory." Then he looks to Roberta. "Tell me about her."

20 · Nelson

The Juvey-cop turned parts pirate has outdone himself this time! Not one, but two AWOLs!

Nelson attributes his success to the ingenuity of his tactics. He caught the girl at a food court by posing as a resistance worker. Gullibility has always been his greatest ally. The girl's hair isn't quite red, as Divan requested, but it could be strawberry blond in a certain light. As for the boy, Nelson used the girl as bait, securing her to a drainpipe near an abandoned factory in an umber neighborhood that was known to be AWOL-infested. He waited until her cries drew someone from the dark recesses of the building, and he watched as the boy freed her. Then, from his vantage point in a building across the street, Nelson tranq'd them both as they ran.

His DNA analyzer pegged them both as known AWOLs, which is always better for his conscience than catching kids who actually had a life to go back to.

The drive back to Divan's auto dealership is filled with anticipation for Nelson. He was never an overachiever, so doing twice the job with half the effort is a rare thing indeed!

When he arrives, Divan is surprised but thrilled to see him so soon after the last delivery. "What a catch," he exclaims, and for once, doesn't even dicker—he gives Nelson the price he asks. Perhaps because Nelson doesn't ask for his trophies this time. The girl's eyes have fading purple pigment injections that are just plain ugly, and Nelson never did see the boy's eyes. He rarely covets what he doesn't see.

In a rare show of gratitude, Divan treats Nelson to dinner in the kind of restaurant he hasn't frequented in quite a while.

"Business must be picking up," Nelson comments.

"Business is business," Divan says, "but prospects are good."

Nelson can tell that the black marketeer has something on his mind. He watches and waits as Divan dips a spoon into his coffee, stirring slowly, methodically. "At our last encounter," Divan says, "I spoke to you of rumors, did I not?"

"Yes, but you failed to share them with me," Nelson says, drinking his own coffee much more quickly than Divan. "Are these rumors something I'll enjoy hearing?"

"Not at first, I'm sure. I've heard it spoken of more than once now. I didn't want to bring it to your attention until I had heard it from more than one source." He continues to stir his coffee. Not drinking, just pondering the swirling liquid. "They are saying that the Akron AWOL is still alive."

Nelson feels the little hairs on the back of his neck rise and embed themselves in his collar.

"That's impossible."

"Yes, yes—you're probably right." Then Divan puts down his spoon. "However, did anyone actually see or identify the body?"

"I wasn't at Happy Jack. I imagine it was a mess."

"Exactly," says Divan slowly. "A mess." Then he picks up his coffee and takes a long, slow sip. "Which means that any number of things could have happened." Then he puts down his coffee and leans closer. "I believe these rumors may be true. Do you have any idea how much the parts of the Akron AWOL would go for? People will pay obscene amounts for a piece of him." Then he smiles. "I'll pay you ten, maybe twenty times what I paid you for today's catch."

Nelson tries not to react, but he knows that by not saying anything, his greed has expressed itself. But for him, this particular moment of greed is not about money. Bringing in Connor Lassiter wouldn't just be about the cash, it would even out a very imbalanced score.

It's as if Divan can read his mind. "I am telling you this before any of my other suppliers. It would bring me great pleasure if *you* were the one to catch him, considering your history with him."

"Thank you," Nelson says, genuinely grateful for the head start.

"Word has it that there are some sizable AWOL populations in hiding. It would be wise to find those places, as there's a good chance he's working for the Anti-Divisional Resistance now."

"If he's alive, I'll catch him and bring him to you," Nelson tells him. "One thing, though."

Divan raises an eyebrow. "Yes?"

Nelson levels his stare, making it clear that this is nonnegotiable, and says, "I get his eyes."

Part Four

Leviathan

SURGEONS HARVEST ORGANS AFTER EUTHANASIA

by Michael Cook, May 14, 2010, BioEdge web journal

How often is this going on in Belgium and the Netherlands? Bioethics blogger Wesley Smith drew our attention to a conference report by Belgian transplant surgeons about organ procurement after euthanasia. As the doctors from Antwerp University Hospital explained in the 2006 World Transplant Congress (in a section called "economics"), they killed a consenting forty-six-year-old woman with a neurological condition and took her liver, two kidneys, and islets.

In a 2008 report, the doctors explained that three patients had been euthanased between 2005 and 2007. . . .

At the time of writing the article, the doctors were enthusiastic about the potential for organ donation in countries where euthanasia is legal. . . .

The curious thing about this is how little publicity this has received, even though the Belgian doctors published their achievement in the world's leading journal of transplant surgery. ~ *Transplantation*, July 15, 2006; *Transplantation*, July 27, 2008.

Full article is available at:

http://www.bioedge.org/index.php/bioethics/bioethics_article/8991/

21 · Lev

It's a very rare thing that a clapper doesn't clap, because by the time one gets to the stage of being willing to make one's own blood explosive enough to take out a whole building, that soul is far beyond the point of no return.

There had still been a spark of light in Levi Jedediah Calder, however. Enough to ignite a powerful change of heart.

The clapper who didn't clap.

It made him famous. His face was known nationwide and beyond. WHY, LEV, WHY? magazine headlines read, with his life story spread out like a centerfold, ready to be ogled and gobbled by a world greedy for dirt and personal tragedy.

"He was always the perfect son," his parents were quoted as saying more than once. "We'll never understand it." To see their teary interviews, you'd think Lev had actually blown himself up and truly was dead. Well, maybe in a way he was, because the Levi Calder he had been on the day he was sent to be tithed no longer existed.

Almost a year after his capture at Happy Jack Harvest Camp, Lev sits in a detention center rec room on a rainy Sunday morning. He is not a resident of the detention center; he's a visitor on a mission of mercy.

Across from him sits a kid in an orange jumpsuit, his arms crossed. Between them are the sorry ruins of a jigsaw puzzle left from the last person to sit at the table, one of many unfinished projects that plague this place. It's February, and the walls are halfheartedly hung with Valentine's Day decorations that are supposed to add a sense of festivity but just seem sadistic, because in an all-boys' detention center, only a select few are finding romance this year.

"So you're supposed to have something useful to say to me?" the kid in the orange jumpsuit says, all attitude, tattoos, and body odor. "What are you, like, twelve?"

"Actually, I'm fourteen."

The kid smirks. "Well, good for you. Now get out of my sight. I don't need spiritual guidance from baby Jesus." Then he reaches out and flicks up Lev's hair, which, over the past year, has grown to his shoulders in a very Jesus-like way.

Lev is not bothered. He gets this all the time. "We still have half an hour. Maybe we should talk about why you're in here."

"I'm in here because I got caught," the punk says. Then his eyes narrow, and he takes a closer look at Lev. "You look familiar. Do I know you?"

Lev doesn't answer. "I would guess you're sixteen, right? You're labeled a 'divisional risk,' you know that, don't you? It means you're at risk for being unwound."

"What, you think my mother would unwind me? She wouldn't dare. Who'd pay her friggin' bills?" Then he rolls up a sleeve, revealing that the tattoos visible on his wrists go all the way up to his shoulder. Bones and brutality painted on his flesh. "Besides, who's gonna want *these* arms?"

"You'd be surprised," Lev tells him. "People actually pay extra for ink as good as yours."

The punk is taken aback by the thought, then studies Lev again. "Are you sure I don't know you? You live here in Cleveland?"

Lev sighs. "You don't know me, you just know *of* me."

Another moment, then the punk's eyes go wide with recognition. "No way! You're that tithe kid! I mean the clapper! I mean the one who didn't blow up! You were all over the news!"

"Right. But we're not here to talk about me."

Suddenly the punk seems like a different kid. "Yeah, yeah, I know. I'm sorry I was an ass before. So, like, why aren't you in jail?"

"Plea bargain. Not allowed to talk about it," Lev tells him. "Let's just say talking to you is part of my punishment."

"Damn!" says the kid, grinning. "They give you a penthouse suite, too?"

"Seriously, I'm not allowed to talk about it . . . but I can listen to anything you want to tell me."

"Well, all right. I mean, if you really wanna hear it."

And then the kid launches into a confessional life story that he probably never told anyone before. It's the one positive thing about Lev's notoriety—it gets him respect among those who usually don't give it.

These kids in detention always want to know all about him, but the terms of the settlement were very clear. With so much sympathy from some people, and so much anger from others, it was "in the public's best interest" to get Lev out of the news as quickly as possible and keep him from becoming the national voice against unwinding. In the end, he was sentenced to house arrest, complete with a tracking chip embedded in his shoulder, and 520 hours of community service every year, until his eighteenth birthday. His service consisted of picking up trash in local parks and ministering to wayward youth about the ills of drugs and violent behavior. In return for the relative lightness of his sentence, he agreed to give them all the inside information he knew about clappers and other terrorist activities. That part was easy—he knew very little beyond his own clapper cell, and the other members were all dead. He was also put under a permanent gag order. He could never speak in public about unwinding, tithing, and what happened at Happy Jack. He was basically sentenced to disappear.

"We should call you the little mermaid," his brother Marcus had joked, "because they let you magically walk, in exchange for your voice."

So now every Sunday, Pastor Dan picks Lev up at Marcus's town house, and they share their own brand of spirituality with kids in juvenile detention.

At first it was painfully awkward, but within a few months Lev became very good at reaching into the hearts of strangers, figuring out what made them tick, and then defusing them before the tick became a countdown.

"The Lord works in mischievous ways," Pastor Dan once told him, taking an old adage and giving it a necessary tweak. If Lev has any heroes, they would be Pastor Dan and his brother Marcus. Marcus not just for standing up to their parents, but also for going the distance and taking Lev in, even though it got him cut off entirely from their family. They were both outcasts now from a family so rigid in their beliefs that they'd rather pretend Marcus and Lev were dead than face the choices the two had made.

"It's their loss," Marcus often tells Lev, but he can't say it without looking away to hide the sorrow it makes him feel.

As for Pastor Dan, he's a hero to Lev for having the courage to lose his convictions without losing his faith. "I still believe in God," Pastor Dan told him, "just not a God who condones human tithing." And in tears, Lev asked if *he* could believe in that God too, never having realized he had such a choice.

Dan, who no one but Lev calls "Pastor" anymore, listed himself as a nondenominational cleric on the form they had to fill out before they began meeting with kids at the detention center.

"So then what religion are we?" Lev asks him each week as they walk in. The question has become a running joke, and each time Pastor Dan has another answer.

"We're Pentupcostal because we're sick of all the hypocrisy."

"We're Clueish, because we finally got a clue."

"We're PresbyPterodactyl, because we're making this whole thing fly against all reason."

But Lev's favorite was, "We're Leviathan, because what happened to you, Lev, is at the heart of it all."

It made him feel both terribly uncomfortable and also a little bit blessed to be at the core of a spiritual movement, even if it was only a movement of two.

"Isn't a leviathan a big, ugly monster?" he pointed out.

"Yes," said Pastor Dan, "so let's hope you never become one."

Lev is never going to become a big anything. The reason why he doesn't quite look fourteen is more than just looking young for his age. In the weeks after his capture, he endured transfusion after transfusion to clean out his blood, but poisoning his body with explosive compounds had damaged him. For weeks Lev's body was bound in puffy cotton gauze like a mummy, yet with arms stretched wide to keep him from detonating himself.

"You've been cruci-fluffed," Pastor Dan told him. At the time, Lev didn't find it very funny.

His doctor tried to mask his disdain for Lev by hiding it behind a cold, clinical demeanor.

"Even when we purge your system of the chemicals," the doctor said, "they'll take their toll." Then he'd chuckled bitterly. "You'll live, but you'll never be unwound. You have just enough damage to your organs to make them useless to anybody but you."

The damage also stunted his growth, as well as his physical development. Now Lev's body is perpetually trapped at the age of thirteen. The wage of being a clapper who doesn't clap. The only thing that will still grow is his hair—and he made a conscious decision that he would just let it grow, never again becoming the clean-cut, easily manipulated boy he had once been.

Luckily, the worst predictions didn't come true. He was told he would have permanent tremors in his hands and a slur in his speech. Didn't happen. He was told that his muscles would atrophy and he'd become increasingly weak. Didn't happen. In fact, regular exercise, while it hasn't bulked him up like some, has left him with fairly normal muscle tone. True, he'll never be the boy he could have been—but then, he would never have been that boy anyway. He would have been unwound. All things considered, this is a better option.

And he doesn't mind spending his Sundays talking to kids who, once upon a time, he would have been afraid of.

"Dude," the tattooed punk whispers, leaning over the rec room table and pushing some stray puzzle pieces to the floor. "Just tell me—what was it like at harvest camp?"

Lev looks up, catching a security camera trained on the table. There's one trained on every table, every conversation. In this way, it's not all that different from harvest camp.

"Like I said, I can't talk about it," Lev tells him. "But trust me, you want to stay clean till seventeen, because you don't want to find out."

"I hear ya," says the punk. "Clean till seventeen—that oughta be the motto." And he leans back, looking at Lev with the kind of admiration Lev doesn't feel he's earned.

When visiting hours are over, Lev leaves with his former pastor.

"Productive?" Dan asks.

"Can't tell. Maybe."

"Maybe's better than not at all. A good day's work for a nice Clueish boy."

There's a jogging path in downtown Cleveland that runs along the marina on Lake Erie. It curves around the Great Lakes Science Center and along the back side of the Rock and Roll Hall of Fame, where the memories of those who are notorious for rebellion far hipper than Lev's are immortalized. Lev jogs past it every Sunday afternoon, wondering what it must be like to be both famous and infamous, yet more adored than hated, more admired than pitied. He shudders to think what type of museum exhibit would feature him, and hopes he never finds out.

It's relatively warm for February. Temperatures in the forties. Rain instead of snow that morning, and a dreary afternoon drizzle instead of flurries. Marcus runs along with him, winded, his breath coming in puffs of steam.

"Do you have to run so fast?" he calls after Lev. "It's not a race. And anyway, it's raining."

"What does that have to do with it?"

"You could slip and lose control—there are still slushy spots."

"I'm not a car."

Lev splashes through a slush puddle, splattering Marcus, and grins while his brother curses. Years of fast food and endlessly hitting the books in law school has left Marcus not exactly flabby, but certainly out of shape.

"I swear, if you keep showing me up, I won't run with you anymore. I'll call the feds back in. They always keep up with you."

Ironically, it had been Marcus's idea that Lev begin an exercise routine once he was released into his brother's custody. In those early days of recovery, when his blood was still poisoned, just getting up and down the stairs in Marcus's town house was a workout for Lev—but Marcus had the vision to see that the rehabilitation of Lev's soul was closely tied to rehabilitating his body. For many weeks it had been Marcus pushing Lev to cover just one more block. And yes, when he first began, there were G-men escorting him. At first they escorted him everywhere on his Sundays out, perhaps to show that there was no leniency to house arrest. Eventually they began to trust the tracking chip and allowed Lev to be out without an official escort, as long as either Dan or Marcus was with him.

"If I have a heart attack, it'll have your name all over it!" Marcus calls from farther back.

Lev was never a distance runner. Once upon a time, he was all about baseball; a real team player. Now a more individual sport suits him.

As the rain gets heavier, he stops, only halfway through the run, and lets Marcus catch up with him. They buy Aquafina from a die-hard vendor outside the Rock and Roll Hall of Fame, who'll probably still be selling bottled water and Red Bull as the world is ending.

Marcus catches his breath as he drinks, then mentions casually, "You got a letter from Cousin Carl yesterday."

Lev holds his reaction inside, giving no outward indication that this is any big deal. "If it came yesterday, why are you telling me today?"

"You know how you get."

"No," Lev says a bit coldly. "Tell me how I get."

But Marcus doesn't have to, because Lev knows exactly what he means.

The first letter from Cousin Carl was a complete mystery at first, until Lev realized it was a coded message from Connor. With the possibility that Lev's mail is being monitored by one government agency or another, it was the only way Connor could get him a message and hope that Lev was clever enough to figure it all out. One arrives every few months, always postmarked from someplace different, so it can't be traced back to the Graveyard.

"So what does he say?" Lev asks Marcus.

"It's addressed to you. Believe it or not, I don't read your mail."

When they arrive home, Marcus hands the letter to him but holds it out of reach for a moment. "Promise me you won't go into some black-hole brooding funk where you sit and do nothing but play video games for a week."

"When do I ever do that?"

Marcus just gives him his "Are you kidding me?" scowl. Fair enough. Being under house arrest leaves Lev with little to do to occupy his time. But it's true that hearing from Connor always gets him thinking, and thinking gets him spiraling, and spiraling sends him to places it would be better not to go.

"It's a part of your life you need to leave behind you," Marcus reminds him.

"You're right, and you're wrong, " Lev tells him. He doesn't try to explain himself, because he's not even sure what he means, except to know that it's true. He opens the letter. The handwriting is the same, but he suspects it's not Connor's, to prevent it from being analyzed and linked to him. The paranoia that engulfs them has no end.

Dear Cousin Levi,

A belated birthday card for you. I know fourteen means more to you than to most, what with the things you've been through. The ranch has been busy. The big beef companies keep threatening to take us over, but it hasn't happened yet. We got a business plan that could save us from that, should it come to pass.

Hard work since I took over the ranch, and not much help from the neighbors. Wish I could just up and leave it, but who could handle these ranch hands but me?

*We know of your current situation, and how you can't
come visit. Wouldn't want you to. A lot of mad cow going
on around here. Best to stay away and hope for the best.*

*Take care, and say hello to your brother for us. He's almost
as much of a lifesaver as you.*

Sincerely,

Cousin Carl

Lev reads the letter four times, trying to parse out the
various possible meanings. The Juvies' looming threat to take
the place out. The difficulty of running a sanctuary without
enough help from the resistance. Lev's daily life has grown
so distant from that underworld of desperate souls, hearing
about it is like listening to ice crack beneath his feet. It makes
him want to run—anywhere. Run to Connor, or run away from
him. He doesn't know which direction, only that he can't stand
running in place. He wishes he could write back but knows
how foolhardy that would be. It's one thing receiving a random
letter from a generic "cousin," but sending one to the Graveyard might as well be painting a target on Connor's back. To
Lev's frustration, communication with "Cousin Carl" can only
be one-way.

"How are things on 'the ranch'?" Marcus asks.

"Troubled."

"We do what we can do, right?"

Lev nods. Marcus is no slouch when it comes to the resistance. He volunteers time pulling AWOLs off the street and
getting them to safe houses, and gives a healthy share of the
money he makes as a legal assistant to the cause.

178

He hands Marcus the letter to read, and Marcus seems as bothered by it as Lev does. "We'll have to wait and see how it all shakes out."

Lev paces the living room. There are no bars on his window. Still, they might as well have put him in solitary for the sudden claustrophobia he feels.

"I should speak out against unwinding," Lev says, dispensing with all their coded talk. There's nobody listening anymore anyway. Now that his life has settled into this reclusive version of normal, surveillance feels like a nonissue. The Juvey-cops have better things to do these days than to keep their eyes on a kid who's not doing anything but hanging around his brother's house, trying to disappear.

"If I speak up, people will listen to me—they had sympathy before, didn't they? They'll listen!"

Marcus slaps the letter down on the table. "For a kid who's been through as much as you, you're still so damn naive! People don't have sympathy for you—they have sympathy for the little kid who became a clapper. They look at you like you're the one who killed him."

"I'm tired of sitting here and doing nothing!" Lev storms into the kitchen, trying to distance himself from the truth in Marcus's words, but Marcus follows him.

"You're not doing nothing—you still have your weekend ministries with Dan."

The thought of it just makes Lev furious. "That's my punishment! You think I like being partners with the Juvey-cops? Keeping kids in line for them?" If there's one thing he knows, it's that Connor would never do the Juvies' dirty work.

"You've done more than anyone to change things, Lev. It's time for you to have your own life, which is more than you could have hoped for a year ago. So if you want any of it to mean anything, live your life, and let the rest of us take over."

Lev storms past him again.

"Where are you going?"

Lev picks up a headset and game controller. "My head. You wanna follow me in there, too?"

In a moment, he's losing himself in Firepower and Magic—a game that takes him far from his life and memories—but even so, he knows Marcus has indeed followed him into his head. And so have Connor, and Risa, and Mai and Blaine, and Cleaver and CyFi, all fighting for space. He'll never lose them, he'll never leave any of them behind, and he's not even sure he wants to.

Everything changes the day the Girl Scout comes.

It's a frigid Monday morning, after another Sunday of ministering to divisional-risk kids and jogging in spite of the cold. Dan, whose car has ignition issues, stayed overnight rather than being stranded on the road on a Sunday night. He cooks breakfast while Marcus gets ready for work.

"You know I'm against unwinding, but the ADR is a little too antiestablishment for me," Dan tells Lev as he serves up scrambled eggs. "I'm too old to rage against the system. I just whine at it."

Lev knows he does a little more than that. He speaks out against unwinding to anyone who will listen—something Lev is not allowed to do and, according to Marcus, will do no good anyway.

"I've been approached by the resistance, of course," Dan says, "but I've had enough of organizations for a while, no matter how good the cause. I prefer being a free-agent rabble-rouser."

"So . . . ," asks Lev, "what do you think I should do?"

The former pastor ponders the eggs that tenaciously cling to his spatula. "I think you should clean your room. I've seen it, and it appears to be unwinding itself into God knows what."

"I'm serious."

"So am I." He puts down the spatula and sits beside him. "You're fourteen, Lev. Most fourteen-year-olds aren't actively trying to fix the world. Cut yourself some slack and try dealing with normal fourteen-year-old things. Believe me, compared to saving the world, cleaning your room will be a vacation."

Lev picks at his eggs. "Back before everything happened, my room used to be spotless."

"That's not necessarily a good thing either."

Marcus comes to sit at the kitchen table just as the doorbell rings. He sighs and looks at Lev, who has just finished eating. "Can you get it?"

Lev figures it's Darcy, his state-appointed tutor—because even former terrorists must know their quadratic equations. She usually doesn't come this early, though.

He opens the door to find a Girl Scout standing there, carrying a carton full of multicolored cookie boxes.

"Hi, would you like to buy some Girl Scout cookies?"

"Aren't you a little old to be a Girl Scout?" Lev asks with a smirk.

"Actually," the girl says, "you're never too old, and anyway, I'm only fourteen. But yes, usually it's the younger girls who sell cookies, so you're right in a sense. I'm helping out my younger sister, if you must know. So can I come in? It's cold out here."

The girl is kind of cute, and kind of funny, and Lev does have a weak spot for Samoas, as well as cute, funny girls. "Sure, come on in—let's see what you've got."

She practically waltzes through the door and sets the box down on the dining room table, pulling out one of each variety.

"Hey, Marcus," Lev calls, "you want some Girl Scout cookies?"

"Sure," his brother calls from the kitchen. "Get me the peanut butter."

"Make that two," calls Dan.

Lev turns to the girl. "Okay, so two of the peanut butter ones, and a box of Samoas."

"Yum-yum!" she says. "The Samoas are my favorite too." She hands him the boxes. "That'll be eighteen dollars—are you sure you don't want any Thin Mints? They're our bestseller!"

"No thanks." He pulls out his wallet, pretty sure he doesn't have enough cash, but he wants to check before asking Marcus. As he looks through his wallet, the girl has time to look at him.

"I know you, don't I?" she says.

Lev suppresses a heavy sigh. Here it comes.

"Yeah—you're that guy—the clapper! Wow, I'm selling cookies to the clapper kid!"

"I didn't clap," Lev tells her flatly, and mercifully finds a twenty in his wallet and hands it to her. "Here. Thanks for the cookies. Keep the change."

But she doesn't take the money. Instead she puts her hands on her hips, continuing to look him over. "A clapper who doesn't clap. Kind of defeats the purpose, don't you think?"

"You should go now." He waves the money at her, but she still won't take it.

"Keep your money. The cookies are my gift to you."

"No. Just take the money and go."

Her eyes are locked on his now. "A clapper who doesn't clap. I imagine that would really tick off people in high places. People who put their time and money into making sure every clapper mission goes off without a hitch."

Lev suddenly gets a feeling in the pit of his stomach that goes straight down to China.

"They're very proactive, these organizers, and a clapper who doesn't complete his mission gives all of us a bad name."

Then she smiles and holds out her hands wide.

"Marcus! Dan!" yells Lev. "Get down!"

"Here's another gift," says the girl. "Let me unwrap it for you." And she swings her hands together.

Lev leaps over the sofa for cover as her hands connect. All it takes is a single clap. The explosion blows Lev back against the wall, and the sofa flips on top of him, pinning him there. Shattering glass, crumbling timbers—and a shooting pain in his ears so bad he's convinced his skull has split open. Then, in a few moments, the sounds of the explosion fades, leaving behind an intense ringing in his ears, and a clear sense that the world has just ended.

Smoke begins to burn his lungs and make his eyes tear. He forces the sofa off himself, and as he looks across the room, he sees his bed, which was upstairs just a few moments ago, now lying in the living room like a shipwreck. There is no upstairs now—and there is no roof beyond that, only the cloud-filled sky, while all around him flames eagerly fight to consume the wreckage.

Dan, who was on his way out into the living room when the girl clapped, was blasted backward against the wall. A huge bloodstain in the rough shape of his body marks his impact, and now he lies a lifeless heap on the floor. Pastor Dan—the man who told Lev to run on his tithing day, the first one to visit him once he was in police custody, the man who had become more of a father to him than his own father—is dead.

"No!!"

Lev crawls over the ruins toward Dan's body, but then sees his brother in the kitchen. A beam has fallen in the middle of the room, shattering the glass breakfast table and embedding itself in his brother's gut. There's blood everywhere—but Marcus is still alive. He's conscious, and he shudders as he tries to speak, choking on blood.

Lev doesn't know what to do, but he knows if he doesn't clear his head enough to act, his brother will die too.

"It's okay, Marcus, it's okay," he says, even though it's not.

With all his strength, Lev lifts the beam. Marcus screams in pain, and Lev, holding the beam up with his shoulder, pushes Marcus out of the way, then lets the beam go. The whole rest of the beam comes down, taking out what little was left of the table with a loud crash. Lev reaches into Marcus's pocket, pulls out a blood-soaked phone and, praying it still works, dials 911.

Lev, covered in soot and ears still ringing, refuses his own ambulance. He insists on riding with Marcus and makes such a stink that they let him.

His left ear flutters with every sound, like a moth has found its way inside. His vision is blurry, and time itself seems to have altered. It's like Lev and Marcus have been thrust into an alternate dimension where cause and effect are all confused. Lev can't figure out if he's here because the girl blew up, or if the girl blew up because he's here.

The paramedics work on Marcus as they speed to the hospital, injecting him with God knows what.

"L-L-Lev," Marcus says, his eyes struggling to stay open.

Lev grabs his hand, sticky and brown from drying blood. "I'm here."

"Keep him awake," the paramedic tells him. "We don't want him to go into shock."

"L-listen to me," Marcus says, fighting to get the words out. "Listen to me."

"I'm listening."

"They'll want to . . . to give me stuff. Unwind stuff."

Lev grimaces to prepare himself. He knows what Marcus will say. Marcus would rather die than get parts from Unwinds.

"They're gonna . . . they're gonna wanna give me kidneys . . . a liver . . . whatever . . . parts from Unwinds . . ."

"I know, Marcus, I know."

Then he opens his half-shut eyes wider, locks his gaze on Lev, and grips Lev's hand more tightly.

"Let them!" he says.

"What?"

"Let them do it, Lev. I don't wanna die. Please, Lev," Marcus begs. "Let them give me unwound parts. . . ."

Lev squeezes his brother's hand. "Okay, Marcus. Okay." And he cries, thankful that his brother didn't just condemn himself to death, and hating himself for feeling that way.

Lev is examined thoroughly and told that he has a broken eardrum, various lacerations and contusions, and possibly a concussion. They bandage his wounds, which are minor, put him on antibiotics, and hold him for observation. He hears no word of Marcus, who was rushed into an operating room the moment they arrived. Aside from the nurse taking his pulse and blood pressure every hour, there's no one to visit Lev but the police, who have questions, questions, and more questions.

"Did you know the girl who perpetrated this attack?"

"No."

"Did you recognize her from your clapper training?"

"No."

"Was she a part of your clapper cell?"

"I told you I didn't know her!"

And of course, the stupidest question of all:

"Do you know any reason why they would target you?"

"Isn't it obvious? She told me it was retribution for not clapping—that the people in charge weren't happy."

"And who are the people in charge?"

"I don't know. The only ones I ever knew were a bunch of

other kids who are dead now because they all blew up, okay? I never met anyone in charge!"

Satisfied, but not really, the police leave. Then the FBI shows up and asks him the same questions the police did—and still no one will tell him anything about Marcus.

Finally, later in the afternoon, during one of her routine checks, his attending nurse takes pity on him.

"I was told not to speak to you about your brother, but I'm going to anyway." Then she sits in a chair close to him, keeping her voice down. "He had a lot of internal damage. But luckily, we happen to have one of the best-equipped organ lockers in the state. He received a new pancreas, liver and spleen, and a sizeable segment of small intestine. He had a punctured lung, and rather than letting it heal, your parents opted to replace that, too."

"My parents? They're here?"

"Yes," the nurse said. "They're in the waiting room. Would you like me to get them?"

"Do they know I'm here?" Lev asks.

"Yes."

"Did they ask to see me?"

She hesitates. "I'm sorry, hon, they didn't."

Lev looks away, but there's nothing to look at. The TV in his hospital room has been disconnected, because there's so much coverage of the explosion. "Then I don't want to see them."

The nurse pats his hand and offers him an apologetic smile. "Sorry there's so much bad blood there, hon. I'm sorry all this had to happen to you."

He wonders if she knows the whole of it, and figures that she does. "I should have realized they'd come after me eventually. The clappers, I mean."

The nurse sighs. "Once you get wound in with bad people, the unwinding never ends." Then she catches herself. "I'm sorry—that was a very unfortunate choice of words, wasn't it? I should just sew my lips shut right now."

Lev forces a smile. "It's okay. Once you've almost blown up twice, you're not so sensitive about word choices."

She smiles at that.

"So what happens now?"

"Well, I understand your brother is your legal guardian. Is there anyone else who might come forward to help you? Somewhere else you can go?"

Lev shakes his head. Pastor Dan was the only other person he could count on. He can't even think of Dan now. It simply hurts too much. "I was under house arrest. I can't go anywhere without permission from the Juvenile Authority, even if there was someone to go with."

The nurse stands up. "Well, that's way out of my department, hon. Why don't you just relax for now? I know they want to keep you overnight—it can all be sorted out in the morning."

"Could you maybe tell me what room my brother's in?"

"He's still in recovery," she tells him, "but as soon as they assign him a room, I promise you'll be the first to know." She leaves, and in comes a detective, with more ways to ask the same questions.

True to her word, the nurse tells him that Marcus is in room 408, and so after dark, when all the questioning is over and the halls have quieted, Lev ventures out of his room, ignoring the aches that fill most of his body. Just outside his door, he sees that the cop assigned to guard him is down the hall, flirting with one of the younger nurses. Lev quietly slips away to visit Marcus.

As he pushes open the door to room 408, the first thing he sees is his mother sitting in a chair, her eyes fixed on Marcus, who is unconscious and intubated, and connected to a hissing breathing machine. His father is there too, his hair looking a little grayer than it did a year ago. Lev feels tears threatening to rise, but he wills them away, sucking his emotions in and locking them tight.

His mother sees him first. She reaches over to get his father's attention. They look at each other for a moment, sharing whatever pseudo-telepathy married couples have. Then his mother stands, crosses to Lev, and never once looking at him, hugs him awkwardly, then leaves the room.

His father doesn't look at him either. Not at first anyway. He just looks to Marcus, watching his chest rise and fall in a slow, steady, machine-regulated rhythm.

"How is he?" Lev asks.

"He's in an induced coma. They said they'll keep him like this for three days, so the nanos can speed the healing."

Lev has heard that the pain of nano-healing is unbearable. It's best that Marcus sleeps through it. Lev is certain that his parents gave Marcus all tithed organs. The most expensive. He knows this, but he won't ask.

Finally his father looks at him. "Are you satisfied now? Are you happy with the results of your actions?"

Lev has imagined this conversation between him and his father a hundred times. In each of those mental confrontations, Lev has always been the one making accusations, not the other way around. How dare he? How *dare* he? Lev wants to lash out, but he refuses to take the bait. He says nothing.

"Do you have any idea what you've put this family through?" his father says. "The shame? The ridicule?"

Lev can't maintain his silence. "Then maybe you shouldn't surround yourself with people as judgmental as you."

His father looks to Marcus again. "Your brother will come home with us," he decrees. And since any guts that Marcus now has have been paid for by their father's money, he won't have much of a choice.

"And me?"

Again, his father won't look at him. "My son was tithed a year ago," he says. "That's the son I choose to remember. As for you, you can do as you please. It's not my concern." And he says no more.

"When Marcus wakes up, tell him I forgive him," Lev says.

"Forgive him for what?"

"He'll know."

And Lev leaves without saying good-bye.

Farther down the hallway, he spots his mother again, and other members of his family, in the fourth-floor waiting room. A brother, two sisters, and their husbands. In the end, they came for Marcus. None of them are there for him. He hesitates, wondering if he should go in there. Will they behave like his father, bitter, rigid, and cold—or like his mother, offering a pained hug, yet refusing to look at him?

Then, in that moment of indecision, he sees one of his sisters bend down and pick up a baby. It's a new nephew Lev never even knew he had.

And the baby is dressed all in white.

Lev races back to his room, but even before he gets there, he feels the eruption begin. It starts deep in his gut, sobs rising with such unexpected fury, his abdomen locks in a cramp. He must struggle the last few feet to his room doubled over, barely able to catch his breath as the tears burst from his eyes.

Somewhere deep, deep down in the most irrational corner of Lev's mind—perhaps the place where childhood dreams go—he held out a secret hope that he might actually be taken back. That he might one day be welcomed home. Marcus had told him to forget about it—that it would never happen, but nothing could wipe out that stubborn hope that hid within him. Until today.

He climbs into his hospital bed and forces his face into his pillow as the sobs crescendo into wails. A full year's worth of suppressed heartache pours forth from his soul like Niagara, and he doesn't care if he drowns in the killing whiteness of its churning waters.

Lev wakes without ever remembering having slept. He knows he must have, because there's morning light streaming into the room.

"Good morning, Lev."

He turns his head toward the voice a little too sharply, and the room spins around him. An aftereffect of the explosion. His ears are still ringing, but at least the flutter in his left ear has settled down.

Sitting in a chair near the foot of his bed is a woman a little too well-dressed to be part of the hospital staff.

"Are you FBI? Homeland Security? Are you here to ask me more questions? Because I don't have any more answers."

The woman chuckles slightly. "I'm not with any government agency. I represent the Cavenaugh Trust. Have you heard of it?"

Lev shakes his head. "Should I have?"

She hands him a colorful brochure, and as he looks at it, he gets a shiver.

"It looks like a harvest camp brochure."

"Hardly," she says, clearly insulted. The right response, as far as Lev is concerned. "To put it simply," she tells him, "the Cavenaugh trust is a whole lot of money, set aside by what was once a very wealthy family to help wayward youth. And we can think of few youth as wayward as you."

She gives him a twisted little smile, thinking herself funny. She's not.

"Be that as it may," she says, "we understand you have no place to go once you're released, and rather than leave you at the mercy of Child Protective Services, who certainly cannot protect you from any future clapper attacks, we are prepared to offer you a place to live—with the full approval of the Juvenile Authority, of course—in exchange for your services."

Lev pulls his knees up beneath his covers and shrinks away from her. He doesn't trust well-dressed people who make offers with strings attached. "What kind of services?"

She smiles at him warmly. "Just your presence, Mr. Calder. Your presence and your winning personality."

And although he can't think of anything that his personality has won, he says, "Sure, why not?" Because he realizes he has absolutely nothing left to lose. He thinks back to the days after he left CyFi, and before he arrived at the Graveyard. Dark days, to be sure, but punctuated by a bit of light when he found himself on a reservation, taken in by People of Chance. The Chance folk had taught him that when you have nothing to lose, there's no such thing as a bad roll of the dice. And then something occurs to him. Something that has been in the back of his mind for a while, but today has risen to the forefront.

"One thing, though," Lev says.

"Yes?"

"I want to have my last name legally changed. Can you do that?"

She raises her eyebrows. "Of course, if that's what you want. May I ask what you would like to change it to?"

"It doesn't matter," he tells her. "Just as long as it's not Calder."

22 · Trust

There's a home on a street in northern Detroit. It is now the official legal residence of one Levi Jedediah Garrity. It's a small home, but adequate, and comes through the generosity of the Cavenaugh trust, dedicated to helping wayward youth. There is a full-time valet to take care of Lev's needs, and a new tutor to take care of his lessons. The trust has even planted a permanent rent-a-cop out front to deter any unwanted guests and suspicious solicitors. No clappers are getting anywhere near the front door here.

It would be a perfect situation for Lev, except for the fact that he doesn't actually live there. True, there's that subcutaneous tracking chip embedded in his neck that swears he does, but the chip was easily compromised. Now the chip can ping out a signal from wherever they want Lev to appear to be.

No one knows he's being brought to the Cavenaugh mansion, almost forty miles away.

The Cavenaugh mansion is a behemoth of a building resting on seventy-five secluded acres in Lake Orion, Michigan. It was designed to look like Versailles and was built with motor money in the days before the American automotive industry had done its own version of clapping and applauded itself into nonexistence.

Most people don't know the mansion is still there. They're mostly right, because it's barely there at all. Exposure to the elements all these years has left it one storm short of surrender.

The mansion served as the Midwest headquarters for the Choice Brigade during the Heartland War, until it was captured and became headquarters for the Life Army. Apparently both the Lifers and Choicers saw great value in having their own personal Versailles.

The place was under attack constantly until the day the Unwind Accord ended all battles, putting forth the worst possible compromise and yet the only one both sides could agree to: sanctity of life from conception to thirteen, with the option of unwinding teenagers whose lives were deemed to have been a mistake.

For many years after the war, the Cavenaugh mansion lay

crumbling, too expensive to repair yet too large to tear down, until Charles Cavenaugh Jr., to assuage his guilt at still having old money in new times, donated the mansion to a trust fund, which was owned by another trust fund, which was laundered through yet another trust fund, which was owned by the Anti-Divisional Resistance.

23 · Lev

Charles Cavenaugh Jr. meets Lev personally at the entrance of the crumbling mansion. He's dressed like he's too rich to worry about how he's dressed. Even with the Cavenaugh family fortune long gone, Lev figures there must be enough residual wealth to keep at least his generation living elite. The only thing that betrays his allegiance to the resistance is his thinning hair. Nowadays the rich don't have thinning hair. If they do, they just replace it with someone else's.

"Lev, it's an honor to meet you!" He grasps Lev's hand with both of his, shaking it firmly and maintaining a steady eye contact that Lev finds awkward.

"Thanks. Same here." Lev isn't sure what else to say.

"I was so sorry to hear about the loss of your friend and your brother's injuries. I can't help but think if we had approached you earlier, the tragedy never would have happened."

Lev looks up at the mansion. Barely a window is intact. Birds fly through the jagged, broken panes.

"Don't let it fool you," Cavenaugh says. "She still has some life in her—and the way she appears is actually an asset. It's camouflage for anyone who tries to look too closely."

Lev can't imagine anyone looking too closely. The place is on seventy-five fenced-in acres, in the middle of a weedy field that was once a lawn, which is surrounded on all sides by dense woods. The only way to even see the mansion would be from above.

Cavenaugh pushes open a rotted door and leads Lev into what was once a grand foyer. Now the foyer has no roof. Two sets of stairs climb to the second floor, but most of the wood on the stairs has caved in, and weeds grow through cracks in the floor, pushing up the marble tiles, making it randomly uneven.

"This way." Cavenaugh leads him deeper into the ruined building, down a dim hallway in equally awful condition. The smell of mildew makes the air feel gelatinous. Lev is about to conclude that Cavenaugh is a madman and run in the other direction when the man unlocks a heavy door in front of them, swinging it open to reveal a grand dining hall.

"We've restored the north wing. For now it's all we need. Of course, we've had to board all the windows—lights at night in an abandoned ruin would be way too conspicuous."

The place is nowhere near in the condition it must have once been in. There's still peeling paint, and water stains on the roof, but it's far more livable than the rest of the sprawling estate. The dining hall has two mismatched chandeliers that were probably salvaged from other areas of the mansion. Three long tables and benches suggest that a lot of people are served their meals here.

At the far end of the room is a huge fireplace, and above it a full-length portrait, larger than life. At first Lev takes it to be a painting of one of the Cavenaughs as a boy, until he looks more closely.

"Wait—is that . . . me?"

Cavenaugh smiles. "A good likeness, isn't it?"

As he crosses toward it, Lev can see how good a likeness it really is. Or at least a fine rendering of how he looked a year ago. In the portrait, he's wearing a yellow shirt that seems to glow like gold. In fact, the portrait is painted so that his skin gives off a sort of divine radiance. The expression on his painted face speaks of wisdom and peace—the kind of peace Lev has yet to find in life—and at the base of the portrait are tithing whites metaphorically trampled beneath his feet.

His first reaction is to laugh. "What's this all about?"

"It's about the cause you fought for, Lev. I'm pleased to say we've picked up where you left off."

On the mantel just below the portrait are everything from flowers to handwritten notes, to bits of jewelry and other trinkets.

"These things spontaneously began to appear after we put up the portrait," Cavenaugh explains. "We didn't expect it, but maybe we should have."

Lev still struggles to process this. Again, all he can do is giggle. "You're joking, right?"

Then off to his right, at a doorway to an adjacent hallway, a woman calls out to them. "Mr. Cavenaugh, the natives are getting restless. Can I let them in?"

Lev can see kids craning to see around the rather heavyset woman.

"Give us a moment, please," Cavenaugh tells her, then smiles at Lev. "As you can imagine, they're very excited to meet you."

"Who?"

"The tithes, of course. We held a contest, and seven were chosen to personally greet you."

Cavenaugh talks like these are all things Lev should already know. It's all too much for him to wrap his mind around. "Tithes?"

"Ex-tithes, actually. Rescued before their arrival at their respective harvest camps."

Then something clicks, and it dawns on Lev how this is possible. "Parts pirates—the ones who target tithes!"

"Oh, there are certainly parts pirates," Cavenaugh says, "but to the best of my knowledge, none of them have taken any tithes. It's a good cover story, though. Keeps the Juvenile Authority barking up the wrong tree."

The idea that tithes are being rescued rather than sold on the black market is something that has never occurred to Lev.

"Are you ready to meet our little squad of ambassadors?"

"Sure, why not."

Cavenaugh signals the woman to let them in, and they enter in an orderly procession that doesn't hide the high-voltage excitement in their step. They're all dressed in bright colors—intentionally so. Not a bit of white in the whole bunch. Lev just stands there dazed as they greet him one by one. A couple of them just stare and nod their heads, too starstruck to say anything. Another shakes his hand so forcefully Lev's shoulder has to absorb the shock. One boy is so nervous, he stumbles and nearly falls at Lev's feet, then goes beet red as he steps away.

"Your hair is different," one girl says, then panics like she's gravely insulted him. "But it's good! I like it! I like it long!"

"I know everything about you," another kid announces. "Seriously, ask me anything."

And although Lev is a bit creeped out by the thought, he says, "Okay, what's my favorite ice cream?"

"Cherry Garcia!" the kid says without the slightest hesitation. The answer is, of course, correct. Lev's not quite sure how to feel about it.

"So . . . you were all tithes?"

"Yes," says a girl in bright green, "until we were rescued. We know how wrong tithing is now."

"Yeah," says another. "We learned to see the way you see!"

Lev finds himself giddy and caught up in their adoration. Not since his days as a tithe has he felt "golden." After Happy Jack, everyone saw him either as a victim to be pitied or a monster to be punished. But these kids revere him as a hero. He can't deny that after all he's been through, it feels good. Really good.

A girl in screaming violet can't contain herself and throws her arms around him. "I love you, Lev Calder!" she cries.

One of the other kids pulls her off. "Sorry, she's a little intense."

"It's okay," Lev says, "but my name's not Calder anymore. It's Garrity."

"After Pastor Daniel Garrity!" the know-it-all kid blurts. "The one who died in the clapper blast two weeks ago." The kid is so proud that he has all the information down, he doesn't realize how raw Dan's death still is for Lev. "How's your broken eardrum, by the way?"

"Getting better."

Cavenaugh, who has been standing back, now steps in to gather them and send them on their way. "That's enough for now," he tells them. "But you'll all get your chance to have a personal audience with Lev."

"Audience?" Lev says, chuckling at the thought. "Who am I, the pope?" But no one else is laughing—and it occurs to him that his inside joke with Pastor Dan has actually become a reality. All these kids are Leviathan.

Sixty-four. That's how many ex-tithes are being sheltered and given sanctuary in the Cavenaugh mansion. It gives Lev a hope he hasn't felt since the passage of the Cap-17 law, which turned out to be as many steps backward as it was forward.

"Eventually we'll give them new identities and place them with families we trust to kept their secret," Cavenaugh tells Lev. "We call it the Wholeness Relocation Program."

Cavenaugh gives Lev the grand tour of the reclaimed north wing. On the walls are framed photos and news clippings about Lev. A banner in one hallway proclaims they should all LIVE LIKE LEV! His giddiness begins to turn to butterflies in his stomach.

How can he live up to all this buildup? Should he even try?

"Don't you think it's kind of . . . overkill?" he asks Cavenaugh.

"We've come to realize that by pulling these kids from their tithing, we've removed from them the focus of their lives; the one immutable thing they believed in. We needed to fill that space, at least temporarily. You were the natural candidate."

Stenciled on the walls are quotes and expressions attributed to Lev. Things like "To celebrate an undivided life is the finest goal of all," and "Your future is 'wholly' yours." They are sentiments he agrees with, but they never came out of his mouth.

"It must feel strange to be the focus of such lofty attention," Cavenaugh says to him. "I hope you approve of how we've used your image to help these children."

Lev finds himself in no position to approve, or disapprove, or even to judge the wisdom of it. How do you judge the brightness of a light when you're the source? A spotlight can never see the shadows it casts. All he can do is go with it, and take his place as some sort of spiritual figure. There are worse things. Having experienced several of them, there is no question that this is better.

On his second day there, they begin to arrange his personal audiences with the ex-tithes—just a few a day so as not to overwhelm him. Lev listens to their life stories and tries to give advice, much the same way he did for the incarcerated "divisional risk" kids he used to visit on Sundays with Pastor Dan. For these kids, though, no matter what Lev says, they take it as divinely inspired. He could say the sky is pink, and they would find some mystical, symbolic meaning to it.

"All they want is validation," Cavenaugh tells him, "and validation from you is the greatest gift they could hope for."

By the end of the first week, Lev has settled into the rhythm of the place. Meals don't begin until he arrives. He's usually called on to say a nondenominational grace. His mornings are spent in audiences, and in the afternoon, he's allowed time to himself. He's encouraged by Cavenaugh and the staff to write his memoirs, which feels like an absurd request of a fourteen-year-old, but they're completely serious. Even his bedroom is absurd—a kingly chamber far too large for him, and one of the few that has an actual window to the outside that isn't boarded over. His room is larger than life, his image larger than life and death combined, and yet all these things only serve to make him feel increasingly small.

And to make it worse, at each meal he is faced by that portrait. The Lev they believe he is. He can fill that role for sure, but the eyes of that portrait, which follow him through the room, carry an accusation. *You are not me,* those eyes say. *You never were, you never will be.* But still flowers and notes and tributes appear on the mantel beneath the painting, and Lev comes to realize that it isn't just a portrait . . . it's an altar.

During his second week, he's called in to greet new arrivals—the first since his own arrival. They're fresh off the hijacked van, and all they know is that they've been kidnapped and tranq'd. They do not yet know by whom.

"It would be our wish," Cavenaugh tells him, "that you be the first thing they see upon their unveiling."

"Why? So they can imprint on me like ducklings?"

Cavenaugh exhales in mild exasperation. "Hardly. To the best of their knowledge, you are the only one who escaped being tithed. You don't realize the visceral effect your presence has on another child slated for that same fate."

Lev is directed to the ballroom, which remains in a sorry state and is probably beyond salvation. He is sure there is some researched psychological reason for greeting the kids here, but he doesn't really want to ask.

When he gets there, the two new arrivals are already there. A boy and a girl. They've been tied to chairs and blindfolded, making it clear what Cavenaugh means by "unveiling." The man is way too theatrical.

The boy sobs, and the girl tries to calm him. "It's all right, Timothy," she says. "Whatever's going on, it's going to be okay."

Lev sits across from them, feeling awkward and frightened by their fear. He knows he needs to put forth confidence and comfort, but facing a pair of terrified kidnap victims is different from facing adoring ex-tithes.

Cavenaugh is not present, but two adults in his employ stand at the ready. Lev swallows and tries to keep his hands from shaking by gripping the arms of his chair. "Okay, you can take off their blindfolds."

The boy's eyes are red from crying. The girl is already looking around, surveying the situation.

"I'm really sorry we had to do it this way," Lev says. "We couldn't risk you getting hurt, or figuring out where you were being taken. It was the only way to safely rescue you."

"Rescue us?" says the girl. "Is that what you call this?"

Lev tries to deflect the accusation in her voice, but can't. He forces himself to hold eye contact the way Cavenaugh does, hoping he can sell it as confidence.

"Well, it might not feel that way at the moment, but yeah, that's exactly what we've done."

The girl scowls in absolute defiance, but the boy gasps, and his wet eyes go wide.

"You're him! You're that tithe who became a clapper! You're Levi Calder!"

Lev offers a slim, apologetic smile, not even bothering to correct the last name. "Yes, but my friends call me Lev."

"I'm Timothy!" the boy volunteers. "Timothy Taylor Vance!

Her name is Muh—Muh—I can't quite remember, but it starts
with an *M*, right?"

"My name is my business and will stay my business," she says.

Lev looks at the little cheat sheet he'd been given. "Your
name is Miracolina Roselli. It's a pleasure to meet you,
Miracolina. Do you go by Mira?"

Her continuing glare makes it clear that she doesn't. "All
right, Miracolina then."

"What gives you the right?" she says. It's almost a growl.

Lev forces eye contact again. She knows who he is, but she
hates him. Despises him even. He's seen that look before, but
it surprises him to see it here.

"Maybe you didn't hear me," Lev says, getting a little bit
angry. "We just saved you."

"By whose definition of 'save'?"

And for an instant, just an instant, he sees himself through
this girl's eyes, and he doesn't like what he sees.

"I'm glad you're both here," he says, trying to hide the
quaver in his voice. "We'll talk again." Then he signals for the
adults to take the kids away.

Lev sits there in the ballroom alone for a good ten minutes. There is something about Miracolina's behavior that feels
disturbingly familiar. He tries to think back to when Connor
pulled him from his limo on his own tithing day. Was he that
belligerent? That uncooperative? There is so much from that
day that he's blocked out. At what point did he begin to realize
that Connor wasn't the enemy?

He will win her over. He has to. All the ex-tithes have been
turned eventually. Un-brainwashed. Deprogrammed.

But what if this girl is the exception? What then? Suddenly
this whole rescue operation, which had felt like a grand and
glorious idea, feels very small. And very personal.

24 · Miracolina

Born to save her brother's life and to be gifted back to God, Miracolina will not stand for this violation—the corruption of her sacred destiny into the profane life of a fugitive. Even her own parents became weak at the end, willing to break their pact with God and save her from her tithing. Would this please them, she wonders, for her to be captured and forced to live whole? Denied the holy mystery of the divided state?

Not only must she suffer this indignation, but she must suffer it at the hands of the boy she practically considers to be Satan incarnate. Miracolina is not a girl given to hatred and unfair judgment—but to be faced with this boy proves she is not nearly as tolerant as she had thought.

Perhaps that's why I have been put on this path, she thinks, *to humble me and make me realize that I can be a hater, just like anyone else.*

On that first day, they try to trick her by putting her in a comfortable bedroom in much better condition than most of the mansion. "You can rest here until the last effects of the tranqs wear off," says a plump, kindly woman, who also brings her a meal of corned beef and cabbage, with a tall, heady glass of root beer.

"Saint Patrick's Day, don'tcha know," she says. "Eat up, dearie. There's more if you want seconds." It's a blatant attempt to win her over. She eats, but refuses to enjoy it.

There are videos and books in her room to entertain her, but Miracolina has to laugh, because just as the harvest camp van had only happy, family-friendly movies, the titles she has to choose from here have a clear agenda as well. They're all about kids being mistreated, but rising above it, or kids empowering themselves in a world that doesn't understand them. Everything from Dickens to Salinger—as if Miracolina Roselli could possibly have anything in common with Holden Caulfield.

There are also drawers filled with clothes in bright colors— all her size, and she shudders to think that they took her measurements and prepared a wardrobe while she was unconscious. Her tithing whites have become dirty, but she won't give them the satisfaction of changing out of them.

Finally a bald middle-aged man comes in with a clipboard and a name tag that just says BOB.

"I used to be a respected psychiatrist until I spoke out against unwinding," Bob tells her after the obligatory introductions. "Being ostracized was a blessing in disguise, though, because it allowed me to come here, where I'm truly needed."

Miracolina keeps her arms folded, giving him nothing. She knows what this is all about. They call it "deprogramming," which is a polite term for undoing brainwashing with more brainwashing.

"You *used* to be respected, which means you're not anymore," she tells him, "and I don't have respect for you either."

After a brief psych evaluation, which she refuses to take seriously, Bob sighs and clicks his pen closed. "I think you'll find," he says, "that our concern for you is genuine, and we want you to truly blossom."

"I'm not a potted plant," she tells him, and hurls her glass of flat root beer at the door as it closes behind him.

She quickly discovers that her door is not locked. Another trick? She goes out to explore the halls of the mansion. She can't deny that even in her anger at having been abducted, she's curious about what goes on here. How many other kids have been torn from their tithing? How many captors are there? What are her chances of escape?

It turns out there are tons of other kids. They hang out

in dorm rooms or public areas. They work to repair the unre-pairable damage and rot around the mansion, and they have classes taught by other Bob-like people.

She wanders into a social area with a sagging floor and a pool table propped up with wood to keep it level. One girl glances at her, singling her out, and approaches. Her name tag says JACKIE.

"You must be Miracolina," Jackie says, grabbing her hand to shake, since Miracolina won't extend it. "I know it's a tough adjustment, but I think we're going to be great friends." Jackie has the look of a tithe, as do all the other kids here. A certain cleanness and elevation above worldly things. Even though no one wears a stitch of white, they can't hide what they once were.

"Are you assigned to me?" Miracolina asks.

Jackie shrugs apologetically. "Yeah, kind of."

"Thanks for being honest, but I don't like you, and I don't want to be your friend."

Jackie, who is not a formerly respected psychiatrist, but just an ordinary thirteen-year-old girl, is clearly hurt by her words, and Miracolina immediately regrets them. She must not allow herself to become callous and jaded. She must rise above this.

"I'm sorry. It's not you I don't like, it's what they're making you do. If you want to be my friend, try again when I'm not your assignment."

"Okay, fair enough," Jackie says. "But friends or not, I'm supposed to help you get with the program, whether you like it or not."

An understanding reached, Jackie returns to her friends but keeps an eye on Miracolina as long as she's in the room.

Timothy, the boy she was kidnapped with, is in the room as well, with a former tithe who was apparently assigned to him.

The two talk like they're already great friends. Clearly Timothy has "gotten with the program," and since he was not too keen on being unwound anyway, all it took to deprogram him was a change of clothes.

"How could you be so . . . so shallow?" she says to him, when she catches him alone later in the day.

"If that's what you want to call it," he says, all smiles, like he's just been given a new puppy. "But if it's shallow to want a life, then heck, I'm a wading pool!"

Deprogramming! It's enough to make her sick. She despises Timothy and wonders how anyone's lifelong faith could be traded for corned beef and cabbage.

Jackie seeks her out later in the day—after Miracolina has determined that her "freedom" ends at a locked door, which keeps all the ex-tithes in a single wing of the mansion. "The rest is still uninhabitable," Jackie tells her. "That's why we're only allowed in the north wing."

Jackie explains that their days are spent in classes designed to help them to adjust.

"What happens to the kids who fail?" Miracolina asks with a smirk.

Jackie says nothing—just looks at her like it's a concept she hasn't considered.

Within a few days, Miracolina has all she can stand of the classes. The mornings begin with a long emotional group therapy where at least one person bursts into tears and is applauded by the others for doing so. Miracolina usually says nothing, because defending tithing is frowned on by the faculty.

"You have a right to your opinion," they all say if she ever speaks out against their deprogramming. "But we're hoping you will eventually see otherwise." Which means she really doesn't have a right to an opinion.

There's a class in modern history—something few schools actually teach. It includes the Heartland War, the Unwind Accord, and everything surrounding them, right up to the current day. There are discussions about the splinter groups within many major religions that took upon themselves the act of human tithing, becoming socially sanctioned "tithing cults."

"These weren't grassroots movements," the teacher tells them. "It began with wealthy families—executives and stockholders in major corporations—as a way of setting an example for the masses, because if even the rich approve of unwinding, then everyone should. The tithing cults were part of a calculated plan to root unwinding in the national psyche."

Miracolina can't keep herself from raising her hand. "Excuse me," she tells the instructor, "but I'm Catholic and don't belong to a tithing cult. So how do you account for me?"

She thought the teacher might say, *You're the exception that proves the rule,* or something equally insipid, but she doesn't. Instead she only says, "Hmm, that's interesting. I bet Lev would love to talk to you about that."

To Miracolina, that's the worst threat the teacher could make, and she knows it. It keeps Miracolina quiet. Even so, her resistance to the resistance is well known in the mansion, and she is called in for an unwanted audience with the boy who didn't detonate.

It happens on Monday morning. She's pulled out of her intolerable therapy group and taken to a section of the mansion she hasn't seen before—escorted by not one, but two resistance workers. Although she can't be sure, she suspects at least one of them is armed. They take her to a plant-filled arboretum, all curved glass and sunshine, kept heated and restored to its former glory. In the center is a mahogany table and two chairs. He's already there, sitting in one of the chairs, the boy at the center of this bizarre hero worship. She sits across from him and waits for him to speak first. Even before he speaks, she can tell he's genuinely interested in her: the only square peg in the whole mansion who can't be whittled round.

"So what's up with you?" he says after studying her for a few moments. She's offended by the informality of the question—as if her whole stance on everything occurring in this place is a matter of "something being up." Well, today she'll make it clear to him that her defiance is more than just attitude.

"Are you actually interested in me, clapper, or am I just the bug you can't squash beneath your iron boot?"

He laughs at that. "Iron boot—that's a good one." He lifts his foot to show her the sole of his Nike. "I'll admit there may be some stomped spiders between the treads, but that's about it."

"If you're going to give me the third degree," she tells him, "let's get it over with. Best to withhold food or water; water is probably best. I'll get thirsty before I get hungry."

He shakes his head in disbelief. "Do you really think I'm like that? Why would you think that?"

"I was taken by force, and you're keeping me here against my will," she says, leaning across the table toward him. She considers spitting in his face, but decides to save that gesture as punctuation for a more appropriate moment. "Imprisonment is still imprisonment, no matter how many layers of cotton you wrap it in." That makes him lean farther away, and she knows she's pushed a button. She remembers seeing those pictures of him back when he was all over the news, wrapped in cotton and kept in a bombproof cell.

"I really don't get you," he says, a bit of anger in his voice this time. "We saved your life. You could at least be a little grateful."

"You have robbed me, and everyone here, of their purpose. That's not salvation, that's damnation."

"I'm sorry you feel that way."

Now it's her turn to get angry. "Yes, you're sorry I feel that way, everyone's sorry I feel that way. Are you going to keep this up until I don't feel that way anymore?"

He stands up suddenly, pushing his chair back, and paces, fern leaves brushing his clothes. She knows she's gotten to him. He seems like he's about to storm out, but instead takes a deep breath and turns back to her.

"I know what you're going through," he says. "I was brainwashed by my family to actually want to be unwound—and not just by my family, but by my friends, my church, everyone I looked up to. The only voice who spoke sense was my brother Marcus, but I was too blind to hear him until the day I got kidnapped."

"You mean *see*," she says, putting a nice speed bump in his way.

"Huh?"

"Too blind to *see* him, too deaf to *hear* him. Get your senses straight. Or maybe you can't, because you're senseless."

He smiles. "You're good."

"And anyway, I don't need to hear your life story. I already know it. You got caught in a freeway pileup, and the Akron AWOL used you as a human shield—very noble. Then he turned you, like cheese gone bad."

"He didn't turn me. It was getting away from my tithing, and seeing unwinding for what it is. That's what turned me."

"Because being a murderer is better than being a tithe, isn't that right, clapper?"

He sits back down again, calmer, and it frustrates her that he is becoming immune to her snipes.

"When you live a life without questions, you're unprepared for the questions when they come," he says. "You get angry and you totally lack the skills to deal with the anger. So yes, I became a clapper, but only because I was too innocent to know how guilty I was becoming."

There is an intensity about him now, and a moistness to his eyes. Miracolina can tell that he is sincere, and that this is not just a show for her. Maybe he's even saying more than he meant to say. She begins to wonder if she has misjudged him, and then gets angry at herself for wondering such a thing.

"You think I'm like you, but I'm not," Miracolina says. "I'm not part of a religious order that tithes. My parents did it in spite of our beliefs, not because of it."

"But you were still raised to believe it was your purpose, weren't you?"

"My purpose was to save my brother's life by being a marrow donor, so my purpose was served before I was six months old."

"And doesn't that make you angry that the only reason you're here was to help someone else?"

"Not at all," she says a little too quickly. She purses her lips and leans back in her chair, squirming a bit. The chair feels a little too hard beneath her. "All right, so maybe I do feel angry once in a while, but I understand why they did it. If I were them, I would have done the same thing."

"Agreed," he says. "But once your purpose was served, shouldn't your life be your own?"

"Miracles are the property of God," she answers.

"No," he says, "miracles are gifts *from* God. To call them his property insults the spirit in which they are given."

She opens her mouth to reply but finds she has no response, because he's right. Damn him for being right—nothing about him should be right!

"We'll talk again when you're over yourself," he says, and signals a waiting guard to take her away.

The next day a class is added into her schedule, to keep her from having too idle a mind. It's called Creative Projection. It takes place in a classroom that was once some kind of parlor, with faded, moth-eaten portraits on peeling walls. Miracolina wonders if the stodgy faces in the paintings look down on the lessons here with approval, disapproval, or absolute indifference.

"I want you to write a story," says the teacher, a man with annoying little round glasses. Glasses! Objects of antiquity no longer needed by anyone, what with laser procedures and affordable eye-replacement surgery. There is a certain arrogance to their quaintness. As if people who choose to wear glasses feel they are somehow superior.

"I want you to write the story of you—your biography. Not the life you've lived but the life you're *going* to live. This is the biography you might write forty, fifty years from now." The teacher wanders the room, gesticulating into the air, probably imagining himself to be Plato or someone equally lofty. "Project yourselves forward. Tell me who you think you'll be. I know that'll be hard for all of you. You've never dared think of the future—but now you can. I want you to enjoy this. Be as wild as you want. Have fun with it!"

Then he sits down and leans back in his chair with his hands behind his head, very satisfied with himself.

Miracolina taps her pen impatiently on the page while the other kids write. He wants her dream future? Fine. She'll give these people something honest, even if it isn't what they want to hear.

It is years from now, she writes, *and my hands belong to a mother who lost her hands in a fire. She has four children. She comforts them, bathes them, brushes their hair, and changes their diapers with those hands. She treasures my hands because she knows how precious they are. She gets manicures weekly for me, even though she doesn't know who I was.*

My legs belong to a girl who was in a plane crash. She had been a track star, but found that my legs simply weren't built for that. For a while she mourned the loss of her Olympic dream, but then realized that my legs could dance. She learned to tango, and one day she met a prince while dancing in Monaco, and she danced her way into his heart. They married, and now the royal couple have a grand ball every year. The highlight of the ball is her stunning tango with her prince.

With every word she writes, Miracolina is filled with deeper fury at all the possibilities stolen from her.

My heart went to a scientist on the verge of discovering a way to harness starlight and solve the world's energy needs. He was so close—but then suffered a major heart attack. Thanks to me, though, he survived and completed his life's work, making the world a better place for all of us. He even won the Nobel Prize.

Is it so strange to want to give of yourself totally and completely? If that is what's in Miracolina's heart, why should it be denied her?

And as for my mind—my memories, which are full of a loving childhood—they all went to troubled souls who had no such memories of their own. But now with that part of me in them, they are healed of the many hurts in their lives.

Miracolina turns in her paper, and the teacher, perhaps more curious about hers than anyone else's, reads it while the other kids are still writing. She watches his face, full of thoughtful expressions as he reads. She doesn't know why she should care, but she's always cared what her teachers think. Even the ones she didn't like. Then, when he's done, he comes over to her.

"Very interesting, Miracolina, but you've left out one thing."

"What?"

"Your soul," he says. "Who gets your soul?"

"My soul," she tells him with confidence, "goes to God."

"Hmm . . ." He strokes some graying whisker stubble. "So it goes to God, even if every part of your body is still alive?"

Miracolina stands firm against his questioning. "I have a right to believe that, if I want to."

"True, true. One problem with that, though. You're Catholic, isn't that right?"

"Yes."

"And you want to be unwound voluntarily."

"So?"

"Well . . . if your soul leaves this world, then voluntary unwinding is no different from assisted suicide—and in the Catholic religion, suicide is a mortal sin. Which means that by your own beliefs, you'd be going to hell."

Then he leaves her to stew with an A-minus on her essay. Minus, she assumes, due to the eternal damnation of her soul.

25 · Lev

Miracolina has no idea how deeply her obstinance affects him. Most kids here are either terrified of Lev, or worship him, or both—but Miracolina is neither intimidated nor reverent; she just hates him, plain and simple. It shouldn't bother him. He's gotten used to being hated—for just as his brother Marcus said, as much as the public mourned for poor, corrupted, little-boy-Lev, they also despise the "monster" that he has become. Well, he was innocent, and he was a monster, but here in the Cavenaugh mansion, none of that matters, because here he is one step short of being a god. There's a heady, awkward kind of fun to that, but Miracolina is the pin that pops the bubble.

His next encounter with her is the following week, at an

Easter dance. Tithes are notoriously inept when it comes to male/female interaction. Knowing that dating and all that goes with it won't be a part of their limited future, tithes and their families don't give boy/girl stuff much attention. In fact, it's downplayed, since it would create the kind of wistful longing that a tithe should not have.

"These kids are all smart as a whip," Cavenaugh exclaims at the weekly meeting of the tithe rescue staff, "but they have the social skills of six-year-olds." It's a fair description of how Lev was on his tithing day as well, and he's not all that sure he's come much further. He's still never been on a date.

There are about twenty staff members, and Lev is the only one under thirty. Each of their faces are filled with concern that's so long-lived, it seems burned into their expressions. He wonders if their passion comes from their own experiences with unwinding. Did they, like the Admiral, unwind their own child, and come to regret the decision? Was it personal for them, or did their dedication to the cause come from a general disgust with society's status quo?

"We shall have an Easter dance," Cavenaugh proclaims from the head of the meeting table, "and encourage our ex-tithes to behave like normal teenagers. Within reason, of course." Then he singles Lev out. "Lev, can we count on you, as our goodwill ambassador, to join in the festivities?"

Everyone waits for his answer. It bothers him that they're hanging on his response. "What if I say no?"

Cavenaugh looks at him incredulously. "Why on earth would you? Everyone loves a party!"

"Not really," Lev points out. "The last parties these kids had were their tithing parties. Do you really want to remind them of that?"

The others around the table mumble to one another, weighing what Lev has said, until Cavenaugh dismisses it. "Tithing parties are farewells," he says. "Ours will be about new beginnings. I'm counting on you to attend."

Lev sighs. "Sure." There is no challenging of ideas in the Cavenaugh mansion when those ideas come from the man who shares the mansion's name.

It is decided that the ballroom is in too poor shape for an adolescent gala, so they use the dining hall, clearing away the tables and chairs and setting up a DJ station beneath the portrait. With attendance mandatory, the entire population of ex-tithes is there.

As Lev expected, they gather by gender on either side of the room like it's a game of dodgeball, boys against girls. Everyone busies themselves drinking punch and eating cocktail weenies while stealing secret glances at the opposing team, as if being caught looking will get them disqualified.

One of the adults does his best impersonation of a DJ, and when encouragement doesn't work, he demands that everyone form a circle on the dance floor to do the Hokey Pokey. However, ten seconds into the dance, he suddenly realizes how ill-advised it is for ex-tithes to be putting various body parts in and out. The DJ becomes flustered and tries to skip right to the "you put your whole self in" part, but the kids are so amused by all this that they continue singing and dancing part by part even after the music has stopped. Ironically, it ends up being the perfect icebreaker, and when the dance music starts up again, there are actually kids dancing.

Lev is not one of them. He's more than satisfied to be an observer, in spite of the fact that he can have his pick of dance partners—although he suspects if he actually did ask one of these girls to dance, she might spontaneously combust on the spot.

But then from across the room he spots Miracolina leaning back against the wall with her arms resolutely crossed, and he decides that this is a challenge worth taking.

The moment she sees him approaching she looks away, a bit panicked, hoping he's headed toward someone else. Then she takes a visible breath when she realizes she is the subject of his attention.

"So," says Lev, as casually as he can, "you wanna dance?"

"Do you believe in the end of the world?" she responds.

Lev shrugs. "I don't know. Why?"

"Because the day after that is when I'll dance with you."

Lev smiles. "You're funny. I didn't think you had a sense of humor."

"I'll tell you what. If you run out of girls who worship the ground you walk on, you can ask me again. The answer will still be no, but I'll give you the courtesy of pretending to think about it."

"I read your essay," he tells her, which gets a nice head-snapping reaction out of her. "You have a dancing princess fantasy—don't deny it."

"My *legs* have a dancing princess fantasy."

"Well, to dance with your legs, I guess I'll have to put up with the rest of you."

"No, you won't," she says, "because not a single part of me will be here." Then she glances toward Lev's portrait, which is now weirdly lit by colorful strobe lights. "Why don't you dance with your portrait?" Miracolina suggests. "The two of you deserve each other." Then she storms out. The adults at the door try to stop her from going back to her room, but she gets past them anyway.

After she's gone, Lev hears the grumbling around him.

"She's such a loser," someone says.

Lev turns to the kid with a vengeance. It's Timothy, the boy who arrived with her. "I could say the same about you!" he snaps. "All of you!"

Then he shuts himself up before he goes too far. "No,

that's not true. But you shouldn't be judging her."

"Yes, Lev," says Timothy obediently. "I won't, Lev. I'm sorry, Lev."

And then a shy girl, apparently less shy than all the other shy girls, steps forward. "I'll dance with you, Lev."

So he goes out onto the dance floor and obliges her and every other girl there with a dance, while his portrait looks down on them with its irritating gaze of holy superiority.

The next day the portrait is vandalized.

Something rude is tagged in spray paint right across the middle of it. Breakfast is delayed until the portrait can be removed. There is a spray paint can missing from the storeroom, but no smoking gun as to who could have done it. Everyone has a theory, though, and most of those theories point to the same person.

"We know it was her!" the other kids try to tell Lev. "Miracolina's the only one here who has something against you!"

"How do you know she's the only one?" Lev asks them. "She's just the only one with guts enough to say it out loud."

Out of respect for Lev's wishes, the other kids don't accuse her to her face, and the adults are diplomatic enough to keep their opinions to themselves.

"Perhaps we need more surveillance cameras," Cavenaugh suggests.

"What we need," Lev tells him, "is more freedom to express opinions. Then things like this wouldn't happen."

Cavenaugh is genuinely insulted. "You talk like this is a harvest camp. Everyone's free to express themselves here."

"Well, I guess not everyone feels that way."

26 · Miracolina

After a day of being cold-shouldered by every living thing in the mansion, there's a knock on her door. She doesn't say anything, because whoever it is will just come in anyway; the bedrooms here have no locks.

The door opens slowly, and Lev steps in. There's a quickening of her heart when she sees him. She tells herself it's anger.

"If you're here to accuse me of vandalizing your portrait, I confess. I can't hide the truth anymore. I did it. Now punish me by taking away all my inspirational movies. Please."

Lev just keeps his arms limply by his side. "Stop it. I know you didn't do it."

"Oh—so you finally caught the naughty tithe?"

"Not exactly. I just know it wasn't you."

It's a bit of a relief to be vindicated, although she did take some guilty pleasure in being a prime suspect. "So what do you want?"

"I've been meaning to apologize for the way you were brought here. Tranq'd and blindfolded and all. I mean, what they're doing here is important, but I don't always agree with how they do it."

Miracolina notes that this is the first time she's heard him say "they" instead of "we."

"I've been here for weeks," she says. "Why are you telling me this now?"

Lev reaches up and flips his hair out of his eyes. "I don't know. It was just bothering me."

"Soooo . . . you're going around apologizing to every kid here?"

"No," Lev admits. "Just you."

"Why?"

He begins pacing the small room, raising his voice. "Because you're the only one who's still angry! *Why are you so angry?*"

"The only angry person in this room is you," Miracolina says, with antagonizing calm. "And there are plenty of angry kids here. Why else would your portrait get vandalized?"

"Forget about that!" shouts Lev. "We're talking about you!"

"If you don't stop yelling, I'll have to ask you to leave. In fact, I think I'll ask you to leave anyway." She points to the door. "Leave!"

"No."

So she picks up a hairbrush and throws it at him. It beans him on the head and ricochets to the wall, where it wedges behind the TV.

"Ow!" He grabs his head, grimacing. "That hurt!"

"Good, it was supposed to."

Lev clenches his fists, growls, then turns like he's going to storm out, but he doesn't. Instead he turns back to her, unclenching his fists and holding his palms out to her, pleading like maybe he's showing off his stigmata. Well, there might be blood on his hands, but it sure isn't flowing from his palms.

"So is this how it's going to be?" he asks. "You're just going to stew and bitch and make things miserable for everyone here? Don't you want something more out of life?"

"No," she tells him, "because my life ended on my thirteenth birthday. As far as I'm concerned, from that moment on I was supposed to be a part of other people's lives. I was fine with that. It's what I wanted. It's what I still want. Why do you find that so hard to believe?"

He looks at her for a moment too long, and she tries to imagine him all dressed in white as a tithe. She could like that boy; still pure and untainted. But the kid before her now is a different person.

"Sorry," she says, not sorry at all. "I guess I failed deprogramming school." She turns her back to him and waits a few moments, knowing he's just standing there, then turns again—only to find that he's not. He has left, closing the door so quietly she didn't hear.

27 · Lev

Lev sits in on yet another meeting of the tithe rescue staff. He doesn't know why they include him; Cavenaugh never listens to what he says. These meetings truly make him feel like a mascot, a favorite pet. This time, however, he's determined to make them listen.

Even before they begin, Lev speaks loudly enough to get everyone's attention, stealing the floor from Cavenaugh before he has the chance to take it. "Why is the portrait of me back in the dining hall?" he asks. "It was already vandalized once—why put it back?" The question quiets everyone down and brings the room to order.

"I ordered it restored and returned," says Cavenaugh. "The comfort and focus it provides the ex-tithes is invaluable."

"I agree!" says one of the teachers. "I think it draws their focus toward the positive." Then she punctuates her remark with a brownnosing nod toward Cavenaugh. "I, for one, like it and approve."

"Well, I don't like it, and I don't approve," Lev tells them, for the first time voicing his feelings out loud. "I shouldn't be some sort of god-thing. I shouldn't be put a pedestal. I'm not and never have been this image you're trying to make me."

There's silence around the room as everyone waits to see how Cavenaugh will react. He takes his time and finally says, "We all have our jobs here. Yours is very clear and very simple: to be an example for the other ex-tithes to follow. Have you noticed kids have been letting their hair grow? At first I thought your hair would be off-putting, but now they are modeling themselves on you. It's what they need at this juncture."

"I'm not a role model!" Lev yells. He stands up, not even realizing he's come to his feet. "I was a clapper. A terrorist! I made awful decisions!"

But Cavenaugh remains calm. "It's your *good* decisions we care about. Now sit down and let us get on with this meeting."

Lev looks around the table but sees no support. If anything, he sees them all tallying this outburst as one of his bad decisions, best forgotten. He boils with the same kind of anger that once turned him into a clapper, but he bites it back, sits down, and remains silent for the rest of the meeting.

It's only as the meeting breaks up that Cavenaugh takes his hand. Not to shake it, but to flip it over and scrutinize his fingers—or more specifically, to look under his fingernails.

"Best clean those a little better, Lev," he says. "Spray paint comes out with turpentine, I think."

28 · Risa

Risa does not have an Easter social. She can't even be sure which day is Easter—she's lost track of the days. In fact, she can't even be sure where she is. At first she's held by the Juvenile Authority in Tucson, then transferred in a windowless armored vehicle to another detention facility about two hours away—in Phoenix, she presumes. Here is where they send in interrogators to ask her questions.

"How many kids are in the Graveyard?"

"A bunch."

"Who sends your supplies?"

"George Washington. Or is it Abraham Lincoln? I forget."

"How often do you receive new arrivals?"

"About as often as you beat your wife."

The interrogators are infuriated by her lack of cooperation, but she has no intention of telling them anything useful. Besides, she knows they're asking her questions they already know the answers to. The questions are merely tests to see whether she'll tell the truth or lie. She doesn't do either. Instead she makes a mockery of each interrogation.

"Your cooperation might make things easier on you," they tell her.

"I don't want things easy," she responds. "I've had a hard life. I'd rather stick with what's familiar."

They let her go hungry but don't let her starve. They tell her they have Elvis Robert Mullard in custody and they're cutting him a deal for information—but she knows they're lying, because if they had him, they'd know it's not Mullard at all, but Connor.

This is how it goes for two weeks. Then one day in walks a Juvey-cop. He aims a gun at her and unceremoniously tranqs her—not in the leg, where it would hurt the least, but right in the chest, where it stings until she loses consciousness.

She awakes in a different cell. A little newer and larger, perhaps, but still a cell. She has no idea where she has been transported this time, or why. This new cell is not at all designed for a paraplegic, and her captors have offered no help since she arrived. Not that she'd accept it if they did, but it's as if they want her to struggle over the lip of the bathroom threshold, or onto her bed, which is abnormally high—just enough to make getting into it an ordeal.

She suffers a week of food brought in by a silent guard in a rent-a-cop uniform. She knows she's no longer in the hands of the Juvenile Authority, but who her new captors are is a mystery. These new jailers ask no questions, and that concerns her the same way that Connor is always concerned by the fact that the Graveyard has never been taken out. Are they so unimportant in the grand scheme of things that the Juvenile Authority won't even torture her to get the information they want? Have they been deluding themselves into thinking they're making a difference?

All this time she's forced out thoughts of Connor, because it simply hurt too much to think about him. How horrified he must have been when she turned herself in. Horrified and stunned. Well, fine, let him be; he'll get over it. She did it for him just as much as she did it for the injured boy, because as painful as it is to admit, Risa knows she had become just a distraction to Connor. If he's truly going to lead those kids in the Graveyard like the Admiral did, he can't be giving Risa leg massages and worrying whether her emotional needs are being met. Maybe he does love her, but it's obvious there's no room in his life at this moment to pay it any more than lip service.

Risa has no idea what her future holds now. All she knows is that she must focus on that future and not on Connor, no matter how much that hurts.

A few days later Risa finally has an actual visitor: a well-dressed woman with an air of authority.

"Good morning, Risa. It's a pleasure to finally meet the girl behind the hullabaloo. "

Risa immediately decides that anyone who uses the word "hullabaloo" cannot be her friend.

The woman sits down in the single chair in the cell. It's a chair that has never been used, because it's not exactly designed for a paraplegic. In fact, it seems specifically designed *not* to be accessible to Risa, like most everything else in her cell. "I trust they've been treating you well?"

"I haven't been 'treated' at all. I've been ignored."

"You haven't been ignored," the woman tells her. "You've just been allowed some time to settle. Some time alone, to think."

"Somehow I doubt I've ever been alone. . . ." Risa throws a glance to a large wall mirror, through which she can occasionally see shadows. "So am I some sort of political prisoner?" She asks, getting right to the point. "If you're not going to torture me, do you just plan to leave me here to rot? Or maybe you're selling me to a parts pirate. At least the parts that work."

"None of those things," says the woman. "I'm here to help you. And you, my dear, are going to help us."

"I doubt that." Risa rolls away, although she can't roll very far. The woman doesn't get up from her chair. She doesn't even move; she just sits there comfortably. Risa wanted to be in control of this situation, but this woman keeps control with her voice alone.

"My name is Roberta. I represent an organization called Proactive Citizenry. Our purpose, among other things, is to do good in this world. We seek to advance the causes of both science and freedom as well as to provide a sense of spiritual enlightenment."

"And what does that have to do with me?"

Roberta smiles and pauses a moment, holding her smile before she speaks. "I'm going to have the charges against you dropped, Risa. But more importantly, I'm going to get you out of that wheelchair and give you a new spine."

Risa turns to her, filled with more mixed emotions than she can sort right now. "No, you will not! It's my right to refuse the spine of an Unwind."

"Yes, it is," Roberta says, way too calmly. "However, I firmly believe you will change your mind."

Risa crosses her arms, her belief more firm than Roberta's that she won't.

She's given the silent treatment again—but they must be getting impatient, because it's only for two days this time instead of a week. Roberta returns and sits once more in the chair designed for people who can walk. This time she has a folder with her, although Risa can't see what's inside.

"Have you given any thought to my offer?" Roberta asks her.

"I don't need to. I already gave you my answer."

"It's very noble to stand on principle and refuse an unwound spine," Roberta says. "It does, however, represent a wrongful mind-set that is neither productive nor adaptive. It's backward, actually, and it makes you part of the problem."

"I plan to keep my 'wrongful mind-set' as well as my wheelchair."

"Very well. I won't deny you your choice." Roberta shifts in her chair—perhaps a little irritated, or maybe just in anticipation. "There's someone I'd like you to meet." Then she stands and opens the door. Risa knows that whoever it is has been waiting in the other room, watching through the one-way mirror.

"You can come in now," Roberta says cheerfully.

A boy steps in cautiously. He seems sixteen or so. He has multicolored skin and multicolored streaks in his hair. At first she assumes it's some sort of extreme body modification, but she quickly realizes it's more than that. There is something profoundly wrong about him.

"Hi," he says, and smiles tentatively with perfect teeth. "I'm Cam. I've been looking forward to meeting you, Risa."

Risa backs away, her wheelchair bumping the wall. Now it strikes her exactly what she's seeing—exactly why this boy seems so "off." She has seen a news report about this creation. Her flesh starts to crawl. If it could, it would crawl right through the air vents to escape what she's seeing.

"Get that thing away from me! It's disgusting! Get it away!"

His expression mirrors Risa's horror. He backs away and hits the wall as well.

"It's all right, Cam," Roberta says. "You know people always have to get used to you. And she will." Roberta offers him the chair, but suddenly Cam doesn't want to be there, he wants to escape just as much as Risa does.

Risa looks to Roberta so she doesn't have to look at Cam. "I said get it out of here."

"I'm not an it," Cam insists.

Risa shakes her head. "Yes, you are." She still won't look directly at him. "Now get it out of here, or I swear I will rip every stolen part out of its body with my bare hands."

She tries not to catch his gaze, but she can't stop herself. The thing has begun to cry tears from someone else's stolen tear ducts, and it just makes her angry.

"Dagger plunged deep," he says. Risa has no idea what he's talking about but doesn't really care.

"Get it out of my sight," she yells at Roberta, "and if you have any decency in you at all, you'll kill it!"

Roberta looks at her sternly, and then turns to Cam. "You can go, Cam. Wait outside for me."

Cam quickly, awkwardly, leaves, and Roberta closes the door. Now she's fuming. If Risa can take anything positive out of this, it's that she's gotten the better of Roberta.

"You're a cruel girl," Roberta says.

"And you're a monster to create a thing like that."

"History will be the judge of who we are, and what we've done." And then she puts a piece of paper down on the table. "This is a consent form. Sign it and you can have a new working spine by the end of the week."

Risa picks it up, tears it to shreds, and throws the pieces in the air. Roberta must have been expecting this, because she instantly pulls out a second consent form from her folder and slaps it down on the table.

"You *will* be healed, and you *will* make up to Cam for how badly you've treated him today."

"Not in this life, or any other."

Roberta smiles like she knows something Risa doesn't. "Well then . . . here's hoping you have a sudden change of heart." Then she exits the room, leaving the pen and the consent form on the table.

Risa looks at the consent form long after Roberta has gone. She knows she won't sign it, but the fact that they want her to intrigues her. Why is it so important to them that her broken body be repaired? There's only one answer to that: For some reason Risa is much more important than she ever dreamed she was. Important to both sides.

29 · Cam

He sits in the observation room. He's been there more often than he'd like to admit, spying on Risa—although when it's officially allowed through a one-way mirror, it's not called spying. It's called surveillance.

On the other side of the glass, Risa stares at the contract Roberta put before her. Her face is stony, her jaw clenched. Finally she picks up the page . . . then folds it into a paper airplane and throws it at the mirror. Cam jolts in spite of himself. He knows she can't see him, but still she looks into the mirror at almost the right spot to make eye contact. For a moment Cam feels like she can see not only through the glass, but through him as well, and he has to look away.

He hates the fact that she hates him. He should have expected it, but still, her words hurt him deeply and make him want to hurt her back. But no. That's just the reaction of the various Unwinds in his head; kids who would lash out at the slightest provocation. He won't give in to those impulses. There are enough sensible parts of him to balance things and allow him to control those parts that threaten to disturb the peace. He reminds himself that, as Roberta has said, he is the new paradigm—the new model of what humanity could, and should, be. The world will get used to him, and in time revere him. And so will Risa.

Roberta comes into the room behind him and speaks quietly. "There's no point staying here."

"Jericho," he says. "She's a wall, but she'll crumble. I know she will."

Roberta smiles at him. "I have no doubt that you'll win her over. In fact, I suspect she'll change her mind sooner than you think."

Cam tries to read between the lines of her smile, but she reveals nothing. "Cat that ate the canary—I don't like when you keep secrets."

"No secret," Roberta tells him. "Just an undying faith in human nature. Now come, it's almost time for your photo shoot."

Cam sighs. "Another one?"

"Would you prefer a press conference?"

"A sharp stick in the eye? No thank you!"

Cam has to admit that this new approach to the media is far better than press conferences and interviews. Roberta and her friends at Proactive Citizenry have cooked up a first-class advertising campaign. Billboards, print ads, digital, the works. All just photos, but even so, the ads are powerful.

The first round of ads will feature extreme close-ups of various parts of him. An eye; streaks of his multicolored hair; the starburst of flesh tones on his forehead. Each image will be accompanied by a pithy but enigmatic caption like, "The Time Has Come," or "The Brilliant Tomorrow," with no other clue as to what's being advertised. Then, when public curiosity is piqued, they move to phase two, where the ads will feature his face, his body, and finally his whole self.

"We'll create a mystique around you," Roberta told him. "Play into their puerile fascination with the exotic until they're champing at the bit to see more."

"Striptease," Cam had said.

"An elevated version of the same concept, I suppose," Roberta admitted. "Once the ad campaign has rolled out, you will enter the public eye not as an oddity, but as a celebrity— and when you finally deign to do interviews, it will be on our terms."

"My terms," Cam corrected.

"Yes, of course. Your terms."

Now, as Cam watches Risa through the one-way glass, he wonders what could possibly make her live by his terms too. Roberta has told him that he can have anything he desires, but what if the thing he desires most is Risa choosing to be with him of her own free will?

"Cam, please—come now, or we'll be late."

Cam stands, but before he leaves, he spares one last glance through the mirror at Risa, who has struggled onto her bed. Now she lies stretched out on her back, looking morosely at the ceiling. Then she closes her eyes.

The eternally sleeping princess, thinks Cam. *But I shall free you from those poisoned brambles that surround your heart. And then you will have no choice but to love me.*

30 · Nelson

The Juvey-cop turned parts pirate makes a side trip to check one of his most successful traps. It is, however, in an unfortunate location. Unfortunate because it's in a field that floods during storms. Nothing's more irritating than a drowned AWOL. Except maybe disposing of one. He would rather continue searching for safe houses, with hopes of finding Connor Lassiter in one of them, but with major storms projected throughout the Midwest, checking this particular trap is worth the effort.

The trap is a piece of drainage pipe—a concrete cylinder five feet high and twenty feet long, lying in a fallow field that no one has farmed for years. Half a dozen such pipes rest in the field, surrounded by weeds—all abandoned when some public works project got canceled. It's a nice hiding spot for runaway Unwinds—and in fact, one of the tunnel segments has a store of canned food right in the middle. The inside surface of that same cylinder, however, is painted with super-adhesive resin that sticks to clothes and flesh with such tenacity that anyone caught in the pipe might as well be nailed to the concrete. It tickles Nelson that he can catch Unwinds the way other people catch roaches.

Sure enough, there's a kid stuck in the pipe. "Help me!" the boy shouts, kind of like the Fly caught in the spiderweb. "Help me, please!" The kid is scrawny and acne-ridden, with crooked teeth yellowed from chewing tobacco or just bad genetics. Either way, he's not a prime specimen and won't fetch much on the black market. His hair is plastered with glue, although Nelson suspects it doesn't look much better clean.

"My God! What happened to you?" Nelson says, feigning concern.

"It's like glue or somethin'! I can't get out!"

"Okay," Nelson says, "I think I can get you out of there. I have some adhesive remover in the van." Actually he already has it with him. He pretends to jog away and jog back, then soaks a foul-smelling rag with the fluid, climbs into the tunnel, and begins dabbing the kid's clothes and skin. Bit by bit the boy comes free from the adhesive.

"Thanks, mister," says the kid. "Thanks a lot!" Nelson climbs out and waits at the mouth of the tunnel as the gooey, glue-covered kid slides himself out, just as nasty as a baby being born. Then, as he comes into the light of day, something finally occurs to this dim bulb. "Hey, wait a second . . . why would someone have that there adhesive remover stuff unless—"

Nelson doesn't give him the chance to finish his thought. He grabs the boy, wrenches his arms behind his back, and tugs a plastic cable tie around his wrists. Then Nelson pushes him to the ground and pricks him with the DNA reader.

"William Yotts," Nelson announces, and the kid groans. "AWOL for four days. Not too good at hiding, are ya?"

"You ain't takin' me in," Yotts screams. "You ain't takin' me in!"

"You're right, I'm not," Nelson tells him. "You're not going 'in,' you're going 'up.' As in 'up' on the black market auction block. Ka-ching!"

The kid seems to go both pale and red in the face at the same time, making him all blotchy. Nelson surprises him with a hypodermic. Not tranqs, though. "Antibiotics," he tells the boy. "Clean out whatever diseases crawled into your system while you were in that pipe. Even the ones that were there before. Most of them, anyway."

"Please, mister, you don't gotta do this. Please . . ."

Nelson kneels down and takes a good look at him.

"I'll tell you what," he says. "I like your eyes, so I'll make you a deal."

He cuts the cable tie, and offers the same deal he always offers. A countdown. A chance to run. These AWOLs never realize that the game is rigged. It never occurs to them that Nelson can count as fast as he chooses, and they don't know that he's a very, very good shot.

This boy, like all the others, thinks he'll be the one to escape. He takes off, tripping in the field and picking himself up while Nelson counts. He nears the road as Nelson gets to "eight" and raises his gun. "Nine." He has a clear target—the clothing logo on the kid's back. "Ten!" Then Nelson lowers the gun and doesn't fire. Instead he watches as the kid races across the road, nearly getting hit by a car—but the car swerves around him. The kid then disappears into the woods.

Nelson applauds his own restraint. It would have been so easy to take the kid down. But he has other plans for this AWOL. The injection he gave the kid wasn't an antibiotic at all, but a delivery system for a microscopic tracking chip. The kind they used to monitor the populations of endangered species. This is the fourth AWOL Nelson has tagged and released into the wild since his new mission began. With any luck they'll get picked up by the resistance and give him a clear path to the AWOL sanctuary where Connor Lassiter is holed up. But in the meantime, there are plenty of local leads to follow up on. Nelson smiles. It's good to have a goal. Something joyful to look forward to.

31 · Miracolina

Miracolina endures her captivity and deprogramming at the hands of the Anti-Divisional Resistance for weeks but never surrenders her core. She never gives in to the things they try to teach her. Oh, she's learned to function within their little world of ex-tithes, doing what's expected, if only so they'll leave her alone. More tithes are brought in, others are placed with families and given new identities. There's no such plan for Miracolina. Even semi-cooperative, she's still too much of a risk. They have no idea, however, what she's really planning.

Miracolina considers herself up for any challenge. While she is a tithe, she has not lived the same sheltered life as most other tithes, and although she's not a girl from the hard streets, she considers herself street-smart and world savvy. Escaping from the velvet-gloved fist of the resistance will be a challenge, but not an insurmountable one.

Early on Lev personally warned her of the futility of an escape attempt. "There are sharpshooters with tranq rifles everywhere," he said, making it sound hopeless. Yet every bit of information helps her, because Lev let it slip that although there's a fence, it isn't electrified. Good to know.

She explores every corner of the huge mansion to which she has access, paying special attention to the many unused, dilapidated rooms and corridors too far gone to be restored. Most of the windows are boarded over, and all the doors to the outside are locked. But the more forgotten an area is, the less reliable those locks will be—and a padlock hasp is only as good as the wood it's screwed into. Such as the lock on the garden door, which has an unpleasant termite infestation. Once she finds the door, she files the information away for future reference.

The ex-tithes' meals are usually served on chipped china that must have been part of the Cavenaugh collection in better days, but on Sundays, the finest stuff is brought out, including silver platters just large enough to fit beneath her shirt, like armor. Again, she files the information away for future reference.

Now all she needs is a diversion—not just inside the mansion, but outside as well. Unfortunately, that's not something she can create, so she bides her time, confident that an opportunity will present itself. An opportunity such as a tornado watch on a Sunday night.

The wind is already picking up at dinnertime. Talk of the coming storm rumbles throughout the crowd of kids. Some are scared, some are excited. Lev is notably absent. Maybe he's left to avoid the storm, whisked away by his protectors to a place of greater safety. When the meal is over, Miracolina clears her plate, taking with her a couple of silver serving platters, presumably to bring to the kitchen.

"You don't have to do that, Miracolina," says one of her teachers.

"It's okay, I don't mind," she says with a smile, and the teacher smiles back, glad to see her finally settling in.

The storm hits like spring storms do, a warning wind, then a deluge like heaven itself has ruptured. Rain pours through holes in the roof into the areas that have yet to be repaired. The ballroom, where Miracolina was first greeted by Lev, is at least an inch deep with water. Pans set up beneath leaks in bedrooms fill and must be dumped. It's like bailing out a sinking ship. The Weather Channel shows a grid of Michigan counties blinking angry red with tornado alerts.

"Don't worry," says one of the teachers, "there's a storm cellar if they call a tornado alert in our area." Which they do, at exactly 8:43.

Immediately the staff begins rounding up the kids. With lightning striking and agitated kids, it's hard to keep track of everyone. That's when Miracolina slips away with several serving platters and disappears down a side passage, hurrying toward the termite-ridden door.

Standing in front of the door, she shoves the larger platters under her shirt, both front and back. They're cold and uncomfortable but very necessary. She slips two smaller platters down the back of her sweatpants, turning them into protectors for her rear. She waits for a powerful burst of lightning to fill the sky in uneven, strobing flashes, and the moment the thunder rolls in a few seconds later, she smashes the door with her shoulder. It gives on the second attempt, while the thunder is still rolling, hiding the sound of the door as it bursts open.

There is still the remains of a path left in the middle of the ruined garden. She races down the path, immediately drenched and almost blinded by rain. Then she races from the garden into the weedy clearing that leads to the woods, in clear view of any sharpshooter, and she wonders if infrared lenses can see through sheets of rain. She knows metal is a conductor of electricity, and in the back of her mind she fears that the lightning might seek her out—but she has to believe that won't happen. She has to believe that God has brought this storm for her, so she can escape—so she can do what she was meant to do. And if she does get struck by lightning, well, that would be a sign from above too, wouldn't it? So she says a silent prayer.

"Lord, if what I'm doing is wrong, then by all means strike me down. Otherwise set me free."

32 · Lev

A lightning strike is provided. Not one to strike Miracolina down, but to illuminate her for all to see. Or at least for anyone who happens to be looking.

Most everyone is already in, or en route to the storm cellar, which may or may not stand the force of a tornado, considering how old it is. Lev, however, who has always loved storms, and actually has a window in his room to view it, is slow to leave.

He stalls, taking a few moments to watch the raw violence of nature. A gust of wind rattles the old windows almost enough to break them, and a particularly long flash of lightning hits. In that flash he sees someone running across the grass and into the woods. It's only a brief glimpse, but it's enough for him to know exactly who it is, even if he can't see her face.

33 · Miracolina

She doesn't hear the first rifle fire, but she feels the tranq dart as it hits the silver platter strapped to her back, its barbed tip caught in the fabric of her sweatshirt. She doesn't know where the shooter is, except that he's behind her. She was hoping that the sharpshooters had left their stations to shelter from the storm, but at least one, maybe more, are still on the lookout—perhaps knowing that a storm like this is a clear flight opportunity for any kids not yet deprogrammed.

Another dart whizzes past her, inches away, and from a different direction. There is more than one shooter still in place. She knows they're going after her body because they wouldn't risk a shot to the head, so she pulls in her arms, making herself a smaller target. Another dart hits one of the smaller platters covering her rear. She almost didn't put those there because they hampered her ability to run. Now she's glad she did. This time the dart doesn't stick, it just bounces free.

In a moment she's in the woods with the trees whipping around her. If there are any sharpshooters here in the woods, she would be really surprised. More than likely the shots came from the mansion itself. She doubts even the most dedicated snipers would hold their positions in the woods in the middle of a tornado threat. She has no idea in what direction she's running, but any direction is the right one if it's away from the mansion. She knows that eventually she'll come to a fence. She can only hope that it's not too high to climb.

The only view ahead of her comes from freeze-frame glimpses in flashes of lightning. Her clothes are torn and her face scratched by whipping branches. She stumbles into mud but picks herself up and continues. Then, in a flash of light, she sees a chain-link fence up ahead. It's about eight feet high—not too hard to climb, but there's barbed wire across the top. More scrapes, more cuts, but she'll deal with that. She's sure any injuries will heal before she's unwound.

Out of breath and near the end of her stamina, she hurls herself at the fence, but just before she reaches it, she's hit by someone even faster than she is, who takes her down, tackling her to the wet ground. She catches only a glimpse of his face, but it's enough to know who it is. The golden child himself has come to capture her.

"Get off me!" she says, pushing Lev, scratching at him. She tears the platter from her chest and swings it. It connects with his head with a heavy bang. He falls, but he's right back up again.

"I swear I will take your head off with this if I have to!" she says. "Let me go. I don't care if they worship you, I don't care if you're their patron saint. I'm leaving, and you can't stop me!"

Then Lev backs off, breathing heavily, and says, "Take me with you."

It's not what she expected to hear.

"What?"

"I can't be a part of this anymore. I can't be what they want me to be. I'm no one's patron saint, and they can rescue tithes fine without me. So I'm getting out too."

Miracolina doesn't have the time to figure out whether this is a trick. She doesn't even have the time to process what he's saying, but if he's telling the truth, she can test his resolve.

"Give me a boost up the fence."

He does it without hesitation. He helps her up, and she scratches herself on the barbed wire coming down the other side, but at least she's on the other side! Then Lev, the boy who she saw as her jailer, climbs over and joins her.

"There's a road," he says, "maybe a hundred yards or so through the woods. We can flag down a ride."

"Who would be driving on a night like tonight?"

"There's always someone desperate to go somewhere."

The wind dies down a bit by the time they reach the road, but in tornado weather that could be a good sign or bad. They haven't seen hail yet, and hail's a sure sign that something worse is on the way.

Sure enough, there's traffic on the two-lane road—not much, just a car every minute or two, but all they need is one.

"They won't know we're gone until after the storm passes," Lev says. "If someone picks us up, promise me you won't tell them about the mansion and what we're doing there."

"I won't promise anything," Miracolina tells him.

"Please," Lev begs her. "The other kids there aren't like you. They don't want to be tithed. Don't condemn them to something that was never their choice."

Although it goes against her instincts, right now the line between right and wrong is blurry enough for her to say, "Fine. I won't tell."

"We'll make up a story," Lev says. "We were out biking and got caught in the storm. Just go along with anything I say. Then when we're dropped off, if you really want to be tithed, go turn yourself in. I won't stop you."

And although she doubts he'll make it that easy, she agrees.

"What about you? Where will you go?"

"I have no idea," he tells her, and there is such a spark in his eye when he says it, she can tell having no idea is exactly the way he wants it.

Headlights approach, and the wind picks up again. They wave their arms and the vehicle, a van, pulls over to the side of the road. A window rolls down, and they hurry to the van.

"My God. What are you two doing out here in this?" says the driver.

"We were on our bikes—we didn't know a storm was coming," Lev says.

"Where are the bikes?"

"We left them way back," Miracolina chimes in.

"We'll come get them after the storm," Lev says. "There's a tornado watch—we just need to get out of here. Can you help us?"

"Of course I can." He unlocks the car, and Lev pulls open the side door. As he does, the dome light comes on, illuminating the man's face for the first time. Although the moment calls, quite literally, for any port in a storm, Miracolina can't help but be a bit troubled by the man's face as she gets in. There's something odd about it. Or maybe it's just his eyes.

34 · Lev

Lev doesn't pay much attention to the driver. He's just glad to be out of the storm and to have transportation away from his gilded cage. He has lied to Miracolina. He has no intention of letting her turn herself in to the Juvenile Authority. He knows he might not be able to stop her, but that doesn't mean he can't try.

A gust of wind almost pushes the van off the road as they drive, and the driver fights it with both hands on the wheel. "Some storm, huh?" The man says as he glances at Lev in the rearview mirror. Lev averts his gaze. The last thing he wants is to be recognized as "that clapper kid."

"Comfy back there?" the man asks. He hasn't asked them

where they're headed yet. Lev runs though his mind the names of towns he knows in the area for when the question is inevitably asked.

Outside the rain slices at the windshield at such a violent angle, the wipers are defeated, and they have to pull over. The man turns to them.

"Tornado watch, you say? Do you suppose we'll be taken to Oz?" He seems far too jovial under the circumstances.

"The sooner we all get home the better," Miracolina offers.

"Yes, but you're not headed home," he says, the same happy tone to his voice. "We all know that, don't we?"

Miracolina throws Lev a worried glance. The man has locked his gaze on Lev, and only now does Lev see how very mismatched his eyes are. The sight gives him a chill that has nothing to do with the storm.

"I know you don't remember me, Mr. Calder, because you were unconscious at our last encounter. But I certainly remember you."

Lev reaches for the van door, but it's locked, with no visible way to unlock it.

"Lev!" shouts Miracolina, and when he looks back, he sees the man has pulled out a tranq pistol, which looks extremely large and nasty in such close quarters. Heavy hail begins to pummel the van, and the man must shout to be heard over it.

"The first time I shot you, it was an accident," he says. "This time it's not." Then he tranqs both of them before they can say a word. Lev catches sight of Miracolina's eyes rolling back and her slumping in the seat before he begins to drown in his own tranquilizer cocktail, spinning down, down, down, while outside the sound of hail gives way to a roar like a freight train barreling through hell.

35 · Nelson

In a flash of lightning, he sees a glimpse of the tornado. It tears out trees from the side of the road not a hundred yards ahead of him. It tears up the road itself—chunks of asphalt flying into the sky. Something—a piece of road or a tree limb—puts a dent in the roof like the angry stomp of a giant. A side window shatters, and the van is dragged sideways from the shoulder and into the middle of the road.

Nelson feels no fear, only awe. The van begins to lean to the left. He feels the entire vehicle straining in a tug-of-war between the wind and gravity. Finally gravity wins, and the car remains a heavy, earthbound object instead of a two-ton airborne projectile. Then in a moment the tornado is gone, tearing a jagged line toward someone else's misery. The roar fades, and it's just a torrential downpour once more.

This, Nelson knows, is his second great defining moment. The first was the tranq bullet that stole his life. But now his life has been spared. Not just spared, but validated, all in the same moment. The capture of Lev Calder is no accident. Nelson has never believed in divine providence, but he is open to the idea of balance, that there is somehow justice in the grand scheme of things. If that's true, then justice will be visiting him very soon, delivering Connor Lassiter into his waiting hands.

Part Five

Matters of Necessity

From the *Independent*, a UK news journal:

"HOODIES, LOUTS, SCUM":
HOW MEDIA DEMONISES TEENAGERS

By Richard Garner, Education Editor, Friday, 13 March 2009

The portrayal of teenage boys as "yobs" in the media has made the boys wary of other teenagers, according to new research.

Figures show more than half of the stories about teenage boys in national and regional newspapers in the past year (4,374 out of 8,629) were about crime. The word most commonly used to describe them was "yobs" (591 times), followed by "thugs" (254 times), "sick" (119 times) and "feral" (96 times). Other terms often used included "hoodie," "louts," "heartless," "evil," "frightening," "scum," "monsters," "inhuman" and "threatening."

The research—commissioned by Women in Journalism—showed the best chance a teenager had of receiving sympathetic coverage was if they died.

"We found some news coverage where teen boys were described in glowing terms—'model student,' 'angel,' 'altar boy' or 'every mother's perfect son,'" the research concluded, "but sadly these were reserved for teenage boys who met a violent and untimely death."

The full article can be found at:

http://www.independent.co.uk/news/uk/home-news/hoodies-louts-scum-how-media-demonises-teenagers-1643964.html

36 · Connor

Connor takes out his aggression on the punching bag at least twice a day. He has to. If he doesn't, he might take it out on someone's face. The lazy kid who won't clean the latrines. The moronic girl who smuggled in a cell phone so she could call her friends and tell them where she is. And the kid who makes jokes after every clapper bombing. Connor hits the bag so hard, and so much, it's a wonder the thing doesn't burst.

Risa is gone.

It's been almost a month now. For all he knows she's dead at the hands of the Juvenile Authority, or Proactive Citizenry, or whoever has their clutches on her. It doesn't matter that she's seventeen and disabled—unable to be unwound. The all-seeing government can be very nearsighted when it comes to scrutinizing the actions of its own appendages.

Connor is not the same as he was.

He feels his old patterns and habits returning. The same ones that earned him an Unwind Order to begin with. He thinks back to the days before he was AWOL—when he was just a problem kid. He's back in that place again, only now he's a problem kid responsible for hundreds of other problem kids. He can't help but think that it's not all him. His anger always seems to settle in Roland's hand.

"If you want out, no one would blame you," Starkey tells him over a game of pool one evening. "You should go and try to find Risa. There are others who could take over this place. Trace could do it. Even Ashley or Hayden." He leaves himself out, far too conspicuously. "Maybe we could put it to a vote, once you're gone. Make the whole thing democratic."

"And you're already guaranteed at least a quarter of the vote, aren't you?" says Connor, charging through the bush Starkey keeps beating around.

Starkey doesn't break his gaze, nor does he deny it. "I could run this place if I had to." Then he sinks the eight ball too soon and loses the game. "Damn, you win again."

Connor takes a good look at Starkey, who from the beginning always appeared straightforward and honest. But then, so did Trace. Only now does Connor begin to suspect that Starkey's motives might be more like designs.

"You're good at getting food on the table, and you gave the storks some self-respect," Connor tells Starkey, "but don't think that makes you God's gift to Unwinds."

"No," says Starkey. "I guess that spot's reserved for you." Then he puts down his cue stick and leaves.

Connor mentally smacks himself for being so paranoid. The truth is, he might actually want to groom Starkey to replace him someday—but who is he to be grooming anybody for anything?

Used to be he could share his private insecurities with Risa. She was good at shoring him up by putting Band-Aids on his questionable sense of character long enough for him to heal and get the job done. He could try to confide in Hayden, but Hayden makes a joke out of everything. Connor knows it's a defense mechanism, but still it makes it hard to talk to him about some things. Now his only real confidant is Trace. Connor hates that Trace remains his closest ally, even after revealing himself as a traitor to both sides. But if Risa was a Band-Aid, then Trace is alcohol on an open wound.

"We've all lost people one way or another, and Risa is no different, so stop your bellyaching and do your job."

"I'm not a boeuf," Connor tells him. "I wasn't trained to have no feelings."

"It's not that we don't have feelings, we just know how to harness them and direct them toward specific goals."

Which Connor might be able to do if he had a goal, but life at the Graveyard feels more and more directionless. A treadmill that hurls kids off when they turn seventeen.

Someone—Connor suspects it's Hayden—alerts the Admiral that he's not taking Risa's capture well, so the Admiral pays a surprise visit.

He arrives at the Graveyard in a black limo waxed to such a smooth sheen it doesn't collect the dust it kicks up. Connor barely recognizes him when he steps out. The Admiral's thin. Not just thin but gaunt. His skin, once bronzed from his years in the Graveyard sun, has gotten pale, and he's dressed not in his medal-covered uniform, but in slacks and a plaid shirt, like he's out for a round of golf. He still stands tall, though, and has the unmistakable bearing of a commanding officer.

Connor expects the Admiral will tear him a new one, giving him a reprimand more severe than he himself gave Starkey—but as always, the Admiral's strategy cannot be predicted.

"You've put on some muscle since I last saw you," the Admiral tells him. "I hope to God you're not shooting up those damn military steroids they have the boeufs on; they shrink your testicles down to peanuts."

"No sir."

"Good. Because your genes might actually be worth passing on."

He invites Connor to join him in his plush, air-conditioned limo, and they sit idling on the runway like the thing could sprout wings and take off at any given moment.

They make small talk just a bit. The Admiral tells him of the Great Harlan Reunion: a huge party with all the people who had received his son's parts.

"I'll swear till the day I die that Harlan was there, alive

in that garden, and no one can prove he wasn't."

He tells Connor how, when all the "parts" went their separate ways, Emby, his asthmatic friend, had nowhere to go, so the Admiral kept him on and is now raising him like a grandson.

"Not the shiniest Easter egg on the lawn," the Admiral says, "but he's very sincere."

He also tells Connor that due to his damaged heart, the Admiral was given six months to live.

"Of course, that was almost a year ago. Doctors are mostly imbeciles."

Connor suspects that the Admiral will be alive and kicking for years to come.

Finally he gets down to the real reason for his visit. "I hear that this thing with Risa is getting to you," the Admiral says, then holds his silence, knowing Connor will eventually feel compelled to break it, which he does.

"What do you want me to do? Just go on like it never happened? Like she never existed?"

The Admiral holds a steady demeanor, in spite of Connor's frustration. "I hadn't pegged you as the kind of young man who wastes his time feeling sorry for himself."

"I'm not feeling sorry! I'm angry!"

"Anger is only our friend when we know its caliber and how to aim it."

That makes Connor give out a sudden guffaw that's loud enough for the driver to glance back. "Good one! Someone oughta quote you."

"Someone did. It's on page ninety-three of the *Military Academy Freshman Ordinance Manual*, fifth edition." The Admiral turns to look out of the tinted windows at the activity of the Graveyard. "The problem with all you AWOLs is that you use your anger like a grenade, half the time blowing off your own hands." Then he looks at Connor's arm. "No offense."

"None taken."

But now that the Admiral's attention has been drawn to the arm, he looks at it more closely. "Do I know that tattoo?" Then he snaps his fingers. "Roland. Wasn't that his name? A real pain in the ass."

"That's the one."

The admiral ponders the shark a moment more. "I don't suppose it was your choice to get his arm."

"It wasn't my choice to get any unwound arm," Connor tells him. "If I had a choice, I would have refused it, the same way you refused an unwound heart. The same way Risa refused a new spine." Connor feels goose bumps rise on the arm from the near-arctic chill of the air conditioner. "But now I've got it, and it's not like I'm gonna hack it off."

"And well you should keep it!" the Admiral says. "Roland may have been a miscreant, but he was a human miscreant, and deserved better. I'm sure he'd be satisfied to know that his arm is ruling the Graveyard with an iron fist."

Connor has to laugh. Leave it to the Admiral to make sense of the senseless. Then the man gets quiet. Serious. "Listen here," he says. "This business about Risa—for everyone's sake, you've got to let it go."

But there are some things Connor just can't let go. "I should never have let her make that trip to the hospital."

"If she hadn't, from what I understand an innocent boy would have been unwound."

"So? Let him be unwound!"

The Admiral quietly bristles. "I'm going to forget you said that."

Connor sighs. "You should never have put me in charge. You wanted the Akron AWOL running this place, but he doesn't exist. He never did. He's just a legend."

"I stand behind my decision. You see yourself as failing—but that's not what I see. Sure, when you're in the midst of your own suffering, it's easy to convince yourself that you're no good—but we are all tested in this life, Connor. The measure of a man is not how much he suffers in the test, but how he comes out at the end."

Connor lets his words sink in, wondering when this particular "test" will be over and how many undiscovered layers it might still have. It makes him think about all the things Trace has told him.

"Admiral, have you heard of something called Proactive Citizenry?"

The Admiral thinks about it. "Sounds somewhat familiar. Don't they fund some of those blasted pro-unwinding advertisements?" He shakes his head in disgust. "They remind me of the old 'terror generation' ads."

That catches Connor like a barbed hook. "Terror generation?"

"You know—the Teen Uprisings? The Feral Flash riots?"

"I'm drawing a total blank."

The Admiral looks at him like he's an idiot. "Good God—don't they teach you anything in those poor excuses for schools anymore?" Then he calms down, but only a little. "No, I suppose they wouldn't. History is written by the victors—and when there are no victors, it all winds up in corporate shredders." He looks out the window with the sad resignation of a man who knows he's too old to change the world.

"You must educate yourself, Mr. Lassiter," he says. "They may not teach it, but they can't blot it out entirely. It's the very reason why people were so willing to accept the Unwind Accord. The very reason for our twisted way of life."

"Sorry to be so ignorant," Connor says.

"Don't be sorry. Just do something about it. And if you're

curious about this Proactive Citizenry, educate yourself on that, too. What is it you've heard about them?"

Connor considers telling him everything he learned from Trace but realizes it couldn't be good for the man's heart. The Admiral is retired, and while he can be called on to give Connor a swift and necessary boot, it would be wrong of Connor to involve him in things now.

"Nothing," Connor tells him. "Rumors."

"Then leave it to those who have nothing better to do than gossip," the Admiral tells him. "Now man up, get the hell out of my limo, and save these kids' lives."

Once the Admiral is gone, Trace respectfully requests a private meeting with Connor. In spite of his admission that he's working for the Juvies and Proactive Citizenry, he still treats Connor with the full respect of a commanding officer. Connor doesn't know what to make of this. He can't tell whether it's a scam or if Trace is being sincere. Although Connor can't stomach being a pawn for the Juvies by maintaining their vault of Unwinds, he can't deny that receiving privileged information from Trace makes him feel that he's the one pulling the wool over the eyes of the Juvenile Authority, and not the other way around. The truth hasn't set Connor free, as Trace has suggested, but at least it has given him a sense of power over his captors.

They ride down one of the eastern aisles, past rows of fighter jets so dusty the cockpit windows don't even look like glass. They're far enough away from any activity in the Graveyard that their meeting is very private.

"You need to know that things are brewing," Trace tells him.

"What kinds of things?"

"From what intelligence I've been able to gather, there's dissent in the Juvenile Authority. There are some who want to take this place out—they just need a reason."

"If they want to take us out, the fact that we're here is reason enough."

"I said *some* want to take us out. The suits I work for don't— and as long as everything stays smooth here, they can keep the Juvies muzzled. I've been a good little stool pigeon and continue to tell them that Elvis Robert Mullard is running a tight ship."

Connor laughs. "They still have no clue that Elvis has left the building?"

"None whatsoever—and I've given them no reason to doubt my word." Trace pauses for a moment. "Did you tell the Admiral about me?"

"No," Connor tells him. "I haven't told anyone."

"Good. A leader should know things no one else does, and spoon out information on a need-to-know basis."

"Spare me the military classroom," Connor tells him. "So is that all you wanted to talk about?"

"There's more."

They reach the end of the aisle, and Trace stops before turning into the next one. He pulls out a slip of paper from his pocket and hands it to Connor. There's a name on it, scrawled by hand. *Janson Rheinschild.*

"Is this someone I'm supposed to know?" Connor asks.

"No. He's someone nobody's supposed to know."

Connor has little patience for this. "Don't waste my time with riddles."

"That's the point," Trace says. "He *is* a riddle." He puts the Jeep in gear, and they turn down the next aisle.

"Do you remember the other week when I went up to Phoenix to get components for the Dreamliner's electrical system?"

"You didn't go to Phoenix," Connor says. "You went to meet with your bosses at Proactive Citizenry. Don't you think I know that?"

Trace seems a bit surprised, then a bit pleased. "I didn't

tell you because I didn't know whether you trusted me."

"I don't."

"Fair enough. Anyway, it was different this time. They didn't just meet with me, they flew me out to their main head-quarters in Chicago. They had me give a full report to a packed conference room. Of course I left out some key things, like our escape plan. I told them the Dreamliner is a new dormitory jet, and that the cockpit was dismantled and sold."

"Oh, so it's not just me that you lie to?"

"They're not lies. It's disinformation," Trace says. "After the meeting, I did some snooping. There was a marble wall in the lobby commemorating former presidents of the organization—some names you'd probably recognize—giants of business both before and after the war . . . but there was one name missing. It had been gouged right out of the marble, with no attempt to patch it up. And then again, out in the garden there was a sculp-ture of the founders. Five of them, but clearly the pedestal was built for six. There were still rust stains from where that sixth statue had once been."

"Janson what's-his-face?"

"Rheinschild."

Connor tries to work it out but can't. "It doesn't make sense. If they wanted to disappear him, why not patch the marble? Why not get a smaller pedestal?"

"Because," says Trace. "They didn't just want to disappear him . . . they wanted to make sure their members never forgot that they disappeared him."

Connor gets a chill in spite of the desert heat. "So what does all this have to do with us?"

"Before they flew me back, a couple of the friendlier suits took me to their private club—a place that served the kind of alcohol you can't even get on the black market. Real Russian vodka. Tequila from before the agave extinction. Stuff that must cost thousands of dollars a shot, and they were guzzling it like water. When they were fairly wasted, I asked about the missing statue. One of them blurted out the name Janson Rheinschild, then became worried that he had said it. After that, they changed the subject, and I thought it was over. . . ." Then Trace stops the Jeep so he can look Connor dead in the eye as he speaks. "But then, as I was leaving, one of them said something to me that I still haven't been able to get out of my mind. He clapped me on the shoulder, called me his 'friend,' and told me that unwinding is more than just a medical process, it's at the very core of our way of life. 'Proactive Citizenry is dedicated to protecting that way of life,' he said, 'and if you know what's good for you, you'll forget you ever heard his name.'"

37 · Risa

PUBLIC SERVICE ANNOUNCEMENT

"I was a ward of the state about to be unwound, so I went AWOL. That means I shouldn't be here right now. You might think I'm lucky . . . but because I stayed whole, fourteen-year-old Morena Sandoval, an honor student with a bright future, died because she was denied the liver I would have provided. Jerrin Stein, a father of three, died of a fatal heart attack because my heart wasn't available when he desperately needed it. And firefighter Davis Macy lost his life to pulmonary asphyxiation because my lungs weren't there to replace his burned ones.

"I'm alive today because I ran from unwinding, and my selfishness cost these, and many others, their lives. My name is Risa Ward, AWOL Unwind, and now I must live knowing how many innocent people I've killed."

—Sponsored by Citizens for AWOL Justice

38 · Hayden

Hayden stares at the computer screen, trying to believe Risa's "public service announcement" is some kind of sick joke, but he knows it's not. He wants to be furious at Tad, the busy little net-raker who brought it to his attention, but he knows it's not the kid's fault.

"What do we do now?" Tad asks.

Hayden looks around the ComBom. The eight kids on communications duty all look at him as if he can make the video go away.

"She's a goddamn traitor!" Esme shouts.

"Shut up!" Hayden yells. "Just shut up, let me think." He tries to come up with alternate explanations. Maybe it's not real—just a digital image. Maybe it's a trick designed to demoralize them . . . but the truth screams louder than any conjecture. Risa is publicly speaking in favor of unwinding. She's gone to the other side.

"Connor can't know about this," Hayden says.

Tad shakes his head doubtfully. "But it's been on TV, and trending over the net since this morning. It's not just one, either. She made a whole bunch of public service announcements— and there's an interview, too."

Hayden paces the cramped space of the plane, trying to pull together a coherent thought. "Okay," he says, forcing himself to calm down. "Okay . . . All the computers with web access are here in the ComBom and the library, right? And the Rec Jet TVs all get their feed directly from here."

"Yeah . . ."

"So, can we route everything through facial recognition software before it goes out and scramble it every time she turns up? Do we have a program that can do that?"

No one answers for a few seconds; then Jeevan speaks up. "We have tons of old military security programs, there's got to be facial recognition stuff in there. I'll bet I can patch something together."

"Do it, Jeeves." Then he turns to Tad. "Cut the feeds to the Rec Jet and library until it's done. No incoming broadcasts or web connections at all. We'll tell everyone the satellite is out, or an armadillo mated with the dish, or whatever. Got it?" Agreement all around. "And if any one of you breathes a word of this to anyone, I will personally make sure you spend the next few years of your life shoveling crap out of the latrines. The Risa-bomb stays in the ComBom, *comprende*?"

Again total agreement—but Tad isn't quite ready to let it go. "Hayden, there was something about it I don't know if you noticed. Did you see how she—"

"No, I didn't!" says Hayden, shutting him down. "I didn't see a thing. And neither did you."

39 · Connor

The man with Proactive Citizenry said that unwinding was at the core of the country's way of life.

It sticks in Connor's gut just as it did in Trace's. Connor knows that things haven't always been the way they are now—but when the world's been one way for your entire life, it's hard to imagine it being any different. Years ago, before he was even of unwinding age, Connor got bronchitis, and it just kept coming back. There was actually talk about getting him new lungs, but the problem cleared up. He remembers feeling so sick for so long, after a while he had forgotten what being well even felt like.

Could it be that way for an entire society?

Does a sick society get so used to its illness that it can't remember being well? What if the memory is too dangerous for the people who like things the way they are?

Connor makes the time to go to the library jet to do some research, but the computers are off-line, so he goes straight to Hayden.

"You're telling me everything's down?" he asks Hayden.

Hayden hesitates before answering. "Why? What do you need?" He almost seems suspicious, which is not like him.

"I need to look something up," Connor tells him.

"Can it wait?"

"*It* can, but *I* can't."

Hayden sighs. "Okay, I can get you online in the ComBom—on the condition that you let me do the surfing."

"What, are you afraid I'll break the web?"

"Just humor me, okay? We've had a lot of computer issues, and I'm very protective of the equipment."

"Fine, let's just do this before I get dragged off to deal with someone's idea of an emergency."

The kids in the ComBom are noticeably stressed as soon as they see Connor. He had no idea he inspires that level of fear. "Take it easy," he says. "No one's in trouble." And then he adds, "Yet."

"Take ten," Hayden tells them, and the kids file out and down the stairs, happy to be freed, at least temporarily, from their stations.

Hayden sits down with Connor, who pulls out the slip of paper Trace gave him. "Do a search on this name."

Hayden types in "Janson Rheinschild," but the results are not promising.

"Hmm . . . There's a Jordan Rheinschild, an accountant in Portland. Jared Rheinschild—looks like he's a fourth grader who won some art contest in Oklahoma. . . ."

"No Janson?"

"A few J. Rheinschilds," offers Hayden. He checks them out. One's a mother with a low-hit blog about her kids; another's a plumber. Not a single one seems to be the kind of person who would have a bronze statue erected to them, then destroyed.

"So who is he?"

"When I find out, I'll let you know."

Hayden swivels his chair to face Connor. "Is that all you were looking for?"

Then Connor remembers something. Didn't the Admiral talk about events leading to "our twisted way of life" too? What were those things he said Connor should educate himself about?

"I want you to look up 'the terror generation.'"

Hayden types it in. "What's that? A movie?"

But when the results begin popping up, it's clear that it's not. There are tons of references. The Admiral was right—all the information is right there for anyone to find, but buried among the billions of web pages on the net. They zero in on a news article.

"Look at the date," says Hayden. "Isn't that right around the time of the Heartland War?"

"I don't know," Connor says. "Do you know the actual dates of the war?"

Hayden has no answer. Strange, because Connor can remember key dates of other wars, but the Heartland War is fuzzy. He's never been taught about it, has never seen TV shows about it. Sure, he knows it happened, and why, but beyond that there's nothing.

The first article talks about a spontaneous youth gathering in Washington, DC. Hayden plays a news clip. "Whoa! Are those all people?"

"Kids," Connor realizes. "They're all kids."

The clip shows what must be hundreds of thousands of teens packing the Washington Mall between the Capitol Building and the Lincoln Memorial, so dense you can't even see the grass.

"Is this part of the war?" Hayden asks.

"No, I think it's something else. . . ."

The reporter calls it "The Teen Terror March," already putting a negative spin on the rally. *"This is by far the largest flash riot anyone has ever seen. Police have been authorized to use the new, controversial tranquilizer bullets to subdue the crowd. . . ."*

The idea that tranq bullets could be controversial sets Connor reeling. They're just an accepted part of life, aren't they?

Hayden scrolls down. "The article says they're protesting school closings."

That also throws Connor for a loop. What kid in their right mind would protest their school closing? "There," he says, pointing to a link that says "Fear for the Future."

Hayden clicks on it, and it brings up an editorial clip by some political pundit. He talks about the struggling economy and the collapse of the public education system. *"A nation of angry teenagers with no jobs, no schools, and too much time on their hands? You bet I'm scared—and you should be too."*

More reports—those same angry kids calling for change, and when they don't get it, they hit the streets, forming random mobs, burning cars, breaking windows, letting loose a kind of communal fury. In the midst of the Heartland War, President Moss—just a few weeks before his assassination—calls an additional state of emergency, this time ordering a curfew on everyone under the age of eighteen. *"Anyone caught breaking curfew will be subject to transport to juvenile detention camps."*

There are reports of kids who have either left or been thrown out of their homes. "Ferals," the news calls them. Like stray dogs. Then comes a shaky video of three kids swinging their hands together. A sudden white flash, and the image becomes static. *"Apparently,"* says the news anchor, *"these feral suicide bombers have altered their blood chemistry, so that bringing their hands together triggers detonation."*

"Holy crap!" says Hayden. "The first clappers!"

"All this was going on during the Heartland War," Connor points out. "The nation was tearing itself apart over pro-life and pro-choice but completely ignored the problems of the kids who were already here. I mean, no schools, no work, no clue if they'd even have a future. They just went nuts!"

"Tear it all down and start over."

"Do you blame them?"

Suddenly it was obvious to Connor why they don't teach it. Once education was restructured and corporatized, they didn't want kids knowing how close they came to toppling the government. They didn't want kids to know how much power they really had.

The various links lead Connor and Hayden to an image that's much more widespread and familiar: hands being shaken at the signing of the Unwind Accord. In the background is the Admiral as a much younger man. The report talks about peace being declared between the Life Army and the Choice Brigade, giving everyone hope for domestic normalization. Nowhere are the teen uprisings mentioned—yet within weeks of the Accord, the Juvenile Authority was established, feral detention centers became harvest camps, and unwinding became . . . a way of life.

That's when the truth hits Connor so brutally he feels light-headed. "My God! The Unwind Accord wasn't just about ending the war—it was also a way to take down the terror generation!"

Hayden leans away from the computer like it might start

clapping and blow them all up. "The Admiral must have known that."

Connor shakes his head "When his committee proposed the Unwind Accord, he never believed people would actually go for it, but they did . . . because they were more terrified of their teenagers than their consciences."

Connor knows that Janson Rheinschild, whoever he was, must have played into this somewhere, but Proactive Citizenry was extremely thorough in wiping him off the face of the earth.

40 ·Starkey

Mason Starkey knows nothing of Janson Rheinschild, the terror generation, or the Heartland War. If he did, he wouldn't care. The only teen uprising he has any interest in will involve the Stork Club.

His motives are a complex weave of self-interest and altruism. He truly wants to raise his storks to glory, as long as they all know *he's* the one who's done it. Credit where credit is due, and honor to the trickster whose illusions finally become real.

Starkey's hoping for a silent coup, but is prepared for anything. It will either be gracious, and Connor will see the wisdom of stepping aside for a more able leader . . . or he'll be steamrolled. Starkey will bear no guilt if it comes to that. After all, Connor, in spite of all his pretenses of fairness, still refuses to rescue storks from their unwindings.

"We save the kids we're most likely to get away with saving," Connor told him. "It's not our fault that storks are in bigger families and more complicated situations." It was the same excuse that Hayden had given him, but as far as Starkey is concerned, that's no excuse at all.

"So you're happy just letting them be unwound?"

"No! But there's only so much we can do!"

"So little, you mean."

Connor lost his temper then, which he does more and more often now. "If it was up to you, we'd be blowing up harvest camps, wouldn't we? That's not how this battle is going to be won! It will just make them come down harder on every Unwind, every AWOL."

Starkey wanted to take his argument all the way to the wall and nail Connor to it for letting storks go unsaved, but instead, Starkey backed down.

"I'm sorry," he told Connor. "You know I get passionate when it comes to storks."

"Your passion's a good thing," Connor told him, "when you keep it in perspective."

He could have slammed Connor for that, but instead he just smiled, agreed, and left—secure in the knowledge that someday soon Connor would be faced with an entirely new perspective.

While Connor has a history lesson with Hayden in the Com-Bom, Starkey relaxes at the Rec Jet, teaching kids simple card tricks and dazzling them with close-up magic he could do in his sleep. It's Stork Hour. Seven to eight p.m. Prime time. There's a nice breeze blowing under the Rec Jet. It's a perfect time of day. He has one of the storks bring him a drink so he doesn't have to get out of his comfortable chair. It's been a hard day dishing slop—and although he doesn't actually do the dishing, supervision can be a bitch.

Drake, the farm boy who runs the Green Aisle, passes and gives them a dirty look. Starkey glares back and makes a mental note. When he takes over, the new Holy of Whollies will be made up of all storks. Drake will be demoted to picking beans, or cleaning chicken crap. Many things will change when Starkey takes over, and God help anyone who's not in his good graces.

"You gonna get off your ass and play me a game of pool?" Bam asks, pointing her cue at him like a harpoon. "Or do my superior skills challenge your masculinity?"

"Watch it, Bam," Starkey warns. He will not play her, because he knows she'll win. First rule of competition—never accept a losing proposition. He loses when he plays Connor, of course, but that's different. It's intentional, and he makes sure the other storks know it.

Farther down the main aisle, Connor comes down the stairs of the ComBom with Hayden.

"What do you think that's all about?" Bam asks.

Starkey keeps his opinion to himself.

"I think they're hot for each other," says one of the other storks.

Starkey turns to him. "You're the only one I know who keeps checking out Connor's butt, Paulie."

"That ain't true!" But by the way Paulie goes red, it's clear that it is.

Finally Starkey stands up to get a better look at the situation. Connor and Hayden say their good-byes. Hayden heads toward the latrine, and Connor goes back to his own little jet.

"He's been having private meetings with Trace, too," Bam points out. "But he hasn't been sharing any secrets with you, has he?"

Starkey hides his fury at being left out of whatever Connor is plotting. "He must be happy with food service."

"A regular fatted cow," Bam says with a grin. "Just about ready for slaughter."

"I will not have you bad-mouthing our commander in chief."

Bam turns and spits on the ground. "You're such a freakin'

hypocrite." Then she goes back to playing pool against kids who never beat her.

Starkey, however, has no need to bad-mouth Connor. Griping is for those without a plan of action—and tonight Starkey has something new up his sleeve. A gift for Connor. It comes in the person of Jeevan, whose skill with computers got him assigned to the ComBom, and who happens to be a loyal Stork Club member. Of course, no one but Starkey knows that fact. "Jeeves" is one of two well-positioned "sleeper agents," whose allegiance is to him, rather than Connor. And what a gift Jeeves has provided! Starkey's been saving it for just the right moment. He concludes that now—when Connor seems to be getting his balance back—is the perfect time to unwrap it . . . and while the gift is in his arms, pull the rug out from under him.

41 · Connor

Connor sits alone in his jet, staring into space, trying to process everything he's just learned. *We can't stop unwinding,* the Admiral once told him. *The best we can hope to do is save as many of these kids as we can.* But somehow, after seeing those old news reports, Connor is starting to feel that maybe the Admiral was wrong. Maybe there *is* a way to end unwinding. If only he can figure out how to truly learn from the past . . .

Connor is still pondering the dark specter of history late into the evening, when Starkey shows up at his jet. Connor opens the hatch for him. "What's up? Is there a problem?"

"You'll have to tell me if it's a problem," Starkey says enigmatically. "Can I come in?"

Connor lets him in, "It's been a killer day—this had better be good."

"There's a TV here, right?"

Connor points to it. "Yeah, but there's no line in, and the color sucks."

"Don't need a line, and color's not gonna matter when you see what I've got." Starkey pulls out a microdrive and plugs it into the TV's data port. "You should sit down."

Connor laughs. "Thanks, but I'll stand."

"You sure?"

Connor gives him a funny look, continues standing, and waits for an image to come on the screen.

He recognizes the show immediately. It's a weekly news magazine he has seen many times before. A familiar TV journalist discusses the featured story. The logo screened in behind her says ANGEL OF DIVISION.

"A little over a year ago," she begins, "clappers took out an unwinding facility in Happy Jack, Arizona. The social and political fallout from that event still resonates today, but one girl—an infamous player in that event—is speaking out. Her message, however, is not what you think. You may have seen her in various public service announcements blitzing the airwaves. In a short time, she's gone from being one of the Juvenile Authority's most wanted to becoming the poster child for the cause of unwinding. Yes, you heard me right: FOR unwinding. Her name is Risa Ward, and you're not going to forget her anytime soon."

Connor takes a deep, shuddering breath and realizes that Starkey was right—he needs to sit down. His legs practically fall out from under him as he sinks into the chair.

The studio shot cuts to Risa being interviewed in some plush location by the same journalist. There's something different about her, but Connor can't yet tell what it is.

"Risa," begins the journalist, "you were a ward of the state slated for unwinding, became a coconspirator with the notorious Akron AWOL, and were even present at Happy Jack Harvest

Camp to witness his death. After all that, how is it that you now speak in favor of unwinding?"

Risa hesitates before answering, then says, *"It's complicated."*

Starkey crosses his arms. "Yeah, I'll bet it is."

"Quiet!" snaps Connor.

"Could you walk us through it?" the journalist asks, with a disarming grin that Connor wants to punch right off her face with Roland's fist.

"Let's just say I have a different perspective now than I had before."

"You've come to see unwinding as a good thing?"

"No, it's a terrible thing," she answers, which gives Connor hope . . . until she says, *"But it's the least of all evils. Unwinding is there for a reason, and the world would be very different without it."*

"Pardon me for pointing this out, but that's easy for you to say, now that you're seventeen and beyond unwinding age."

"No comment," says Risa, and it's like a dagger slowly twisting in Connor's gut.

"Let's talk about the charges against you," the journalist says, looking at her notes. *"Theft of government property, namely yourself; conspiracy to commit acts of terrorism; conspiracy to commit murder—and yet all these charges against you have been dropped. Does that have anything to do with your change of heart?"*

"I won't deny that I was offered a deal," Risa says, *"but the dropping of those charges is not the reason why I'm here today."* Then she does something very simple—something that no one else would notice in the slightest, except for those who know her. . . .

Risa crosses her legs.

For Connor, it's as if the air has been sucked out of the

jet. He half expects oxygen masks to drop from the ceiling.

"If you think that's bad, listen to this next part," says Starkey, actually seeming to enjoy it.

"Risa, would you call your change of heart a matter of convenience or a matter of conscience?"

Risa takes time to craft her answer, but that doesn't make it any less devastating. *"Neither,"* she says. *"After all I've been faced with, I find I have no choice. For me, supporting unwinding is a matter of necessity."*

"Turn it off," Connor says.

"There's still more—you really should hear the end."

"I said turn it off!"

Starkey reaches over and turns off the TV, and Connor feels his mind slamming shut like a fire door to keep out all the things too hot to handle—but he knows it's too late; the fire has already leaped inside. In this moment he wishes he had been unwound a year ago. He wishes Lev hadn't come in to save him, because then he would never have to feel what he's feeling now.

"Why did you show me this?"

Starkey shrugs. "I thought you had a right to know. Hayden knows, but he's been keeping it from you. I think that's wrong and completely unfair to you. Knowing who's your friend and who's your enemy can only make you stronger, right?"

"Yeah, yeah, sure," Connor says absently.

Starkey grips his shoulder. "It's okay, you'll get over it. We're all here to support you." Then he leaves, his mission of enlightenment accomplished.

Connor sits for a long time without moving. Although he knows he needs to be strong enough to carry this burden, he feels so shredded inside, he doesn't know how he can make it through the night, much less take care of hundreds of Unwinds in the days ahead. All those lofty ideas of exposing history to end unwinding implode into a single desperate thought.

Risa. Risa. Risa.

He is hobbled. How could Starkey not know how devastated he would be? Either he's stupider than Connor thought . . . or he's much, much smarter.

42 · Starkey

Jeeves brings Starkey a copy of the list of local unwind orders. There are only three kids on this list deemed savable, and none of them are storks. But today is the day that things change. There is a storked kid on the list, ignored and forgotten.

Jesus LaVega
287 North Brighton Lane

Well, Connor doesn't have a monopoly on rescuing Unwinds. It's high time Starkey took things into his own hands.

"Hey, we're saving Jesus, instead of him saving us," someone says when Starkey tells the Stork Club his plan. Another kid raps him on the head. "It's pronounced *Haysoos*, moron."

But regardless of how he pronounces his name, Jesus is about to get a wholly visitation.

At eleven o'clock p.m., one day before the Juvies are due to come for Jesus, Starkey and nine Stork Clubbers storm the house at 287 North Brighton Lane. They have weapons, because Starkey picked the arsenal lock. They have cars, because the kid in charge of vehicle maintenance is a loyal member of the Stork Club.

They don't knock, they don't ring. They break down the doors, front and back, crashing the place like a SWAT team taking down a crack house.

A woman screams and herds two younger kids to a back room. Starkey doesn't see anyone the right age to be the target of their rescue. He goes into the living room in time to see a man pull down a curtain rod and turn to him—it's the closest thing to a weapon the man can find on such short notice. Starkey easily disarms him and pushes him up against the wall with the muzzle of a submachine gun to his chest. "Jesus LaVega. Tell me where he is. Now!"

The father's eyes dart back and forth in panic, then fix on something behind Starkey. Starkey turns in time to see a baseball bat swinging at him. He ducks, and the bat breezes past an inch from his head. The kid holding the bat is the size of a linebacker.

"No! Stop! You're Jesus LaVega, right? We're here to save you!"

But that doesn't stop him from swinging the bat again. It connects with Starkey's side. An explosion of pain. Starkey goes down, his weapon flies behind a sofa, and now the kid is over him, hefting the bat once more. Starkey can't catch his breath. His side hurts so much he can only breathe shallow gulps of air.

"Juvies! Here! Tomorrow!" Starkey gasps. "Your parents! Unwinding you!"

"Nice try!" he says, and pulls back the bat, ready to swing again. "Run, Dad! Get out!" The man tries to scramble away but is cornered by other storks. Doesn't this kid get it? Doesn't he realize they already signed the order to have him unwound? Jesus LaVega tenses his muscles to swing just as one of Starkey's storks comes up behind him with a large football trophy and swings the marble base at his head. The heavy stone connects with the back of Jesus's head, and he crumples to the ground instantly. The trophy falls to the floor, broken.

"What did you do?" screams Starkey.

"He was gonna kill you!" screams the stork.

Starkey kneels down beside Jesus. Blood pours out of his

head, soaking the carpet. His eyes are half-open. Starkey feels for a pulse but can't find one, and when he turns the kid's head, he can see how badly his skull was crushed by the heavy trophy base. One thing is certain: Jesus LaVega is not going to be unwound. Because he's dead.

Starkey looks to the kid who did it, who panics under Starkey's gaze. "I didn't mean it, Starkey! Honest! I swear! He was gonna kill you!"

"It's not your fault," Starkey tells him, then turns to the kid's father, who's cornered like a spider.

"You did this!" Starkey screams. "You kept him here all his life just so you could unwind him. Do you even care that he's dead?"

The man is horrified by the news. "D-dead? No!"

"Don't pretend you care!" Starkey can't hold it in anymore. He can't hold back. This man—this monster who would unwind his stork-brought son—has to pay for what he's done!

Ignoring the pain in his side, Starkey swings his foot, connecting with the man's torso. *He should feel this pain, not me. He should feel all of it!* Starkey kicks again and again. The man screams, the man moans, but Starkey keeps swinging his foot, unable to stop—it's as if he's channeling the fury of every doorstep baby, every unwanted child, all kids everywhere who were treated like something less than human just because they were born to mothers who didn't want them.

Finally one of the other storks grabs Starkey, pulling him away.

"That's enough, man," he says. "He gets the idea."

The man, bloody and beaten, still has enough strength to crawl out the door. The rest of his family has escaped too, running to neighbors. They've probably called the police, and Starkey realizes that he can't stop now, he's gone too far—he has to take this all the way. This isn't what he wanted, but somehow he can use it. Yes, the kid they came to rescue is dead, but this night can't end with that. It has to stand for something. It has to be worth something. Not just for Starkey, but for all storks.

"Let this be a warning," he yells out the front door as the man stumbles away. He spots neighbors on their porches. Strangers are there to hear his words. Good! It's time for people to listen. "Let this be a warning," he says again, "to anyone who would unwind a stork! You will all get what's coming to you!" Then, in a flash of inspiration, he runs through the house and into the garage.

"Starkey!" one of the others yells after him. "What the hell are you doing?"

"You'll see."

In the garage he finds a gas can. It's only half-full, but half is enough. He runs through the house pouring gasoline everywhere, and on the mantel above the fireplace he finds a book of matches.

Moments later he's racing across the lawn away from the house, toward his friends in the waiting Jeeps, while an ominous glow rises within the house behind him. By the time he climbs into a Jeep, flames are rising in the windows, and the moment the Jeeps screech away into the night, those windows begin to explode, and smoke pours forth from the rising inferno. The entire house has become a blazing beacon to let the world know that Mason Starkey was here, and people are going to pay.

43 · Avalanche

This document I sign of my own free will.

That was the last line of the consent form that Risa Ward signed, just as Roberta had predicted she would. Signing that form has given her a new spine and the use of her legs, but that's not all it did. It set into motion a cascading series of events that Risa could not have predicted, and yet was expertly orchestrated by Roberta, her associates, and their money.

. . . I sign of my own free will.

Risa has never gone skiing—such frivolous activities were not offered to state wards—yet lately she's been dreaming that she's skiing down a triple black diamond slope, chased by the leading edge of an avalanche. There's no stopping until she either reaches the bottom, or sails off a cliff to her doom.

. . . my own free will.

Before the news interviews, before the public service announcements, before she knows any of what she'll be asked to do, Risa's damaged spine is replaced, and she awakes from a five-day medically induced coma into her brave new life.

44 · Risa

"Tell me if you can feel this," a nurse says, scraping Risa's toe with a strip of plastic. Risa gasps in spite of herself. Yes, she feels it—and it's not just a phantom sensation. She can feel the sheets brushing against her legs. She can feel her toes again. She tries to move them, but just moving her toes makes every part of her body ache.

"Don't try to move, dear," the nurse tells her. "Let the healing agents do their job. We're using second-generation healing agents. You'll be up and walking in two weeks."

It speeds her heart to hear those words. She wishes the connection between her heart and her mind could be more direct—that the part of her that wants this could be firmly ruled by the part of her that doesn't—because although her mind wants to despise what they've done for her, the part of her that knows no reason is filled with joy at the prospect of holding her own balance and moving under the power of her own legs.

"You'll require a lot of physical therapy, of course. Not as much as you might think, though." The nurse checks the devices that are attached to her legs. They are electrical stimulators, which cause her muscles to contract, awakening them from their atrophied state, building them back to prime body tone. Each day she feels like she's run miles, although she hasn't left the bed.

She's no longer in a cell. It's not really a hospital, either. She can tell it's some sort of private home. She can hear the roar of ocean surf outside her window.

She wonders if the staff knows who she is and what happened to her. She chooses not to bring it up, because it's too painful. Better just to take it day by day and wait until Roberta comes for her again, to tell her what more she has to do to fulfill the terms of her so-called contract.

It's not Roberta who visits her, though, it's Cam. He's the last person she wants to see, if she indeed can call him a person. His hair has filled in a bit since the time she first saw him, and the scars on his face from the various grafts are slimmer. You can barely see the seam where the different skin tones touch.

"I wanted to see how you were feeling," he says.

"Sick to my stomach," she tells him, "but that only started when you walked in."

He goes to the window and opens the blinds a bit more, letting in bars of afternoon light. A particularly loud wave crashes on the shore outside the window. "'The ocean is a mighty harmonist,'" he says, quoting someone she's probably never even heard of. "When you can walk," Cam tells her, "you should look at your view. It sure is pretty this time of day."

She doesn't answer him. She just waits for him to leave, but he doesn't.

271

"I need to know why you hate me," he asks. "I've done nothing to you. You don't even know me, but you hate me. Why?"

"I don't hate you," Risa admits. "There's no 'you' to hate."

He comes up beside her bed. "I'm here, aren't I?" He puts his hand on hers, and she pulls away.

"I don't care who or what you are, nobody touches me."

He thinks for a moment, then says, in all seriousness, "Would you like to touch *me* then? You can feel all the seams. You can see what makes me me."

She doesn't even dignify that with a response. "Do you think the kids who were unwound to be a part of you wanted it?"

"If they were tithes, they did," Cam says, "and some of them were. As for the other ones, they had no choice . . . any more than I had a choice in being made."

And for a moment, within the fury she feels toward the people who created him, Risa realizes that Cam, as much as all the kids who were unwound to make him, is a victim too.

"Why are you here?" she asks him.

"I have lots of answers to that one," Cam says proudly. "'The sole purpose of human existence is to kindle a light in the darkness of mere being.' Carl Jung."

Risa sighs, exasperated. "No—why are you here, in this place, talking to me? I'm sure Proactive Citizenry has more important things for their beta test to do than talk to me."

"Where the heart is," he says. "Uh—I mean—I'm here because this is my home. But I'm also here because I want to be."

He smiles at her, and she hates the fact that his smile is sincere. She has to keep reminding herself that it's not his smile at all. He's just wearing the flesh of others, and if it was all peeled away, there'd be nothing in the center. He is little more than a cruel trick.

"So did your brain cells come preprogrammed? A head full

of ganglia implants from the best and the brightest?"

"Not all of them," Cam says quietly. "Why do you keep holding me responsible for the things I had no control over? I am what I am."

"Spoken like a true god."

"Actually," he says, returning a little bit of her attitude, "God said, 'I am *that* I am,' if you're going by the King James version."

"Don't tell me—you came programmed with the entire Bible."

"In three languages," Cam says. "Again, not my fault, it's just there."

Risa has to laugh at the audacity of his creators—did it occur to them that filling him with biblical knowledge while playing God was the ultimate hubris?

"And anyway, it ain't like I can regurgitate it verbatim, I just got a workin' knowledge of a whole lotta stuff."

She looks at him, wondering whether the sudden change in speech pattern from advanced-placement to country-casual is a joke, but she can tell it's not. She supposes as connections spark through the various and sundry bits of his brain, he kicks out all kinds of talk.

"May I ask you what made you change your mind?" he asks. "Why did you agree to the operation?"

Risa looks away. "I'm tired," she tells him, even though she's not, and shifts to face away from him. Even this action of rolling sideways in her bed was something she could not easily accomplish before the operation.

When it becomes clear that she's not going to answer him, he asks, "May I come see you again?"

She keeps her back to him. "No matter what I say, you'll come anyway, so why bother asking?"

"Well," he says as he leaves, "it would be nice to have permission."

She lies there in that position for a long time, trying not to give a foothold to any of the thoughts swimming through her mind. Finally she dozes off. This is the first night she dreams of the avalanche.

Roberta is off somewhere taking care of business on the day Risa first walks—and only a week after waking up, instead of two. It's a day that brings to a head all her conflicted emotions. She wants this to be a personal moment, not something shared, but as usual, Cam comes uninvited.

"Milestone! This is a momentous occasion," he tells her cheerily. "It should be witnessed by a friend."

She throws him an icy gaze, and he does a verbal backpedal.

"Aaaand since no friends are present, I'll have to do."

A male nurse who looks more like a steroid-pumped boeuf grabs Risa's upper arm and helps her swing her legs off the bed. It's an unearthly sensation to actually feel them cantilevered out over the floor. She bends her knees shakily until she feels the tips of her toes touch the wooden floor.

"They should have a rug on the floor," Cam tells Nurse Beefcake. "To make it softer for her."

"Rugs slip," Nurse Beefcake replies.

With the nurse holding her on one side, and Cam on the other, she rises to her feet. The first step is the hardest. It's like dragging her foot through mud, but the second step comes with remarkable ease.

"Atta girl!" says the nurse, like he's talking to a baby taking her first step—and in a sense she is. She has no balance whatsoever, and her knees feel like they'll give out at any moment, but they don't.

"Keep going," Cam says. "You're doing great!" By the fifth step, she can't hold back the visceral joy she's been suppressing. A smile fills her face. She becomes short of breath and giggles giddily at the simple joy of walking.

"That's it," says Cam. "You're doing it! You're whole again, Risa! You have a right to enjoy it!"

And although she doesn't believe that's true, she can't fight the moment. "The window!" she says. "I want to look out the window."

As they turn slightly to angle toward the window, Nurse Beefcake tentatively lets go, and now it's just Risa with her arm around Cam's shoulder and his arm around her waist—and she wants to be furious that she wound up stuck in this position with him, but that feeling is overridden by giddy sensory overload from her feet, her ankles, her shins, her thighs; parts of her body that just a few short days ago felt nothing at all.

45 · Cam

For Cam this is nothing short of heaven. She's holding him. Relying on him. He convinces himself that this is the moment that all the barriers will fall. He's convinced she will turn to him and kiss him even before they reach the window.

She grips his neck tightly for support. Her hold on him pinches the seam there, but it's a good feeling. He imagines her putting pressure on all his seams, making them ache. No pain could ever feel so good.

They reach the window. No kiss, but she hasn't let go of him either. She can't or she'll fall, but Cam wants to believe she'd hold him anyway.

The sea is rough this morning. Spray launches high into the air with the pounding of eight-foot rollers. An island can be seen in the distance.

"No one ever told me where we are."

"Molokai," Cam tells her. "In Hawaii. The island used to be a leper colony."

"And Roberta owns this place?"

Cam detects unveiled bitterness in the way Risa says her name. "It's owned by Proactive Citizenry. Actually, I think about half the island is. This place was some rich guy's summer home once, but now it's their medical research center—and Roberta is the head of medical research."

"Are you her only project?"

It's a question Cam has never even considered before. As far as he knows, he is the center of Roberta's universe. "You don't like her, do you?"

"Who, me? No, I love her dearly. Evil scheming bitches are my favorite kind of people."

Cam feels a sudden protectiveness and an unexpected spike of anger. "Red light!" he blurts. "She's the closest thing I have to a mother."

"You'd be better off storked."

"Easy for you to say. A ward like you doesn't even know what a mother is."

Risa gasps, then brings her hand back and slaps him hard across the face. The momentum of the slap pushes her off balance, and she falls backward—but the nurse is there to catch her. He gives Cam an accusing glance, then returns his attention to Risa. "Enough for now," the way-too-muscular male nurse says. "Back into bed."

He helps Risa back to bed while Cam stands impotently at the window, not sure who to be mad at—himself, her, or the nurse for taking her away from him.

"Did the slap sting evenly, Cam," she asks with a nasty bite in her voice, "or do the kids in your face all feel it differently?"

"Teflon!" he says, refusing to let her comment stick.

"Muzzle!" He cannot let himself lash out again. He cannot! He takes a deep breath, picturing the tumultuous sea calming to a glassy lake.

"I know I invited that slap," he tells her calmly, "but watch what you say about Roberta. I do not speak unkindly of the people you love—have the same courtesy for me."

Cam gives Risa some space. He knows this change in her life must be as traumatic as it is wonderful for her. He still doesn't quite understand what made Risa change her mind about allowing the operation, but he knows Roberta can be persuasive. He likes to pretend that some of it had to do with him—that deep down, beneath her initial repulsion, was a curiosity, perhaps even an admiration for the mosaic that had been created from all his disparate parts. Not the one they put together for him, but how he took what he was given and made it all work.

They eat one meal a day together. "It is imperative," Roberta tells him, "if the two of you are ever going to bond, that you dine together. Meals are when the psyche is most vulnerable to attachment."

He wishes Roberta didn't make it all sound so clinical. Growing accustomed to each other's company shouldn't be about Risa's "vulnerability to attachment."

Risa does not yet know that she is here to be his companion.

"Do not rush this," Roberta has told Cam. "She must be groomed for the role, and we have other things planned for her first. We're turning her folk-legend status to our advantage, creating a powerful media presence before we link the two of you together publicly. That will take time. In the meantime, be your wonderful, charming self. She is yours to win."

"And if I don't?"

"I have every confidence in you, Cam."

Risa is in his thoughts through each activity of the day. She

277

becomes a thread weaving through all the seams of his mind, binding them together more tightly. And she's thinking of him, too. He knows because of the way she watches him secretly. He plays basketball one afternoon with an off-duty guard. He has his shirt off, revealing not only his seams, but his musculature, in tip-top shape. A boxer's six-pack abs, a swimmer's powerful pecs—flawless muscle groups reined in by a finely tuned motor cortex to produce the perfect layup. Risa watches him play from a window in the main living room. He knows, but he doesn't let on—he just delivers spectacular game, allowing his body to speak for itself. Only when he's done playing does he glance up at her, to let her know that her stolen glimpses of him aren't stolen at all—they're given freely. She backs away from the window into shadows, but they both know she was watching. Not because she had to but because she wanted to, and Cam knows that makes all the difference in the world.

46 · Risa

Risa walks up the spiral staircase. Risa walks down the spiral staircase. Risa works with Kenny the physical therapist, who keeps telling her how quickly she's gaining strength. She hears no news of the outside world. For all she knows it no longer exists, and this island clinic—which is not a clinic at all—quickly feels like home. And she hates that.

As much as Risa dreads the daily meal with Cam, she also finds herself looking forward to it. It's out on the veranda, weather permitting, and whichever meal it is, it's always the best meal of the day. Cam, who has been happy to show off his remarkable physique to her from a distance, is awkward at the meals, and just as uncomfortable as she is to be thrust together like it's some sort of arranged marriage. They don't speak of the day she slapped him. They don't speak about much of any-thing. Risa puts up with him. Cam puts up with her putting up with him. Finally he breaks the ice.

"I'm sorry about that day," he says as they eat steaks together on the veranda. "I was just upset. There's nothing wrong with being a state ward. In fact, parts of me know what it's like. I have memories of state homes. More than one."

Risa looks down at her food. "Please don't talk to me about that, I'm eating."

But he doesn't stop. "They're not the nicest of places, are they? You have to fight for every bit of attention, otherwise you live a life of bare adequacy, which is the worst life of all."

She looks up at him. He's put into words the feelings she's always had about the way she grew up.

"Do you know which homes you were in?" she asks.

"Not really," he tells her. "There are images, feelings, spe-cific memories, but for the most part, my language center didn't come from state wards."

"I'm not surprised," Risa says. "Language skills are not a strong point at state homes." She grins.

"Do you know your history?" Cam asks. "How you ended up there? Who your birth parents are?"

Risa feels a lump in her throat and tries to swallow it down. "No one knows that information."

"I can get it for you," Cam tells her.

It leaves her with a feeling of dread and anticipation. And this time she's very pleased to say that the dread wins out.

"It's not something that I've ever needed to know, and I don't need to know now."

Cam looks down, a little disappointed. Maybe a little bit crushed, and Risa finds herself reaching across the table to clasp his hand. "Thank you for offering. It was very kind of you, but it's something I've come to terms with." It's only when she lets go of his hand that she realizes that it's the first time she has voluntarily made physical contact with him. The moment is not lost on him, either.

"I know you were in love with the boy they call the Akron AWOL," Cam says.

Risa tries not to react.

"I'm sorry he died," Cam says. Risa looks at him in horror until he says, "That must have been a horrible day at Happy Jack Harvest Camp—to be there when it happened."

Risa takes a deep, shuddering breath. So Cam doesn't know he's alive. Does that mean that Proactive Citizenry doesn't know either? It's something she can't speak of, can't ask about, because it would provoke too many questions.

"Do you miss him?" Cam asks.

Now Risa can tell him the truth. "Yes, I do. Very much."

It's a long time before Cam speaks again. And when he does, he says, "I would never ask to take his place in your heart, but I hope there's room for me in there as a friend."

"I make no promises," says Risa, trying to sound less vulnerable than she truly feels.

"Do you still think I'm ugly?" Cam asks her. "Do you still think I'm hideous?"

Risa wants to answer him truthfully, but it takes a while to find the right words. He takes her hesitation for an attempt to spare his feelings. He looks down. "I understand."

"No," Risa says, "I don't think you're hideous. It's just that there's no way to measure you. It's like looking at a Picasso and trying to decide if the woman in the painting is ugly or beautiful. You don't know, but you can't stop looking."

Cam smiles. "You see me as art. I like that."

"Yeah, well, I never cared for Picasso."

That makes Cam laugh, and Risa does too, in spite of herself.

The cliffside plantation estate has a rose garden filled with well-pruned hedges and exotic, aromatic flowers.

Risa, having been raised in the concrete confines of an inner-city state home, was never much of a garden girl, but once she was allowed access, she began coming out daily, if only to pretend that she isn't a prisoner. The sensation of walking again is still new enough to make every step in the garden feel like a gift.

Today, however, Roberta is there, preparing some sort of miniature production. There is a small camera crew, and smack in the middle of the garden sits her old wheelchair. The sight of it brings back a flood of too many emotions to sort through right now.

"Would you mind telling me what this is all about?" Risa asks, not sure she really wants to know.

"You've been on your feet for almost a week now," Roberta tells her. "It's time to deliver on the first of the services you've agreed to perform."

"Thank you for wording it just the right way to make me feel like I'm prostituting myself."

For a moment Roberta is flustered, but she's quick to recover her poise. "I meant it no such way, but you do have a knack of taking things and twisting them." Then she hands Risa a sheet of paper. "Here are your lines. You'll be recording a public service announcement."

Risa has to laugh at that. "You're putting me on TV?"

"And in print ads, and on the net. It's the first of many plans we have for you."

"Really, and what else do you have planned?"

Roberta smiles at her. "You'll know when it's your time to know."

Risa reads over the single paragraph, and the words go straight to the pit of her stomach.

"If you're unable to memorize them, we have cue cards prepared," Roberta says.

Risa has to read the paragraph twice just to convince herself she's actually seeing what she's seeing. "No! I won't say this, you can't make me say this!" She crumples the page and throws it down.

Roberta calmly opens her folder and hands her another one. "You should know by now that there's always another copy."

Risa won't take it. "How dare you make me say this?"

"Your histrionics are uncalled-for. There's absolutely nothing in there that isn't true."

"It doesn't matter. It's not the words, it's what's implied!"

Roberta shrugs. "Truth is truth. Implications are subjective. People will hear your words and draw their own conclusions."

"Don't try to doublethink me, Roberta. I'm not as stupid or naive as you'd like to think."

Then the expression on Roberta's face changes; she becomes coolly direct. No more posturing. "This is what is required of you, so this is what you will do. Or perhaps you've forgotten our arrangement. . . ." It's a threat as thinly veiled as the sheerest silk. Then out of nowhere they hear—

"What arrangement?"

They both turn to see Cam coming out into the garden. Roberta throws Risa a warning glance, and Risa looks down to the crumpled piece of paper at her feet, saying nothing.

"Her spine, of course," Roberta says. "In return for very expensive and state-of-the-art spinal replacement surgery, Risa has agreed to become a part of the Proactive Citizenry family. And every member of the family has a role to play." Then she holds out the paragraph to Risa again. Risa knows she has no choice but to take it. She looks to the video crew, who wait impatiently to do their job, then back to Roberta.

"Do you want me to stand beside the wheelchair?" Risa asks.

"No, you should sit in it," Roberta tells her, "then rise halfway through. That will be more effective, don't you think?"

PUBLIC SERVICE ANNOUNCEMENT

"I was paralyzed—a victim of the clapper attack at Happy Jack Harvest Camp. I used to hate the very idea of unwinding, then overnight *I* was the one with a desperate medical need. Without unwinding, I would have been denied a new spine. Without unwinding, I would be confined to this wheelchair for the rest of my life. I was a state ward. I was an AWOL. I was a paraplegic—but now I'm none of those things. My name is Risa Ward, and unwinding changed my life."

—paid for by the National Whole Health Society

Risa has always thought of herself as a survivor. She managed the treacherous waters of Ohio State Home 23 until the day she became a "budget cut" and was pruned for unwinding. Then she survived as an AWOL, then at harvest camp, and then even survived a devastating explosion that should have killed her. Her strength has always been her keen mind and her ability to adapt.

Well, adapt to this:

A life of minor celebrity, all the comforts you could desire, a smart and charming boy infatuated with you . . . and the abandonment of everything you believe, along with the abdication of your conscience.

Risa sits on a plush lawn chair in the backyard of the cliffside estate, looking out at the tropical sunset, pondering these things and trying to infuse perspective and peace back into her mind. There's a powerful surge against her soul, as relentless as the waves crashing below, reminding her that in time the strongest of mountains is eroded into the sea, and she doesn't know how much longer she can resist it, or even if she should.

There was a news interview this morning. She tried to answer questions in a way so that she never actually had to lie. It's true that her support of unwinding is "a matter of necessity," but no one but she and Roberta know what has made it so necessary. No matter how hard she tries, though, things come out of her mouth that she can't believe she's said. *Unwinding is the least of all evils.* Is there actually a part of her that believes that? The constant manipulation has left her internal compass spinning so wildly, she's afraid she'll never find true north again.

Exhausted, she dozes, and it seems only seconds later she's awakened by someone gently shaking her shoulder. It's night now—just the slightest trace of blue on the horizon holds the memory of dusk.

"Sawing wood," Cam says. "I didn't know you snored."

"I don't," she says groggily. "And I'm sticking to my story."

Cam has a blanket with him. It's only as he wraps it around her that she realizes how chilled she has gotten while she slept. Even in this tropical environment, the air can get cool at night.

"I wish you wouldn't spend so much time alone," he says. "You don't have to, you know."

"When you've spent most of your life in a state home, solitude feels like a luxury."

He kneels beside her. "We have our first interview together next week—they're flying us to the mainland—has Roberta told you?"

Risa sighs. "I know all about it."

"We're supposed to be a couple. . . ."

"So I'll smile and do my job for the camera. You don't have to worry."

"I was hoping you wouldn't see it as a job."

Rather than looking at him, she looks up to see a sky full of stars—even fuller than the sky over the Graveyard, but there, she rarely had the time or the inclination to look heavenward.

"I know all their names," Cam offers. "The stars, that is."

"Don't be ridiculous; there are billions of stars, you can't know them all."

"Hyperbole," he says. "I guess I'm exaggerating—but I do know all the ones that matter." Then he begins pointing them out, his voice taking on just the slightest Boston accent as he accesses the living star chart in his head. "That's Alpha Centauri, which means 'foot of the centaur.' It's one of the closest stars to us. That bright one to the right? That's Sirius—the brightest star in the sky. . . ."

His voice begins to feel hypnotic to her, and it brings her a hint of the peace she's been craving. *Am I making this more difficult than it has to be?* Risa wonders. *Should I find a way to adapt?*

"That dim one is Spica, which is actually a hundred times brighter than Sirius, but it's much farther away. . . ."

Risa has to remind herself that her choice to get with Proactive Citizenry's program was not out of selfishness—so shouldn't her conscience be appeased? And if not—if her conscience is the only thing dragging her to dark depths, shouldn't she be able to cut it loose in order to survive?

"That's Andromeda, which is actually a whole galaxy. . . ."

There is a sense of arrogance to Cam's bragging, but also an innocence to it, like a little kid wanting to show off what he learned in school that day. But he never learned any of this, did he? The accent with which he now speaks makes it clear that the information was someone else's that got shoved into his head.

Stop it, Risa! she tells herself. Perhaps it's time to let the mountain erode, and so to spite the part of herself that would resist, she gets out of her chair and lies on the grass beside him, looking up at the spray of stars.

"Polaris is always easy to find. It's directly over the North Pole—so if you know where it is, you can always find true north." Hearing him say that makes her gasp. He turns to look at her. "Aren't you going to shut me up?"

Risa laughs at that. "I was hoping you'd put me back to sleep."

"Oh, am I that boring?"

"Only slightly."

Then he reaches over and gently brushes her arm.

Risa pulls away and sits up. "Don't! You know I don't like to be touched."

"Is it that you don't like to be touched . . . or that you don't like to be touched by me?"

She doesn't answer him. "What's that one?" she asks, pointing. "The red one?"

"Betelgeuse," he tells her. Then, after an awkward silence, he says, "What was he like?"

"Who?"

"You know who."

Risa sighs. "It's not a place you want to go, Cam."

"Maybe I do."

She doesn't have the strength to fight it, so she lies back down and fixes her eyes on the stars as she speaks. "Impulsive. Brooding. Occasionally self-loathing."

"Sounds like a real gem."

"You didn't let me finish. He's also clever, loyal, passionate, responsible, and a strong leader, but is too humble to admit all that to himself."

"Is?"

"Was," she says, covering. "Sometimes it feels like he's still here."

"I think I would have liked to have known him."

Risa shakes her head. "He'd hate you."

"Why?"

"Because he was also jealous."

Silence falls between them again, but this time it's not awkward at all.

"I'm glad you shared that with me," Cam says. "There's something I'd like to share with you, too."

Risa has no idea what he's going to say, but she finds she's actually curious.

"Did you know a kid named Samson when you were back at the state home?" he asks.

She searches her thoughts. "Yes—he was on the harvest camp bus with me."

"Well, he had a secret crush on you."

At first it boggles Risa how he would know this, and when the truth dawns on her, a surge of reflexive adrenaline triggers her fight-or-flight response. She gets up, fully prepared to run back to the mansion, or jump off the cliff, or whatever it will take to get away from this revelation, but Cam eclipses her like a moon before one of his precious stars.

"Algebra!" he says. "He was a math whiz. I got the part of him that does algebra. It's just a tiny part, but when I came across your picture, well, I guess it was enough to make me stop and take notice. Then, when Roberta heard that you'd been captured, she pulled strings to get you here. For me. So it's my fault that you're here."

She doesn't want to look at him, but she can't stop. It's like looking at a traffic accident. "How am I supposed to feel about this, Cam? I can't pretend not to be horrified! I'm here because of some whim you had, but that whim wasn't even yours! It was that poor kid's!'"

"No, it wasn't like that," says Cam quickly. "Samson was like . . . like a friend who taps you on the shoulder to get your attention . . . but what I feel for you—it's all me. Not just algebra, but, well, the whole equation."

She turns her back to him, grabbing the blanket and wrapping it around herself. "I want you to go now."

"I'm sorry," he says, "but I didn't want there to be any secrets between us."

"Please leave."

He keeps his distance, but he doesn't go. "'I'd rather be partly great than entirely useless.' Wasn't that the last thing he said to you? I feel it's my responsibility to make that wish come true."

And finally he goes inside, leaving her alone with way too many people's thoughts.

Ten minutes later Risa still stands with the blanket wrapped around her, not wanting to go inside, but the circular pattern of her own thoughts begins to nauseate her.

I can't give in to this—I must give in to this—I can't give in to this, over and over until she just wants to shut herself down.

When she finally steps into the house, she hears music, which is not unusual, but this music isn't being pumped through the sound system. Someone is playing classical guitar. The piece sounds Spanish, and although many things sound Spanish when played on a classical twelve-string, this has a definite flamenco feel.

Risa follows the tune to the main living room, where Cam sits, curled over the instrument, lost in the music he's playing. She didn't even know he played—but she shouldn't be surprised; he came loaded with a veritable full house of skills.

Still, playing guitar like this requires the melding of many things: muscle memory, combined with cortical and auditory memory, everything linked through a brain stem capable of coordinating it all.

The music lulls her, disarms her, enchants her, and she begins to realize that these are not just other people's parts. Someone is pulling those parts together. For the first time Risa truly begins to see Cam as an individual, struggling to pull together the many gifts he's been given. He didn't ask for these things, and he couldn't refuse them if he wanted to. As horrified as she was by him five minutes ago, this new revelation soothes her. It compels her to sit at the piano across the room and begin a simple accompaniment.

When he hears her, he brings his instrument closer, and sits beside her. No words are spoken; instead they communicate through the rhythms and harmonies. He lets her take control of the piece, lets it evolve at her hand, then she seamlessly gives it over to him again. They could go on for hours, and soon realize that they actually have, but neither one wants to be the first to stop.

Maybe, Risa thinks, there is a way to make this life work, and maybe there's not—but right now, in the moment, there's nothing more wonderful than losing herself to the music. Until now, she had forgotten how good that feels.

47 · Audience

Back from commercial, the studio audience applauds on cue, as if the viewers at home missed something.

"For those of you just tuning in," says one of the show's hosts, "our guests today are Camus Comprix and Risa Ward."

The young man with multiple skin tones that are exotic yet

pleasing to the eye waves to the audience with one hand. With
the other he clasps the hand of the pretty girl next to him. The
couple looks perfect—as if they were meant to be. Camus, the
audience quickly learns, prefers to be called Cam. He's even
more interesting to behold in person than in the many teaser
ads they've seen—ads that prepared them for something mysterious and wonderful. But this boy isn't mysterious at all—just
wonderful, and they are certainly not shocked by his appearance, because the ads have fermented shock into intoxicating
curiosity.

The studio audience, as well as the audience at home,
is more than primed, because they know this is something
special—this is Cam's first major public appearance. And
what better way to welcome him into the spotlight than on
Brunch with Jarvis and Holly, a friendly, nonthreatening
morning talk show? Everyone loves Jarvis and Holly, who
are so funny together and are in such comfortable command
of their fashionably decorated faux living room set.

"Cam, there's quite a controversy as to how you . . . 'came
to be.' I wonder how you feel about that?" asks Holly.

"Not my problem," Cam says. "It used to bother me when
people would say terrible things about me, but I came to realize it only matters what one person thinks."

"Yourself," Holly prompts.

"No, her," he says, and glances at Risa. The audience
laughs. Risa offers a humble smile. Then Holly and Jarvis go
into some cute little banter about who wears the pants in various relationships. Jarvis poses the next question.

"Risa, you've been through a lot yourself. A ward of the
state, a rehabilitated AWOL . . . I'm sure our audience would
love to know how you and Cam met."

"I got to know Cam after my spinal surgery," Risa tells the
world. "It was the same clinic where he got put together. He

came to see me every day to talk to me. Eventually I came to realize that . . ." She hesitates for a moment, perhaps choked up by her emotions. "I came to realize that his whole was greater than the sum of his parts."

It is just the type of thing people love to hear. The whole audience releases a collective "Aw . . ." Cam smiles at Risa and clasps her hand tighter.

"We've all seen your public service announcements," says Holly. "I still get chills when I see you rise out of that wheel-chair." Then she turns to the audience. "Am I right?" The audience applauds in agreement; then she turns back to Risa. "Yet I would think when you were an AWOL you must have been very much against unwinding."

"Well," says Risa, "who wouldn't be against it when you're the one being unwound?"

"So exactly when did your feelings change?"

Risa takes a visibly deep breath, and Cam squeezes her hand again. "It isn't so much that they changed . . . but I found myself having to accept a broader perspective. If it hadn't been for unwinding, Cam wouldn't exist, and we wouldn't be here together today. There's always going to be suffering in the world, but unwinding takes suffering away from those of us"— she hesitates again—"those of us living meaningful lives."

"So then," Jarvis asks, "what would you say to kids out there who are AWOL?"

Risa looks down rather than at Jarvis when she speaks. "I would say if you're running, then run—because you have every right to try to survive. But no matter what happens to you, know that your life has meaning."

"Maybe even more meaning if they're unwound?" prompts Jarvis.

"Maybe so."

Then they segue into an introduction of a top fashion

designer, here to present a whole new line of trend-setting patchwork clothes inspired by Camus Comprix. Designs for men and women, boys and girls.

"We call it Rewind Chic," says the designer, and models parade out to gleeful applause.

48 · Risa

Once their appearance with Jarvis and Holly is over, Risa holds Cam's hand until they are backstage and out of view of the audience. Then she releases it in disgust. Not disgust at him, but at herself.

"What is it?" Cam asks. "I'm sorry if I did something wrong."

"Shut up! Just shut up!"

She looks for the bathroom but can't find it. This blasted studio set is a maze, and everyone from the interns to the crew stares at them as they pass, as if they're royalty. These people must get celebrities on this show every day, so what makes them any different? But she knows the answer to that: After a while a celebrity is just a celebrity, but there is only one Camus Comprix. He is the new golden child of humanity, and as for Risa, well, it's "gilt" by association.

Finally she finds the bathroom and locks herself in, sits on the toilet, and buries her head in her hands. To have to defend unwinding—to have to say that the world is a better place because innocent kids are being unwound—shreds her inside. Her self-respect, her integrity are gone. Now, not only does she wish she hadn't survived the explosion at Happy Jack, she wishes she had never been born at all.

Why are you doing this, Risa?

It's the voices of all the kids at the Graveyard. *Why?* It's the voice of Connor, accusing her, and rightfully so. She wishes she could explain her reasons to him, and the deal with the devil she made with Roberta. A she-devil with the power to build herself a perfect boy.

And perfect, he very well may be. At least by society's definition. Risa can't deny that with each day, Cam grows more and more into his potential. He's smart and strong, and has the capacity to be profoundly wise when he's not being profoundly self-centered. The fact that she's starting to see him as a real boy and not a piecemeal Pinocchio bothers her almost as much as the things she said today on camera.

There is an urgent banging at the bathroom door.

"Risa," Cam calls, "are you okay? Please come out, you're scaring me."

"Leave me alone!" Risa shouts.

He says nothing more, but when she finally leaves the bathroom five minutes later, he's still standing there, waiting. He would probably have waited all day and all night. She wonders whether such unyielding resolve came from his parts, or if it's something he's developed on his own.

She suddenly finds herself bursting into tears and throwing herself into his arms, not even knowing why. She wants to tear him to bits, yet she desperately wants him to comfort her. She wants to destroy everything he represents, and yet she wants to cry on his shoulder because she has no other shoulder to cry on. Around them, people ogle them, trying to be inconspicuous about it. Their hearts are warmed by what appears to be the embrace of two souls in love.

"Unfair," he says. "They shouldn't make you do these things if you're not ready to do them." And the fact that he, the subject of all this attention, understands her, empathizes with her, and is somehow on her side, confuses everything inside her even more.

"It's not always going to be like this," Cam whispers to her. She wants to believe that, but right now she can only imagine it being worse.

49 · Cam

There are things that Roberta hasn't told him. Her control over Risa is more than a mere matter of wills. It's not as simple as gratitude for a new spine, because Risa isn't grateful at all. It's very clear that her spine is a burden she wishes she didn't have to bear. Then why did she consent?

Every moment they're together the question hangs heavy in the air, but when he broaches the subject, all Risa says is, "It was something I had to do," and when he tries to probe deeper, she loses patience and tells him to stop pushing. "My reasons are my own."

He wants to believe that he's the reason why she's doing all the things she's doing—all these things that clearly go against her grain. But if there are any parts of him that are naive enough to believe that she'd do these interviews and ads for his sake, they are outnumbered by the parts of him that know better.

Their appearance on *Brunch with Jarvis and Holly* made it painfully clear that whatever pain Risa is feeling over her part in all this runs very deep. The fact that she allowed him to comfort her didn't change that. If anything, it made him feel a responsibility to get to the bottom of it—not just for his own sake, but for hers. For how could anything between them ever be real without a full disclosure?

It all comes down to the day she signed that consent form—but asking Roberta about it is a useless endeavor. Then Cam realizes he doesn't have to . . . because Roberta is the queen of surveillance videos.

"I need to see the surveillance records from April seventeenth," Cam tells the security guard he's most friendly with—the one he plays basketball with—after they return to Molokai.

"No can do," he tells Cam, right off the bat. "No one sees those without permission from you-know-who. Get her permission, and I'll show you whatever you want."

"She'll never know."

"Don't matter."

"But it'll matter if I tell her I caught you trying to steal from the mansion." That makes the guard stutter. "Allow me," Cam says. "You say, 'You son of a bitch, you can't do that,' and I say 'Yes, I can, and who do you think she'll believe, me or you?'" Then Cam hands him a flash drive. "So just put the files on this, and everyone's life will be easier."

The guard looks at him incredulously. "You're a real piece of work, you know that? The apple doesn't fall far from the tree."

And although Cam knows who he's referring to, he says, "I've got lots of trees, you'll have to be more specific."

That evening the drive turns up in his desk drawer, packed with video files. He doubts he'll have a basketball partner anymore, but it's a small sacrifice to make. When it's late enough to know he won't be interrupted, he loads the files onto his personal viewer—and witnesses something he was never supposed to see. . . .

50 · Risa

April 17. Almost two months ago. Before the interviews and the public service announcements, before the operation that replaced Risa's severed spine.

Risa sits in her wheelchair in a sparse cell with nothing to occupy her time but her own thoughts. A consent form folded into a paper airplane lies on the floor beneath a one-way mirror.

She spends her time thinking about her friends. Of Connor, mostly. She wonders how he'll fare without her. Better, she hopes. If she could only get word to him that she's alive, that she hasn't been tortured at the hands of the Juvies—and that she's not even in their hands, but in the hands of some other organization.

Roberta comes in, as she did the day before, with a new consent form. She sits down at the table and slides the consent form and a pen toward Risa again.

She smiles at Risa, but it's the smile of a snake about to coil around its prey.

"Are you ready to sign?" she asks.

"Are you ready to see me fly another paper airplane?" Risa responds.

"Airplanes!" says Roberta brightly. "Yes, why don't we talk about airplanes? Particularly the ones in the aircraft salvage yard. The place you call the Graveyard. Let's talk about your many friends there."

At last, thinks Risa, *she's going to question me.* "Ask whatever you want," she says. "But if I were you, I wouldn't trust a thing I say."

"No need to ask you questions, dear," Roberta says. "We know all we need to know about the Graveyard. You see, we allow your little AWOL sanctuary to exist because it serves our needs."

"Your needs? You're telling me you control the Juvenile Authority?"

"Let's just say we have substantial sway. The Juvenile Authority has wanted to raid the Graveyard for quite a while, but we're the ones holding them back. However, if I give the word, the Graveyard will be cleaned out, and all those children who you fought so valiantly to save will be transported to harvest camps and unwound."

Risa can sense the rug being pulled out from under her. "You're bluffing."

"Am I? I believe you know our inside man. His name is Trace Neuhauser."

The news completely blindsides her. "Trace?"

"He's provided us with all the information we need to make a takedown of the airplane Graveyard quick and painless." She pushes the consent form just an inch closer to Risa. "However, it never needs to happen. None of those AWOLs need be unwound. Please, Risa. Accept a new spine, and do all we ask of you. If you do, I will personally guarantee that all seven hundred nineteen of your friends will be unharmed. Help *me*, Risa, and you'll save *them*."

Risa looks at the paper, seeing it in a terrible new light. "What types of things?" she asks. "What types of things will you ask me to do?"

"It will begin with Cam. You will put aside your feelings, whatever they may be, and learn to be kind to him. As for what other things we may ask of you, you will know when it is your time to know."

She waits for Risa's response, but she has none. The shrapnel of this bombshell has yet to come to rest.

Risa's silence seems to satisfy Roberta, so she stands, leaving Risa with the form and the pen. "As you pointed out before, I won't take away your choice—it remains in your rights to refuse . . . but if you do, I hope you can live with the consequences."

Risa holds the pen in her hand and reads the document for the fourth time. A single page filled with incomprehensible legalese. She doesn't need to decipher the fine print—it's pretty obvious what it says. By signing it, she gives her express permission to replace her damaged spine with a healthy one, harvested from an anonymous Unwind.

How many times has she imagined what it would be like to walk again? How many times has she relived that moment at Happy Jack Harvest Camp when the roof collapsed and crushed her back, and wondered what it would be like to have that moment erased?

The way Risa saw it, however, the cost of the new spine would be her soul. Her conscience couldn't allow it, not then, not ever. Or so she thought.

If she looks at the big picture and refuses to sign it, she makes a personal statement against a world that's lost its way . . . but no one will ever know, and her statement will cause hundreds of her friends to be unwound.

Roberta claims that Risa has a choice, but what choice does she really have? She holds the pen firm, takes a deep breath, and signs her name.

51 · Cam

Roberta is overjoyed by the response to the *Jarvis and Holly* appearance. She's already fielded dozens of interview requests.

"We can afford to be choosy," she tells Cam the morning after he views the surveillance video. "Quality versus quantity!"

Cam says nothing, and Roberta is so wrapped up in her own plans, she fails to notice that Cam isn't himself.

You will put aside your feelings, whatever they may be, and learn to be kind to him.

He takes his frustration out alone on the basketball court, and when that doesn't calm him down, he takes it to the source. He searches the sprawling manor for Risa. He finds her in the kitchen, making herself a late-morning sandwich. "I get tired of being served all the time," she says casually. "Sometimes all I want is a PB&J that I make myself." She holds out the sandwich to him. "You want this one? I'll make another."

When he doesn't take it, she looks at his eyes and sees how off he is. "What's the matter? Have a fight with Mommy?"

"I know why you're here," he tells her. "I know all about your deal with Roberta, and your friends at the Graveyard."

She hesitates for a moment, then begins to eat her sandwich. "You have your deal with her, I have mine," she says in a peanut-butter-muffled voice. She tries to walk away, but Cam grabs her. She quickly pulls out of his grasp and pushes him against the wall. "I've come to accept it!" she yells at him. "So you might as well too!"

"So was it all just pretend? Was being nice to the freak just a performance to save your friends?"

"Yes!" snaps Risa. "At first."

"And now?"

"Do you really think so little of yourself? Do you really think I'm that good of an actress?"

"Then prove it!" he demands. "Prove that you feel anything but contempt for me!"

"Right now that's all I feel for you!" Then she storms out, hurling her sandwich into the trash.

Five minutes later, Cam swipes a pass card from an inattentive guard and uses it to get past the security door into the garage. Then he steals a motorcycle and takes off down the winding path out of the estate.

He has no destination, just a burning need for acceleration. He's sure there is at least one speed freak in his head, maybe more. He knows several of his constituents drove motorcycles. He takes every turn too fast until he finally gets to the town of Kualapuu, giving satisfaction to every self-destructive impulse that resides within him. Then he takes a turn too sharply, loses control, and flies from the bike, rolling over and over on the pavement.

He's hurt, but he's alive. Motorists stop and get out of their cars to help him, but he doesn't want their help. He gets to his feet and feels a sharp pain in his knee. His back feels shredded; blood from beneath his hairline clouds his eyes.

"Hey, buddy, you okay?" yells some tourist. Then he stops short. "Hey! Hey, it's you! You're that rewind kid! Hey, look, it's that rewind kid!"

He hurries away from them and gets on the motorcycle again, riding back the way he came. By the time he arrives, there are already police cars out front. Roberta sees him and runs to him.

"Cam!" she wails. "What did you do? What did you do? My God! You need medical attention! We'll get the doctor right away!" Then she turns angrily to the house guards. "How could you let this happen?"

"It's not their fault!" yells Cam. "I'm not a dog that got off its leash, so don't treat me like one!"

"Let me look at your wounds. . . ."

"Back off!" he yells loudly enough for her to actually back off. Then he pushes past everyone, goes up to his room, and locks the world out.

A few minutes later there's a gentle knocking at his door, as he knew there would be. Roberta, trying to handle her volatile boy with kid gloves. But it's not Roberta.

"Open up, Cam, it's Risa."

She's the second-to-last person he wants to see right now, but the fact that she came surprises him. The least he can do is open the door.

She stands at his threshold with a first aid kit in her hand. "It's really stupid to bleed out just because you're pissed off."

"I'm not 'bleeding out.'"

"But you *are* bleeding. Can I at least take care of the worst of it? Believe it or not, I was the chief medic at the Graveyard. I dealt with stuff like this all the time."

He opens the door wider and lets her in. He sits at his desk chair and allows her to clean the wound on his cheek. Then she has him take off his torn shirt and begins cleaning his back. It stings, but he bears it without wincing.

"You're lucky," she tells him. "You have lacerations, but none of them need stitches, and you didn't tear any of your seams."

"I'm sure Roberta will be relieved."

"Roberta can go to hell."

For once Cam agrees with her. She takes a look at his knee and tells him that whether he likes it or not, he's going to need to have it x-rayed. When she's done assessing his wounds, he takes a good look at her. If she's still angry at him from before, it doesn't show. "I'm sorry," he says. "Going out like that was stupid."

"It was human," she points out.

Cam reaches out and gently touches her face. Let her slap him for it. Let her rip his arm out of its socket, he doesn't care.

But she doesn't do either of those things. "C'mon," she says. "Let's get you over to your bed so you can get some rest."

He stands but puts too much weight on his knee and almost goes down. She holds him, giving him support, the way he once gave her support on the first day she walked. She helps him all the way to the bed, and when he flops onto it, her arm is looped around him in such a way that she's pulled down onto the bed too.

"Sorry."

"Stop apologizing for everything," she tells him. "Save it for your more important screwups."

Now they lie side by side on his bed, his aching back stinging even more pressed against the blanket. She could get up, but she doesn't. Instead she rolls slightly toward him and brushes her fingers across a scrape on his chest, checking to see if it needs a bandage, then determining it doesn't.

"You're quite the freak, Camus Comprix. How I got used to that is a mystery to me. I did, though."

"But you still wish I was never made, don't you?"

"But you were, and you're here, and I'm here with you." Then she adds, "And I only hate you sometimes."

"And other times?"

She leans toward him, thinks about it for a moment, then kisses him. It's more than a peck, but only slightly more. "Other times, I don't." Then she rolls onto her back and stays there beside him.

"Don't read too much into this, Cam," she tells him. "I can't be what you want."

"There are lots of things I want," he points out. "Who says I have to have all of them?"

"Because you're Roberta's spoiled little boy. You always get whatever your rewound heart desires."

Cam sits up so he can look at her. "So unspoil me. Teach me to be patient. Teach me that there are some things worth waiting for."

"And some things you might never have?"

He thinks about his answer, then says, "If that's what you have to teach me, then that's what I'll have to learn—but what I want most is something I think I can have."

"What might that be?"

He takes her hand and holds it. "This moment, right now, in a thousand different ways. If I can have that, then the rest won't matter as much."

She sits up and pulls her hand away from his, but only so she can brush it through his hair. She seems to be just looking at the wound on his scalp, but maybe not.

"If that's really what you want most," she says gently, "maybe you can have it. Maybe we both can."

Cam smiles. "I'd like that very much."

And for the first time since being wound, he feels tears welling in his eyes that he knows are truly his own.

Part Six

Fight or Flight

Google search: "Feral teenagers." About 12,100 results (0.12 seconds)

Global Faultlines | World Politics, Political Economy, Contemporary . . . "Nihilistic and **feral teenagers**" the Daily Mail called them: the crazy youths from all walks of life who raced around the streets mindlessly and . . .

The Black Flag Cafe© • View topic - feral teenagers attack . . . 3 posts - 2 authors - Last post: Jul 7, 2007—**feral teenagers** attack once more........ » Fri Jul 06, 2007 10:31 pm. WEST PALM BEACH, Fla. - Two teenagers were accused of . . .

Feral007's Blog—Random rants about feral teenagers » teenagers Random rants about **feral teenagers**. Day to day problems of a single parent with teenagers! What to do?

Feral Teenagers Attack Strangers in Philadelphia Aug 18, 2011—The word "wilding" refers to gangs of teenagers assaulting strangers for fun and . . .

"Feral" teenagers beat man to death - News - Wigan Today Apr 4, 2007—Two **"feral" teenagers** who subjected a harmless and deeply vulnerable Wigan man to months of bullying before savagely . . .

Silver Spring, Singular: Coveting thy Neighbor's Restaurants Jun 30, 2010—Bethesda has far fewer packs of **feral teenagers**, which makes the whole downtown experience over there vastly more pleasant . . .

52 · Lev

Lev is woken by a burst of ice water in his face. At first he thinks he's out in the storm again. A tornado was coming—did he get hit by a tree? He has to get up. Must keep running. Running.

But he's not in the storm. He's not outside. His focus is blurry, but he can see enough to know he's in some sort of room, looking at a dirty wall. No, not a wall, a ceiling. A water-stained ceiling. And he's lying on a bed. And his hands are tied above his head. Tied to the bed frame. His mouth tastes like battery acid, the air smells like mildew, and his head pounds, pounds, pounds. Now he remembers! He was in a van with Miracolina. Hail was pummeling the van. Then they were tranq'd by—

"Awake?" Nelson says. Lev remembers his name now. Nelson. Officer Nelson. Lev had never seen the man's face, but his name was in the news almost as much as Lev's. He doesn't look much like a Juvey-cop now.

"Sorry for the water alarm. I'd have given you a wake-up call, but there's no phone service here."

On a bed next to Lev is Miracolina, still unconscious. Like him, her hands are tied to her bed frame with plastic cable ties.

Lev coughs up some water. Nelson sits a few feet away, his legs crossed, holding his tranq gun.

"You know, I've been staking out the Cavenaugh mansion for days. Just had a hunch. See, everything pointed to a major safe house in the area, but no one could nail down the location. But the Cavenaugh estate—there's that guard gate made to look abandoned that's not abandoned at all. And all those state-of-the art surveillance cameras in the trees that border the property. I didn't know the resistance had that kind of money!"

Lev says nothing, but Nelson doesn't seem to care. Apparently he's just happy to have a captive audience.

"So, imagine my surprise when I find you and your friend practically gift-wrapped by the side of the road!" Nelson pops the clip from his tranq gun, slides out the dart bullets one by one, then reloads it, snapping the clip back in. On the other bed, Miracolina groans, finally beginning to stir out of her deep sleep.

"Here's what I think." Nelson leans closer to Lev. "You were escorting this poor little AWOL girl to the Cavenaugh mansion and into the arms of your scofflaw friends, but on the way you got caught in the storm. Am I right?"

"Not even close," Lev croaks.

"Ah well, the particulars don't really matter. The point is, you're here."

"And where is here?"

"Like I said," says Nelson, waving the gun, "the particulars don't matter."

Lev looks over toward Miracolina again. Her eyes are half-open, but she's still not entirely conscious. "Let her go," he says. "She's got nothing to do with this."

Nelson smiles. "How noble of you—thinking of the girl before yourself. Who says chivalry is dead?"

"What do you want?" Lev asks, his head aching too much to dance around the point. "I can't get you your job back, and it's not my fault Connor tranqed you, so what do you want from me?"

"Actually," says Nelson, "it *is* your fault. If you weren't being used as a human shield, none of us would be here today."

Lev realizes how true that is. Had he not inadvertently taken Nelson's bullet meant for Connor, then both of them would have been unwound on schedule.

"So, shall we play?" Nelson asks.

Lev swallows, and his throat feels like it's coated with wood shavings. "What's the game?"

"Russian roulette! My clip is loaded with five tranq bullets and one nickel-plated lead shell with an explosive tip. I can't recall in what position I put Mr. Bad Bullet—I was too busy talking to you to notice. I will ask you questions, and if I don't like an answer, I shoot."

"This game could last for days if I keep going unconscious."

"Or it could be over very quickly."

Lev takes a deep breath and tries not to show any more fear than he has to. "Sounds exciting. I'm in."

"Well, it's not quite the thrill of clapping, but I'll try to keep you from getting bored." He takes the safety off the weapon. "Question one. Is your friend Connor still alive?"

Lev suspected he might ask this, so he does his best to lie as honestly as he can. "I've heard the rumors too," he says, "but I'm out of that loop. He was taken away, bloody and unconscious, from Happy Jack, and I was arrested. Beyond that, I have no idea."

Nelson smiles at him, then says, "Wrong answer," and swings the gun toward Miracolina.

"No!"

Nelson fires without hesitation. Miracolina arches her back as she's hit, releasing a semiconscious gasp, then falls silent. Lev's heart feels like it's about to explode, until he sees the tiny telltale tranq flag sticking out of her shirt.

Nelson stands and shakes his head at Lev. "I'd better like your next answer." Then he leaves, closing the door.

53 · Nelson

Nelson decides to give Lev plenty of time to think about it. In the meantime, he sits in an adjoining room of the cottage, researching the leads he already has. Not that many. He has tagged nearly a dozen AWOLs, letting them think they've escaped from him. Some are still on the streets not far from where he originally captured them. Others are at harvest camps, having been caught by the Juvies. One appears to be in Argentina, although he suspects the kid was caught by another parts pirate and unwound on the black market, which means only his tagged part went to South America. There are two signals pinging from Arizona at the site of an old defunct air force base. This he finds the most curious. He heard talk of some sort of AWOL sanctuary in the Southwest when he was still with the Juvies, but details were sketchy, and he hadn't had high enough security clearance to learn any more about it, or interest at the time to care. In any case, Arizona is too far away for him to jump to any conclusions. Unless, of course, his little clapper boy places Connor there.

The tranq bullets Nelson loaded in his pistol are the mildest kind, with the shortest half-life. When he returns about two hours later, he lingers outside the door, listening. The girl is awake but groggy, and Lev is all about apologizing for getting her involved in this. No talk of Connor or any potential AWOL hideouts.

Nelson kicks open the door for effect, then sits calmly in the chair between them, brandishing his pistol, just in case there's any question about his intentions.

"Are we ready?" Nelson says. "Five bullets left. A twenty percent chance that the next one is lethal."

Lev avoids eye contact with him, struggling to keep his breathing under control. As he already knows the surprise ending of the game, Nelson aims the gun at the girl even before asking the question.

"You think I'm afraid to die, but I'm not," the girl says. However, the warble in her voice says otherwise.

"Please," Lev begs. "You don't have to do this."

"I believe I do," Nelson cheerfully tells him. He clears his throat. "Round two. The question is . . . Where is the Akron AWOL hiding? You have three seconds before the buzzer."

"Please don't," Lev pleads again.

"One!"

"Turn it on me! She has nothing to do with this!"

"Two!"

"I'm the one with the wrong answers! Not her!"

"Three!"

"No! Wait! I'll tell you! I'll tell you!"

He cocks the trigger. "Better make it quick."

Lev takes a deep, shuddering breath. "Indian Echo Caverns. In Pennsylvania. It's where the AWOLs from the East Coast are hidden. They take them deep in the caverns and keep them there until they turn seventeen. Connor's helping them run it."

"Hmm," says Nelson, considering it. "It's on an Indian rez. I'll bet stinking Slotmongers are always giving sanctuary to AWOLs."

He puts the gun across his lap and leans back in his chair. "Now I have a dilemma. Of all the AWOLs I've tagged, none of them have gone in that direction. So who should I believe? You or my data?"

"Where were you tagging them?" Lev asks quickly. "If they're west of Pittsburgh, they probably go someplace else if the resistance picks them up—and don't ask me where, because I don't know!"

Nelson smiles. "You know, I'm so glad you didn't blow your-self to smithereens last year, young man. Because you've just saved this girl's life. Assuming, of course, that you're telling the truth."

"If I'm lying," says Lev, "you can come back and kill us both."

That makes Nelson laugh. "If it turns out you're lying, I would have done that anyway, but thank you for giving me per-mission."

Then he leaves, making no attempt to free them from their bonds.

54 · Lev

"Were you telling the truth?" Miracolina asks,

"Of course I was," Lev says, just in case Nelson is still listen-ing. A few moments later he hears Nelson's van start and drive off. The fact is, it hadn't mattered what Lev told him—what mattered was Nelson believing it. Lev pulled the location out of his memory—he had been to Indian Echo Caverns with his fam-ily many years before. He remembered the guide saying that it used to be a hideout for outlaws. Lev stayed close to his mother, fearing that those outlaws might still be lurking in shadowy crev-ices. Lev has no idea if AWOLs really are hiding there. He hopes not, now that he's unleashed Nelson on the place.

"So what do we do?" Miracolina asks. "If he catches your friend, he won't be back, and we'll starve to death, and if your friend's not there, he'll come back and kill us."

"I thought you weren't afraid of dying."

"I'm not. I just don't want to die a senseless death."

"We won't. Not if I can help it." Then he begins to roll back and forth on his bed. His hands are secured tightly to two of the metal bedposts with the cable ties, but his feet are able to build a kind of rocking momentum. He throws his weight left, then right, over and over again, and the bed begins to scrape on the ground beneath him as he does. He tries to flip the bed but can't build the momentum, and eventually he has to rest.

"It's not working," Miracolina says, stating what's more than obvious.

"Then maybe you should start praying. I sure am."

After a few minutes' rest, he tries it again. This time he's able to slide the bed over a little bit more with his rocking, until one of the legs catches on an uneven floorboard. Now when he rocks the bed, the legs on the other side rise slightly off the ground. He loses his strength, and the pain of the plastic ties digging into his wrists gets to him. He has to stop, but after a few minutes of recovery he tries again, and again, each time getting closer to the exact force, and the exact torque it will take. Then finally, releasing a clenched-jawed groan, he hurls all his weight toward the far wall, practically wrenching his arms out of their sockets—and the bed rises, its future dangling like a coin between heads and tails—and then it flips upside down. The metal frame and the mattress land on top of him. Lev's elbows smash painfully on the rotting wooden floor, splinters digging in. With the bed lying on top of him, he has a momentary flashback to the explosion in the town house and being pinned beneath the sofa. His brother's face, and Pastor Dan's. He tries to draw strength from the moment, rather than let himself be overwhelmed by grief.

"You did it! That was great!" he can hear Miracolina saying, although he can't see her. "Now what?"

"Not sure yet."

Lev's hands are still painfully tied to the metal headboard bars. He can see how badly his wrists are bleeding, and there's rust on his hands too. He thinks about tetanus, and how they

NEAL SHUSTERMAN

always want you to get a tetanus shot when you step on a rusty nail or something. He thinks about how, at his family's beach home, the iron fence had rusted into nothing from exposure to salt air. *Rusted into nothing . . .* He looks to where the head-board bars connect to the bed frame. The bar to which his left hand is attached is practically rusted all the way through. Ignoring the pain again, he tugs and he tugs until finally the pole breaks and his hand comes free.

"What's going on down there?" Miracolina asks.

He reaches up and grabs her hand instead of telling her, and she gasps.

The bar that secures his right hand is not in the same weak state as the other, but it is rusty also, and rough. He knows he can't break this pole like the other one, so he tries a different tactic. He begins to move his wrist back and forth, scraping the plastic tie against the jagged, rusted metal. Bit by bit the plastic is worn away, until finally the tie shreds apart and his hand comes free. He wipes the blood from his wrists on the mattress and stands up.

"How did you do it?" she asks.

"Superpowers," he tells her. He looks at Miracolina's bonds, then reaches beneath her mattress to find the same rusted metal. He pulls the bed away from the wall and, stand-ing behind it, kicks at the bars until the ones Miracolina are attached to break free. She pulls her hands away, peeling the plastic loops over her knuckles.

"You okay?" Lev asks, and she nods. "Good. Let's get out of here." But the moment he puts weight on his right ankle, he grimaces and starts to limp.

"What is it?" Miracolina asks.

"I think I sprained my ankle kicking out the bars," Lev tells her. She lets him put his weight on her, and she helps him walk.

As they open the front door, it becomes clear where they're being held. It's a cottage in the woods, so isolated they could have screamed at the top of their lungs for days and no one would have heard them.

There's a dirt path leading out to what Lev hopes is a major road. He tries putting weight on his ankle and grimaces again—so she continues to let him put his arm over her shoulder, and he gratefully accepts her assistance.

Then, when they're a good distance away from the shack, he says, "I'm really going to need your help now. You have to help me warn my friend."

She steps away from him, and he almost topples, but manages to keep his balance.

"I'll do no such thing. Your friend is not my problem."

"Please, look at me. I can barely walk—I can't make it there on my own."

"I'll get you to a hospital."

Lev shakes his head. "When I went to Cavenaugh, I broke the terms of my parole. If I get caught, I'll get locked away for good."

"Don't blame me for that!"

"I just saved your life," Lev reminds her. "Don't repay me by destroying mine."

She looks at him almost as hatefully as the day they first met. "That parts pirate will get to the caverns before we do. What's the point?" Then she studies him for a moment as if reading Lev's mind, and says, "Your friend's not in the caverns, is he?"

"No."

She sighs. "Of course not."

55 · Miracolina

Miracolina is not a girl given to impulsive behavior. All things must be planned and have sufficient time to settle before being carried out. Even her escape from the Cavenaugh mansion was not a wild bolt, but the result of careful preparation. Therefore, she is completely unprepared for the madness that overtakes her as she stands in that dirt path with Lev.

"I will contact my parents before I help you get anywhere," she tells him, realizing that by saying this, she's entered into negotiation. She's actually considering going with him. Perhaps it's post-traumatic stress disorder.

"You can't call your parents. If you do, they'll know your tithing bus wasn't attacked by parts pirates. It will compromise the entire Cavenaugh operation."

"If you care so much about it," she asks him, "then why did you run?"

He takes a moment before answering, shifting his weight and grimacing again. "Their work is good," he says. "It just isn't mine."

This baffles her. His motives—his hazy integrity. It was easy to dismiss Lev as "part of the problem" when she did not know him, but now it's not so easy. He's a paradox. This is a boy who almost blew himself to bits in an attempt to kill others, and yet he offered himself to the parts pirate in order to save Miracolina's life. How could someone go from having no respect for one's own existence to being willing to give himself as a sacrifice for someone he barely knows? It flies in the face of the truths that have defined Miracolina's life. The bad are bad, the good are good, and being caught in between is just an illusion. There is no gray.

"I will contact my parents and let them know that I am alive," she demands, holding firm. "Just knowing I'm alive will make them happy."

"A call can be traced."

"We'll be moving, won't we? If my parents report it to the Juvenile Authority, they'll only know where we've been, not where we're going." And then she asks, "Where *are* we going?"

"I guess you can get in touch with your parents," Lev says, giving in, "but don't ask where we're going. The less you know, the better."

And although that sends a red warning flag flying to the top of her mast, she says, "Fine." Then she puts her hands on her hips. "And you can stop pretending your ankle hurts. That will just slow us down."

Lev puts his full weight on the ankle and offers her up an impish little grin. It's in this moment that Miracolina realizes she lost this negotiation before it began. Because even before he asked her to come along with him, a part of herself—secret even to her—had already decided that she would.

56 · Lev

The journey to the Graveyard is different for Lev than his first time. That first trek had no definite destination beyond a slow downward spiral, and was made while his wounded spirit was so raw, he had been ripe for recruitment by the Clappers. He had been lost with no real way to cope with his anger.

First there was CyFi, and the kid in CyFi's head who didn't even know he had already been unwound. Then Lev was left alone to fend for himself, prey for bottom-feeders as stealthy as mosquitoes. They would offer help, or shelter, or food—but they all had some bloodsucking agenda. A brief stint in a

Chance folk rez bolstered his strength, but even that ended with a nasty run-in with a parts pirate. Lev's time surviving under the radar had made him street-smart and resourceful. He had been toughened by a brutal baptism of life experience. In those bleak days, the idea of blowing himself up and taking as much of the world with him as he could didn't sound like such a bad idea.

But he is not in that dark place now, and he knows that no matter what happens to him, he'll never be in that place again.

To honor Miracolina's wishes, Lev slips a cell phone out of the coat pocket of a businessman so she can call home. The call is brief, and as promised, she gives no more information than the fact that she's alive, cutting off her mother's rapid-fire inquiry by quickly hanging up.

"There, are you happy?" she snaps at Lev. "Short and sweet." She insists he return the phone to the same business-man's pocket, but he's long gone, so he drops it in the pocket of a similar man.

With no money of their own, everything they need must be stolen. Lev uses milder versions of the survival tricks he learned his first time on the streets. Smash and grab without the smash. Breaking and entering without any actual breaking. Oddly, Miracolina has no problem with them stealing.

"I am making a list of all the things we take, and where we take them from," she tells him. "All will be paid for in full before I am unwound."

However, the fact that she is allowing for the bending of her personal moral code gives Lev hope that it may bend enough to break her of her tithing fixation.

He knows that time is of the essence. Nelson is the kind of human bloodhound who won't give up—and he'll be even more relentless once he realizes Lev has lied to him. They have to warn Connor.

Neither Lev nor Miracolina can drive, or look old enough to get away with it if they could—and kids their age traveling on conventional transportation stick out like sore thumbs. So they ride in the shadows of the world. The containers of eighteen-wheelers, when they can get inside; the beds of pickups when there are tarps under which to hide. More than once they're chased away, but never seriously pursued. Luckily, most people have more important things to do than run after a couple of kids.

"I hate what we're doing, and how we're doing it!" Miracolina yells, after running from a particularly aggressive trucker who chased them with a tire iron for all of ten yards. "I feel dirty! I feel subhuman."

"Good," Lev tells her. "Now you know how a real AWOL feels."

He has to admit that being back on the fringe is exhilarating. That first time it was all about betrayal, alienation, and survival. He hated it, and still has nightmares about it—but now giving in to instincts, impulses, and the rush of adrenaline feels far more like home than being a caged bird in the Cavenaugh mansion. Some of that survival excitement seems to be rubbing off on Miracolina—for every time they get away with something, she loosens up. She even smiles.

The longest leg of their journey is in the baggage compartment of a Greyhound bus—having climbed in behind luggage when no one was looking. The bus, out of Tulsa, is bound for Albuquerque, just one state away from their destination.

"Are you ever going to tell me where this journey ends?"

"We're going to Tucson," he finally tells her, but nothing more specific than that.

The bus leaves at five in the evening and will travel through the night. They create a reasonably comfortable place for themselves among the luggage. Then, about two hours into the trip, Lev realizes he's in trouble. Even in the pitch dark of the cramped compartment, Miracolina can tell something's wrong, because she asks, "What's the matter?"

"Nothing," Lev says. Then he confesses. "I gotta pee."

"Well," says Miracolina in a superior voice that must have taken years to cultivate, "*I* thought ahead and went at the bus station."

Within ten minutes Lev realizes this is not going to end well.

"Are you going to wet your pants?" Miracolina asks.

"No!" says Lev. "I'd rather blow up."

"So I've heard."

"Very funny."

But as the bus hits a patch of rough road, it becomes painfully clear that holding it in is not an option. He will not foul the compartment . . . then he realizes that absorbency is only a luggage zipper away. He moves away from Miracolina and begins to unzip a suitcase.

"You're going to pee in someone's suitcase?"

"Do you have any other ideas?"

And suddenly Miracolina begins to snicker, then giggle, then cackle uncontrollably. "He's going to pee in someone's suitcase!"

"Quiet! Do you want the people in the bus to hear you?"

But Miracolina is beyond help. She's entered into a fullfledged laughter fit—the kind that leaves your stomach hurting. "They're gonna open their suitcase," she blurts between bursts of glee, *"and their clothes'll be full of pee!"*

For Lev this is no laughing matter. He opens the suitcase and feels around to make sure it's just clothes and nothing electronic, because that would be really bad—and Miracolina can't catch her breath. *"And I thought it was bad when shampoo spilled in mine!"*

"Shampoo!" says Lev. "You're a genius."

Lev rifles blindly through one suitcase, then a second,

until he comes up with a nice-size shampoo bottle. Then he frantically dumps the shampoo out in the corner of the luggage compartment and, without a second to lose, refills it with sweet relief. When he's done, he caps the bottle tightly. He considers putting it back in the suitcase, but decides it's best to just leave it rolling around at the far corner of the luggage compartment.

Lev releases a shivering sigh, then returns to his space next to Miracolina.

"Did you wash your hands?" she asks.

"Wash them?" Lev tells her. "They're covered with shampoo!"

Now they're both laughing, and when they breathe in, the cloying smell of cherry blossom shampoo fills the air around them, which just makes them laugh harder, until they're all laughed out.

And in the silence that falls afterward, something changes. The tension that has been strung taut between them since the moment they met now goes slack. Soon the motion of the bus begins lulling them to sleep. Lev feels Miracolina lean into his shoulder. He doesn't move for fear of waking her. He just enjoys the feeling of her there—certain that she would never do such a thing if she were awake.

And then she says, with no hint of sleep in her voice, "I forgive you."

Lev feels it begin deep inside him, just as it did on the day he realized his parents would never take him back. It's an emotional swell that can't be contained, and there's no bottle in the world big enough to hold it. And although he fights to keep his sobs silent, his chest begins to heave with them, and he knows he won't be able to stop any more than Miracolina was able to stop laughing. Although she must know he's racked with tears, she says nothing, just keeps her head on his shoulder as his tears fall into her hair.

All this time, Lev never realized what he needed. He did not need to be adored or pitied. He needed to be forgiven. Not by God, who is all-forgiving. Not by people like Marcus and Pastor Dan, who would always stand by his side. He needed to be forgiven by an unforgiving world. By someone who once despised him. Someone like Miracolina.

Only once his silent sobs have stopped does she speak to him. "You're so weird," she says. He wonders if she has any idea of the gift she has just given him. He's pretty sure she does.

Lev knows his world is different now. Maybe it's exhaustion, or stress, but in that rattling, bouncing, greasy, shampooey compartment, his life suddenly feels like it couldn't be any better.

Both he and Miracolina close their eyes and fall asleep, blissfully unaware of the brown van with a dented roof and shattered side window that has been following the bus since it left Tulsa.

57 · Connor

"Chatter," Hayden tells Connor. "All kinds of chatter."

Hayden paces the tight space in Connor's jet, hitting his head on the ceiling more than once. Connor has rarely seen Hayden this agitated. Until now, he always managed to keep the world at smirking distance.

"Is it just on the Tucson police bands, or the juvey bands too?"

"Everywhere," Hayden tells him. "Radio, e-mails, every communication we can intercept. The analysis programs have us shooting to red alert."

"They're just programs," Connor reminds him. "It doesn't necessarily mean—"

"There's chatter specifically about us. Code words mostly, but they're easy to crack."

Connor begins to wonder if his own paranoia has infected Hayden as well. "Just calm down and give me specifics."

"Okay," says Hayden, pacing and trying to slow his breathing. "There have been three house fires over the past two weeks. Three homes in different Tucson neighborhoods got burned to the ground, and they're blaming us for it."

Connor's grafted hand balls into a fist. That iron fist the Admiral had spoken of, perhaps. Didn't Trace say that there were people itching for a reason to take the Graveyard out? If they couldn't find a reason, it would be pretty easy to manufacture one.

"Where's Trace?" Connor asks. "If something's really going on, he would know."

Hayden just looks at him, confused. "Trace? Why would Trace know?"

"Never mind why, he just would. I have to talk to him."

Hayden shakes his head. "He's gone."

"What do you mean 'gone'?"

"No one's seen him since yesterday. I figured you sent him on some mission."

"Damn it!" Connor punches the wall, cracking the fiberglass interior of the corporate jet. So Trace finally decided which side he's on—and without him, they have no escape plan. No one but Trace can fly the Dreamliner.

"There's more," Hayden says, hesitating long enough for Connor to know that there's yet another round of bad news. "All three homes had Unwinds—and they burned the day before the Juvey-rounders were due to take them to Harvest camp. I checked, and the kids were on our list. And all three of them were storks."

• • •

"What the hell were you thinking?"

Connor doesn't hide his fury as he storms into GymBo, where Starkey works out like he doesn't have a care in the world.

"I don't know what you're talking about."

"Like hell you don't!"

Around them other kids leave their equipment and slowly approach, taking menacing positions. Only now does Connor realize that Starkey has completely surrounded himself with members of the Stork Club. There's not a single bio-raised kid there.

"How many of you were with him?" Connor demands. "How many of you are as crazy as he is?"

"Let me show you something, Connor." Starkey saunters over to a kid sitting on a side bench, who looks both angry and scared at the same time. "I'd like you to meet Garrett Parks, the newest member of the Stork Club. We liberated him last night."

Connor looks the kid over. He has a black eye, a swollen lip. He was pretty roughed up during his "liberation."

"They burned down your house—you know that, don't you?" Connor asks him.

The kid can't look Connor in the eye. "Yeah, I know."

"He also knows," adds Starkey, "that his so-called parents were about to have him unwound. We saved him, and sent a message."

"Yeah, you sent a message, all right. To the Juvies. You told them that it's time to take every last one of us out. You didn't save him, you've condemned him. You've condemned all of us! Do you really think they'll stand for us burning down homes?"

Starkey crosses his arms. "Let them try to take us down. We've got weapons. We'll fight them off."

"How long do you think we can last? An hour? Two? No

matter how many weapons we have, they have more, and they'll just keep coming and coming until we're all dead or captured."

Finally Starkey begins to show a hint of uncertainty.

"You're just a coward," shouts Bam, glowering at him just as she did the day Connor fired her.

"Yeah, yeah, a coward," the others echo.

The chorus of support gives Starkey all the justification he needs to bury any doubts beneath his own blind confidence. "I've been here long enough to know that you're nothing but a babysitter. We need more than that. We need someone who's not afraid to take this battle to the streets. I gave you every chance to leave on your own, but you wouldn't go. You leave me no choice but to take you down."

"Not gonna happen."

Connor is clearly outnumbered. Starkey's inner circle of storks advance on him—but Starkey's not the only one with tricks up his sleeve. Suddenly Hayden and half a dozen others, who've been waiting outside, begin piling through the door, firing tranq pistols at every stork in their path until half of Starkey's inner circle is unconscious on the floor of the jet, and the others drop their weapons.

Connor looks straight into Starkey's eyes. "Cuff him."

"With pleasure," says Hayden, pulling Starkey's hands behind his back and cuffing them together.

Connor has been foolish enough to trust him, and to believe that Starkey's ambition was healthy, not blind.

"The difference between me and you, Connor," Starkey says, still defiant, "is that—"

"—is that you're in handcuffs and I'm not. Get him out of here."

Hearing the gunfire of tranq pistols, dozens of kids have gathered in front of GymBo, as they haul Starkey out and down the stairs.

"Put his little mutiny team in the detention jet with two armed guards," Connor says.

"Starkey, too?" Hayden asks.

Connor knows he can't put Starkey in the same holding pen as his coconspirators. It would just lead to more plotting.

"No. Lock him in *my* jet," Connor orders, and one of the kids holding Starkey throws him to the ground, but Connor pulls the kid back.

"No! We are not the Juvies. Treat him with dignity. Whether he deserves it or not."

They obey, although no one helps Starkey up. With his hands cuffed behind his back, he has to wiggle and contort himself to get to his feet.

"This isn't over!" Starkey yells.

"Yeah, that's what they always say when it is."

Starkey is taken away, and Connor begins damage control. He tunes in to the rumbles of conversation on the perimeter. Some kids are just wondering what the hell happened, but there are other voices. Disapproving voices. The Stork Club. He wonders how much support Starkey has. It might be a mile wide, but Connor hopes it's only an inch deep.

"Listen to me, all of you," Connor says, knowing he has to sell himself as their leader more than ever. "Whether you're a stork, or a ward, or bio-raised, we have to stand united now. What we do now will decide whether we live or die. The Juvies are about to make a move. We have to work together, unless you want to end up in pieces."

His speech meets with affirmations and a sense of solidarity until someone in the back asks, "What about Starkey?"

Then everyone waits to see what Connor will say.

"Starkey is one of us," Connor tells them. "And I won't let a single one of us be unwound."

• • •

With no one to fly the Dreamliner, there is no escape plan, so Connor calls together Hayden, Ashley, and half a dozen others—some from the Holy of Whollies, and other kids he knows he can trust. They meet in the ComBom—a makeshift war room for an unlikely general—and Connor pulls plan B out of thin air.

"We set up two fronts—here, and here." He points to a hand-drawn map of the Graveyard. "The Juvies will come in through the north gate. Once they're in, we drive them right down the main aisle, then ambush from both sides, with about fifty of us."

"Live ammo?" Hayden asks.

"We hit them with everything we have. Live ammo, tranqs, everything."

"They'll have more than us," Ashley points out. "No matter what we do, they'll outlast us."

"Yes, but it's all about buying time," Connor tells her. "When our ammo runs low, we retreat to here—behind the fuel tanker, east of the fighter jets."

"Won't they corner us?" another kid asks.

"When they start to close in, we blow the tanker and run east."

"We'll never make it!" says Ashley.

"Here's the thing, though. The second the fifty take on the Juvies, more than six hundred fifty will be scattering to the south." And on the map, Connor draws a dispersal pattern of kids spreading out like a fan toward the remote southern fence. "That fence is full of holes."

Hayden nods, getting it, and points to the main aisle. "So if the fifty do their job here and then draw the Juvies to the east, keeping them engaged and distracted, by the time they realize everyone else is on the run, they'll never be able to catch them."

"They might be able to round up some, but the others will make it. They'll all be on their own again, but at least they'll be alive, and whole."

And then comes the big question. "What about the fifty?"

Finally Connor has to answer. "We'll be the sacrifices so the others can survive."

He can actually hear the click in Hayden's Adam's apple as he swallows. "So much for a future in broadcasting," Hayden says.

"Any of you who aren't up for it, I won't hold it against you if you leave," Connor says, but everyone knows that's like the minister asking if anyone objects to the wedding.

"All right, good," he says when no one raises a hand. "Each of you put together a team of your most trusted friends who are willing to stand against the Juvies, then let the others know to start running when the alarm sounds, and not to stop running until they're either caught or turn seventeen."

"Why wait until the alarm sounds?" someone asks. "Why not abandon the Graveyard now?"

"Because," Connor points out, "they're watching our every move now. If they see us starting to bail, they'll have squad cars lining that perimeter fence before we even get there, and they can pick us off like rabbits—but if all their forces are tied up in a single forward offensive, that's when we'll have a back door."

They all approve of Connor's logic. He seems to be the only one who knows he's flying by the seat of his pants.

"How much time do we have?" Ashley asks.

Connor lets Hayden field that one.

"Days if we're lucky," Hayden tells her. "Hours if we're not."

58 · Trace

While Connor has his summit meeting, Trace breaks all speed limits racing back to the Graveyard. He had been called for an emergency meeting with his "employers," to confirm that

Graveyard AWOLs were responsible for the house fires in Tucson. There was enough evidence to lay the attacks on the Graveyard's doorstep—it made no sense to deny it. What the suits from Proactive Citizenry wanted to know was why Trace hadn't told them about these attacks ahead of time. After all, that was his entire purpose there—to let them know everything before it happened. They refused to believe that he had been just as blindsided by it as they were.

"Do you have any idea the position this puts us in?" they asked him. "The Juvenile Authority wants to clean the place out, and with these attacks on civilian neighborhoods, we won't be able to stop them."

"I thought you controlled them."

The suits bristled in unison. "Our relationship with the Juvenile Authority is more complex than your simplistic boeuf understanding." Then they told him they were ending his assignment, effective immediately.

But to Trace, this wasn't an assignment anymore. And the time of playing both sides had come to an end.

So, preparing himself for battle, he sped off to the Graveyard like a surfer riding ahead of a tsunami.

Now, at dusk, he screeches to a halt before the locked gate and honks nonstop until the two teen guards on duty come out to see what the commotion is. When they see it's Trace, they unlock the gate.

"Jesus, Trace, do you want to wake all of Tucson?"

The other kid on duty chuckles. "Ain't nothing gonna wake Tucson."

Poor bastards, thinks Trace. *They have no idea what's coming.* He looks at the rifles they wield limply, like fashion accessories. "You got tranq bullets in those?" he asks.

"Yup," says the first kid.

"Replace them with these." Trace reaches over onto his

passenger seat of his Jeep and hands them two boxes of the deadliest military ammunition made. Shells that could take the head off an elephant.

The kids look at the shells like they've been handed a new-born they're afraid they'll drop.

"Load them quick—and the next time you see someone headed for the gate, shoot first, and don't stop until you're out of bullets, do you hear me?"

"Y-yes, sir," says the first kid. The other kid just nods mutely. "Why, sir?"

"Because the Juvies are right behind me."

59 · Lev

It's the fading edge of dusk when Lev and Miracolina arrive on the road that skirts the northern edge of the Graveyard. They're on foot now. An old rusted road sign points ahead toward what was once Davis Air Force Base. The faint shape of aircraft can be seen rising in the desert more than a mile beyond the fence.

"An air force base? Your friend is holing up in an air force base?"

"It's not a base anymore," Lev tells her, "and hasn't been since the war. It's an aircraft salvage yard."

"So the Akron AWOL is hiding in one of those planes?"

"Not just him, and not just one plane."

The fence seems to go on forever. Every few minutes a car zooms past on its way to or away from Tucson. Lev knows that drivers must see them and wonder what two kids are doing way out here, but he doesn't care. He's too close to waste time hiding from headlights now.

"I know the gate's up here somewhere. It's guarded, but they'll recognize me and let us in."

"You sure about that? Not everyone in the world is like your worshipful tithes."

At last the gate comes into view, and Lev picks up the pace.

"Slow down!" Miracolina yells.

"Catch up!" Lev yells right back.

As he nears the gate, he sees one of the kids on guard duty hurrying to greet him. There's something in the kid's hands, but it's gotten too dark to see just what it is until it's too late, and a single rifle shot explodes through the dying dusk.

60 · Starkey

From the moment the cuffs are on Starkey's wrists, he begins his escape act. He has no secret key, no penknife in his shoe to pick the lock, but a true master knows how to improvise.

He keeps his wits about him as they bring him to Connor's jet, suppressing his fury at the humiliation of being collared in front of the entire Graveyard. The arrogance of Connor! Allowing him to "preserve his dignity" was anything but dignified. Starkey would rather have fought as they dragged him through the dirt. *That* would be dignified—but to treat him with such limp pity? It was the ultimate insult.

The two kids assigned to guard him are bigger than him and are armed. Once inside the jet, they relock the handcuffs around a steel support strut so he stays in one place. Satisfied, the two kids leave, one of them dangling the key in front of him to taunt him, before shoving it in his pocket. They close the door, and Starkey finds himself an official prisoner of war.

He watches the two guards from the window of the jet, sizing them up. They're chatty with each other—probably friends. Of course, neither of them are storks; Connor made sure of that. Storks are now the enemy. Well, if Starkey has his way, Connor will see what a formidable enemy they are.

This, Starkey knows, is the turning point of his life. Not his escape from the Juvies, not his arrival at the Graveyard, but this moment alone, handcuffed in a plane. Everything depends on getting out of this jet, and no mistakes can be made. If he's going to lead the storks to greatness, he's going to have to dazzle everyone with his escape.

Starkey squats, getting his feet on the chain between the cuffs. He knows they're tempered steel. Not even bolt cutters would separate them. As for the support strut, it's part of the plane's airframe and can't be torn loose. The weakest link here is flesh and bone.

Starkey takes a few deep breaths to steady himself. Every escape artist is someday faced with an impossible escape; however, the true artist knows that nothing is impossible if you're willing to do the unthinkable.

Getting himself leverage and locking his jaw to keep from shouting out, Starkey brings the heel of his boot down on his left hand. The pain is excruciating, but he swallows his scream. He brings it down again, this time feeling the fine bones of his hand begin to break. The pain makes him weak. His body resists, but his will countermands that biological order, and he brings his heel down again.

Quickly, before blood flows into the area, making it swell, he shifts the cuff slightly and brings his heel down on his wrist. The bones of his wrist shatter on the metal of the cuff. He feels his vision begin to go as dark as if he's been tranq'd, but he forces away the cloudiness and nausea, breathing slowly, deeply, forcing himself to stay conscious and transforming the pain into action. He's bit his tongue; blood fills his mouth, but he spits it out. The job is done. With his right hand, he twists his left cuff. This time he's unable to hold back the wail of pain as he forces his shattered left hand through the small hole.

61 · Noah

Being assigned to guard a guy who's handcuffed and closed inside a jet isn't exactly a difficult job, but hey—if Connor feels Starkey needs two guards, who is Noah Falkowski to argue? This is the first assignment given to Noah directly by Connor since he was rescued from his unwinding nearly four months ago, and he's not gonna screw it up. Inside the jet, Starkey lets out a guttural scream.

"What the hell?" asks the other kid who's guarding Starkey.

"That is one pissed-off dude," says Noah.

Right about then a Jeep comes speeding toward them, its headlights making the twilight seem darker around them.

"What the hell?" says the other kid. Clearly his favorite expression.

The Jeep screeches to a halt, and out steps Trace. He heads straight for Connor's jet.

"Whoa, Trace, hold up. Connor's not in there," Noah says.

"Where is he?"

Noah's not quite sure. All he knows is that Connor has called the remaining members of the Holy of Whollies for a meeting after the Starkey incident. "He left the main aisle. One of the supply jets, maybe?"

"You're useless." Trace hops back into his Jeep and speeds toward the outlying planes. Only once he's gone does Noah hear a banging sound from inside Connor's jet—but it's not the kind of sound he'd expect Starkey to make. The emergency exit above the wing begins to open.

"What the hell? How did he get loose?"

"Shh!" Noah cocks his pistol. He's never fired it and knows it's just a tranq, but it will do the job. He never really liked

Starkey and won't mind being the one to tranq him as he tries to escape from the jet. The emergency door falls inward. Both kids hold their weapons at the ready, but Starkey doesn't come out. Cautiously they get closer, and when Noah looks inside, he sees straight through the plane to the darkening desert on the other side. While they were staring at this emergency exit, Starkey had climbed through the other one on the opposite side of the plane and is gone.

"Aw crap!"

Noah is less worried about Starkey than he is about having to tell Connor he screwed up his first real assignment.

62 · Starkey

He wears a hooded coat pulled from Connor's closet to hide his face. His left hand feels like a twenty-pound weight on the end of his wrist. With every heartbeat it pounds so painfully that his knees wobble, but somehow he keeps himself moving. He knows that Trace is back, and that's a game changer. Connor doesn't know yet, which means Starkey can use Trace's return to his advantage.

The Graveyard is scrambling. Kids race every which way. An aisle over, there's a crowd at the arsenal. Hayden hands out weapons; not just one or two, but everything. No one notices Starkey.

A Stork Club member passes, carrying a load of weapons, and Starkey grabs him with his good hand. When the kid sees who it is, he almost shouts out his name, but Starkey stops him.

"Shut up and listen. Get a message out to the Storks. On my signal, we storm the escape jet."

"But . . . that's not the plan."

"It's *my* plan, do you understand?"

"Yeah, yeah, sure, Starkey." Then he looks at Starkey's hand, like he might ask a question about it, but decides not to. "What's the signal?"

Starkey looks at the kid's load of weapons and pulls out a flare gun. "This," he says. "Go now!"

The kid races off to spread the word.

Starkey can see Trace's Jeep speeding back toward the main aisle from the supply jets, having been given bad information from the idiots guarding him. Starkey's not sure where Connor is—perhaps the ComBom, which will probably be the next place Trace will check.

Then Starkey spots Ashley racing from the arsenal with a nasty-looking machine gun, and he intercepts her. Her eyes go wide when she sees him.

"What the hell are you doing out? Does Connor know?"

"He will if you don't keep your voice down!"

Ashley moves closer to him. "Forget it, Starkey. Why don't you just make a run for it? Connor won't care, as long as you're out of his way when the Juvies come."

"Are you a stork, Ashley, or are you one of Connor's lackeys after all?"

When it's put that way, there's really only one response that Starkey's key "sleeper agent" could give.

"What do you want me to do?"

63 · Trace

Unable to find Connor, Trace speeds back to the main aisle, headed for the ComBom, ready to sound the alarm himself. He sees kids carrying weapons away from the arsenal, but they're not moving nearly fast enough.

He's so distracted, he nearly runs down Ashley, who's standing right in his path. He screeches to a halt.

"Trace! There you are!"

"Where's Connor? The Juvies are coming with a full takedown force."

"We know, Hayden heard the chatter," Ashley tells him. "Connor wants you to power up the escape jet."

"He knows I'm back?"

"Of course—he saw you racing off to the supply jets in a panic."

"It wasn't panic," Trace says, although he knows it was. "I'll get the Dreamliner ready for flight. If we're fast enough, we may not need to fight them. Tell Connor to start loading kids onto the plane."

"Sure thing, Trace." But she does no such thing. She watches Trace race to the Dreamliner and climb up the stairs. Then she goes to tell Starkey that her mission has been accomplished.

64 · Lev

The rifle shot explodes through the Graveyard gate, ringing in Lev's ears. "Down!" he yells. "They're shooting at us!"

But Miracolina is already down. Not just down, but crumpled. She lies lifelessly in the dirt by the side of the road.

"No!" He falls to his knees beside her, afraid to look, afraid to touch her. "Please, God! No!" This can't be happening. Not again! Everyone Lev gets close to is either killed or maimed, and it can't happen again! He prays for the impossible. He prays for it not to be true. . . .

Then he rolls Miracolina over to find there's no gaping hole in her chest. But there is a small spot of blood on her shoulder.

And the tiny flag of a tranq bullet. He doesn't know whether to be relieved or horrified.

"Looks like you've got trouble from both sides, Lev," says Nelson, somewhere in the dark behind him. "What to do . . . what to do?"

Then, from the gate, he hears a shaky voice say, "Stay away, whoever you are, or I'll shoot again!"

But before the teen guard can even aim his rifle, Nelson fires a second tranq bullet out of the darkness and takes the guard down right through the fence.

"Enough of him," Nelson says calmly. "Now, where were we?"

Lev still can't see Nelson, but Nelson can clearly see him, because Lev hears the telltale *pffft* of a tranq being fired. It hits his pant leg, deflecting off a rivet in his jeans, and lands in the gravel beside him. Lev knows he has no defense against Nelson now, so thinking quickly, he grabs the dart, digs it into the fabric of his jeans, careful not to nick his skin, and collapses on top of Miracolina. He closes his eyes. He hears the second guard panicking by the fence, and hears Nelson's footsteps approaching from the other direction on the gravel. Lev's heart races like it might explode in his chest, but he holds still, playing possum for his life, and prays for a second miracle in as many minutes. He prays that Nelson will fall for his act.

65 · Nelson

He never went to Indian Echo Caverns. Nelson merely drove his van to a roadside café a few miles away, then monitored his laptop and waited for the tracking nanites in Lev and Miracolina's blood to show movement away from the cabin. Then he followed. It was no accident that the bed frames were nearly rusted all the way through. Nelson had wanted

NEAL SHUSTERMAN

them to escape. For a while he worried that Lev might be too stupid to figure out how to break free, but in the end the boy rose to the occasion.

Lev didn't give away the location of Connor Lassiter that day, but Nelson heard enough to know that they were on their way to warn him about the big bad parts pirate. All Nelson had to do was give them a leash and let them lead the way.

Now that he knows Lassiter is at the defunct air force base, he has no use for these two anymore, but killing them would require too much disposal time. Besides, knowing Lev will wake up and have to live with the knowledge that he was responsible for Connor being unwound on the black market is a far sweeter revenge than the numb silence of death.

Nelson is not seriously concerned about the skittish AWOL still manning the gate. The first one fired wild, and he's confident the second doesn't really know how to wield a rifle with live ammo either. Most likely they were trained on tranq bullets, which have no kick and shoot lower. Nelson, who can use both, is well armed for this mission. In fact, he has a romantic notion that, for this capture, he will be like an old-fashioned gunslinger—his singular purpose reflected in a tour de force of firepower. He has three pistols at the ready and a semiautomatic rifle slung across his back. All but one pistol are loaded with fast-acting tranqs, which are far more effective than bullets. A bullet can graze a target, hit a limb—even inflict a body shot, and still the target can return fire. With a tranq, no matter where it hits, it takes a target out of the equation instantly. As for the live-ammo pistol, well, Nelson considers that his insurance policy.

He's about to check Lev to make sure he made an accurate and effective hit, when the situation takes a drastic turn that no gunslinger could have predicted.

66 · Gate Guard

The one remaining kid at the gate has no idea what has taken his comrade down. Their job usually consists of giving directions to people who are lost, because no one comes to the Graveyard intentionally at night. Trace has put the fear of God into both of them, however, and now his friend is lying on the ground right in front of the gate, possibly dead.

He hurries to him, fully expecting to be killed on the way. Although he heard voices outside the gate, they're silent now. No one shoots at him. And he's relieved to find his friend still breathing.

The only warning he has is the sudden rev of an approaching engine. Then out of nowhere, a police battering ram, its headlights dark, crashes through with such speed that the gates fly off their hinges. He dives out of the way just in time, and when he looks back, he sees his unconscious friend turned to roadkill by the wheels of the battering ram. Flowing in behind the ram is a flood of Juvey squad cars and armored riot trucks, followed by the chilling sight of Unwind transport trucks—it's just as Trace said. This is a full takedown force!

Only now that they've crashed the gate do their headlights come on, illuminating the desert before them, glinting off the planes in the distance. After the last transport truck passes through the gate, a brown van barrels through, following the Juvies, and then some kid races through the ruined gate, running after the van.

What comes next? thinks the gate guard. *An elephant?*

When the running kid realizes there's no way he's going to catch up with the party crashers on foot, he spots the guard and runs toward him. The guard reflexively raises his rifle but realizes that like an idiot, he's holding it upside down. By the time he rights it, the kid is there, ripping it away from him.

"Don't be stupid, I'm not the enemy," he says. There's something familiar about his face. Like maybe he's seen him before, but with shorter hair. "You have a Jeep or something?"

"Behind the trailer . . ."

"Good. Give me the keys."

And this younger kid's voice is so commanding, the guard obeys, reaching into his pocket and handing him the keys.

"Listen to me," the kid says. "There's a girl outside the gate. She's been tranq'd. I want you to get her and run. Take her someplace safe. Do you understand?"

The guard nods "Yeah, sure. Someplace safe."

"Promise me you'll do that."

"Yeah, yeah, I promise."

Satisfied, the kid gets into the Jeep and drives off toward the main aisle, where gunfire can already be heard. Clearly he doesn't know how to drive, but that really doesn't matter much when there's no road, only hardpan desert.

Once he's gone, the guard takes a moment to look at the remains of his fallen comrade, then bolts. Somewhere in the bushes just outside the gate is a tranq'd girl. He doesn't care. Every man for himself in a Juvey crackdown. Every girl, too. So rather than even looking for her, he takes off running as fast as he can, and leaves the girl to the Juvies, or the coyotes—whichever come first.

67 · Connor

With his volunteer defense force fully armed—about sixty kids in all—Connor dispatches half of them to hide behind Rip, the largest boys' dormitory. It's a C-130 cargo plane with its wings ripped off and a belly slung so low to the ground that a small militia can hide behind it. "You're the left defense flank," he tells them. "Do what you can to draw the Juvies' fire and keep them in the north end of the main aisle."

"Maybe we'll get lucky for once," one kid says. "Maybe the Juvies won't come after all."

Connor tries to offer him a reassuring smile. He doesn't know the boy's name. He tried his best to learn as many names as he could, but there was only so much he could do. If this kid gets killed, or worse, unwound, who will remember him? Who will remember any of them? He wishes he could have been wise enough to have had each kid carve his or her name into the steel of the old Air Force One, as a testament to the fact that they existed. Even if no would ever see it, at least it would be there. But now it's too late.

Connor takes the rest of his fighting force to the Rec Jet, directly across the main aisle from Rip. "We'll set up a barricade beneath the wings," he tells them, "and shoot out from behind it."

"Where will you be?" a girl asks.

"Right beside you, Casey," Connor tells her, happy to have remembered her name.

"No," says another kid. "The king should never be on the front lines. In chess, I mean."

"This isn't chess," Connor points out. "It's our lives."

"Yeah," he says, "but I kinda like to picture myself as a knight."

"Well, you got the horse face," says Casey, and everyone laughs. That they can laugh in the face of this says more about their courage than anything else.

Connor and his left flank fighters race to push couches, tables, and arcade machines into a barricade. Then, while Connor's upending a pool table, Hayden's voice blares in his earpiece.

"Connor, something's wrong. I can't raise the guards at the gate—no one's responding."

"It can't be! We're not ready!"

Then the horse-faced kid says, "We'll never be ready. So I guess that means we're as ready as we'll ever be."

Connor climbs to the hatch of the Rec Jet and looks north across the dark desert to see a wall of approaching headlights fanning out . . . getting wider. "Sound the alarm," he tells Hayden. "Here we go."

68 · Vessels

To look at an airplane head on, one might get the uncanny feeling that it has eyes. No doubt the planes of the Graveyard have witnessed many things, and perhaps they are the only ones with a clear perspective of fight and folly on the day the Juvenile Authority invades.

GymBo, the northernmost jet on the main aisle, has the best view of the approaching Juvey force. Its fuselage resonates with the monotone blare of the general alarm. On the ground around it, kids who had been trying to save what they can from the salvage yard drop what they're doing and run south, as they've been told. What was an organized chaos now becomes full-fledged panic around the stalwart rows of retired aircraft.

The medical jet has a clear view of the Dreamliner and its engines, which are powering up, preparing for flight. If Connor could see what the medical jet sees, he might alter his plan and call for everyone to get onboard before the Juvies arrive, but he has no idea that the escape jet is back in play.

The Dreamliner has an unobstructed view of Starkey, who is no longer bothering to hide his face as he prepares to signal the storks to abandon Connor's plan and follow his. But Trace in the cockpit is too involved in prepping the plane to share the jet's vision.

Toward the south end of the main aisle, Hush Puppy, the stealth bomber, watches as panicking Whollies running beneath its wings and belly stop as they hear the Dreamliner's engines begin to power up. "What's this?" they cry. "Are we flying out of here after all?" And rather than running south they hesitate, unsure of what to do.

And Dolores, the Korean War bomber, stares blankly at Connor, unable to tell him how badly he's about to be blindsided by mutiny. Although he's in radio contact with Hayden in the ComBom, who monitors videocams all around the Graveyard, none of those cameras can see what the planes already know—that this graveyard of gutted, dismantled aircraft is about to become a human graveyard as well.

The Juvey squad cars part left and right as they approach the main aisle, revealing behind them four armored riot trucks, black and angular like diesel engines. They stop at the head of the main aisle, and out of them flood dozens of armed officers in ballistic riot gear.

In the ComBom, Hayden flips from one surveillance camera to another, hoping that a new view might make the situation look less dire.

"Connor, are you seeing this?" he says into his headpiece. "It's not just Juvies—they've brought a freaking SWAT team!"

"I can see that. The squad cars are breaking off. Where are they going?"

"Hold on." Hayden flips to a different camera. "The aisles on either side of you. They're trying to surround us."

Connor orders a handful of kids from both the left and right flank to intercept the squad cars before they can get past, but keeps the larger part of his force hiding, waiting to ambush the riot team as soon as they're far enough down the main aisle. "We don't have to beat them," Connor reminds everyone. "We just have to keep them fighting us, instead of going after the others."

Just then a panicked kid runs out of the shadows into the main aisle in a frenzy to escape. A riot cop raises a gun and tranqs him, and as he drops to the dust, Connor gives the order to attack.

The riot squad is hit from both sides by everything Connor's team has. They take cover and return fire.

Meanwhile, on the side aisles, the kids Connor sent to take out the Juvey squad cars fire round after round, blowing out tires and shattering the windshields. One car careens into the forward landing gear of an old fighter jet and bursts into flames.

"Yes!" Hayden shouts. "No squad car has gotten past the third plane in the aisle, on either side," he tells Connor. "They're scrambling out of their cars, firing into the dark. Connor? Connor, are you there?"

Connor's there, but his brain won't give rise to words. Beside him Casey lies draped over the leg of the upended pool table with a tranq bullet in her neck—but worse than that is the horse-faced boy. He took a real bullet to the forehead.

"My God!" screams one of the others. "They're not just tranqing us, they're killing us too!"

And this kid's panic—Connor's *own* panic—is the reason why. Sure, the Juvenile Authority wants to save them for unwinding—but a bullet through the brain of the kid next to you is enough to make anyone panic and run. So Connor digs down into his own fortitude and finds courage enough to stand his ground, and following his example, so do the others.

Starkey, at the foot of the Dreamliner's forward staircase, jabs himself with a morphine hypodermic brought to him by a medic who also happens to be a stork. In seconds he begins to feel dizzy and distant, but he fights the wooziness. He climbs the stairs and waits at the jet's open door. His hand is already numbing from the morphine, and although the powerful pain-killer wants to put him to sleep, his own adrenaline rush fights back. What remains is a calm in the midst of the chaos that is almost transcendent. He is untouchable. He raises the flare gun and fires, lighting the sky in shimmering pink. The storks, who had been hiding rather than running south, all come out and surge toward the Dreamliner, streaming up the two sets of stairs.

Farther south, kids who have reached the fringe planes of the Graveyard see the wave of Whollies flooding toward the escape jet.

"Hey, there's someone in there! Someone's flying it! Come on!" They double back, heading toward the Dreamliner instead of running south, and as more escaping kids see others do an about-face, mob mentality takes over. They all run toward the waiting jet.

On the battlefront, Connor's force is outnumbered and out-classed by the weapon skills of the riot team. But this was expected. This is all part of the plan. About a third of Connor's team is down on both flanks. He doesn't want to know who's been tranq'd and who's been killed.

"You're clear for phase two," Hayden tells him, and Connor prepares to order the right flank to abandon their position and race toward the fuel tankers, drawing the invaders' attention away from the kids breaking south.

"No . . . no, wait," Hayden tells him. "Something's wrong!"

Suddenly the riot squad is no longer interested in Connor and his defense force. They're pushing forward, racing down the main aisle—and only now, with the bursts of deafening crossfire gone, does Connor hear the whine of jet engines. He turns to see kids rushing the escape jet.

"No! What are they doing?"

Then Connor sees him. Starkey. He stands atop the forward staircase, shepherding in his flock of storks—but it's not just storks who are trying to get on. Now a massive push of kids crowds the base of both staircases in a panic. It's perhaps the entire population of the Graveyard, fighting one another to get onto those narrow stairs.

Even before the riot police get down to them, Juvies come in on either side and start taking kids down with tranqs, like a shooting gallery. Connor can do nothing but watch as his plan—and all hope—crumbles into desert dust.

For once storks come first. For once storks will be victorious. And to hell with everyone else. The bio-raised world never did anything for Starkey. Well, now it will. Those bio-raised kids will be targets and draw the fire of the Juvies while his storks get onboard.

The exodus doesn't move as quickly or as smoothly as he wants it to, but at least it's moving. The riot police are still a ways off, but the Juvey-cops themselves have taken up positions much closer and have begun taking out the swarms of kids fighting to get on the stairs. Most of his storks, however, are already onboard.

Then a Juvey targets one of the kids on the stairs. He's tranq'd and goes down, slowing the storks behind him. They trample over him, and he seems to vanish beneath everyone's feet.

Ashley, the secret weapon stork, is the last stork up the stairs. She smiles at Starkey.

"Made it!" she says, reaching for him to help her up the last few steps.

But just then one of the Juvies on the ground locks eyes with Starkey and takes aim at him. Thinking quickly, he smoothly pulls Ashley over just a bit. The tranq bullet embeds in her back instead of his chest. She locks eyes with him in shock.

"Sorry, Ashley."

And before she can slump unconscious in his arms, he strategically pushes her back down the stairs, causing a domino-tumble of kids behind her. It gives Starkey just enough time to close the door.

The kids inside are both excited and terrified. Seeing that the front hatch is closed, they close the rear hatch as well. With the seats removed from the plane, no one quite knows what to do. Some kids sit, some stand, some look out of windows.

Starkey goes straight to the cockpit, where he finds Trace, focused and single-minded.

"Is everyone aboard?" Trace asks.

"Yeah, yeah, everyone's here," Starkey says. "Go!"

Only now does he realize Starkey's in charge. "You? Where's Connor?"

"He didn't make it, now let's get out of here."

Instead Trace stands up, looks out the window, and sees the panic outside. Kids still flood the stairs even though the doors are closed, and a quick glance into the cabin makes it clear exactly which kids were saved and which weren't.

"You son of a bitch!"

This is no time for arguments. Starkey pulls out a gun but keeps his distance so that Trace can't use one of his fancy boeuf disarming maneuvers. "You'd save Connor's kids, but you won't save storks, is that it? Fly this plane or I shoot."

"Kill me and no one gets out of here."

But Starkey doesn't lower his weapon because he's not bluffing, and Trace knows it.

Trace's glare could melt iron. He sits back down and eases the throttle forward. "When we land," Trace says, "I'm going to kill you with my bare hands."

Starkey's pretty sure he's not bluffing either.

The Dreamliner pulls forward, knocking over both sets of metal stairs. Kids and cops scramble to get out from under the huge plane's wheels as it picks up speed, taxiing at nearly thirty miles per hour. Connor had positioned it with a clear path to the runway, and the Juvies try unsuccessfully to head it off.

On the ground, the stranded kids try to break away and go back to the old plan of running south, but now they're surrounded. Juvies and riot police tranq them. They don't even have to aim; just shoot into the crowd and someone goes down.

Connor watches in horror as it all goes wrong. A Juvey fires at him, and Connor deflects the tranq bullet with his rifle. Before the man can fire again, Connor charges him, taking him down with a single swing from the butt of his rifle. When Connor looks up, he sees the stork-filled Dreamliner begin to accelerate down the runway—but he quickly sees that there's a problem.

Far, far away, barely visible in the night, is a dark, rectangular shape on the runway. It's nearly a mile away, but as the plane picks up speed and closes the distance, its headlights illuminate an armored riot truck that has pulled right into the plane's path, playing chicken with a 112-ton jet.

In the cockpit Trace sees it, but it's too late to abort liftoff.

In the truck, the driver realizes a moment too late that this is a game he's going to lose.

As the jet's nose lifts off the ground, the truck swerves to get out of the way, but the driver isn't fast enough. The starboard landing gear clips the truck, sending it tumbling like a toy, and a huge chunk of the landing gear rips loose, just as the plane leaves the ground. The Dreamliner lists precariously to one side, threatening to fall from the sky, but then stabilizes. Its broken landing gear, twisted and useless, retracts sluggishly into the wheel well.

On the ground, hundreds of earthbound kids are "tranq'd and yanked" by the Juvies, finding neither salvation nor sanctuary in the flightless vessels around them, while up above, the only vessel ever to be resurrected from the Graveyard carries 169 souls into the sky: 169 souls with no possible way to land.

69 · Lev

Lev has the advantage of being behind the action. He can see where the battlefront is, he can see the tactics of the Juvey attack force, and since no one has yet to graft eyes in the back of their head, Lev can move behind the battle without being caught.

And so can Nelson.

It's before the escape jet has taxied away, when the focus is still on the armed AWOLs toward the north end of the main aisle. Lev spots Nelson leaving his van at the far western aisles of the Graveyard and moving in on foot. The parts pirate now wears a Juvey uniform he must have pulled from a real Juvey that he tranq'd. He'll blend in. He'll pass for one of them. The only thing Lev can pass for is an AWOL, and that won't get him anything but unconscious. He knows he has to be careful.

Lev tries to figure out where Connor might be in this war zone, and suddenly he realizes that he doesn't even know this Connor. The old Connor was all about saving himself, and he was good at it. But will he still be that way now that he's responsible for every kid here? Connor saved a baby once. He also saved Lev. No, he won't be running or hiding. He'll be here until the last AWOL is taken down, and that last one may very well be him.

Nelson doesn't know that. He sees Connor in only one dimension: a lowly AWOL. He won't look for Connor at the battlefront, he'll look for him on the fringes—and sure enough, Lev sees Nelson on the edges; places where stray kids have been tranq'd. Like a vulture pecking at carrion, Nelson lifts their heads off the ground, looks at each of their faces, then drops them back down again, moving on to the next one.

Lev circles behind Nelson in shadows, giving him a wide berth, and makes his way closer to the danger zone, where riot police clash with armed AWOLs. This is where Connor will be— but how can Lev save him from both Nelson *and* the Juvies?

When the answer comes to Lev, he grins in spite of the dire battle around him. The answer is simple. It's terrifying. It's impossible. It might work!

Lev nears the main aisle just as the Dreamliner begins to move and riot police advance on the crush of kids who never made it onboard.

A hundred yards away, on the failed front line, Lev sees a figure in off-color camouflage fearlessly charge a Juvey shoot- ing at him. The kid takes the Juvey out—not with a bullet, but with the butt of his rifle—and there's something about the way this kid moves that's familiar.

Lev charges against a panic of escaping kids running toward him, ignoring the sound of gunfire, the roar of jet engines, and the crunch of crushing metal as the Dreamliner takes out a riot truck on takeoff.

The tumbling truck bursts into flames as the plane rises into the sky, and the light of the explosion illuminates the face of the kid in camouflage. Lev knows he's found him.

"Connor!"

But Connor's eyes are fixed on the escaping plane. "Don't just stand there, run!" Connor tells him. "You were all supposed to run!"

"Connor, it's me. It's Lev."

Even when Connor looks at Lev, he doesn't seem to recognize him at first, and Lev knows it's more than just the hair. Neither of them are the kids they were a year ago.

"Lev? What are you doing here? What, has the whole world gone nuts, and I've lost my mind?"

"I'm sure both are true, but I'm really here." Lev bends down and takes the tranq gun away from the cop Connor has just rendered unconscious. "I came to save you."

"That's the stupidest thing I've ever heard!"

"That's probably true too, but I have to warn you: There's a parts pirate after you."

"That's the least of my problems right now!"

Another kid with an automatic rifle hurries up to Connor. "We're out of ammunition! What do we do?"

"Sticks and stones and airplane parts," Connor tells him. "Or you can take your chances and run. Starkey didn't leave us many choices."

"Freakin' Starkey!" The kid drops his spent weapon. "Good luck, Connor," he says, and hurries away, trying to lose himself in the night.

Farther away, the mob that has been trying to get on the Dreamliner is now lit by the spotlight of a police helicopter and is fully surrounded. There are maybe four hundred kids corralled and helpless, while huge transport trucks roll down the main aisle to gather them and take them away.

"There's nothing you can do for them now," Lev tells Connor.

"I won't leave them."

"That's why I'm not giving you a choice." Then Lev raises

the tranq pistol he took from the unconscious Juvey and shoots Connor in the arm.

Connor's spun away by the force of the blast and goes down, the tranqs taking effect in seconds. Lev catches him as he falls, and he looks up at Lev with half-open, fading eyes.

"It didn't work, Lev," he says weakly. "My plan didn't work."

"I know," Lev tells him as Connor slips from consciousness, "but maybe mine will."

70 · Nelson

He has no idea how many kids are here, how deep the airplane graveyard goes, or where his target might be in the midst of the chaos. No matter. If the Juvies do their job, and it looks like they will, the whole nest of AWOLs will be rounded up, tranq'd, and yanked. Lassiter will be among them. Nelson just needs to keep his eyes open and his head low, because some of these kids have weapons, and by the sound of them, they're deadly.

Methodically he checks the AWOLs who have already been tranq'd and takes down a few himself, just so he really looks like a Juvey-cop doing his job. He keeps a safe distance from the heart of the battle, knowing that the Akron AWOL will do the same.

One of the Juvey-cops spots him looking at the faces of the fallen AWOLs. "Don't waste your time," he says. "It's our asses if any of these kids get past us and into the desert."

"I'm looking for an AWOL neighbor kid," Nelson tells him without missing a beat. "Favor for the wife."

But the cop is suspicious. "Do I know you? What unit are you with?"

"Unit Sixteen, down from Phoenix."

"There *is* no Unit Sixteen in Phoenix."

Deciding this has gone quite far enough, Nelson tranqs him, then tranqs an escaping AWOL who saw him do it. Then gets back to the task of finding the Akron AWOL.

It's only when he sees the Dreamliner taking off that he begins to worry. What are the chances that Lassiter's on that plane? Then he realizes that the riot squad isn't just tranq'ing and yanking—they're going against procedure, loading the mob into the transport trucks conscious. If Lassiter gets loaded into a truck before Nelson can get to him, it's over.

Now he's worried. He moves closer to the riot roundup, pulling out binoculars, scanning the faces. A gaggle of scared teenagers. No Lassiter. Sure, he might be in the swarm, but if he is, Nelson can't spot him. He puts down the binoculars.

"Crap!"

He knows that with every passing second his chances get slimmer. Around him, kids who were either too slow to get there or smart enough to stay away from the corralled mob race in all directions to escape. Some get tranq'd as they run, but the farther they are away from the main action, the better their chances.

Up ahead Nelson sees the dark silhouette of one smaller kid struggling to carry an older tranq'd kid on his back—reminding Nelson of the way ants will carry off their wounded. But apparently this kid has better sense than an ant, because he gives up, drops the bigger kid in the dust, and takes off into the shadows.

Nelson almost doesn't check the dropped kid. He almost walks on past, because he doesn't want to miss a single face running by, but Nelson is nothing if not thorough. He grabs the unconscious the kid by the hair, lifts his head out of the dirt, and practically yells with triumphant surprise. It's him! It's Lassiter! Brought to him like a gift, right in his path!

Nelson wastes no time. He hefts him onto his back, gets

his bearings, and weaves through the aircraft, heading toward his waiting van. As he crosses an outer aisle, he's spotted by another Juvey.

"Forget him," the cop says. "Leave him for Sanitation and Transport. Our orders are to take out the bolters." And to emphasize his point, he fires at a girl bolting between two fighter jets, tranqing her into the dust.

"Special orders on this one," Nelson tells him, trying to get past, but the other cop won't yield.

"Why? Is he the one who's been starting the fires in town?"

"Yeah," Nelson says. "He's the one."

Then behind them, three kids try to break for the outer aisles, and their attempted escape pulls the cop's attention long enough for Nelson to get past him.

The farther from the main aisle, the fewer AWOLs, and the fewer cops. Transport trucks are already here on the outskirts, gathering whatever tranq'd kids they find before moving into the high-density zone. The San & Tran workers treat the fallen kids with much more care than the Juvies, zipping them into padded transport bags—constrictive sleeping bags in either powder blue or pink that cover everything but their faces, so that their precious parts are protected in transit.

Nelson reaches his van, dumps Connor in the back, and drives out the way he came, heading toward the north gate, knowing he's not in the clear yet.

As he nears the gate, there's a small showing of Juvey squad cars—as if any of the AWOLs will be stupid enough to try to get out through the main gate. They stop Nelson, and he flashes a stolen badge. "Orders to take this van to HQ. It's being impounded as evidence."

"What, are you kidding me? The whole damn place is being impounded as evidence! They couldn't wait for a tow truck?"

"When can they wait for anything?"

The cop shakes his head. "Incredible!" And he waves Nelson through.

As Nelson leaves the Graveyard behind, he turns on the radio, surfs until he finds a song he knows, and sings with rare joy.

Divan, his black market dealer, will pay a fortune—and the dollar signs Nelson now sees will soon be seen through the Akron AWOL's eyes. That's the real reward, far more important than the cash. Nelson doesn't even remember what this kid's eyes are like, but it doesn't matter. Whatever their color, whatever their acuity, they'll be the last pair Nelson will ever need. They will be perfect!

He's still thinking of Connor's eyes when he hears the high-pitched blast of a tranq pistol and feels a sudden sharp pain in his leg, then a second, then a third.

His hands, suddenly lead-heavy, fall from the steering wheel, and with his last bit of strength, he forces his head to turn so he can see his attacker.

Rising from behind him in the van is Lev, wearing a smile as big as the desert around them.

"Tranq'd by your own gun," Lev says. "How pathetic."

71 · Lev

Nelson had used Lev to help him find Connor—and now Lev has returned the favor. With so many Juvies, and so many riot police, getting anyone out of the Graveyard would be a miracle. And then Lev realized that, at least for the moment, Nelson was his greatest ally. Both Nelson and Lev had the same objective: get Connor away from the Juvies and out of the Graveyard alive. So Lev carried an unconscious Connor right into Nelson's path. Lev risked exposing his identity, but with so many kids running, and the only lights from head-lights and spotlights, it was easy to keep his face in shadows, then drop Connor and run, letting Nelson do the hard work of getting Connor out.

While Nelson carried Connor off, Lev raced ahead and slipped into his van, keeping low—hoping that Nelson would be distracted by the events around him and euphoric enough at his catch to never notice that Lev was hiding in the backseat.

Now, half a mile from the Graveyard, Nelson slumps in the driver's seat, unconscious, and Lev hurries to take the wheel, keeping the truck from flying off the road. Then, push-ing Nelson aside, he stomps on the brakes, and the van comes to a halt.

Only one thing left to do.

Leaving the van, Lev doubles back on foot to the gate. From his position on the floor of the van, he hadn't been able to see how many Juvies were at the gate. Now, as he gets close, he sees there are only a handful—all the rest are in the battle zone. The scant chaparral of the desert doesn't provide enough cover to hide him, but he has to get closer.

He told the kid at the gate to get Miracolina and take her someplace safe. The kid said he would do it, but Lev has to be sure.

There's a squad car right in front of the spot where Miracolina had been, and a Juvey-cop leans against it, talk-ing on his radio. The moment the Juvey-cop looks away, Lev darts behind the car, keeping low, and checks behind the dry bushes.

She's not there.

He breathes a silent sigh of relief, then turns and hurries back to the van. Once there, he pulls Nelson out and leaves him unconscious in a ditch. Then Lev does his best to drive the van down the narrow two-lane road—which is much different from driving a Jeep off-road, across open desert. *How stupid would it be*, he thinks, *if, after all this, Connor and I both die in a car accident because I don't know how to drive?* He can only thank God that the road is straight.

For once he's batting a thousand, and although he knows he may never see Miracolina again—and that she may, in the end, submit herself for tithing—he knows that he's done everything within his power to save her. To free her.

Be safe, Miracolina, he says to himself, hoping that by saying it, he can make it true, never knowing that the kid at the gate was only interested in saving himself, and that Miracolina was still unconscious just a few feet away from where Lev was searching . . . because he didn't think to look in the backseat of the squad car.

72 · Starkey

"Well, Starkey, what do we do now?"

"If you ask me one more time, I'll rip your freaking head off."

Bam storms away in frustration.

"At least we got out of there!" Starkey yells after her. "We're probably the only ones who did!"

Although it's not going to mean much if they crash.

Kids sit in groups on the floor of the seatless cabin, some of them crying at the ordeal they've been put through and the friends left behind.

"Suck it up!" he yells at them. "We're storks—we're better than that." Then he holds up his crushed hand, which is now so swollen and purple it barely resembles a hand at all. "Do you see me crying?" This war wound, he realizes, has already become a symbol of his power and a talisman of respect.

The whimpers subside, but not entirely. The truth is, in

spite of the morphine swiped from the medical jet, his hand still aches too much to have patience for anything or anybody.

"Where are we going?" someone asks.

"A better place," Starkey says, then realizes that's what they say when you die.

He storms to the cockpit, and storks clear out of his way. Trace sits at the controls with no copilot, and Starkey begins with a threat.

"If you as much as touch that radio . . ."

Trace looks at him, disgusted, then back to the control panel. "Just because you're the one leading these kids, it doesn't mean I want them to be unwound. I haven't, nor will I notify anyone."

"Good. Tell me the plan. Tell me what you schemed up with Connor."

Trace grips the controls to maintain stability as they hit a patch of turbulence. More whimpers from the cabin. Once the turbulence subsides, Trace says, "We'll be over Mexican airspace in a few minutes, which buys us time, because our military can't pursue without permission, and theirs won't until they see us as a threat. Next we fly within a mile of another jet headed north, switch signatures, and when that other jet hits American airspace, they'll think it's us."

"We can do that?"

Trace doesn't even answer the question. "The plan was to double back into the U.S. and land in an abandoned airfield in the Anza-Borrego Desert, east of San Diego—but there's a problem with the landing gear."

Starkey already knows this. They all felt the collision as the plane smashed the truck in its path. Everyone heard something rip loose. There's no question that there's damage, but it's impossible to know how much. All they have is an idiot-light on the control panel that says LANDING GEAR FAILURE.

"So what do we do about it?"

"We die." Trace lets the thought linger for a moment, then says, "I can try to set us down in a body of water. I'm thinking the Salton Sea."

"In Utah?"

"No, that's the Great Salt Lake, moron. The Salton Sea is a huge dead lake south of Palm Springs. There's a town there that's the asshole of the armpit of the world. You'd fit right in."

Starkey snarls at him, then decides he's not worth it. "How long?"

"I have to find a passing jet and do the signature switch first. Figure an hour and a half till we're there."

"Fine, I'll tell the others." He turns to go, then pauses at the cockpit door, looking back at Trace. "And if you call me moron one more time, I'll blow your brains out."

Trace turns to him and smiles. "Then *you* can land this plane . . . moron."

73 · Risa

Risa sits in a network studio dressing room, staring at the monitor. The late-night news show on which she and Cam are about to appear has just reported some breaking news: a crackdown on a massive AWOL hideout in Arizona. None other than the airplane graveyard. Kids are already being shipped to harvest camps.

"It is believed that these same AWOL Unwinds are responsible for a rampage of violence in the city of Tucson," says the anchorman. *"The Juvenile Authority hopes this raid will allow the citizens of Tucson to rest easy once more."*

How could this happen? After all the horrific things Risa has done for the past two months to prevent this raid—to keep

Connor and Hayden and everyone there safe—the Juvies raided anyway. Maybe it was always going to happen, and Roberta's bargain was a lie from the beginning. How could Risa have been so stupid as to trust anything that woman said?

The assistant stage manager pokes his head in the door. "Three minutes, Miss Ward."

Risa never considered herself a violent girl. Sure, she's always been more than able to defend herself, but she was never the kind of girl to initiate or enjoy brutality. Yet in this moment, she knows she would kill Roberta if she had the means to do it.

Then she realizes she doesn't have to. In less than three minutes Risa will be broadcasting live to a national audience. She doesn't have to kill Roberta. She can unwind her. . . .

Bright, unnatural light. A TV studio with no audience. A well-known news personality in a suit and tie, looking smaller and older in person than he does on TV. Three cameras—one on him, one on Risa, one on Cam. As they wait for the show to come back from commercial, News Guy briefs them.

"I'll be asking both of you questions. First about Risa's decision to support unwinding, then about the process of rewinding that ostensibly led to Cam's 'birth,' if you will, and finally I'll ask about your relationship, and how you two found each other. I know they're all questions you've been asked before, but I'm hoping you can give me something fresh."

"Well, we'll certainly do our best," Risa says, with a grin that's a little too pleasant.

Cam leans over to her and whispers, "We should hold hands."

"There's no wide shot," she points out. "No one will see."

"We should anyway."

But this time Cam will not get his way.

The stage manager counts down from five. The red light on camera one comes on.

"Welcome back," says News Guy. "Considering the current police action in Arizona, our guests tonight have a certain . . . resonance, if you will. A militant AWOL turned unwinding advocate, and a young man who, were it not for unwinding, would not even exist. Risa Ward and Camus Comprix."

A moment of pleasant welcomes, and he starts his questioning, as he promised, with Risa, but hits her with something designed to throw her off balance.

"Miss Ward, as a former AWOL yourself, what's your take on the raid in Arizona? Do you support the unwinding of these runaways?"

Nothing he asks can fluster her, because she already knows exactly what she's going to say. Risa turns to look right into camera two, which has just come on.

"I feel it's important that I set the record straight," Risa begins. "I am not now, nor have I ever been, in favor of unwinding. . . ."

74 · Roberta

Had Roberta been paying attention, things might have gone down differently, meaning they wouldn't have gone down at all. To her credit, her bargain with Risa was an honest, if intensely manipulative one. She made a few calls, pulled a few strings, and was able to confirm with the Juvenile Authority that there were no imminent raids planned on the airplane graveyard. Should that change, Roberta would be given ample warning—which meant ample time to pull further strings to prevent such a raid. Roberta has never been about deceit. She's about results.

However, she has been so wrapped up in the media campaign to make Cam the darling of modern times, she's not aware of the homes set on fire in Tucson, and the brazen youth who set them, claiming to be the avenger of all unwound storks. Yes, the Juvenile Authority was supposed to notify Roberta of the raid through her associates at Proactive Citizenry. But like any spiderlike organization, the fangs of Proactive Citizenry don't know what the spinneret is doing. Once the news hit the airwaves, of course, her phone began to ring her pocket off—but she's been too fed up with too many people wanting too much of her time to answer it.

Thus, Roberta does not know about the raid until the interview with Risa and Cam begins. And by then it's too late.

Roberta sits in the greenroom, the studio's pleasant little ready room replete with stale danishes and weak coffee, watching a monitor that broadcasts from the studio down the hall. Her expression of horror could curdle the nondairy creamer.

"I am not now, nor have I ever been, in favor of unwinding," Risa says. *"Unwinding may be the single most evil act sanctioned by the human race."*

The newsman, famous for being cool under fire, stammers for a moment. *"But all those public service announcements you made—"*

"They're lies. I was being blackmailed."

Roberta bursts out of the greenroom into the hall and storms toward the studio door. The red light is on. It's supposed to be a warning not to go in, since the cameras are live, but it's a warning she has no intention of heeding.

In the corridor around her are a series of monitors broadcasting Risa's diatribe. Her face is on every screen, looking at Roberta from half a dozen different directions.

"I was threatened and blackmailed by a group called Proactive

UnWholly

Citizenry. Oh, they have lots of other names, like the Consortium of Concerned Taxpayers and the National Whole Health Society, but it's all smoke and mirrors."

"Yes, I'm aware of Proactive Citizenry," the newsman says, "but isn't it a philanthropic group? A charitable organization?"

"Charitable to whom?"

Just as Roberta nears the stage door, she's intercepted by a security guard.

"I'm sorry, ma'am, you can't go in right now."

"Let me pass, or I promise you, you'll be out of work by morning."

His response is to stand firm and call for backup, so Roberta heads for the control booth instead.

"They claim to control the Juvenile Authority," Risa continues. "They claim to control a lot of things. Maybe they do, and maybe they don't, but believe me, Proactive Citizenry has no one's interests at heart but its own."

The shot cuts to Cam, who looks dumbfounded, or just plain dumb; then it goes back to the newsman.

"So your relationship with Camus . . ."

"Is nothing but a publicity stunt," says Risa. "A publicity stunt carefully planned by Proactive Citizenry to help Cam be accepted and adored."

Roberta bursts into the control booth, where an engineer works the editing bay, and the show's producer leans back in his chair, extremely pleased. "This is mint," he tells his engineer. "The princess of unwinding bites the disembodied hand that feeds her! It doesn't get any better than this!"

"Stop the interview!" orders Roberta. "Stop it now, or I will hold you and your network liable for everything she says!"

The producer is unfazed. "Excuse me, who are you?"

"I'm . . . her manager, and she is not authorized to say what she's saying."

363

"Well, lady, if you don't like what your client has to say, that's not our problem."

"Your viewers need to ask themselves this," Risa says. *"Who stands to benefit most from unwinding? Answer that question, and I think we'll know who's behind Proactive Citizenry."*

Then the security guard comes up behind Roberta and manhandles her out the door.

Roberta is relegated to the greenroom until the interview is over and they cut to commercial.

The guard, still on "intruder alert" mode, won't let her pass. "I have orders to keep you out of the studio."

"I am going to the restroom!"

She pushes past him and bolts for the studio door. Both Risa and Cam are gone, and the next guests are being miked.

Avoiding the guard—who Roberta knows is fully prepared to tranq her—she turns down a side hallway to the dressing rooms. Risa's dressing room is empty, but Cam is in his. His coat and tie are strewn on the ground like he couldn't wait to peel out of them. He sits before the vanity with his head in his hands.

"Did you hear what she said about me? Did you hear?"

"Where is she?"

"Head in the sand! Turtle in its shell! Leave me alone!"

"Focus, Cam! She was on the stage with you. Where did she go?"

"She ran. She said it was over, that she was history, and she ran down the emergency stairs."

"She *will* be history when I'm through with her."

Roberta takes the emergency stairs down. They're on the second floor, and the only place for Risa to go is out into the parking lot, which is mostly empty at this time of night. She can't have had more than a fifteen-second lead, but she's nowhere to be seen. The only person around is their driver, who leans against his limo, eating a sandwich.

"Did you see her?" Roberta asks.

"See who?" he answers.

And Roberta's phone starts ringing like it will never stop.

75 · Cam

Roberta returns from her unsuccessful search for Risa. Cam meets her in the greenroom, where two security guards now wait, eager to escort Roberta out. She's on the phone, already in the throes of damage control.

"Antarctica," Cam says. "I should have said something out there, but I froze."

"What's done is done," she says, then growls at a dropped call. "Let's get out of here."

"I'll meet you at the car," Cam tells her. "My stuff's still in the dressing room."

The guards solemnly escort Roberta out of the building, and Cam goes back to the dressing room. He puts on his sports coat and carefully rolls up his tie, putting it in his pocket. Then, when he's sure Roberta has left the building, he says, "It's okay, she's gone."

The closet door opens, and Risa steps out. "Thank you, Cam."

Cam shrugs. "She deserved it." He turns to look at her. She's breathing rapidly, as if she's been running, but he knows she's only been running in her head. "Will they all be unwound? Your AWOL friends?"

"Not right away," she tells him. "But yes, they will be."

"I'm sorry."

"It's not your fault." Although she doesn't look at him when

365

she says it, like maybe she thinks it somehow is. Like his very existence makes him guilty.

"I can't help what I am," he tells her.

"I know . . . but today you showed me you can help what you do." And then she leans forward and kisses him on the cheek. He feels it like an electric shock in all the seams of his face. She turns to go, but he can't let her. Not yet. Not without saying—

"I love you, Risa."

She glances back at him and offers nothing more than an apologetic smile. "Good-bye, Cam."

And she's gone.

It's only after she leaves that the anger begins to rise in him. Not just a spike, but an eruption, and there's nowhere for it to go. He takes the chair and hurls it against the vanity mirror, smashing it. He hurls everything that's breakable against the walls and doesn't stop until the security guards burst in on him. It takes three guards to restrain him, but still he's stronger. He has the best of the best in him—every muscle group, every synaptic reflex. He tears free from the guards, bolts down the emergency exit stairs, and meets Roberta in the limo.

"What took you so long?"

"Solitude," he says. "I needed some time alone."

"It's all right, Cam," she tells him as they drive away. "We'll get past this."

"Yes, I know we will."

But he keeps his true thoughts to himself. Cam will never accept Risa's good-bye. He will not let her disappear from his life. He will do whatever it takes to have her, to hold her, to keep her. He has all of Roberta's resources at his fingertips to get what he wants, and he's going to use them.

Roberta smiles at him reassuringly between phone calls,

and he smiles back. For now Cam will play the game. He'll be the good rewound boy Roberta wants him to be, but from this moment on, he has a new agenda. He will make Risa's dream come true and take down Proactive Citizenry piece by bloody piece.

And then she will have no choice but to love him.

Part Seven

Landings

Our country is challenged at home and abroad . . . it is our will that is being tried and not our strength.

> —PRESIDENT JOHNSON *on Vietnam and the school campus war protests, 1968*

I have every faith that this devastating national conflict shall be resolved, and that the accord between both sides shall also serve as an ultimate solution to the feral teenage problem. But until that glorious day, I am instituting an eight p.m. curfew for anyone under the age of eighteen.

> —PRESIDENT MOSS *on the Heartland War, two weeks prior to his assassination by militant New Jersey separatists*

76 · Dreamliner

In Southern California, far south of the glitz of Hollywood and far east of the suburban sprawl of San Diego, lies an inland sea as forgotten and as unloved as a state ward AWOL or a harvest camp stork. Hundreds of thousands of years ago it was the northern reach of the Sea of Cortez, before that sea even had a name. But now it's little more than a giant landlocked salt lake, slowly drying into desert. Too saline for vertebrate life, its fish have all died. Their bones cover the shores like gravel.

At ten minutes to midnight, a plane once heralded as the dream of aviation before it was replaced by newer dreams descends toward the Salton Sea. It is flown by a young military pilot with far more confidence than experience. Barely clearing the mountains around the lake, the jet comes in for what airlines ridiculously call "a water landing."

It does not go well.

77 · Starkey

No seatbelts, no seats. No way to brace themselves for a crash landing. "Lock your elbows together! Hook your legs around each other," Starkey tells them. "We'll be one another's seatbelts."

The storks obey, huddling, locking limbs, turning themselves into a tangled colony of flesh and bone. Sitting on the floorboards, no one can see out the windows to know how close the lake is—but then Trace comes on the intercom. "About

371

twenty seconds," he says. Then the angle of their descent changes as he pulls up the nose of the jet.

"See you on the other side," Starkey says, then realizes once more that it's something you say when you're about to die.

Starkey counts down the last twenty seconds in his head, but nothing happens. Was he counting too fast? Did Trace misjudge? If this is twenty seconds, then they're the longest of his life. Then it finally comes—a jarring jolt, followed by calm.

"Was that it?" someone says. "Is it over?"

There's another jolt, then another and another, each one coming closer together, and Starkey realizes the plane is skimming like a stone. On the fifth skim, a wing dips, acting like a rudder that pivots the plane to a diagonal, and suddenly it's the end of the world. The Dreamliner begins to flip end over end, turning cartwheels against the unforgiving surface of the lake.

Inside, the mob of kids is launched from the floorboards and pulled apart by centrifugal force, thrown in two separate clusters to either end of the main cabin. The hooking of arms actually saves many of them, as they're cushioned by the bodies around them, but those on the outside of the tumbling crush of kids—those acting as the cushions—become the sacrifices. Many of them are killed as they're slammed against the hard surfaces of the Dreamliner.

The cache of weapons, which had been stowed in the overhead compartments, flies free as well, as those compartments tear loose and burst open. Pistols and rifles and machine guns and grenades become ballistic, creating casualties without ever having to go off.

Wrapped in the forward twist of bodies, Starkey feels his head hit something hard, leaving a gash on his forehead, but that's nothing compared to the exploding pain in his battered hand.

Finally the tumbling jet comes to rest. The cries and wails

sound like silence compared to the noise of the crash. Then somewhere toward the back of the cabin there's an explosion: a grenade that lost its pin. It blows a hole in the side of the jet, and water begins to pour in. That's when the electrical system fails, and they're plunged into darkness.

"Over here!" Bam calls. She pulls a huge lever and opens the cabin's front port-side door. A life raft automatically inflates and detaches, then drops to the water, and with a "Sayonara," Bam leaps right out after it.

Starkey's instinct is to get out now . . . but if he's going to be seen as the protector of the storks, then he must be their protector in action, not just words. He waits, shooing kids out the door, making it clear he is not the first one out—but neither does he plan on being the last.

Farther back in the foundering jet, kids pull open wing exits and a midship hatch—but only on the left side. On the right, a slick of jet fuel has ignited in the water and burns beyond the windows.

"The weapons!" Starkey shouts. "Take the weapons! We still have to defend ourselves!" And so kids pick up any and all weapons they can find, throwing them out onto the rafts before jumping out themselves.

The fire outside provides enough light for Starkey to see to the far recesses of the main cabin, and he wishes he hadn't looked. The dead are everywhere. Blood is smeared on every surface, sticky and thick. But there are more living than dead, and more kids running than crawling. Starkey determines right then and there to save only those who can make it out on their own. The critically injured are just liabilities.

The angle of the floor has quickly changed as the jet begins to sink tail-first. The rear cabin is already flooded, and the water level rises in a steady, relentless surge past the central bulkhead. Then Starkey hears a muffled voice from the front of the jet.

"I need help here!"

Starkey makes his way to the cockpit door and pulls it open. The windshield is shattered, and the entire cockpit is a mess of smashed gauges, open panels, and exposed wires. The pilot's chair has jammed forward, and Trace is pinned.

Which leaves Starkey in an interesting position.

"Starkey!" says Trace, relieved. "I need you to pull me out of here. I can't do it by myself."

"Yes, that's a problem," Starkey says. But is it *his* problem? They needed Trace to get them this far, but they don't need a pilot anymore—and didn't Trace already threaten to kill him? If Trace survives, from this moment on he'll be nothing but a threat—and a dangerous one, at that.

"I never had the guts to try the great water escape," says Starkey. "It killed Houdini, but I'm sure it'll be easy for a big boeuf like you." Then he backs out of the cockpit and closes the door.

"Starkey!" Trace yells. "Starkey, you son of a bitch!"

But Starkey's decision is final, and as he returns to the main hatch, Trace's muffled voice is drowned out by the sounds of panicking storks. There are about a dozen kids left—the slow ones, the injured ones, the ones afraid to jump because they can't swim.

"What's that awful smell?" one of them whines. "What *is* that out there?"

He's right—there's a stench to this lake like a fish tank left to putrify, but it's the least of their problems. Water's already pooling at their feet, and the floor is at a thirty-degree tilt.

Starkey pushes past the lingering kids. "Jump or drown, you've got no other choice, and I'm not waiting for stragglers." Then he hurls himself out the door and into the foul-smelling brine of the Salton Sea.

78 · Trace

Trace's calls for help go unanswered, and in furious frustration he pounds the console and bucks in the chair, but it doesn't give. He's so tightly wedged in by the accordioned cockpit, not even a boeuf of his strength can get out. He forces himself to calm down and review his options. All he can hear now are the diminishing moans and wails of kids too injured to escape, and of course the relentless rush of water. That's when he realizes there are no options left to him anymore. Starkey made certain of that.

The lake begins to pour in through the broken cockpit window so quickly there's no time to prepare himself. Trace cranes his neck, trying to keep his head above water as long as he can. Then he takes one deep gulp of air, holds it, and he's underwater. Suddenly there's silence all around him except for the metallic complaints of the sinking jet.

His body burns through the last of its oxygen; then, resigned to his fate, Trace releases his final breath. It bubbles away from him in the darkness, and his body gets to the business of drowning. It's as awful as he ever imagined it might be, but he knows it won't last long. Five seconds. Ten. Then the injustice of it all doesn't seem to matter anymore. As the last of his consciousness filters away, Trace holds on to the hope that his choice to fight on the side of the AWOLs instead of the Juvenile Authority will be enough to pay his passage to a truly better place.

79 · Starkey

The water tastes like rubber and rot and is neither warm nor cold, but tepid, like tea left to steep an hour too long. The last of the plane disappears beneath the surface, leaving nothing but white water bubbling up through the brine and the fuel slick, which has almost burned itself out. Starkey looks around to see kids in the water, kids on rafts, and kids who've drifted too far away to see at all, calling out for help.

There's a deserted shore just a few hundred yards way. Trace, rest his soul, knew enough to bring them down near the unpopulated side of the huge lake. Even so, people will have seen the crash and will come to investigate. They have to get away from the scene as quickly as possible—the attention of the locals is the last thing they need.

"This way!" Starkey tells them, and starts swimming, pulling himself forward with his good hand. The kids in rafts paddle, the kids in the water swim, and in a few minutes they're pulling themselves out of the fetid water onto a spongy shore of pulverized fish bones.

Starkey sets Bam to do a head count, and she comes back with 128. They lost forty-one in the crash. Around him the survivors try to tally exactly who is missing, which just makes Starkey angry. Sitting here will do nothing but get them captured. He knows he's cunning enough to make it on his own; somehow he's got to extend his survival smarts to all of them.

"Everybody up! We can't waste our time licking our wounds and mourning the dead. We've got to get out of here."

"Where do you suggest we go?" asks Bam.

"Right now, anywhere but here."

Starkey knows he needs to give these kids direction and purpose. Now that they're free from the holding pen of the Graveyard, their priorities need to change. Connor might have been happy to just keep kids alive, but Starkey has to make this about more than just survival. Under his leadership, his storks can be a force to be reckoned with.

He goes to the nearest kids nursing their exhaustion and

lifts them to their feet by their collars. "Let's move! We'll rest when we're safe."

"When will we ever be safe?" someone asks. Starkey doesn't answer, because he knows they'll probably never be. But that's all right. They've been complacent for too long. Being on the edge will keep them sharp and focused.

As the storks all gather their strength for an uncertain journey on foot, Starkey searches through them until he finds Jeevan, relieved that he's one of the survivors.

"Jeeves, we'll need the same type of setup you had in the ComBom, but mobile. I need you to be our eyes and ears and gather all the intelligence you can from the Juvenile Authority."

Jeevan just shakes his head in panicked disbelief. "That was all high-end military software. We don't have it anymore. We don't even have a computer!"

"We'll commandeer as many computers as you need," Starkey tells him. "And you'll make it work."

Jeevan nods nervously. "Yes, sir."

Even before they leave the shore, Starkey's grand plan begins to take shape. He will step up the campaign of vengeance he began in Tucson—only this time it won't just be a handful of avenging storks, it will be all of them: a guerrilla army 128 strong, heaping punishment on anyone who would unwind a stork. Their numbers will grow with every stork they rescue. He doesn't doubt that in time they could take down entire harvest camps. And then the Akron AWOL will be nothing but a sorry footnote beneath his own legacy.

Drawing strength from his powerful vision, Starkey leads them into the mountains east of the Salton Sea. His first trick will be to make them all disappear, but that's only the beginning. From this moment on, there will be no end to the magic.

80 · Miracolina

Miracolina's head is spinning as she awakes. That's how she knows she's been tranq'd. This is the fourth time she's been tranq'd—she knows the drill by now. Memories of the events leading up to it come back, but slowly and not in order. She suppresses the nausea and sets to the task of determining her current circumstances and defragging her mind.

She's moving. She's in a vehicle. She was traveling with Lev. Is she in the back of a pickup? No. Is she in the baggage compartment of a bus? No.

It's night. She's in the backseat of a car. Is Lev with her? No.

They weren't in a vehicle at the end, were they? They were walking. By a fence. Toward an old air force base. Is there more? There must be, but try as she might, she can't remember anything after walking toward the gate.

Although she knows it will makes her feel as if her brain wants to escape through her ears, she sits up. There's a thick glass barrier between her and the front seat. A police car? Yes— two Juvey-cops are in the front seat. This should be good news for her. It means that she's finally surfaced out of the under- world that Lev has dragged her through. It doesn't feel good at all, though, and it's more than just the tranqs. That she's in a squad car doesn't bode well for Lev, and she can no longer deny that she cares about what happens to him in spite of herself.

The Juvey-cop at the wheel glances in his rearview mirror, catching her gaze. "Well, look who's awake," he says pleasantly.

"Can you tell me what happened?" The sound of her own voice makes her head pound.

"Police action at the aircraft salvage yard," he says. "But you already know that, don't you?"

"No. I was tranq'd outside the gate." And then she adds, "I was out for a walk," which is a stupid thing to say, considering how isolated that road is.

"We know who you are, Miracolina," the cop riding shot-gun says. The news makes her have to lie back down on the sticky leather of the backseat, but she leans the wrong way and ends up slumped against the door.

"He told you?" she asks. She can't imagine Lev voluntarily giving her name to the Juvies.

"No one told us," he says, and holds up a small electronic device. "DNA tester. Standard issue for Juvey-cops since Happy Jack."

"I'd like to know what 'he' she's talking about," says the cop driving.

Well, if they don't know, she's not going to tell them. If Lev hasn't been caught, then he wasn't with her when she was. But would he just leave her? Lev is such a mixed bag of contradict-ing ethics, she can't be sure. But no—that's a lie—the kind of lie she used to tell herself just to demonize him. Deep down she knows he wouldn't leave her voluntarily. If he did, he had no choice. Still, there's no telling whether he's free or has been captured.

"What I want to know," asks the cop riding shotgun, "is how you wound up outside the gate and not inside like the rest of them."

Miracolina decides to tell them an edited version of the truth, since they're not going to believe it anyway. "I escaped from a parts pirate with a friend," she tells them. "We were looking for a place of safety."

The two cops look to each other. "So you had no idea that the airplane graveyard was an AWOL stronghold."

"We were just told to go there—that we would be safe from the parts pirates."

"Who told you?"

"Some guy," she says, which sounds like something any kid would say, and effectively throws a wet rag over the question.

"How did you get tranq'd?"

When she doesn't answer, the driver looks at his partner and says, "Prolly a trigger-happy rookie." His partner just shrugs.

"Well, you're here, and you're safe. Was your friend a tithe too?"

Miracolina has to suppress a smile. "Yes," she says, "he was." She's pleased she can lie to them in complete honesty, because after all it is the best policy.

"Well, no tithes turned themselves in," Shotgun says. "Perhaps he got hauled off with the rest."

"The rest?"

"Like we said, police action. Rounded up a huge nest of AWOLs. A few hundred at least."

Again, something that once would have been good news for Miracolina—justice prevailing, order restored—now brings her nothing but melancholy.

"Any bigwigs brought in?" she asks, knowing that if Lev or his friend, the Akron AWOL, were caught, it would be big news—they'd all know.

"No such thing as a bigwig AWOL, sweetie. They're all nonentities. Otherwise they wouldn't be where they are."

Again she sighs in relief, and the cops assume her sigh is exhaustion from the tranquilizers. "Lie back down, honey. You've got nothing to worry about. The parts pirates can't get you now." But she stays upright, not wanting to slip into a post-tranq stupor. There's something off about the way they're treating her. After all, she is an Unwind with a questionable story—and even though she's a tithe, she's never known Juvies to be so nice to kids about to be unwound. As they said, they see Unwinds as nonentities. You don't call nonentities "honey" and "sweetie."

As they pull into the local Juvey headquarters, she begins to wonder what the process is now. "I was supposed to go to Wood Hollow Harvest Camp," she tells them. "Will I still go there, or to a camp in Arizona?"

"Neither," the driver says.

"Excuse me?"

He parks the car and turns to her. "From what I understand, your parents never actually signed the unwind order."

That leaves Miracolina speechless.

They never signed it. Now she remembers them telling her that as she stood at the door—but she told them it was her choice to go, and she got into the van anyway.

"Even if you had made it to Wood Hollow, you would have just been sent home once they double-checked the paperwork. Can't unwind without an order."

She laughs at the irony of it. All this time fighting to finally be tithed, and not only won't it happen, but it was never going to happen. She wants to be angry—but how can she fault her parents for loving her too much to let her go? She wonders how things would have been different if she had known. Would she still have taken the journey west with Lev after escaping from the parts pirate? Would she have stayed with him long enough to forgive him, granting him that absolution he so desperately needed?

To her amazement, the answer is no.

Had she known she'd never be tithed, that call she made to her parents wouldn't have just been a message that she was alive—it would have been a plea to come and get her. She would have let Lev finish his journey alone—solitary and unforgiven.

"I know how tithes are," says the shotgun cop sympathetically. "If it's what you really want, you can take it up with your parents when they get here."

And although it is what she wants, she's coming to terms with the disappointment of staying whole.

"Thank you," she says. "Thank you so much." But it's not them she's thanking.

Either things happen for a reason, or they happen for no reason at all. Either one's life is a thread in a glorious tapestry or humanity is just a hopelessly tangled knot. Miracolina has always believed in the tapestry, and now she feels blessed to have had a glimpse of its smallest corner. Now she knows her desire to be tithed was not there to leave her in a divided state—it was there to propel her into the right place at the right time to have a hand in the redemption of the boy who would blow himself up.

Who would have thought that the singular whole of her forgiveness was a more valuable gift than a hundred of her parts?

So she will return into the arms of her wildly emotional parents and will live the life they dream for her until she can find her own dream. She had no tithing party, but right now, she resolves that she will have herself a grand celebration someday. Perhaps a sweet sixteen. And she will find Lev, wherever in the world he is, ask him to attend, and refuse to take no for an answer. And then, finally, she will dance with him.

81 · Hayden

To the best of Hayden's knowledge, they're the last ones left. There are fourteen others in the ComBom with him, all kids from the various communication shifts, who put more faith in him than in anyone else—which shocks Hayden. He had no idea there was anyone who looked up to him. One kid is noticeably absent. Before power was cut to the cameras, Hayden saw

Jeevan getting into the Dreamliner with the other storks, his arms packed with pilfered weapons.

Connor had stopped responding in the middle of the battle, and the Juvies had, one by one, taken out the power generators, plunging the ComBom, and every other jet, into darkness.

By midnight it's over. Through the windows of the Com-Bom, Hayden can see the heavy transports, the battering ram, the riot trucks, and most of the Juvey squad cars pulling out: Mission accomplished.

Hayden thinks that maybe they've been forgotten—that they can sit it out for a few more hours, then make a break for freedom. But the Juvenile Authority is smarter than that.

"We know you're in there," they shout through a bullhorn. "Come out, and we promise no one will get hurt."

"What do we do?" the kids around him ask.

"Nothing," Hayden says. "We do nothing." Being that the ComBom was the communications center and brain of the Graveyard, it's one of the few crafts with all its outer doors in place and in working order. It's also one of the few crafts that can only be opened from the inside. When the battle began, Hayden had sealed the airtight hatch, leaving them as self-contained and cut off as a submarine. Their only defense is their isolation and a submachine gun Connor insisted that Hayden have. He doesn't even know how to fire the thing.

"You're in a hopeless situation," the Juvies yell through their bullhorn. "You'll only make matters worse for yourselves."

"What could be worse than all of us getting unwound?" Lizbeth asks.

Then Tad, who from the very beginning has been hanging close to Hayden as if they're joined at the hip, says, "They won't unwind you, Hayden. You're seventeen."

"Details, details," Hayden says. "Don't bother me with details."

"They'll storm us!" warns Nasim. "I've seen it on TV. They'll blow off the door and gas us, and a SWAT team will drag us out!"

The others look nervously to Hayden to see what he'll say. "The riot police have already left," Hayden points out. "We're not important enough to storm. We're just cleanup. I'll bet they just left the fat, stupid Juvies to wait for us." And the kids laugh. He's glad that they can still laugh.

Regardless of IQ and body mass, the Juvies aren't going away. "All right," they announce. "We can wait as long as you can."

And they do.

At dawn they're still there—just three squad cars and a small gray transport van. The media, which the cops held back through the raid, are now camped out just fifty yards away, their antennas and satellite dishes high.

Hayden and his holdout Whollies have spent the night dozing on and off. Now the sight of the media gives some of them a surreal sort of hope.

"If we go out there," Tad says, "we'll be on the news. Our parents will see us. Maybe they'll do something."

"Like what?" asks Lizbeth. "Sign a second unwind order? You only need one."

At seven fifteen, the sun clears the mountains, heralding another scorcher, and the ComBom begins to roast. They manage to scrounge up a few water bottles, but not enough for fifteen kids who are already beginning to sweat out more than there is to take in. By eight o'clock, the temperature hits one hundred, and Hayden knows this can't last. So he comes back to his favorite question, but this time it isn't rhetorical.

"I want you all to listen to me and think about your answer to this," he tells them. He waits until he's sure he has all their attention, then says:

"Would you rather die . . . or would you rather be unwound?"

They all look to one another. Some put their heads in their hands. Some sob dry tears because they're too dehydrated to cry. Hayden silently counts to twenty, asks the question again, then waits for the answers.

Esme, their best password-cracking hacker, is the first to break through the firewall of silence. "Die," she says. "No question."

And Nasim says, "Die."

And Lizbeth says, "Die."

And the answers start to come faster.

"Die."

"Die."

"Die."

Everyone answers, and not a single one of them chooses unwinding.

"Even if there is such a thing as 'living in a divided state,'" Esme says, "if we get unwound, the Juvies win. We can't let them win."

And so, as the temperature soars past 110 degrees, Hayden leans back against the bulkhead and does something he hasn't done since he was little. He says the Lord's Prayer. Funny how some things you never forget.

"Our father, who art in heaven . . ."

Tad and several others are quick to join in. "Hallowed be thy name . . ."

Nasim begins to recite an Islamic prayer, and Lizbeth covers her eyes, chanting the Shema in Hebrew. Death, as they say, doesn't just make all the world kin, it makes all religions one.

"Do you think they'll just let us die?" Tad asks. "Won't they try to save us?"

Hayden doesn't want to answer him, because he knows the answer is no. From the Juvies' point of view, if they die, all they lose are kids no one wanted anyway. All they lose are parts.

"With the news vans out there," suggests Lizbeth, "maybe our deaths will stand for something. People will remember that we chose death over unwinding."

"Maybe," Hayden says. "That's a good thought, Lizbeth. Hold on to it."

It's 115 degrees. 8:40 a.m. Hayden's finding it harder and harder to breathe, and he realizes the heat might not get them at all. It might be the lack of oxygen. He wonders which is lower on the list of bad ways to die.

"I don't feel so good," says a girl across from him. Hayden knew her name five minutes ago, but he can't think clearly enough to remember it. He knows it's only minutes now.

Beside him, Tad, his eyes half-open, begins babbling. Something about a vacation. Sandy beaches, swimming pools. "Daddy lost the passports and ooh, Mommy's gonna be mad." Hayden puts his arm around him and holds him like a little brother. "No passports . . . ," Tad says. "No passports . . . can't get back home."

"Don't even try, Tad," Hayden says. "Wherever you are, stay there; it sounds like the place to be."

Soon Hayden feels his eyesight starting to black out, and he goes places too. A house he lived in as a kid before his parents started fighting. Riding his bike up a jump ramp he can't handle and breaking his arm in the fall. *What were you thinking, son?* A fight his parents had over custody in the heat of their divorce. *You'll have him, all right! You'll have him over my dead body*, and Hayden just laughing and laughing, because it's his only defense against the prospect of his family collapsing around him. And then overhearing their decision to unwind him rather than allowing the other to have custody. Not so much a decision, but an impasse.

Fine!

Fine!

If that's the way you want it!

If that's the way YOU want it!

Don't put this on me!

They signed the unwind order just to spite each other, but laugh, laugh, laugh, Hayden, because if you ever stop laughing, it might just tear you apart worse than a Chop Shop.

Now he's far away, floating in the clouds, playing Scrabble with the Dalai Lama, but wouldn't you know it, all the tiles are in Tibetan. Then for a moment his vision clears and he comes back to the here and now. He's lucid enough to realize he's in the ComBom where the temperature is too hot to imagine. He looks around him. The kids are awake, but barely. They slump in corners. They lie on the ground.

"You were talking about stuff," someone says weakly. "Keep talking, Hayden. We liked it."

Then Esme reaches over and touches Tad on the neck, feeling his pulse. His eyes are still half-open, but he's no longer babbling about tropical beaches.

"Tad's dead, Hayden."

Hayden closes his eyes. Once one goes, he knows the rest of them won't be far behind. He looks at the machine gun next to him. It's heavy. It's loaded. He doesn't even know if he can lift it anymore, but he does, and although he's never used it, it doesn't take a rocket scientist to figure it out. There's a safety, easily removed. There's a trigger.

He looks at the suffering kids around him, wondering where "machine-gun fire" falls on the list of bad ways to die. Certainly a quick death is better than a slow one. He considers his options a moment more, then says, "I'm sorry, guys. I'm sorry I failed you . . . but I can't do this."

Then he turns the machine gun toward the cockpit and blasts out the windshield, flooding the ComBom with cool, fresh air.

82 · Connor

He wakes up in a comfortable bed, in a comfortable room, with a computer, a late-model TV, and sports posters all over the walls. He's groggy enough to think he actually might be in heaven, but nauseous enough to know he's not.

"I know you're pissed at me, Connor, but I had to do it."

He turns to see Lev sitting in the corner, in a chair that's painted with footballs and soccer balls and tennis balls to match the decor of the room.

"Where are we?"

"We're in Sunset Ridge Homes, model number three: the Bahaman."

"You brought me to a model home?"

"I figured we both deserved comfortable beds, at least for one night. It's a trick I learned from my days on the streets. Security patrols are looking for thieves, not squatters. They roll past but never go into model homes unless they see or hear something suspicious. So as long as you don't snore too loud, you're fine." Then he adds, "Of course, we've gotta be out by ten; that's when they open. I stayed too late at a model once and nearly scared a realtor to death."

Connor pulls himself to the edge of the bed. On TV is a news report. Aftermath and analysis of the AWOL raid at the airplane graveyard.

"It's been on the news since last night," Lev tells him. "Not enough to preempt the infomercials and stuff, but at least the Juvies aren't hiding it."

"Why would they hide it?" Connor says. "It's their stinking moment of glory."

On TV, a spokesperson for the Juvenile Authority

announces that the count of AWOLs killed was thirty-three. The number brought in alive is 467. *"With so many, we'll have to divvy them out to various harvest camps,"* the man says, not even realizing the irony in using the word "divvy."

Connor closes his eyes, which makes them burn. Thirty-three dead, 467 caught. If Starkey got away with about a hundred fifty, that leaves maybe sixty-five who managed to escape on foot. Not nearly enough. "You shouldn't have taken me, Lev."

"Why? Would you rather be a trophy to go along with their collection of Unwinds? If they find out that the Akron AWOL is alive, they'll crucify you. Trust me, that's one thing I know about."

"The captain is supposed to go down with the ship."

"Unless the first mate knocks him out and throws him in a lifeboat."

Connor just glares at him.

"Fine," says Lev. "You wanna punch me?"

Connor chuckles at that and looks at his right arm. "Careful what you ask for, Lev—I pack quite a punch these days." Then he shows Lev the tattoo.

"Yeah, I noticed that. There must be a story there. I mean, you hated Roland, right? Why'd you get the same tattoo?"

Now Connor laughs out loud. Hard to imagine that Lev doesn't even know—but then, how could he? "Yeah, there's a story," he says. "Remind me to tell you about it someday."

Onscreen, they've cut live to the Graveyard, where "an unfolding drama" is taking place. One last batch of AWOLs has held off the Juvies by holing up inside an old World War II bomber.

"It's the ComBom! Hayden held them off all night!" For Connor it's almost like victory.

The ComBom hatch opens, and Hayden comes out, carrying

a limp kid in his arms. He's followed by a bunch of other kids, none of them in good shape. The Juvies move in, and so do the media.

"We're witnessing the capture of the final AWOL Unwinds. . . ."

The reporters don't get close enough to stick microphones in Hayden's face, but they don't have to. In spite of the Juvies' attempt to spirit him into the transport van, he shouts loud enough for everyone to hear.

"We are not just AWOLs! We are not just parts! We are whole human beings—and history will look back on these times in shame!"

They shove him and the other kids into the van, but before they slam the door, Hayden shouts, *"To the new Teen Uprising!"*

Then the van carries them away.

"Way to go, Hayden," says Connor. "Way to go!"

The news briefly reports on the plane that got away, but as that's an embarrassment to the Juvies, not much is said. At first they had forced a plane to land in Dallas, thinking it was the AWOL Dreamliner, but it turned out to be a passenger flight from Mexico City. There have been unconfirmed reports of a plane going down in a California lake, but nothing further is said. Connor suspects the plane that went down is the Dreamliner—and as much as he'd like to see Starkey at the bottom of a lake, Connor hopes the storks survived the crash. That would be more AWOLs who got away from the Juvies.

Damn Starkey! He brought the Juvies down on them, then took half the weapons, hijacked their only means of escape, and left everyone else high and dry. And yet as much as Connor wants to blame it all on Starkey, he can't help but feel the brunt of the blame. He was the one who trusted Starkey to begin with, allowing him to amass power among the storks.

When it's clear that the news has moved on to other

subjects—weather woes and celebrities behaving badly—Connor turns off the TV. "Nine thirty. Almost time to move on."

"Actually, there's one more thing I want to show you before we go." Lev goes to the room's computer and pulls up, of all things, a website for hot tubs.

"Uh . . . sorry, Lev, I'm not in the market for a Jacuzzi."

Lev is stymied for a moment, until Connor notices the mistake. "YouTube has an *e* at the end."

"Duh!" Lev types it over. "I was never good at keyboarding."

He tries again and this time gets it right. Lev clicks on a video, and Connor's heart just about stops. It's yet another news interview with Risa.

"I don't want to see it." Connor reaches to turn it off, but Lev grasps his wrist.

"Yes, you do."

And although the last thing Connor wants to see is another sales pitch for unwinding, he gives in, bracing himself for whatever he's about to see.

He can tell right away from the look on Risa's face that she has a single-minded determination she didn't have in the other interview he saw.

He watches in amazement as, in less than two minutes, she blasts Proactive Citizenry, the Juvies, and unwinding so completely there's no doubt which side she's on. The show's anchorman is left scrambling to pick up the pieces.

"They were blackmailing her!" Connor feels his eyes get moist. He knew there had to be an explanation, but he had become so jaded against everyone and everything, he was willing to believe that Risa had chosen to heal herself at everyone else's expense. Now he's ashamed of himself for thinking that.

"Proactive Citizenry has already released a statement denying it," Lev tells him. "They claim *she's* the one who used *them*."

"Yeah, right. Let's hope nobody's stupid enough to believe them."

"Some people are, some aren't."

Connor looks to Lev and smiles, realizing that getting tranq'd kind of put a damper on their reunion. "It's good to see you, Lev."

"Same here."

"What's with the hair?"

Lev shrugs. "It's a look."

They hear a car pulling up in the sales office parking lot. Time to go.

"So what do we do now? Lev asks. "I'm kind of AWOL from the Anti-Divisional Resistance. . . ."

"The ADR has become useless. If the best they can do is send AWOLs to a holding pen for the Juvies, then something's not working. Someone needs to rethink things."

"Why not you?" Lev suggests.

"Why not us?" Connor counters.

Lev considers it. "Well . . . you're a martyr and I'm a patron saint—I can't think of anyone better! So where do we start?"

It's a big question. Where do you begin to change the world? Connor thinks he may have the answer. "Have you ever heard of Janson Rheinschild?"

83 · Nelson

Even before he comes fully to his senses, he knows something has gone terribly, terribly wrong. He opens his eyes to scorching daylight. He's lying in a ditch. His body aches. One side of his face feels as if it's on fire.

He was tranq'd. Not just once, but repeatedly, and by his own damn gun! Enough sedatives to knock him out for maybe twelve hours. It's a wonder he hasn't been eaten alive by desert scavengers—but from the pain in his left leg, and bloody holes in his stolen uniform, clearly something tried. Nelson wonders how long he's been in the sun. Long enough for half his face to be swollen and throbbing from a second-degree sunburn.

He had him! He had Connor Lassiter, and now he has nothing but the tattered clothes on his back. It was the tithe! How could Nelson have been so careless! He should have killed Lev when he had the chance, but out of the kindness of his heart, he had let the boy live.

And here is the result of kindness.

The two will already be far from here, covering their tracks. His laptop held the codes of Lev's tracking nanites. Without his computer, they're useless. Nelson will not give up. He will find them. Tracking has always been his specialty, and this setback? It's nothing! It will only make him more determined, more ruthless in achieving his goal.

He climbs out of the ditch and marches, weak-legged, but strong-willed, like a zombie, toward Tucson. He will catch the Akron AWOL, deliver him to Divan, and be there to witness his unwinding—but the tithe will not meet such a merciful end. When Nelson finds Lev, he will visit upon the boy such wrath it will make the very ground tremble. Of this, Nelson can be sure. Just thinking about it fills him with enough joy and purpose to propel him down the long road to Tucson, and dark destinies beyond.

84 · Connor

"Flagstaff doesn't look much like south Arizona," says Lev. "Looks more like Denver or something."

"Denver doesn't look like Denver," Connor tells him. "I was

there once. It doesn't have crazy mountain views like you'd think. The views here are better." After being so long in the south Arizona desert, Connor is thankful for the dramatic change in scenery. With white-capped mountains to the north and an abundance of pine trees, he knows they can't be too far from the town of Happy Jack and the dead harvest camp, but he tries not to think about that. The past is the past.

They've stopped at a diner on historic Route 66, and, bucking the paranoia that the past year has infused them with, they have dinner in full view of anyone who cares to notice them. No one does.

Their car is a nondescript beige Honda that Connor hot-wired back in Phoenix, after ditching the Ford he hot-wired in Tucson, after ditching Nelson's van. Anyone trying to track them would be hard-pressed to keep up with their transportation switcheroos.

The Rain Valley Diner boasts "the Best Burgers in the Southwest." Connor hasn't had food this good since before his parents signed his unwind order and his life turned upside down. As far as he's concerned, the Rain Valley Diner has the best burgers in the world.

With one hand he eats his burger, and with the other, he does some information gathering on Nelson's laptop, which the parts pirate was kind enough to leave for them in his van.

"Find out anything new?" Lev asks.

"It looks like Risa disappeared after the broadcast last night, and Proactive Citizenry wants her head. Not unwound, just her head. Like on a stake."

"Ew."

"And Hayden's being charged with everything they can charge him with."

"At least they can't unwind him."

"But they can unwind everyone else who got caught."

The thought of the captured Whollies brings Connor waves of anger, chased by sadness that threatens to wash him down into the lightless places within himself. "I should have been able to save them. . . ."

"Hey, you did everything you could—and besides, they're not unwound yet," Lev reminds him. "Maybe what we do now can still make a difference for them."

Connor closes the laptop. "Maybe . . . but what are we going to do now?"

They sit in a long, uncomfortable silence, doing nothing but eating, because that's easier than answering the question. No plans, no destination, no idea what direction to go from here other than "away." Connor's first instinct is to find Risa, but he knows that, like himself, she'll be completely off radar. He wouldn't even know where to start looking.

"I could take you to the Cavenaugh mansion," Lev suggests. "You'd be safe there."

"Safe would be nice for once, but that's not happening. Besides, didn't you bail from there?"

"Yeah, well, if I come back with the one and only Akron AWOL, I think they'll forgive me."

"Keep your voice down!" Connor looks around—they've chosen a corner booth that's relatively secluded, but it's not that big of a diner, and voices carry.

"Maybe we oughta check out that 'You-Tub' place, get a Jacuzzi, and turn into a couple of spa potatoes. We deserve some downtime."

He knows Lev is kidding, but there's something about what he said that triggers a thought. It's a small thought at first, but it grows quickly. An inkling becomes a hunch, becomes an idea, becomes a revelation, and Connor flips open the laptop again, clicking and typing furiously.

"What is it?" Lev asks.

"Janson Rheinschild!"

"But you already told me he was wiped out of digital existence, so what's the point in looking?"

Connor continues to ply the search engines, getting the keyboard slick with french fry grease. "You gave me an idea."

"Me?"

"The hot tub website. The typo."

"Are you gonna make fun of my keyboarding skills again?"

"No. You gotta have skills to make fun of them," Connor tells him. "Anyway, Hayden figured there's a code-eating worm on the net that chewed up every reference to Janson Rheinschild, but it's only looking for his name spelled correctly. . . . So I'm inputting every possible misspelling of his name."

Lev smiles. "Leave it to you to turn someone else's screwup into gold."

Connor orders a second burger and spends twenty minutes misspelling the name. By the last bite of the burger, he's ready to give up hope . . . then suddenly there's a glint of that gold Lev was talking about, and it turns out to be the mother lode.

"Lev—take a look at this!"

Lev comes around to his side of the booth, and they look at a news article dated more than thirty years ago. The article is from a small local paper somewhere in Montana where Rheinschild once lived. Apparently they kept tabs on one of their favorite sons, but consistently misspelled his name as "Reignchild."

Connor and Lev read the article in stunned disbelief. Rheinschild, a research scientist and inventor, was important enough to make quite a name for himself, until that name got erased like a shunned pharaoh from an Egyptian obelisk.

"My God!" Connor says, "This guy pioneered neural bonding and regeneration—the very technology that made unwinding possible! Without Rheinschild, transplants and grafting would be back in the Stone Age!"

"So he was the monster who started this!"

"No, this was right at the beginning of the war—before anyone even thought of unwinding."

Connor plays a video embedded in the article, and they watch an interview with Rheinschild, a middle-aged man with glasses and thinning hair—two clear signs that it was before unwinding.

"We can't even begin to know the uses of this technology," Rheinschild says with an excitement much more youthful than he looks. *"Imagine a world where loved ones who die young don't really die—because every part of them can be donated to ease someone else's suffering. It's one thing to be an organ donor, and another to know that every single part of you will save someone else's life. That's a world I want to live in."*

Connor shivers, for the first time noticing the air-conditioned chill of the diner. The world Rheinschild described is a world Connor would want to live in too . . . but that's not the world they ended up with.

"Of course there are going to be ethical questions," Rheinschild goes on to say, *"which is why I've started an organization to study the ethical issues inherent in this sort of medical advancement. Proactive Citizenry, as I'm calling it, will be a watchdog to make sure there are no abuses of this technology. A conscience to make sure nothing goes wrong."*

Connor stops the video, trying to process it all. "Holy crap! So he founded Proactive Citizenry to protect the world from what he created!"

"And it became the very monster he was afraid of."

Connor thinks back to something he learned in school. Oppenheimer—the man who created the first nuclear bomb—turned against it in the end and became the bomb's greatest opponent. What if Rheinschild was the same, speaking out against unwinding, then was silenced—or worse—was silenced before he even had the chance to speak out. Not even the Admiral remembered the man, which means Rheinschild was either already gone or was prevented from speaking out against the Unwind Accord.

Lev reaches over and starts the video again—just a few more seconds of Rheinschild joyfully, naively waxing on about the glorious future he envisioned. *"This is just the beginning. If we're able to regenerate nerve tissue, we can regenerate anything—it's just a matter of time."*

The interview freezes on his smiling face, and Connor can't help but feel tremendous sorrow for this man; the secret father of unwinding, who paved a road to a place beyond hell with his good intentions.

"That's pretty wild," says Lev, "but how can knowing all this stop unwinding? Isn't that what you said, that finding out about this guy can change life as we know it, or something like that? Even if everyone knew about him, it wouldn't change a thing."

Connor shakes his head in frustration. "There's got to be something we're missing."

He scrolls down to the end of the article, where there's a picture of Rheinschild and his wife in a laboratory—apparently they worked as a team. When Connor reads the caption beneath the photo, his stomach seizes so suddenly, he thinks he might lose both of his Best in the Southwest burgers.

"It couldn't be. . . ."

"What is it?"

Connor can't speak for a moment. He looks at the caption again. "His wife. Her name is Sonia!"

Lev doesn't get it—and why should he? He was never in that first safe house with Connor and Risa. Sonia was the name of the old woman who ran it. Over the years she must have rescued hundreds, maybe thousands, of AWOL Unwinds.

Connor enlarges the picture on the screen, and the more he looks at Mrs. Rheinschild, the more certain he is.

It's the same Sonia!

What was it she said to him? *We move in and out of darkness and light all of our lives. Right now, I'm pleased to be in the light.* Connor had no idea the burden of darkness she must have been carrying all these years.

"I know that woman," he tells Lev. "And now I know where we have to go. We're going back to Ohio."

Lev grows pale at the suggestion. "Ohio?" The thought of home brings a scorpion's nest of emotions neither one of them are ready for, but Sonia's antique shop is in Akron. If there's more to this picture, she's the only one who can give it to them.

Bells above the diner's front door jingle, and a stone-faced deputy saunters in, his eyes immediately scanning the room. While Connor and Lev were absorbed by the news article, two patrol cars had pulled up out front, and officers are all over the stolen Honda.

"You look like a deer in headlights," Connor whispers to Lev. "Stop it."

"I can't help it." Lev lowers his head so his hair hangs over his face, but that looks just as conspicuous as antelope eyes.

Sure enough, the deputy zeroes in on them and makes a beeline across the diner—but to Connor's surprise, their waitress gets to the table first and says, "Tommy, you just about inhaled those burgers! You keep eating like that and you'll burst out of your jeans."

Connor is a little slack-jawed as the deputy arrives, but Lev pulls out of road-kill mode and says, "Yeah, Tommy, you're such a pig. You'll get fat, just like your dad."

"It's in the genes," says the waitress, not missing a beat. "Better be careful!"

The deputy turns to the waitress. "You know these boys, Karla?"

"Yeah, this is my nephew, Tommy, and his friend Evan."

"Ethan," says Lev. "You always get my name wrong."

"Well at least I knew it started with an *E*."

Connor nods politely to the deputy and looks at the waitress. "Your burgers are just too good, Aunt Karla. So if I get fat, it's your fault."

Satisfied, the deputy turns to Karla, concluding that Connor and Lev are somebody else's problem. "Know anything about that car out there?" he asks her.

Karla looks out the window and says, "A couple of kids pulled up, maybe an hour ago. Boy and a girl. I noticed them because they looked to be in a hurry."

"They come in?"

"No, they just ran off."

"I'm not surprised—the car was stolen down in Phoenix."

"Joyriders?"

"Maybe. Could be AWOLs. A bunch of them escaped from that old air force base in Tucson." He jots her statement down in his notepad. "You remember anything else, you be sure to let us know."

Once the deputy is gone, Karla winks at Connor and Lev.

"Well, Tommy and Ethan, your meal's on the house today."

"Thank you," Connor says. "For everything."

She winks at him. "Least I can do for my favorite nephew." Then she reaches into her pocket and, to his amazement, puts a set of car keys in front of Connor, rabbit's foot key chain and all. "Why don't you do me a favor and drive my car 'home' for me today. It's out back."

Lev looks at Connor, astonished, which isn't much different from his deer-in-headlights look. For a moment Connor thinks she might recognize who they are, but he realizes this is not about recognition. It's about the random kindness of a stranger.

"I can't take these keys," Connor whispers.

Karla lowers her voice to match his. "Yes, you can. And anyway, you'd be doing me a favor taking that clunker off my hands. Even better—why don't you total it when you're through? 'Cause I could use the insurance money."

Connor takes the keys from the table. He doesn't even know how to say thank you for something like this. It's been a very long time since anyone has gone so far out of their way to help him.

"You need to know that not everyone's your enemy," Karla says. "Things are changing out there. *People* are changing. It might not be all that obvious, but it's there, and I see it every day. Why, just last week a trucker came in and was bragging all about how last year he picked up that Akron AWOL kid at a rest stop and gave him a ride. Poor guy got arrested for it too, but still he was bragging, because he knew it was the right thing to do."

Connor suppresses a smile. He knows the exact trucker she's talking about. Josias Aldridge, with the grafted card-trick arm. Connor has to clench his jaw to keep himself from telling her all about it.

"There's ordinary people out there doing extraordinary things." Then she winks at them again. "And now you've given me the chance to be one of those extraordinary/ordinary people, so I should be the one thanking *you*."

Connor rubs the rabbit's foot between his fingers, hoping that his own luck has finally changed. "It's too suspicious if you don't report it as stolen."

"I will," Karla says. "Eventually." Then she stands up and starts stacking their empty plates. "I'm telling you, change is on the way," she says. "It's like a plump old peach, ripe and ready to drop." Then she offers them both a warm smile before going back to waiting tables. "You take care now."

Connor and Lev take a few moments to collect their thoughts. Then they head out and around back to find a classic red Charger with some fender damage. Not exactly a show car, but no clunker, either. They get in, Connor starts it, and it purrs like a waking lion. The car smells of rose air freshener, and there are middle-aged-woman accessories everywhere, but that's okay. Connor doesn't mind being reminded of ordinary/extraordinary Karla.

As they pull out onto the road, Lev looks over at Connor. "Ohio?" Lev says. "Does it really have to be Ohio?"

Connor grins at him. "Yes, it does. And when we get there, the first thing I'm gonna do is make you get a haircut."

Then they pull onto Route 66, heading east into a world that's ripe for saving.